CASE CLOSED

STOLEN FROM THE STUDIO

THE CASE CLOSED SERIES

LAUREN MAGAZINER

CASE CLOSED

STOLEN FROM THE STUDIO

PICK YOUR PATH,

CRACK THE CASE

 KATHERINE TEGEN BOOKS
An Imprint of HarperCollins Publishers

Katherine Tegen Books is an imprint of HarperCollins Publishers.

Case Closed #2: Stolen from the Studio
Copyright © 2019 by Lauren Magaziner
Library of Congress Control Number: 2018965817
ISBN 978-0-06-267630-6

Typography by Andrea Vandergrift
19 20 21 22 23 PC/LSCH 10 9 8 7 6 5 4 3 2 1
❖
First Edition

To four special elementary school teachers—
this book is the fruit of all the lessons you taught me and
all the guidance you gave me.

Adam Bloom
4th grade
Thank you for
my love of writing

Sue Berner
1st grade
Thank you for
my love of
learning

Diane Afferton
3rd grade
Thank you for
my love of
reading

Sandy Basanavage
2nd–5th grade math
Thank you for
my love of
puzzles

"**ARE WE THERE** yet?" Frank asks for the millionth billionth time.

"No," I sigh.

"Are we there yet *now*?"

"No," my best friend, Eliza, says through gritted teeth.

"Oh." Frank looks out the window. Then he turns to us again. "How about now?"

"No!" we all shout at him, my mom included. After three hours in the car with Frank, I think Mom's about ready to strangle him. She puts on the radio, and Frank sings along. That'll keep him distracted for two minutes max.

Eliza's little brother, Frank, has always been a wild child. It used to annoy me how he always follows Eliza and me around. But ever since we solved a mystery this past summer that saved my mom's detective agency, I've warmed up to Frank's antics.

"Nine hundred ninety-nine bottles of pop on the wall," Frank sings over the radio, "nine hundred ninety-nine bottles of pop! Take one down, pass it around, nine

1

hundred ninety-eight bottles of pop on the wall—"

Okay, maybe I haven't warmed up to *all* of Frank's antics.

"Frank, shhhhh," Eliza says, putting a hand on her little brother's mouth. "Time for the quiet game."

"I am SO GOOD at the quiet game!" Frank shouts.

Mom and I look at each other in the rearview mirror, and we roll our eyes. Even though Frank is a pain in the bottom, I'm excited to be going on this surprise three-hour road trip to Burbank, California.

Surprise, because yesterday, Mom's detective agency, Las Pistas, got a call from the producer of the hit TV show *Teen Witch*. A show about, well, magical teens. The star of the show, teenage celebrity Layla Jay, has gone missing. She vanished without a trace. And she's supposed to start filming the next season of the show this week.

The show's producer decided to hire a private detective to help find her. So he asked around. And one of the producer's friends just so happens to be Guinevere LeCavalier, Mom's best client.

Eliza and Frank's parents had to leave town for a work conference, and Mom is doing Mr. and Mrs. Thompson a favor. So that's how all four of us ended up together, on this short but (thanks to Frank's annoying singing) *nightmarish* car ride.

2

Mom merges into another lane, and I can't help but feel nervous. This case is the perfect chance to impress Mom with my investigative skills. Ever since the Guinevere LeCavalier case a few months ago, I've been itching to get back into detective work. I mean, it started as a way to save my mom's agency . . . but it turns out I have good detective instincts and a real talent for interviewing suspects.

Eliza wants another case too. I think she misses exercising her logical, problem-solving brain. We've tried to nick a case or two from Mom, but our plans haven't been so successful. Mom keeps me on a tight leash now; she won't let me within fifty feet of a mystery.

But I know that I can change her mind. If only I can prove myself.

I don't remember falling asleep, but the next thing I know, Eliza is shaking me awake.

"We're here, Carlos!" she says. "I can't believe we're going to be on the set of *Teen Witch*! *Eeeeeeeeeee!*"

I hold my ears. "Ow!"

"Sorry, I'm just so excited. We love this show!"

"No, we don't," Frank says.

"Carlos and I," Eliza clarifies.

"Maybe we can find out what season four will be about," I say. "And get an answer to that cliff-hanger at the end of season three with that scene in the graveyard—"

3

"Or maybe they'll let us be extras in the background!"

Mom clicks her tongue. "That's not why we're here. I know you're excited, but this is a very serious situation. Layla Jay could be in trouble."

Eliza and I go silent. Mom's right. As cool as it is to be behind the scenes of my favorite show, I have to stay focused. Whether Layla ran away or was kidnapped, it's up to us to find her and make sure she's safe. Not only does season four of *Teen Witch* need her—the whole world needs her. Layla Jay is a high-profile star. She's, like, the queen of teens. A role model for kids everywhere.

We pull up to the studio, and Mom hands the guard her ID.

"Head to the left—you're going to Stage Eight. You'll see parking outside. Enjoy your meeting with Mr. Westover," he says as he opens the gate for us.

The studio is busy. There are people walking all over the lot, carrying set pieces and costumes into different studio buildings. There seem to be about ten buildings; each has a different plaque on it, indicating what show it belongs to.

Suddenly, Eliza screams. "There he is! *There he is!* Brad Bradley!" She points to a teenage boy with floppy hair just as he disappears through a studio door.

"What is a Brad Bradley?" Frank asks.

4

Eliza doesn't answer. She simply slides down so low in the car seat that her head is beneath the window. "Do you think he saw me?" she whispers, pulling her shirt up by her ears. She crawls into it like a turtle popping back into its shell. "I hope he didn't see me," she groans, her voice muffled.

"Brad Bradley," Mom replies, putting the car into park, "is Layla Jay's costar. Seventeen years old. Blond hair, blue eyes, makes teens and tweens go weak at the knees."

"Exhibit A," I say, gesturing toward Eliza.

Mom laughs, and Eliza elbows me.

We all pile out of the car. My butt is sore after three hours of sitting, and Frank runs in circles around Eliza and me, chanting, "You can't catch me! You can't catch me!" over and over again.

Outside the studio door, a teenage girl is crying hysterically. She's got very in-betweeny features: stringy hair that isn't quite brown but isn't quite blond. Skin that isn't quite pale but isn't quite tan. Close-together brown eyes that hug the bridge of her nose, thin mouth. I don't know who she is—she definitely isn't in the cast of the show—but she must be close to Layla to be this upset.

As we walk by her, I notice she's holding a picket sign that says LAYLA'S NUMBER ONE FAN! XOXO, LOUISE.

Since when do they let fans and groupies hang out on a closed set?

We slide inside the door of Stage Eight, and Mom pauses to write something down in her notebook. Probably about the fangirl we saw outside. Mom chews on the eraser of her pencil, deep in thought.

"Mom, when is your meeting with Wolfgang Westover?"

"A half hour from now," she says cheerily, closing her notebook. "His assistant told me his office is inside the studio, down the second hallway in the back."

Inside, the stage is huge. The ceilings are at least fifty feet high, with lots of lights pointed at the set. And I recognize everything I've seen on TV from *Teen Witch*.

First thing is the ferocious giant robot dragon, which Layla's character had to battle at the end of season two—and then tamed into her pet during season three. It towers over us . . . it's at least twenty feet tall. I guess they use CGI to make the dragon look real.

"COOL," Frank says, looking up at the dragon. "I want to touch it!"

"Don't touch anything, Frank," Mom says, her voice a warning. Frank backs away from the dragon, and I *have* to ask Mom later how she makes Frank obey her. Because whenever *I* say no, Frank hears yes.

Behind the dragon is a classroom with a few desks. And there's a row of lockers—that's part of the witch school. The potions classroom is tucked in the back with all sorts of cauldrons and bubbling concoctions. And there's the set for the principal's office—where Layla's character, Aurelia, ends up a lot.

There's a flimsy cardboard living-room area that looks much smaller in real life than it does on TV. I guess that's Hollywood magic for you.

And then there's something I've *never* seen before: an electric-green room—green floor, green walls. It's a bit of an eyesore. I hope that's not part of season four.

"What's this?" I say. "The show isn't green at all!"

"It's a green screen," Eliza explains. "They can film actors in front of these green screens, and then use digital editing to replace the green with other backgrounds. Look at the mat on the floor—I bet they film a lot of the stunts in that area."

"Oh," I say, feeling a little stupid.

Now that I've taken in the set, I peek at what's behind the cameras. It's a lot colder and more warehouse-y behind the camera. The floor is concrete, and there are chairs set up for some of the cast and crew. Off to the edge, there's a table of snack food, and an open door, leading to a conference room with a long table and several chairs.

"What's that?" I ask Mom, pointing to the conference room.

But it's Eliza who answers. "Probably the writers' room. Oftentimes in television, the writers have to adjust the script during filming if something's not working."

I grin at her.

"What?" she says.

"You know everything about everything, don't you?" I tease her.

"I don't know what that is," Eliza says, pointing to a big garage-looking thing in the corner. There's a big sign on it that says FREIGHT ELEVATOR OUT OF ORDER.

"I wanna ride it!" Frank says.

Mom frowns. "We can't. It's broken."

"So, this is it?" I ask, pivoting around on my toes. "The whole set?"

Eliza shakes her head. "They must film outside too. I saw a grassy square and gazebo on our drive in that looks a lot like Secret Cove." Which is the town in the show.

Mom wanders away, and I turn to Eliza.

"So . . . why are there so many people here?" I ask. "They can't film without Layla. She's the star. She's in almost every scene."

"And even more worrisome," Eliza says with a frown, "is how are we going to narrow down our suspects? There's got to be at least a hundred people here."

I don't have time to answer her—Mom makes a bee-line for a big chair that says DIRECTOR, just as a tall and slim Asian man plops down in it. He has soft round cheeks, a pointy chin, long hair tied back in a pony-tail, and just one earring. Like a pirate. Which doesn't escape Frank's notice.

He points directly at it and says, "ARRRRRR!"

"Excuse me?" the director snaps.

"Arrrrrre you Douglas 'Guillotine' Chen, director of *Teen Witch*?" Mom asks, coming to Frank's rescue.

"Who wants to know?" he demands, pointing a fin-ger at Mom's face. "You're not with the press, are you? I have nothing to say to the press! No comment! None at all!"

Mom smiles, and Guillotine's face softens. It's kind of amazing to watch the master at work. Mom knows just how to manipulate people. Which makes me won-der . . . what kind of manipulation does she pull on *me*?

"I'm Detective Catalina Serrano from Las Pistas Detective Agency. I've been employed to find Layla Jay."

"Oh." He frowns.

"When exactly did she go missing?"

"Thursday," he says. "She never showed up for work."

"Is that like her?" Mom asks.

He snorts. "Layla never misses an excuse to be in front of a camera."

"And did anyone call the police?"

"'Did anyone call the police?'" he mimics. "Of *course* we called the police."

I ball my hands into fists. No one talks to my mom that way! I don't care if he's a famous director.

I open my mouth, but Mom puts a hand on my shoulder.

"And what did the police say?"

Guillotine rolls his eyes. "They have no idea where she might be, and they didn't seem concerned. They said she probably ran away from all the pressures of her famous life, and there wasn't much they could do without any clues to go on. After forty-eight hours, they did send a few officers out here, but it doesn't seem like they're making any progress."

"Do you have any idea where she might be?" I butt in.

"Am I Layla Jay's keeper?" he says. "Ask her agent, Agatha Tuggle. That's *her* job. Though she's clearly not very good at it." Guillotine gestures to the studio door, where a woman has just sauntered in. She is a small lady, but fierce looking in her pantsuit and owlish glasses. Her brown hair is pulled back in a neat bun, and she has three pens sticking out of it.

"Douglas," she says at the director, waving a piece of paper in the air. "What is this ludicrous letter I just received from your office?"

"It's a breach of contract notice. By not showing up to work, Layla Jay has violated the terms of her work agreement!"

"Shhhhh. There, there, Douglas," Layla's agent, Agatha Tuggle, says in a soothing voice. "You know actors. They have flights of fancy sometimes. They're impulsive. They're unpredictable. It's all just part of the creative process. Layla is such a good actress that she's overdue for a . . . erm . . . capricious moment."

"Oh, don't you spin this one, Agatha! Not this time!"

"This time?" I say.

"I'll fire her, Agatha!" Guillotine says over me. "I'll really do it!"

"Now, now, Douglas," Agatha says. "Don't be rash. Layla is your star. Your show would plummet without her. You know that."

"Well, it doesn't seem I have a star either way," he cries, throwing his hands in the air.

"Layla will turn up. I promise." Her cell phone rings. "Hold on, I have to get this." She turns her back on Guillotine. "Hello? No, Leopold, the casting director said you're just not right for that part. But I can get you an audition for a jester on the— Hello? Crummy service, this building is like a black hole for cell reception."

She strides to the side door of the studio and walks out.

"You see what I have to deal with?" Guillotine complains. "We're all in a crisis right now, and she doesn't seem to grasp the severity of the problem. We're in some deep sh—"

"Ac-*hem*!" Mom clears her throat and makes a gesture at Eliza, Frank, and me.

He crosses his arms, then turns away from us. "You'd better get to your meeting. Mr. Westover doesn't appreciate tardiness."

Mom smiles. "Thanks for the tip."

After we're a safe distance away from Guillotine, I try to get a peek at Mom's detective notebook, but she covers her notes with her hand.

"What do you think about Guillotine?" Eliza asks Mom and me.

"I think he's a poop," Frank answers. "A big stinky *poop*."

Mom ruffles Frank's hair. "Well, I've written down my initial thoughts, but I don't like to make hasty decisions. I'll have to investigate more."

I'll investigate him too. Maybe I'll find something

Mom doesn't, and she'll be so amazed that she'll finally understand I was born to be a detective. After all, it's in my blood!

The backstage area is large. There's a long hallway that wraps around the back of the studio, leading to a costume and prop room, a makeup room, Layla's dressing room, Brad Bradley's dressing room. When we turn the corner, there are more offices. We pass Guillotine's, and—in the middle of the hall, across from a potted plant—an office with the nameplate WOLFGANG WESTOVER, EXECUTIVE PRODUCER.

The door is made of blurry glass, so I can't see inside, but I *can* hear a shouting match.

"We're doing everything we can," says a booming voice.

"WELL, YOU'RE NOT DOING ENOUGH!" shouts a woman.

"Please, Miriam, calm down."

"I WILL NOT CALM DOWN, WOLFGANG! NOT UNTIL YOU FIND MY BABY GIRL!"

"I promise—"

A choking sob, then the *thud* of something being thrown. "Yeah, right!"

The door to Wolfgang's office swings open with so much force that I'm surprised the glass doesn't shatter. A large woman storms past us so fast I can't even get a thorough look at her. As she walks away, all I see is her dark brown skin, short curly black hair hidden under a wide-brimmed hat, and a patterned dress that's a bit of an eyesore. Her high-heeled shoes click down the hallway, and then she is gone.

"Sorry about that," a man says at the door. He *must* be the executive producer, Wolfgang Westover. It's strange . . . he seems welcoming and friendly, but there's also something really intimidating about him. He towers over Eliza and me and especially Frank. He even looms over Mom. "Ms. Miriam Jay is obviously distraught."

"That was Layla Jay's mom?" I ask, craning to get another look at her. But she's long gone.

"Indeed," Wolfgang says.

"I'm your twelve o'clock," Mom says, holding out her hand. "Detective Catalina Serrano, at your service."

"Oh. *Oh!*" Recognition dawns on his face. "Of course! My friend Guinevere LeCavalier told me Las Pistas Detective Agency is the best in the business. Come on into my office—we'll chat."

"I would like that very much, thank you," Mom says politely. Wolfgang holds the door open for her, but she doesn't go in yet. Instead she gives me one of those classic mom looks: raised eyebrow, steely stare. "Mijo," Mom says to me, "you, Eliza, and Frank need to wait on the set for me. Park your butts on those chairs behind Director Chen and hang tight."

"Butt." Frank giggles.

"Please, Mom," I say quietly. "Please let me help."

It's a fight we've had a few times since the summer. I know she won't budge. But I need her to hear me . . . to acknowledge me. She needs to hear, again and again, how much I need this.

Mom frowns. "Carlos, I appreciate the help you gave my agency this past summer, but this case is mine to worry about. My job can get very dangerous. I don't want you in harm's way. So, you are to stay on the benches. You can read, do puzzles from Eliza's workbook, talk among yourselves, but you are *not* to talk to anyone on the set. Can you handle that, or do I have to hire an intern to be your babysitter for the day?"

A babysitter! My face gets hot. I look up at Wolfgang Westover, and he is disinterested in the conversation, picking at his hangnails. He must think we're *babies*. I can't think of anything more embarrassing and unprofessional.

"Carlos?" Mom says sternly. "Can I trust you to follow my directions?"

I kick my feet.

"Don't worry, Ms. S," Eliza jumps in. "I'll make sure Carlos stays out of trouble." Her ears turn pink—she is lying. Eliza has been my best friend for years, which means I know her all too well. Her likes? Puzzles. Her strengths? Being a genius. Her habits? She always talks out loud when she's thinking hard about something. And her weakness? She is a terrible liar.

Mom doesn't seem to notice. Maybe because Wolfgang Westover is impatiently looking at his watch. "Thank you, Eliza." Mom pauses to look at Frank, who is taking pictures of TV stars off the wall and rehanging them upside down, cackling madly as he goes down the row. Then Mom says, "Uh . . . keep an eye on Frank too." Then she walks into Wolfgang's office and closes the door behind her.

I turn to Eliza. "Why did you lie to my mom?"

A sly grin creeps up on Eliza's face. "I didn't lie to her. I said I'll make sure you stay out of trouble. And I will."

I scrunch my eyebrows and look at her, and she drapes her arm around my neck. "Come on, Carlos. You know there's no way we could let this case pass us by. This is *Layla Jay* we're talking about—our favorite TV star on our favorite TV show. We can't let her down!"

"So . . . we're going to solve this?" I feel excited . . . but surprisingly, a little squirmy too. I love detective work more than anything else in the world. But the last time I took a case, I broke my mom's trust. And even though my punishment is long over, it's taken her months to trust me again. Am I ready to ruin all that built-up good will?

I want my mom to trust me. And I want to follow my investigative heart. But right now they are polar opposites. If only Mom could see me as a good detective, and not a one-time fluke.

If I crack this case, I'd be breaking her trust again, disobeying her after she told me to wait on the benches. But then again . . . maybe she'd start to trust my detective skills. Maybe she'd let me help with future cases, and believe in Eliza, Frank, and me the way *I* believe in us. If only we prove ourselves.

And I know we can do it. Eliza's genius-level brain and dependable logic, Frank's bravery and wild-card unpredictability, and my people-person talent of getting a good read on suspects. Together, we make a perfect team.

Eliza nudges me. "Carlos?"

I nod. "You're right. We have to do this."

"We're defectives again?" Frank says.

"Detectives," Eliza and I both say.

"So where do we start?" I wonder aloud. "How do we figure out where Layla is? It's not like we have a bread-crumb trail. And we don't even know if she ran away, or if she was kidnapped."

Eliza hums. I can practically see the wheels turning in her head. "Well, we could go snoop through her dressing room. I bet we'll find a clue there that could help us figure out where she went."

Suddenly Wolfgang gets louder, and Frank jumps in alarm. We can hear Wolfgang's muffled voice coming from the door.

That gives me an idea.

"Or," I say to Eliza, "we could eavesdrop on my mom's conversation with Wolfgang Westover. If we hear what Mom hears, we'll be on the same footing with the case."

"Could be risky," Eliza says. "If we get caught."

"So," I reply, "let's not get caught."

TO SEARCH LAYLA JAY'S DRESSING ROOM, TURN TO PAGE 231.

←——→

TO EAVESDROP ON THE CONVERSATION WITH WOLFGANG, TURN TO PAGE 409.

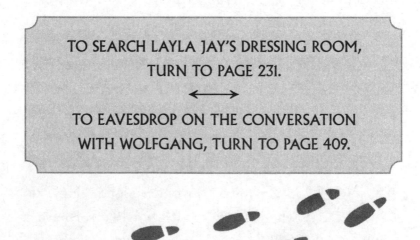

I KEEP STARING at Brad Bradley's phone—and I just can't figure it out. "Eliza, I need more help."

"Hmmm," Eliza says, staring at the phone. "I'm having trouble too. Sometimes trial and error is the best way to proceed when you're stuck. So we have three numbers left: four, five, and six. Which should we put in the middle of the magic square? Pick any random number, Carlos."

"Uh . . . five?" I say. "Because it's the middle of those numbers."

"The middle of the middle!" Frank agrees.

8	3	?
1	5	9
?	7	2

"How do we know if that's right, though?"

"We have to start adding rows and columns," Eliza says, and then she begins muttering to herself. "One plus five plus nine is fifteen. Frank!" she calls louder. "Remember the number fifteen."

"Aye, aye, Captain!"

"And if we just add the middle column, then three plus five plus seven is—"

"Fifteen!" I interrupt. "Eliza! I think every row and every column might have to add up to fifteen."

She looks at me. "If that's true," she says, "then what number would go in the bottom left corner to make the row add up to fifteen *and* the column add up to fifteen? Four or six?"

"Six," I say.

"I'M SIX!" Frank says. "HAPPY BIRTHDAY TO ME!"

"It's not your birthday," Eliza says.

"We've got one number left," I say. "Our magic square is almost complete. You know, Eliza, this was kind of cool."

"Only kind of?" she says. "Math is *magic*."

THE SUM OF EACH ROW, COLUMN, AND DIAGONAL IS THE SAME NUMBER. ADD TWO HUNDRED TO IT, AND TURN TO THAT PAGE.

THE RIGHT PATH is the right way . . . I know it.

"Come on! Follow me!" I say, pulling Eliza and Frank down the path to the right. The hall is just as old, dark, and rickety. Eliza's flashlight has to illuminate the way.

"Carlos, slow down!" Eliza says.

But I can't. I'm too excited. I—

Crack. The rotted wood snaps beneath my feet, and I fall straight into some sort of soft pit, deep down. Eliza and Frank drop right after me, with a shriek of fear and a whoop of pleasure.

At first I think we've landed on a pillow. But then I realize we've fallen straight into a pile of discarded, moth-eaten costumes.

"Well," Eliza says, ripping a costume into pieces and tying the ends together, "it's going to take a lot of work to make a rope long enough to climb out of here. Could take hours."

"Hours?"

"Or days," Eliza says.

"Days?"

"Or months, or years, or decades, or centuries, or millenniums!" Frank adds.

"But probably days," Eliza says, the flashlight sandwiched between her ear and shoulder. "And that's assuming we don't run out of batteries on my light, and assuming that your mom doesn't quit the case to look for us when she discovers we're missing, and assuming that Layla's still . . . *around* to be found by then, and assuming we don't dehydrate or starve, and assuming moths don't lay eggs in our brains, and assuming . . ."

CASE CLOSED.

"OKAY, FINE, MAUREEN. Let's play hide-and-seek," I say. "You hide first!"

"Oh, *wonderful*! You'll never find me! Start counting!"

"One . . . two . . . three . . . ," Frank begins as Maureen scurries off.

I whisper into Eliza's ear. "This is our chance to sneak away. We have to go after Miriam."

"But your mom," she says, concerned.

"Eleven . . . twelve . . . ," Frank continues.

My stomach twists uncomfortably at the thought. Mom betrayed me by hiring Maureen, and I'm about to betray her right back by ditching Maureen. It's an endless cycle of broken trust. "I have to do this. The only way Mom is going to take me seriously as a detective is if I prove myself on my own."

Eliza thinks for a moment. "You're wrong, you know."

"Huh?"

"You're not on your own. You have a team. You have us."

It's quite possibly the nicest thing she could have said. I wrap my arms around her in a giant hug, and when I peel away, I say, "We should go to the front gate and ask if Miriam came into the studio lot this morning. No use looking for her if she isn't here yet. But I think we should start with Miriam."

"Nineteen . . . twenty . . ."

Eliza shakes her head. "We should start with Wolfgang Westover. Tuggle called him untrustworthy, remember? Eavesdropping on your mom's conversation with him isn't enough . . . we need to question him ourselves."

"READY OR NOT, HERE WE COME!" Frank shouts.

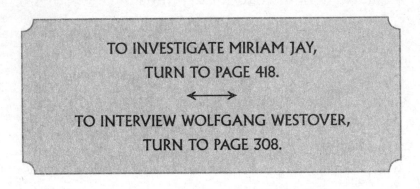

TO INVESTIGATE MIRIAM JAY,
TURN TO PAGE 418.

←——→

TO INTERVIEW WOLFGANG WESTOVER,
TURN TO PAGE 308.

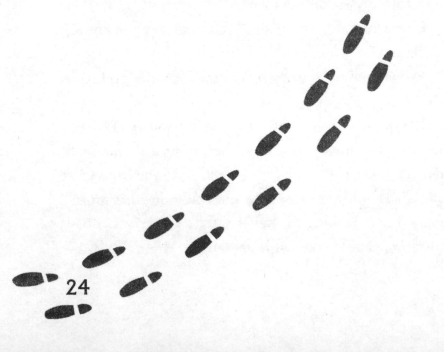

24

WE FIND MIRIAM Jay in Layla's dressing room. And the sight isn't pretty. The room is a *mess*. It looks like a tornado blew through here. Actually . . . it could probably be improved by a tornado. But I can't figure out whether Layla's room is always messy, or whether Miriam Jay caused this mess by rifling through Layla's stuff.

But what is she doing going through Layla's dressing room? Is she looking for something? Layla's mom stiffens as she turns our way. Like Layla, Miriam has brown skin and black hair with tight curls. She looks like an older Layla in every way except one: from every picture I've seen of Layla, she looks fashionable. But her mom is wearing a dress that looks like it's made from a carpet bag.

"Wh-who are you?" Miriam asks, half fear, half outrage. "What are you doing in my daughter's private quarters?"

"I don't see any quarters!" Frank says, dropping to the floor to scour for loose change.

I smack my head with my palm. "Don't mind him," I say. "We three are detectives, trying to find your daughter."

"Detectives," Miriam says. "Did Westover hire you?"

I nod.

"Finally, he's doing *something*! I'm losing my mind

here! I miss Layla *so much*. So, so much! My little baby! I want to hug her and kiss her. I just *miss* her."

"You said that already," I say.

Miriam smiles blankly.

Okay . . . she is halfway creeping me out and halfway making my suspicion radar go wild.

TO ASK MIRIAM WHAT SHE'S LOOKING FOR
IN LAYLA'S ROOM, TURN TO PAGE 412.

TO ASK MIRIAM WHAT SHE'S LOOKING FOR
IN LAYLA'S ROOM, TURN TO PAGE 412.

←→

TO ASK MIRIAM WHERE SHE THINKS LAYLA IS,
TURN TO PAGE 78.

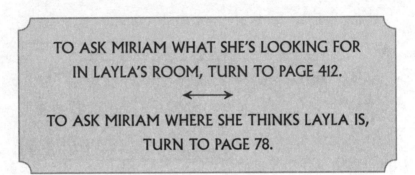

I'M STARING BLANKLY at this scramble—and the more I stare at it, the more worried I get. We're wasting time. Layla depends on us; I have to move faster.

"Help," I say to Eliza, and she starts to fill in the puzzle for me in record time.

ybdnats	S	T	A	N	D	B	Y
lolr	R	O	L	L			
donsu	S	O	U	N	D		
caarem	C	A	M	E	R	A	
etasl	S	L	A	T	E		
arkrem	M	A	R	K	E	R	
nictao	A	C	T	I	O	N	

"Wow," I say.

She blushes and tucks behind her ear a loose strand of hair that fell out of her braid. "We have a lot of high-lighted letters." And she writes them down underneath the scrambled code.

N Y O N E T E I N

"I got it!" Frank says. "Nincompoop!"

"Frank," I say, letting go of an exasperated sigh. "There are no Ps or Cs or Ms in our unscramble!"

"What are you listening to me for? I can't even read yet!"

I turn to Eliza. "Did you figure it out?"

"It's a number," she says quietly. "Just under a hundred. See it?"

Scramble, prepare to meet your match!

> ## THE SOLUTION TO THE PUZZLE WILL
> ## TAKE YOU TO YOUR NEXT PAGE.

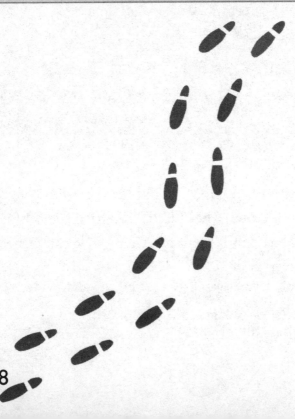

28

WE DECIDE TO wait at the bottom of the ladder. There's only one way down, and we've surrounded it. They can't stay up there forever.

But they do stay a long time. I think they're waiting for us to get bored or fall asleep or go to the bathroom (especially since Frank started doing his pee-pee dance a half hour ago), but we are brick walls. We aren't moving an inch. I'm ready. Eliza and I are holding the ends of the rope she found.

"Who are you?" I call. "What are you doing up there?"

The person shakes their head. And continues to say nothing.

"What do you think?" Eliza whispers in my ear. "Is it our culprit?"

I frown. "Well, it's the middle of the night. And I don't see any reason why they wouldn't answer us if they're doing something innocent. Besides, they're wearing a mask, clearly meant to hide their face."

Eliza nods, and Frank says, "I really gotta go!"

"Then let's move this along." I cup my hands around my mouth and shout to our masked figure. "Hey! You can stay there until morning, when the whole cast and crew shows up for work! It makes no difference to us— you're caught either way!"

The person considers this for a moment, then heads down the ladder.

I grin triumphantly. But Eliza looks worried.

The figure is coming down, getting closer. My stomach twists, and my hands are so sweaty.

The mystery person puts a foot on the floor, then turns around. They're wearing a white mask with no identifying features, no eyeholes, no mouth holes. But the way their head is swiveling? They are clearly looking for an escape route.

"PUT 'EM UP!" Frank hollers, like he's in a Western movie. "STICK 'EM UP, PARTNER!"

The person raises their arms. "P-please don't hurt me!" a female voice says.

"If you follow directions, we won't hurt you," I say.

"Speak for yourself!" Frank says, holding up a stuffed owl prop—it's actually Brad Bradley's father on the show, who got cursed into an owl by the Witch Queen. Long story.

Frank plucks some feathers and says, "GET READY FOR THE TICKLE MONSTER OF A LIFETIME."

"No, Frank. We just need her to remove the mask."

"No, Carlos. I have feathers, and I'm not afraid to use them!"

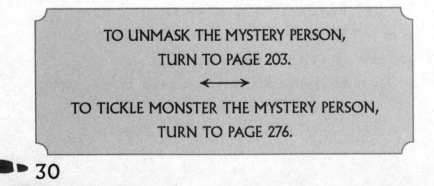

TO UNMASK THE MYSTERY PERSON,
TURN TO PAGE 203.

←—→

TO TICKLE MONSTER THE MYSTERY PERSON,
TURN TO PAGE 276.

I **HAVE TO** keep going with my plan to get into Guillotine's office! It's now or never!

I run so fast my Little League coach would be proud. The door is closing, inching shut—I tuck my left leg behind my right knee and slide. Without my padded baseball pants, it stings, but my foot catches the door *just* before the lock clicks.

Safe!

Eliza and Frank jump over me and let themselves in. Then I get up, brush myself off, and follow.

"Great job, Carlos!" Eliza beams, once we're safely inside.

Guillotine's office isn't quite what I imagined for a big, important television director. It's almost the size of a closet. He's got a tiny desk, a TV cabinet with the world's smallest TV inside, and that's pretty much it. I'm starting to understand why he's mad at Layla for having an executive producer credit and added perks. Her dressing room is twice the size of his private space.

"Look, Carlos," Eliza says, "a filing cabinet."

Frank pulls on the drawer, but it doesn't budge. "IT'S LOCKED!"

"I bet he's got some important information in there. Why else would he lock it?"

"What do you think's inside?" I ask.

"Peanut butter!" Frank suggests. "Socks! Peanut butter and socks!"

31

"Only one way to find out," Eliza says. "We need the key."

TO LOOK IN GUILLOTINE'S DESK DRAWER,
TURN TO PAGE 239.

←→

TO LOOK IN THE TV CABINET,
TURN TO PAGE 332.

"WHO MIGHT HAVE kidnapped Layla?" I ask.

"Aren't *you* the detective?" Tuggle asks, pointing at Mom.

"Humor us," Eliza says.

"Ha ha ha ha ha ha HA HA HA!" Frank hollers. When we look at him, he says, "What? I'm humoring Eliza!"

I groan. Then I turn back to our two suspects. "We have our theories. We want to know what *you* think."

Tuggle and Miriam look at one another. Then they look away real fast, like they're afraid to catch each other's eye.

"I never liked that Brad Bradley kid," Miriam says. "He's a phony little thing, a rotten egg." Her nostrils flare, and for a second I think she's going to throw the table, but she merely folds her arms and says, "He is a social climber. And he uses my Layla like a ladder."

"I don't know anything about Brad," Tuggle says, adding another pen to the collection in her bun.

"That's . . . that's not true," Miriam says, turning on Tuggle. "You seem to be *very* chummy with him lately!"

Tuggle snorts. "Hardly! I'm just trying to smooth things over between Layla and Brad! They've been fighting something fierce lately."

"I see. Shouldn't Brad's agent be smoothing things over with Layla then too? Who is Brad's agent, by the way?" Mom asks.

Tuggle stops fiddling with her bun. "I—I don't know," she says, looking down at the table. It's a clear lie. She *does* know. But I don't know why she'd have to lie about that. Who even cares about Brad's agent?

"Guillotine is a problem!" Miriam continues. "My Layla is not living up to her potential under his direction. Did you even know that Layla can tap dance? But he *refuses* to add in a musical number for her. He says witches don't tap dance—can you believe that?"

Tuggle rolls her eyes. "Beyond that, Guillotine is a difficult man, always yelling at Layla and trying to embarrass her. Sometimes I wonder whether Guillotine wants Layla to quit the show."

"Quit!" I say. "But she's the star!"

"Layla would never quit," her mom says. "She's too persistent for that."

"My mommy is perspirant too," Frank says. "That's why she uses extra-strength deodorant. If Layla's stinky, she should use some."

"How dare you!" Miriam says. "Layla is a STAR. And stars do not *stink*."

"If you need more leads, have you talked to Louise yet?" Tuggle says. "She's been harassing my client for months."

"And look at Wolfgang Westover!" Miriam says. "He's not doing enough to find my daughter—and he admitted to me that her disappearance was great publicity for the show!"

Tuggle presses her hands together. "Look into everyone—"

"Except us!" Miriam finishes. Tuggle glares at her, and Miriam looks stricken. She quickly adds, "Because it would be a waste of your time. Since we're innocent."

What an odd thing to say, considering they're in an interview with a private eye! I look at Mom, and she's failing at trying not to smile. She jots something down in her notebook.

I don't know what to think about Agatha Tuggle *or* Miriam Jay. Maybe I should push them a little bit to see if they crack under the pressure. Maybe one of them is guilty—or knows something—and will fall apart when I turn up the heat. Or maybe I should just end the conversation now. Quit while I'm ahead.

TO ACCUSE THEM OF KIDNAPPING LAYLA,
TURN TO PAGE 460.

←——→

TO END THE CONVERSATION, TURN TO PAGE 160.

"DO YOU KNOW anything about Layla's chest?"

"A super-secret private treasure chest," Frank explains. "*Not* a regular chest."

Guillotine sneers. "You're kidding, right? I don't have time for these silly, juvenile games."

"Hey," I say. "We're very serious about finding Layla. She's our favorite actress! So if you can just help us—"

"I *said* I don't know anything about a secret chest. I have no idea what you're talking about! You are wasting my time, and I have to go."

No! We have to keep him here. I have to ask him something else quick!

TO ASK GUILLOTINE ABOUT LOUISE,
TURN TO PAGE 74.

←——→

TO ASK GUILLOTINE ABOUT BRAD BRADLEY'S
JEALOUSY, TURN TO PAGE 128.

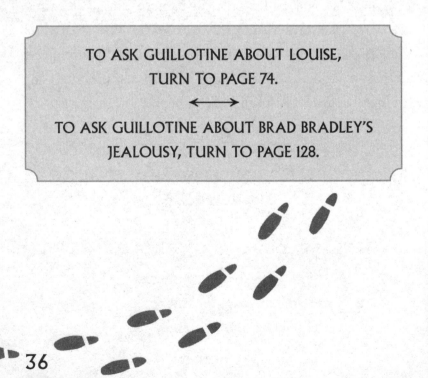

AS MUCH AS Guillotine scares me, we have to talk to him. It seems like he really hates Layla, and we need to find out why.

We find Guillotine with Brad, on the set with all the lockers. He's coaching Brad through his lines. Well, less like coaching and more like bossing Brad around.

"You keep saying, 'Aurelia, I *love* you!' but I need you to read the line like, 'Aurelia, I love *you*!' See how the inflection is different, Brad? You're saying the line wrong."

"But I thought it was better if—"

Guillotine sucks in a sharp breath. "I'm the director. I am the boss, and if you can't do it my way, then get off my set!"

"But—"

"Don't you dare 'but' me!"

To which Frank starts giggling. "Butt."

Guillotine whips around. "No peeps from the peanut gallery!"

Frank twitches, and I put my hands on his shoulders. I know what's happening: the second you tell Frank he can't do something, that's *all* he wants to do.

"PEEEEEEEEEP!" He explodes, and then he pants with relief.

"Can't you see I'm coaching my actor? I'm giving you three seconds to get out of my sight."

"You're very rude," Frank says. "Don't you know your manners? We say thank you, we say please, and excuse me when we sneeze!"

"Three."

Brad frantically shakes his head from behind Guillotine. "Get out!" he whispers. But we can't get out. Not until we get some answers out of this crabby director.

"Two."

"Wait, but we need to ask you a few questions—"

"One."

"—so we can find Layla."

"Security!" Guillotine hollers, and three officers come running up to us. They revoke our badges—the ones that allow us to be on the set. Then they find my mom and kick her off the set too. Bewildered and angry, she drives us straight to military school.

"You ruined my case. I told you not to investigate. I told you to sit quietly. I told you to wait for me. I'm sorry it has to be like this, kids, but maybe *now* you'll learn how to follow directions!"

"Roger that!" Frank says, saluting her.

As Mom drives away, the three of us are face-to-face with the drill sergeant.

"DROP AND GIVE ME TEN THOUSAND!" he spits in our faces.

"Ten thousand what?" Eliza whimpers.

"PUSH-UPS, MAGGOT!"

Up and down, up and down . . . my muscles burn. I'm going to be doing push-ups until my arms fall off, aren't I?

CASE CLOSED.

WE ENTER FORTY into the lock on the side of Layla's mystery box. The box clicks open, and Eliza reaches inside. There's a big stack of papers, which makes Frank groan. "Booooooring," he complains.

"Why don't you count the tiles in the ceiling?" Eliza says. "That's . . . er . . . very important business, and you're the only one I trust, Frank!"

He considers for a moment. "Okay!" he finally replies. "One. Two. Three . . ."

"That will keep him busy for all of ten seconds," I say.

"Then let's read fast."

She hands me a stack. The first thing written at the top of the page is PETITION FOR EMANCIPATION OF A MINOR. Great, I'm already lost.

"Eliza?" I ask, but she gasps at her own paper.

"Notice of termination of representation."

"What?"

"That's what my paper says!" Eliza says excitedly.

"Great, so we *both* have confusing documents."

Eliza lays her paper down on the floor, and we both bend over it. "Notice of termination of representation means that Layla was breaking up with her agent." She thumbs through the contract. "Apparently she is ditching Tuggle, and she put in her sixty-day notice . . . November twentieth."

"The day before she went missing," I say, feeling the wind knocked out of me. But then I pull myself back together, because I have a gut feeling that my document is something different.

I share it with Eliza, whose eyes get wider and wider the farther down she reads. "This is it, Carlos! This is the missing piece in the Miriam puzzle."

"What do you mean?"

"Do you know what legal emancipation is?"

"Should I?"

She points to the paper. "If you're under eighteen, you are considered a minor and need a guardian's permission to do . . . well . . . pretty much anything. But in special cases, the court will allow a teen to divorce their parents. That's called legal emancipation. And that's what Layla is doing with Miriam. She didn't just kick her off the set. She kicked her to the curb . . . permanently."

"Uh, guys?" Frank says.

I pull out the letter we got from Mom—the one we just decoded by reading down the creases. "*That's* why Layla's letter to Wolfgang says, 'Miriam is out of my life now.' And remember how we found that letter in Miriam's glove box about her court date? That's why she's going to court! Because Layla's bringing her there."

"Guys," Frank says.

"And I'm sure the court will allow Layla to be on her

own. She's sixteen, responsible, has adults in her life she can turn to, works a full-time job. *And* her mom has been stealing from her bank account."

"So she's divorcing her mom and her agent at the same time," Eliza says. "That's pretty intense—"

"GUYS!" Frank shouts.

We turn a full one-eighty to look at Frank. And when we do, there are hands wrapped around his tiny neck: Miriam's hands.

TO ACCUSE MIRIAM OF KIDNAPPING LAYLA,
TURN TO PAGE 84.

←——→

TO BEG MIRIAM TO LET FRANK GO,
TURN TO PAGE 143.

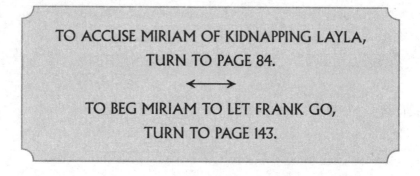

"WHY WERE YOU banned from set?"

Miriam's eyes bulge. *"Excuse* me?"

"Why were you banned from set?" Frank repeats. "Wait, I can say it even louder! WHY WERE YOU BANNED FROM SET?"

"I—I don't know what you're talking about. Layla and I—we're best friends!"

Who is she trying to fool? "We know that your back-stage badge was taken away. It's okay, it happens, but if you could tell us your side of the story . . ."

"We need to know why you were fighting with Layla," Eliza says. Effectively killing my mollycoddle-the-suspect strategy.

Miriam isn't going to like that. In fact, Miriam *doesn't* like that. "I don't see how that's any of your business!" she snaps at Eliza. "I mean . . . Layla and I weren't fighting—we never fight, we are best friends! I mean, how rude and intrusive! You, insulting me like this. Besmirching my character to my face! I will not stand here and continue to be insulted!"

She storms out the door.

"Wait!" I shout after her, but Miriam doesn't stop.

TURN TO PAGE 453.

43

I DECIDE TO climb the tree. Frank is so insistent. And he usually does find good clues, even if by accident.

I go first, and Eliza follows. I'm a little out of practice.

"Come on, you SLOWPOKES! Move it, you SLOTHS!" Frank calls.

A trickle of sweat slides down my forehead, and I keep going.

At the top, I scooch toward Frank, then turn around to pull Eliza up the rest of the way. When we're all nestled on the tree bough, Frank points to the trunk.

"TA-DA!" he says. "And you're welcome!"

There's something carved into the tree:

B.B. ♥s L.J.

"L.J. is clearly Layla Jay," I say. "And B.B. must be . . ."

"Brad Bradley," Eliza finishes. "So, were they a couple? Or were his feelings one-sid—"

Brrrrrrrrrum!

It's a sound I've never actually heard in real life before, but instantly, I know what it is. We all lean over the bough in panic. Near the bottom of the tree, someone is revving up a chain saw.

"HEY! Stop!"

The hooded figure looks at us, and a blank white

mask gleams up. There are no eyeholes, no mouth holes, no indicating features on the mask. Between the mask and the all-black getup, I can't tell if it's a man or woman or boy or girl. All I know is that we have to get out of this tree.

The tree vibrates, and the sound of splitting wood is unmistakable. We scramble to the branches and try to climb down—but the chain saw is too fast. And too good.

Suddenly, the tree sways.

"WE'RE GOING DOWN!" Frank shrieks. "TIMBER!"

CASE CLOSED.

I CHOOSE THE harness. Eliza and I help Frank into it, and I'm tightening the straps as fast as I can. I barely register Eliza, who looks greenish, like she's going to be sick. I can tell she doesn't *love* the idea of pushing her brother off a really tall platform. But it's the best idea we've got.

I hand Frank a second carabiner, attached to a second wire. "Carry this with you."

Eliza's eyebrows raise.

"What for?" Frank asks.

"Pantsuits have belt loops," I tell him. Eliza looks beyond befuddled, but I know Frank understands.

"Aye, aye, Captain!" He salutes.

"Good luck!" I say, and I scoot him off the edge of the bridge.

"I'm a bird! I'm a plane! I'm SUPER FRANK!" he cries as he soars through the air. He heads right for Tuggle, carabiner outstretched in his hands. And he hooks it right onto her belt loop.

"PULL!"

Eliza yanks on the rope, but she needs my help. I put Frank's rope under my feet to keep him suspended and dangling, and with my hands I help yank on Eliza's rope. Tuggle goes flying up off the ground.

"Put me down!" she cries, her legs flailing everywhere.

But we don't. We keep her dangling, suspended and

trapped like a fly in a spider's web.

"Weeeeeeeee!" Frank cries as he swings back and forth.

Boom! The door to the studio bursts open, and a swarm of police officers comes marching in.

"Your mom!" Eliza says.

And sure enough, Mom comes into the studio after the officers, her face swollen like she's been crying.

Louise came through for us!

Once the officers understand what's going on, they run under Frank to catch him.

"HERE I COME!" Frank yells down to them as I release my foot off his rope. He falls into their out-stretched arms.

Then we drop Tuggle, who plunges down. She lands on top of one of the officers and scrambles to make a run for it, but five officers start wrestling her to the ground. Tuggle seems slippery from the paint, and everyone is getting covered with a rainbow of colors. At last a police-woman snaps the handcuffs on, and it's over.

I wave to Mom. And she mimes for us to get to her *right this minute.* I gulp. There's a wormy pit in my stomach as I climb down the ladder and walk over to Mom. I can't meet her eyes because even though we saved Layla, Mom is in the right, and we are in the wrong. I lied to her. I sneaked out. I disobeyed her again. I don't blame her if she hates me.

To my surprise, she starts kissing me rapidly, alternating cheeks.

"You," she says between kisses. "Are. In. So. Much. Trouble."

"I'm sorry," I say once she stops. "I just didn't want you to take me off the case."

"You can't just do whatever you want, whenever you want. If you don't like my parenting decisions, *too bad*. I'm the parent."

"I know."

"And you should have a little faith in me, Carlos. Because I was leaning toward letting you work with me tomorrow."

"But you said . . . you said it was too dangerous."

"I still feel that way. But if you were by my side, I thought maybe I could protect you. Instead, you just throw yourself into harm's way, alone, with reckless abandon!"

"Sorry," I say again.

"Sorry, Ms. S," Eliza echoes, close to tears.

Mom frowns. And then her gaze drifts off to where police officers are helping Frank out of the harness. Behind Mom, a few EMTs are strapping Layla into a stretcher.

"Is Layla going to be okay?" I ask.

Mom escorts us over to the EMTs, who assure us

that Layla will be fine once she wakes up. Layla doesn't seem to be suffering any physical harm or injuries. Apparently Tuggle just gave her something that would knock her out, while she attempted to move her . . . and deal with us.

Between Layla's unconsciousness and the multicolored paint all over the set, I worry for a second that I might have blown it for Mom. Maybe Wolfgang will be mad. Maybe he'll refuse to pay her.

"Did we make a mess out of your case?" I whisper.

"I guess we'll see what Mr. Westover says," Mom says.

As if he were waiting for someone to call his name, Wolfgang kicks the studio door open and rushes in, followed by a handful of people I assume are other producers.

"There you are!" he says to Mom. "I just got the message about Tuggle. *Tuggle!* Who'd have thunk?"

"Hopefully this means you can resume your production schedule," Mom says. "After Layla has recovered, of course. And I . . . I'm very sorry about the mess."

"What mess? Oh, the paint? Pish posh, that's nothing! You should have seen this place after we filmed the season three finale. The dragon burns the school to the ground, spoiler alert! Dust and ashes and scorch marks everywhere. Anyway." He takes a check out of his pocket. "You pulled through for this show. You really deserve this."

Mom takes the check, with a little wink at me. And that's when I know that even though I'm probably grounded until the next century, Mom and I will be okay.

Then Wolfgang links elbows with my mom and starts escorting her toward the door.

"Mr. Westover, where are you taking me?"

"To the press! We're going to put Las Pistas Detective Agency on the map. And we'll make you a STAR."

I stifle a laugh as Mom tries to wiggle away from Wolfgang to avoid greeting the cameras in her pajamas and the hotel bathrobe. But Wolfgang insists. When Mom's out the door, and the police have left with Tuggle, and the ambulance has left with Layla, we three are all alone in a quiet studio.

I put my arms around Eliza and Frank. We don't have the spotlight, but we don't need it. We have each other . . . and the joy of a mystery well solved.

CASE CLOSED.

"FRANK!" I SAY. "Stink bomb!"

He lets it rip.

PFFFFFFFTTTTTT!

Eliza screams, and we both cover our noses and mouths. Wolfgang turns a delicate shade of green, and then moves over to the back of the closet to retch. And Tuggle looks confused, but I know *instantly* the moment the smell hits her—because her eyes water, and her nose twitches.

"That's *foul.* Oh—I taste it! It's on my tongue!"

Frank moves out of the room, butt first, letting loose all sorts of farts in some sort of invisible smell cloud around Tuggle. She even begins to wobble. She loosens her grip on the remote.

"Now, Frank!"

Frank leaps through the air and pulls it out of her hands. "TA-DA!" Frank says.

I grab the tarp covering Layla. Using our shirts as filtering masks, Eliza and I go into the fart cloud. We pull the tarp around Tuggle and tie it tightly closed.

Tuggle just gags.

"Good thing I had beans for lunch today!" he says, even though he actually didn't. "Beans, beans, the musical fruit! The more you eat, the more you toot! The more you toot, the better you feel, so have baked beans at every meal! Beans, beans, they're good for your heart, the more you eat, the more you fart. . . ."

Eliza sings with him, but I'm not in a singing mood—not until I go find Mom.

A few hours later, things are hectic beyond belief.

The paramedics revived Layla Jay, and she was given some juice boxes and a blanket. She seems to be rattled emotionally, but physically mostly unharmed—aside from a few cuts and bruises where she was dragged unconscious across the basement.

I found Mom locked in Layla's dressing-room closet. Turns out Tuggle was bluffing about getting to her first. Mom also has a few scrapes from her brawl with Tuggle. But even while being treated by the paramedics, she didn't forget her detective duty. She made sure that everyone, even the police, gave Layla a few hours' space and privacy, and Layla seemed very grateful for that. Layla was close to tears before she retreated to her dressing room with Mom's phone number, for whenever she was ready.

Meanwhile, the police dragged Tuggle off, and she was tight-lipped. No monologue about her evil villain plan. No explanation of why she did this. Mom whispered in my ear that Tuggle knows that anything she says or admits to while being arrested could come back to bite her in court. And goodness knows they have a *lot* to try her for: kidnapping, arson, attempted murder, slander, fraud . . . the list goes on and on.

"I can't believe Frank's *fart* saved the day," Eliza says as we stand in the sun watching a few police cars drive off.

"I cut the cheese!" Frank says gleefully. "Broke wind! Let it rip! TOOT TOOT!"

I laugh, then go back to watching Wolfgang Westover and Guillotine talk to the press at the studio gate. Brad Bradley is making kissy faces into a mirror. Layla's mom is being escorted from the premises, just like Layla requested.

A hand touches my shoulder. "Come on," Mom says. "Layla just texted—she's ready to talk."

"I'm allowed to go?"

Mom bends over and puts a hand on my shoulder. "I know our walkie-talkie plan didn't work out *quite* the way we wanted to, but you were quick on your feet and smart, and I finally see what you've been trying to tell me this whole time. You're a natural, hijo."

I beam. "So next time—"

"Por Dios, Carlos, we *just* finished with this case. Let's take a ten-minute break, at least!"

I laugh.

"But yes, next time you can help me. Right from the start. That's a promise."

I put out my pinkie, and she links hers with mine. And then she tugs me, by the pinkie, back into the studio—to Layla's dressing room. Eliza and Frank follow in our wake. Through the door, I can hear Layla's loud yelp when we knock.

She lets us in, and I can tell that even though she still looks just as glamorous as ever—with her flawless brown skin and her bright brown eyes and her perfectly coiled corkscrew hair—she's very frightened. "I-is she gone?"

"She's gone," Mom assures her.

"I don't think she meant to kidnap me," Layla says. "She seems to have panicked. Or snapped. I'm not sure which is worse. But even if it wasn't planned, she just held me prisoner for days. She could have let me go! She kept trying to convince me to stay with her agency . . . or at least not to tell anyone about all the bad things she'd been doing. Like I'd do either of those things! I'm going to tell the whole world about this." Her eyes fill up with tears. "Thank you for finding me. I . . . I don't know what I would have done without you."

"Yes," Mom says, beaming. "The junior detectives at Las Pistas Detective Agency are one of a kind."

I don't think my smile could get any bigger.

"I can't wait to see what they'll solve next," Mom says.

I was wrong. My grin gets wider still.

CASE CLOSED.

THIS MAY BE our only chance to search Wolfgang's office. We have to take it.

We slip inside, and the door clicks behind us. Eliza and I start poking around, while Frank sits in Wolfgang's big swivel chair, spinning around and around and around.

"Wheeeeeeeeeee!" Frank says.

"Hey! Look at this."

Eliza comes over to the computer, and we look at a sent email I found.

Douglas,

"Who's Douglas?" Frank says.

"Douglas Chen," Eliza replies. "The director. Everyone calls him Guillotine, remember?"

I know it delays next season's shooting schedule, but don't worry: Layla's disappearance is good news. This is creating so much publicity for Layla and the show. The perfect publicity stunt—my god, why didn't I think of this sooner? Our show has never been googled more. And our ratings have never been higher. Very happy right now.

—W.W.

"Something smells fishy," I say.

"Is it a fish?" Frank says. "Fishes smell fishy."

"You're right," Eliza says. "Wolfgang seems far too happy in this email to Guillotine. Do you think he organized Layla's disappearance?"

Suddenly, the doorknob turns—there's not enough time to hide!

Wolfgang Westover is standing there, his jaw open. "I . . . I forgot something," he says. "What are you doing in here?"

"You're happy about Layla's disappearance, aren't you?"

"I beg your pardon?" His expression is mixed confusion and rage. His chin wobbles.

"It's great *publicity* for the show, isn't it?"

Wolfgang's eyes narrow in on his computer. There's a charged pause, and I hold my breath. For a second, I'm worried Wolfgang's pinched face is going to pop right off his neck.

"First you hide in my closet. Now you snoop through my emails—don't deny it!" he says, as Eliza and I both open our mouths to protest.

Just when I think it can't get any worse, Mom runs in. "What are you doing in here?" she fumes. "Again? I told you to wait by Guillotine's chair!"

"Don't give me that!" Wolfgang snaps. "You put them up to this, didn't you? It's all part of your act, you two-faced scammer! I'm revoking your clearance. Security!"

He presses a button on his fancy watch.

Four security officers come running in and drag us off the lot.

"Carlos, what have you *done*?" Mom shouts.

"LET US GO!" Frank demands.

"Next time, don't mess with me," Wolfgang says coldly. "You see how easy it is for me to get you expelled from the premises?"

I hate to admit it, but it was . . . elementary, my dear Wolfgang.

CASE CLOSED.

WE HAVE TO stay here and guard the prop room. We promised.

But that doesn't mean we have to sit silently and twiddle our thumbs. It's time to examine the scene of the crime.

Frank, Eliza, and I close the door, so that the cast and crew waiting in the hall can't see what we're doing. Just in case we stumble on a big clue.

Eliza and I sit on the floor, combing through the broken props: snapped wands, shredded robes, broomsticks plucked clean of the sweepy parts. Frank squeals over a broken drawer of fake mustaches and beards.

"I don't know if we're going to find anything in here," Eliza says after a while. "It seems like everything is broken, crushed, or hacked to bits."

"We have to keep looking," I say.

"I like this mustache!" Frank says, putting on a mustache with curled tips. "Or do you like *this*?" he says, trying on some muttonchops. Only he puts the fake muttonchops on his forehead.

I roll my eyes.

"Great job, buddy," Eliza says.

"You're not even looking!" Frank whines. "Elizaaaaaa!" He stomps his foot and then jumps up and down. The cracked floor-length mirror on the wall rattles, and the smashed wardrobe creaks.

58

"Frank! Stop!"

"Frank!" Eliza says, her voice shrill. "No temper tantrums."

"YES TEMPER TANTRUMS!" Frank says. Then he picks up debris off the floor and throws it. *Smash! Bang! Crash!*

He hits the floor-length mirror, and it shatters into pieces. A gust of cold wind circles the room. I grab my arms and hug them close to me, and Eliza shivers.

"A ghost!" Frank cries.

"Where is that coming from?" Eliza says.

I walk around the room, hands out in front of me, feeling for the source of the wind. It's difficult to avoid the broken props, but I tiptoe around. First, I check the door, but there's no draft there.

"Over here!" Eliza points. "The shattered mirror."

Standing in front of the mirror, I realize she's right. With the mirror glass gone, there's a strong wind, blowing through the thin wooden backing. I push the mirror frame aside . . . to reveal a small hole. A tunnel, just big enough to crawl through.

"Why is it always tunnels?" Eliza groans.

"Hooray!" Frank says, all signs of his temper tantrum gone. "I love to crawl!"

I pull out the phone in my pocket. I have to text Mom about this. We don't know where this tunnel leads, or what's inside. But I have to let her know where we're going.

Eliza frowns. "Who are you going to call?"

"Ghostbusters!" Frank shouts.

"I'm texting my mom. Just in case."

"Are you sure about that?" Eliza asks. "What if she forbids us from exploring?"

I hesitate. I never like lying to Mom. This feels wrong. But maybe Eliza's right: Mom does get overprotective. But then again, she's been letting us in on the investigation, and keeping our whereabouts from her feels a bit like stabbing her in the back.

I quickly text Mom.

> Following a lead. Hole in the prop room wall to who knows where! Will explain later.

Eliza shakes her head at me. She can judge me all she wants, but I know I did the right thing.

Without a word to Eliza, I drop to my hands and knees—and inch into the darkness.

The tunnel is freezing. The draft keeps blowing right through us, and I'm taking the biggest hit, being in the front. I'm blocking the wind from Frank and Eliza. I'm practically a protective wall.

My teeth chatter, but we can't quit now. Layla Jay

needs us. Because the more we dig into this mystery, the more it seems like there isn't *anyone* who has her back.

"Carlos?" Eliza says softly, after it seems like we've been crawling *forever*. "Are we sure this is the right way? Maybe this is just a mouse hole or something."

"A mouse hole big enough for a person to fit into?"

"A giant mouse!" Frank says. "Like . . . like a rat! Or a squirrel. Have you ever looked at a squirrel? It's just a rat with a tail!"

"Rats have tails, Frank," Eliza reminds him.

"But not bushy tails. Wormy tails."

"But wormy tails are still tails—"

"Shhhhhh!" I interrupt. "I see something!"

Ahead, the tunnel seems to open up enough to let us get to our feet. We're in an empty hollow that feels a lot like the inside of a vault. The ceiling is at least twenty feet above us, and everything is cold. The air, the dirt walls, the dark.

It reminds me a lot of season two, when Layla's character gets kidnapped and taken to a secret cave. She had to solve a puzzle to break free.

Actually . . . *is* this the cave? Could they have filmed it here? Would it be possible to get the cameras into this space under Stage Eight? Clearly, I must investigate.

"Eliza, can I see your flashlight?"

"Sure," Eliza says, her voice echoing around the walls. She slips me the flashlight. "Do you think we are we underground?"

"Yup! In a hidey-hole! Like a mole!" Frank says cheerfully. "Hey—that rhymes!"

I shine the flashlight, and see something carved into the wall:

	1	2	3	4	5
A	A	B	C	D	E
B	F	G	H	I or J	K
C	L	M	N	O	P
D	Q	R	S	T	U
E	V	W	X	Y	Z

B1-C4-D2-A5-E1-A5-D2 E2-B4-C1-C1 E4-C4-D5
D3-D4-A1-E4 B3-A5-D2-A5,
  E2-B4-D4-A3-B3,

B4-C3 A4-A1-D2-B5-C3-A5-D3-D3 C5-C1-A5-
C3-D4-E4, B4-C3
  D3-B4-C1-A5-C3-D4 C5-B4-D4-A3-B3

D5-C3-C1-A5-D3-D3 E4-C4-D5 B3-A1-E1-A5
D4-B3-A5 D3-A5-A3-D2-A5-D4
  B5-A5-E4,

D4-B3-A5 C4-C3-C1-E4 E2-A1-E4 D4-B3-A1-D4
E4-C4-D5 A3-A1-C3 B1-C1-A5-A5:

A1 C2-A1-B2-B4-A3-A1-C1 C3-D5-C2-A2-
A5-D2, D4-B3-A5
    D3-D4-D2-C4-C3-B2-A5-D3-D4 C4-D5-D4
    D4-B3-A5-D2-A5

D4-E2-B4-A3-A5 C2-C4-D2-A5 D4-B3-A1-C3
A1-C1-C4-C3-A5;
    C4-C3-A3-A5 C2-C4-D2-A5 D4-B3-A1-C3 A1
    C5-A1-B4-D2.

D1-D5-A1-D2-D4-A5-D2 A1 A4-C4-E5-A5-C3,
D4-D2-B4-C5-C1-A5 A1 C4-C3-A5,

D3-B3-C4-D5-D4 B4-D4 C4-D5-D4, A1-C3-A4
E4-C4-D5 A1-D2-A5 A4-C4-C3-A5.

It *is* the cave from the show. And we're stuck inside
it—just like Layla's character, Aurelia, was!

"Oh wow!" I say, and I shine my flashlight on the
Thompsons. "Eliza, remember this from season two?"

"Of course I do!" she squeals.

"And . . . do you remember the solution?"

Her face falls. "No, I don't."

"I do!" Frank says.

"Frank, you don't even watch *Teen Witch*."

"I know the password anyway," he brags. "It's zip-perpants."

"That's definitely not it," Eliza says. Then she groans. "I wish I could remember the answer. But I think we're just going to have to do it ourselves . . . just like on *Teen Witch*."

ADD THREE HUNDRED TO THE SOLUTION
TO THIS PUZZLE, AND TURN TO THAT PAGE.

←——→

OR TO ASK ELIZA FOR A HINT,
TURN TO PAGE 234.

I DELETE THE letter L first. Then S, T, A, T, N, G, R. And presto! We're in!

Except . . . we're not in. The box remains locked.

Suddenly, an alarm blares. *WAHHHHH WAHH-HHH WAHHHHH!!!!*

I drop the box, and the screen cracks.

"What are you doing?" says a sharp voice from the doorway. Guillotine is flanked by two security guards. "This is private property!" Guillotine says. "It is illegal to rifle through my things without a search warrant. Step away from my desk!"

"Okay, okay," I say, putting my hands up. Eliza copies me, but Frank sticks his pointer and thumb at Guillotine and says, "This town ain't big enough for the both of us."

"Get them out of here," Guillotine says, snapping his fingers. The guards grab us by the wrists and pull us out of the office. Guillotine has a huge smug smile on his face.

"Where are you taking us?" I ask the guard who's dragging me along. We leave Stage Eight and are being pulled down the path of Burbank Studios, toward an unmarked concrete building.

"Where all the bad actors go . . . to Stage Thirteen: the stage of shame!"

He opens the door and shoves me inside—it's mostly

abandoned, with flickering lights. Except that there are a bunch of actors in there, mulling about aimlessly.

"I forgot my lines!" a woman shouts, seizing Eliza by the shoulders.

"That's nothing!" someone else cries. "I missed my mark."

"I committed the worst crime an actor can commit— I sneezed on the producer!" a man whispers.

"I tripped over a wire."

"I cut my hair an inch too short!"

"The shame! The shame!" all the actors moan. "The horror, the horror!"

They swarm us like zombies—there are too many of them. We're overrun. . . .

CASE CLOSED.

WE DECIDE TO go back inside the studio. Louise gave us so much information, and so many potential suspects to interview that it'd be silly not to start talking to them. We might not find anything in the woods, but I know we'll definitely discover things if we talk to our suspects.

The set is crowded with crew members and cast members, who look like they're filming a scene. There are lots of flying doughnuts, and Brad Bradley is on a stunt broomstick in front of a green screen, trying to catch them in his mouth. I'm not sure why—or what the heck is going on in season four. All I know is that it looks magical to me. And to Frank, who is practically drooling.

"I think I'll watch this show now!" he says. "Let's go get a super doughnut!"

"I think we should interview someone," I say. But as I look around, it seems like everyone's occupied with the show: Brad is acting. Guillotine is filming. Wolfgang is taking notes on his clipboard. Tuggle is on her computer in the corner. Miriam Jay is nowhere to be found. And we left Louise outside. I turn around, and—

I spot the *only* person I did not want to see: Mom.

She walks over to us, and without so much as a hello, Mom swipes Eliza's notebook from her hands. I wish Eliza had put that away before we walked back in the building. But it's too late now. Mom looks between Eliza's notes and me. Then back at Eliza's notes. Then back at me.

I feel like shrinking into the floor.

"You've been investigating," Mom says. "Haven't you, Carlos?"

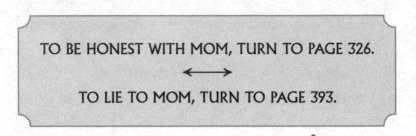

TO BE HONEST WITH MOM, TURN TO PAGE 326.

$\longleftrightarrow$

TO LIE TO MOM, TURN TO PAGE 393.

I DECIDE TO let Guillotine's past-tense error . . . stay in the past. Whether or not it was an honest mistake, I know that it would be a bad call for us to push him too far.

So Guillotine takes a deep breath, nervously reties his ponytail, and continues, "Like I was saying, Layla is a nightmare to work with. Once she was given an executive producer credit, she challenged me on everything. Every directorial decision, she had some question, comment, or complaint. 'No, not that way, Mr. Chen,' he mimics in a high-pitched voice. 'I think my character would be much more likely to cry here.' Who's the director here?" he ends. "In my twenty years in the industry, I've never seen a young girl so bold, insolent, or opinionated!"

Eliza folds her arms, an expression of distaste on her face. I'm sure Eliza didn't take too kindly to his comment about opinionated young girls . . . like it is a *bad* thing.

In fact, I don't take too kindly to that either. "So you're mad that she has thoughts about how her character would react? A character she's been playing for three seasons already?"

Guillotine's nostrils flare. "I'm the director, the boss. Layla Jay is just an actress."

"I thought the producer is the boss," I say. "Wolfgang Westover."

Guillotine doesn't like that. "Don't even get me started on that buffoon!"

"Baboon!" Frank says, scratching his armpits.

"Exactly," Guillotine says. "He may call himself the boss, but he will *never* have my artistic vision for this masterful television show. And worst of all, he doesn't know how to control Layla. He lets her get a big head. He folds to her demands, lets her get whatever she wants. I'm the only one who sees her for what she is: a spoiled brat."

Eliza, Frank, and I inhale sharply. We all know he's gone a step too far, calling a missing girl a brat. Especially after he referred to her in the past tense. Warning bells are chiming in my head—but at the same time, would the culprit be this honest about his hatred of her, knowing we were investigating her disappearance? No one could be that stupid, right?

"Look," Guillotine says, breaking the silence. "If you need even more evidence about Layla's lacking character, you should talk to her agent or her mom."

"Why?"

"Layla's been fighting with both of them, too. Just saying . . . if Layla fights with me, Brad Bradley, Agatha Tuggle, *and* Miriam Jay, then the common denominator here is Layla." He straightens his tie. "If that's all you need, I have to go to the woods now."

70

"The woods?" I ask.

"Well, you don't think we spend *all* day inside, do you?" he says. "It's where we film our outdoor scenes, when we're not using a green screen. It's about a half mile away, still on the studio lot." He steps out the prop-room door, then turns around and says, "Clean this mess."

Then he's gone.

"Wow," I say. "He is terrible."

"A real poo-poo face," Frank agrees.

Eliza starts putting away the props we pulled out of drawers. "I still can't believe you let him get away with referring to her in the past tense. I thought for sure you'd call him out on it."

I shrug. "Sometimes it's better not to back your suspect into a corner. Besides, we know he messed up. And he knows. And he knows we know."

"And we know that he knows that we know that he knows that we know!" Frank says.

"My head is spinning!"

Eliza shuts the trunk of props and turns around to face me. She bites her lip thoughtfully. "So do you think Guillotine had something to do with Layla's disappearance?"

"Too early to tell," I say. "But he's *definitely* suspicious."

"As is Brad Bradley."

"As is Frank!" Frank says. Then he picks up a prop wizard staff—the same one that the Witch Queen had when she battled Aurelia at the end of season one. That staff is practically sacred to Eliza and me. But Frank doesn't care; he swings it around sloppily. Eliza and I jump back to avoid getting whacked.

"Where to now?" Eliza asks.

"We still have to talk to Louise," I remind her. "Come on, Frank. Put the staff down."

"But I was about to destroy all of humankind!" he whines.

Uh-oh. When he starts whining like this, it's a sign that a full-on tantrum is just around the corner. I have to stop it . . . with a bribe. "I'll give you choco—"

"Okay!" he says, before I even finish the sentence.

That was easy. I dig into Eliza's backpack of snacks as we walk out of the dressing room. My head is practically buried in her bag—

BAM.

I look up, and my heart drops to my stomach.

Mom.

She looks at each of us, suspicion written plain on her face. She gives me a once-over, then Eliza, then Frank.

She knows, and my stomach does a somersault again.

"ALERT ALERT ALERT!" Frank shouts. "RUN HIDE PANIC!"

"Hijo," Mom says, narrowing in on me. "I thought I told you kids to stay in the main stage area."

"You did."

"So what are you doing backstage in the prop room?"

This is what I've been afraid of. Ever since we solved our first mystery behind her back, Mom's been harping on about trust and honesty. I haven't been honest, and I've broken her trust . . . again. I don't *want* to lie to her, but she's been blocking Eliza and me from cases left and right, ever since this summer. She just doesn't understand how much being a detective means to me—and how good I am at it. If only there was a way to make her see how much I need this . . .

But if I come clean now, will Mom punish me for lying to her again? Or is it way worse if I keep lying to her?

She squints. "You're hesitating, Carlos. Have you been investigating when I expressly told you not to?"

TO BE HONEST WITH MOM, TURN TO PAGE 326.

⟵——⟶

TO LIE TO MOM, TURN TO PAGE 393.

"WHAT DO YOU think about Louise?" I ask him.

"Entitled, annoying, obsessive thorn in my side—what else can I say?"

"But . . . why is she allowed on set when she clearly bothers Layla?"

"You can do anything when you know the right people." He rolls his eyes. "And that applies to all the children on this set. Layla and Brad included. Spoiled little brats," he mumbles under his breath.

"Do you have a problem with Layla?" I ask.

"No," Guillotine says. "We're just *peachy*."

But it doesn't sound peachy.

Kind of sounds like he's got a major problem with Layla, just like Brad Bradley seems to have some sort of problem with Layla. Does *everyone* have a problem with Layla?

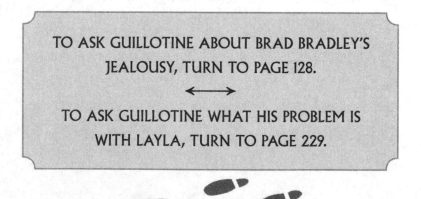

TO ASK GUILLOTINE ABOUT BRAD BRADLEY'S JEALOUSY, TURN TO PAGE 128.

←——→

TO ASK GUILLOTINE WHAT HIS PROBLEM IS WITH LAYLA, TURN TO PAGE 229.

"YOU DIDN'T HAPPEN to get any pictures of Layla before she went missing, did you?"

"You see this?" Louise says, holding up her camera. "This is *old school*. Old-fashioned. Nondigital. I develop my own film, so if you want to see what I've captured, it'll take some time. But I can try to do it quickly, if you think it will help."

"Yes, please," Eliza says.

"But I don't need my camera to tell you what's going on in there," she says, jerking a thumb toward the studio. "It's been bonkers lately. Even before Layla vanished into thin air."

TO ASK LOUISE ABOUT THE ON-SET GOSSIP, TURN TO PAGE 290.

←——→

TO ASK LOUISE WHERE SHE THINKS LAYLA IS, TURN TO PAGE 344.

"WHAT CAN YOU tell us about Louise?" I ask Brad.

"She's disturbing. She creeps everyone out."

"How so?" Eliza whispers, hiding most of her face behind her hands.

Brad crinkles his nose. "When Layla goes out to dinner with her friends or mom, Louise shows up with her camera. She is always following Layla around. Rumor has it Louise even built a Layla shrine in her closet . . . made from Layla's discarded tissues."

"Ewwwww!" Frank says.

"You're telling me, little man!" Brad says. "Like, dude, get a life, right? Oh, and she stole a lock of Layla's hair one time. Did anyone tell you about that? On the red carpet of the Kids' Choice Awards. She just went at Layla Jay with a scissors, and *snip*. Cut one of her curls clean off." Brad smirks. "Security tackled Louise and dragged her away. It was pretty sweet."

"If Louise is such a dangerous presence," Eliza says, "then why is she on the studio lot? That was her outside. The teenager holding the LAYLA'S NUMBER ONE FAN poster, right?"

Brad frowns. No, he *glowers*. "There's not much we can do about Louise. She's the niece of Wolfgang Westover, our producer."

Wow. Okay. Did *not* expect that.

"Does Wolfgang know about her creepy behavior?"

Brad shrugs. "It's no big secret around set. But Mr. Westover hasn't done anything to stop her. So either he knows and doesn't care, or he doesn't care to know. Which one's worse?"

"Do you think," I wonder out loud, "that Louise could have taken Layla?"

"Not a chance. Because Layla wasn't kidnapped."

Eliza and I exchange a glance. The secret note from Layla that we found implies otherwise. But Brad, I'm sure, doesn't know about the cryptic cipher we just decoded, so I don't say anything.

"Layla's *fine*," Brad continues. "I'm sure this is all just a publicity stunt. Some way to get even more famous and more attention," he adds bitterly. "She's an attention hog. And the absolute worst. I'm on Guillotine's side with this one."

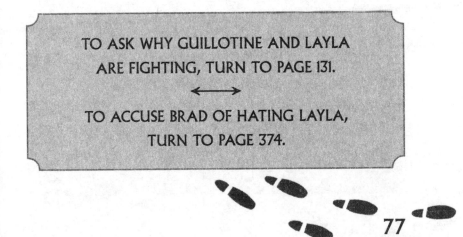

TO ASK WHY GUILLOTINE AND LAYLA ARE FIGHTING, TURN TO PAGE 131.

⟵ ⟶

TO ACCUSE BRAD OF HATING LAYLA, TURN TO PAGE 374.

IF MIRIAM KNOWS Layla like my mom knows me, then maybe she'll have an idea where Layla went. "Where do you think your daughter is?"

"If I knew that, we wouldn't need *you*," Miriam says.

"Take a guess," I say. "Is she at any of her second homes?"

"You *do* know she has a second home, right?" Eliza says. "It was in an interview she did last year before season three."

And I thought *I* was obsessed! Here Eliza is, reading Layla Jay interviews for fun!

"Of course I know about her second home." Miriam bristles. "But she wasn't there."

"Do you think she's hiding? Or do you think she's been kidnapped? Or did she just run away?"

"Like I said, how should I know?" Miriam snaps. "I mean . . . I am just so worried!" She blubbers and snozzes into a tissue.

TO ASK MIRIAM WHY LAYLA BANNED HER
FROM THE SET, TURN TO PAGE 43.

←——→

TO ASK MIRIAM ABOUT LAYLA'S RELATIONSHIP
WITH THE CAST AND CREW, TURN TO PAGE 351.

I CAN'T TAKE a chance that Mom will ban me from detective work . . . forever. There's no way I can tell her what we're up to until I've proven myself.

Mom is giving me her best stink eye. "Well?"

"We haven't been investigating," I say. "We wouldn't do that."

"Is that right?" Mom says, looking at Eliza and Frank now.

Eliza nods but can't seem to meet my mom's eye.

"Everything Carlos said is true," Frank says, and I feel a rush of relief. "ON OPPOSITE DAY."

No, Frank! Noooooooooooo!

Mom whips toward me. "I knew it! Didn't we *just* have a conversation about trust?"

"Uh."

"And two seconds after that conversation, you decide to sneak away from your babysitter?"

"Uh."

"And then you just lied to me about it—*again*—right to my face?"

Well, when she says it like *that*, it sounds really bad.

Mom leads us back to Maureen.

"You lost them," my mom says. "So, just to make sure that you never lose them again . . ." Mom reaches into her bag and pulls out three child leashes.

Before we can run, Mom gets one over my head and

around my torso, and Maureen locks Eliza into one. Frank buckles himself in voluntarily. "Bow wow wow, I'm a dog!" he says.

"Mom, this is *so* embarrassing!"

"Embarrassing, but necessary," Mom replies. "Clearly I need to keep you on a short leash . . . literally."

CASE CLOSED.

THERE'S NO DOUBT about it: when we read the letters only on the crease, it says the papers are under the floorboard. But what papers? And why would she trust Wolfgang with this information? I guess this is stuff I might understand once I look under the floorboard. The only problem is . . .

"Which floorboard?" I say. "There are a ton of floors in this studio."

"Then we'll have to search them ALL!" Frank cries. "Rip up the floors, one by one, until we've looked under every last plank!" He plops down on the floor and starts clawing at the burgundy carpet.

"Stop that, Frank," Eliza says. "It'll be in her dressing room. Why would she hide important papers in someone else's room, or in a room that's used by the whole cast and crew?"

That makes sense to me, so we head toward Layla's room, tiptoeing so we don't draw attention to ourselves. This is good, though—we've been wanting to search Layla's room for a whole day now, ever since we found Miriam Jay sneaking around in there.

I only hope Miriam didn't find whatever's under Layla's floorboards before us.

When we close the door to Layla's dressing room, Frank drops to the floor and starts knocking on the panels.

"Knock on wood!" he says, bursting into cackles. "Get it, guys? *Get it?*"

"Good one, Frank," I say, getting on my hands and knees. Every board I feel is super tight.

"Over here!" Eliza says, prying up a board by the dresser. She reaches under it and pulls up a metal yellow box—a small personal safe.

"Open it!" I say.

"I can't—it's locked!"

We take turns hitting it and smashing it and shaking it—but nothing pops it open. I turn the box over.

"Eliza, look at this!" It has some tiny yellow numbers on it in a triangle shape. Since the box itself is yellow, it's almost impossible to see. And there are two rotating dials underneath that I can push with my thumb . . . both with numbers one through nine on them.

"A combination lock," Eliza says. "I bet this pyramid somehow tells us the right answer. Looking at these dials, we'll definitely need a number to break in."

"Or a sledgehammer!" Frank says. "SMASH! Or a bomb! BOOM! Or a shark! CHOMP!"

"That's not a bad idea, Frank," I say.

Eliza snorts. "A shark? Really?"

I roll my eyes. "Not that part! The sledgehammer—or some sort of tool to break in."

"Or we could just solve the puzzle," Eliza says, running her fingers over the yellow numbers on the yellow safe. "Maybe it's less exciting than smashing a piece of metal to smithereens, but it's more reliable. We just need to figure out the missing numbers in the pyramid."

$$?$$
$$16 \qquad 24$$
$$6 \qquad ? \qquad 14$$
$$2 \qquad 4 \qquad 6 \qquad 8$$

TO SMASH THE SAFE OPEN WITH A HAMMER,
TURN TO PAGE 264.

←—→

TO CRACK THE SAFE USING THE PUZZLE,
THE NUMBER THAT BELONGS AT THE TOP OF
THE PYRAMID IS YOUR NEXT PAGE.

←—→

TO ASK ELIZA FOR A HINT TO THE PUZZLE,
TURN TO PAGE 324.

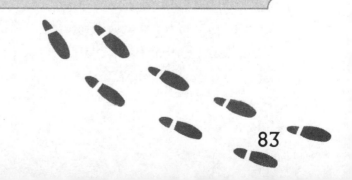

"YOU!" I SHOUT. "You kidnapped your own daughter!"

"First of all, no. Second of all, even if I did, it wouldn't be kidnapping. You can't kidnap your own child."

"Of course you can kidnap your own child!" Eliza says. "That happens all the time!"

"Can't breathe!" Frank says.

"That's the point!" Miriam snaps. "Now, the papers. Pass them to me."

Frank's safety is worth more than any dumb document. I hold the papers out to her. But she's still too far away to reach.

"Closer," she says. "And no funny business."

"What's so important about these papers?" I say, stepping toward her.

"They make me look guilty. I knew Layla had them hidden around here somewhere—I just had to find them. Now I can hide them, and no one will ever have to know that she was trying to divorce me."

"Was?" Eliza says softly.

"You can't really think she's still alive after six days, do you? I know cop shows. Layla even auditioned for cop shows. She's a goner. And I am not wrongfully going to prison for that ungrateful child."

She leans forward and snatches the papers out of my hands and pushes Frank into me. We fall to the ground

84

as Miriam runs. She heads to the left—toward the set. We could follow her, or we could take a shortcut by going right and cutting her off.

TO RUN AFTER HER, TURN TO PAGE 384.

⟵⟶

TO CUT HER OFF, TURN TO PAGE 411.

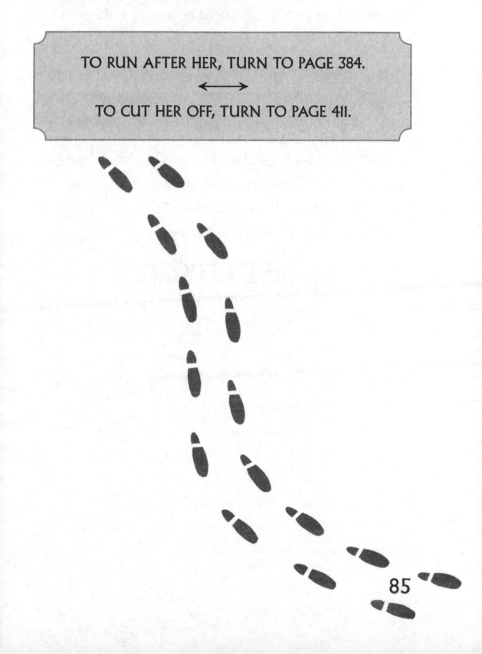

I HAVE TO grab Layla and bring her to safety.

I gather the papers off the floor from when Miriam got thrown aside. Then I move very slowly toward the control center inside the robot dragon. I don't want to make any sudden movements. . . . I have to be calm and steady, so that when I'm close enough, I can make my move.

When I'm a stone's throw away, I lunge, reaching for Layla.

But the dragon lurches forward to block me—it's too fast! I don't have time to jump out of the way!

The last thing I see is the giant tail of the robot dragon, headed straight toward me.

CASE CLOSED.

OKAY . . . THIS ELEVATOR emergency hatch situation is tricky.

"Eliza, I need your help."

She looks up from reading Layla's safe documents. "Hmm . . . it seems like the easiest way to solve it is to dive right in. Want to start with the top left H?"

"We can make *hatch* straight across the top. And then again down the side. Right?"

"Attach the wires, and we'll see," Eliza says. "I'm a visual learner."

"Eliza, you're an *everything* learner," I grumble as I attach the wires to the lettered buttons.

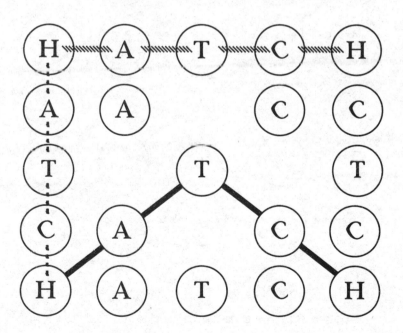

Suddenly, new combinations pop into my head. "Actually, hold back, Eliza. I think I see some more!"

"Yeah! Shut your face, Eliza!" Frank says gleefully.

"That's not very nice, Frank."

"I know you are, but what am I?"

Eliza sighs. "Frank, please. I have to read." And she buries her face back in the documents.

"There!" I say. "While you two were bickering, I found more combinations!"

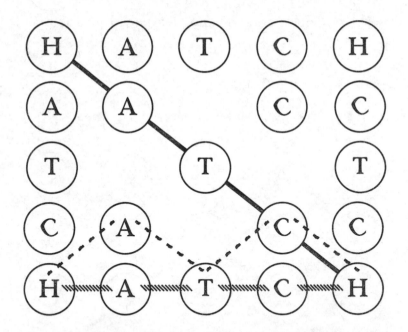

"This is great, Carlos!" Eliza says. "You have six so far! But we still have more to find with the top left H and the bottom left H. I think we can rule out the top right and bottom right H, since there are no As next to them."

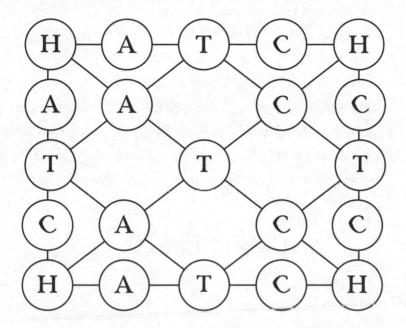

This task is making my head spin. I've connected wires to three hatch combinations starting with the top left H. And then three with the bottom left H. All I have to do is add that to any other hatch connections I see with the bottom left and top left H buttons, and then I'm done. Take that, elevator!

ADD THREE HUNDRED TO THE NUMBER OF TIMES THE WORD *HATCH* CAN BE MADE IN A CONTINUOUS LINE, AND TURN TO THAT PAGE.

I RUN OUT of the closet and charge at Tuggle.

"Auuuugggghhhhhh!" I scream as I grab her around the waist and tackle her.

"Big mistake," Tuggle whispers. "I didn't mean to, but I accidentally pushed the devic—"

BOOM! BOOM! BOOM!

The explosives erupt, and I cover my head to shield myself. I look up when everything is quiet again. But the basement is still rumbling. Suddenly, the dirt ground splinters, then it crumbles. And then the earth swallows us whole.

CASE CLOSED.

THE LAST UNSCRAMBLE gives us a number: ninety-one.

With the passcode in our hands, we head to the door.

"Hold on," Eliza says. "Before we go any farther, we should alert your mom."

"Good idea." I press the walkie-talkie button. "Mom! Code green." Green lets Mom know we found something. "Code green. Over."

"Excellent." Mom's voice rings through the speaker. "I'll be down in a few. Over."

"Can we proceed? Over."

"Use your judgment, over and out!"

Then I slip the walkie-talkie back into my pocket, put the numbers nine and one into the door keypad. The lock clicks open. All we have to do is go through. . . .

I turn around. "Look, we don't know what we're going to find on the other side of this door. It might be dangerous. So if you want to go back—"

"We're going, and that's final," Eliza says. "This is our mystery too."

"YEAH!" Frank says, poking my arm real hard. "You can't hog the fun part all to yourself."

"Okay." I take a deep breath and open the door.

We stumble out into a hallway with exposed pipes and low ceilings. It looks like a cross between an unfinished basement and an evil lair. To the right, the path has just one flickering light bulb that seems to flash toward the broken freight elevator. And to the left, the path descends into total darkness.

Eliza flicks on her flashlight. "Okay," she says matter-of-factly. "Let's go."

We follow. The pipes make clanging noises, and every so often we all jump. The basement is getting colder and darker the deeper we go. I want to call out to Layla, but something inside my gut tells me I shouldn't do that. Eliza seems to be thinking the same thing, and even Frank is dead silent.

At the edge of the basement, we hit a brick wall.

"This is it," Eliza whispers. Something moves behind us, and I grab Eliza's flashlight—but it was just a shadow. "Carlos, stay calm."

"Sorry. Just nervous. I don't like feeling cornered."

"It does seem like we hit a dead end—"

"Muahahahahahahaha!" Frank giggles.

I squint at him. "Frank? Why are you laughing?"

"I know something you don't know!" he sings.

"Okay, what is it?"

"What is it, *please*?"

I sigh. "Okay, what is it, *please*?"

He gestures to the wall.

Eliza grabs my arm with one hand and points with the other. I have to crouch to Frank's level to see it—a small door with symbols carved into the door . . . but a four-digit number code where a doorknob should be.

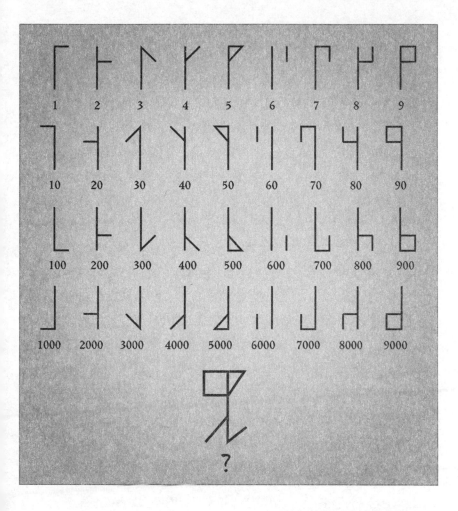

"What is that?"

"I've never seen anything like this," Eliza replies, with a note of awe in her voice. "It seems to be some shorthand way to count from one to nine thousand nine hundred and ninety-nine. There are symbols that represent the thousands, hundreds, tens, and ones. But they combine into one image."

I point to the symbol with the question mark underneath. "I guess we have to figure out what number that is."

"Uh . . . Eliza?" Frank says, tugging on his sister's arm. "There's someone here."

I hold my breath. Frank is right. I didn't hear it before, but now I do: the unmistakable sound of footsteps coming from behind us. Slow but steady footsteps. Careful footsteps blocking our way out. Coming for us. I turn around, but there is too much darkness and too many shadows to see who it is. Which means they can attack us easily.

I gulp. We have to get into this secret door *quick*!

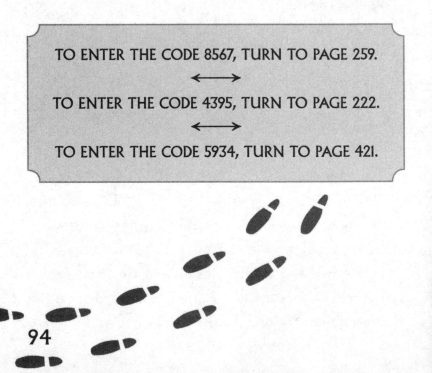

TO ENTER THE CODE 8567, TURN TO PAGE 259.

⟵⟶

TO ENTER THE CODE 4395, TURN TO PAGE 222.

⟵⟶

TO ENTER THE CODE 5934, TURN TO PAGE 421.

WE TURN BOX three, and there's a clicking noise. All the lights on the circuit board go out.

"Did we do it?" Eliza asks.

Mom moves to the center with Frank, and he pulls at the door. "Nope! Still locked."

They go back to the circuit board, and Frank starts twisting every circuit, but no lights turn back on.

"We blew the fuse," Eliza says.

"Isn't that a good thing? Isn't that what we wanted?"

Eliza shakes her head. "We wanted to deactivate the door. But essentially, we killed the circuit while the door was still locked, so it froze like that."

"No way out," Mom whispers.

We blew the fuse, and the case, in one go.

CASE CLOSED.

I CLICK ON Brad's recorder app, and see *New Recording One*. I click the play button, and Brad's voice fills the room.

"Brad, how did you win Emmy, Grammy, Oscar, and Tony awards, all before the age of twenty? That's quite an accomplishment for someone so young!"

He's clearly talking to himself, practicing for an interview. I want to gag.

"That's an amazing question, thank you. It's hard being so wonderful. I guess I attribute all my success to my natural talent. Some people are just born gifted—"

"Yuck."

"Barf."

"Yikes."

All three of us say, back to back, while the recording keeps playing.

"—I'd love to thank the fans. Without ordinary commoners, I'd . . . well, I'd still be a star. But a star with no audi—"

"What are you doing?" says a girl's voice on the recording.

"That's Layla!" Eliza gasps.

I put my finger to my lips for quiet, then point back at the phone.

"Nothing," Brad says quickly.

"I just came to tell you that Guillotine wants to

rehearse the kissing scene before we film it tomorrow. So grab your ChapStick, and let's go."

"Speaking of kissing—"

"No, Brad." Layla's voice is sharp.

"Layla, I promise, one day you'll learn to love me like I love me. Come on. Go out with me."

"Is that a request or a command?"

"We'd be Hollywood's young power couple. We'd be the talk of the town—the tabloids would go nuts. Think of what a relationship would do for our careers! And you'd have the pleasure of going out with *me*, the hottest stud in Hollywood."

"Yeah," Layla snorts. "A real *pleasure*."

"What's your problem?" Brad says.

"You," Layla says. "Not respecting my right to say no. Which I have said. Countless times."

"You think you're hot stuff, don't you? But you're *nothing*. I'm more talented than you. And more famous. And more beautiful. And more powerful. I'm *the total package*, you b—!"

"That's a CURSE WORD!" Frank says, his eyes wide. Eliza and I both shush him.

"This is a really attractive side of you, Brad," Layla says dryly. "Keep it up."

Brad curses at her again—another unforgivably nasty word—and then the recording cuts off.

"Potty mouth, potty mouth!" Frank says.

"Don't you dare repeat that word, Frank," Eliza says, which is a surefire way to make Frank repeat it. He shouts the word, he sings the word, he does a handstand and says the word upside down.

"Brad Bradley is scum," I say.

"This . . . this *can't* be Brad Bradley," Eliza says, shaking her head in disbelief.

"Eliza, you heard him with your own ears! It was all recorded."

"But this just isn't how he seems in interviews. This isn't how he is on TV. I thought I knew him."

"You thought wrong," I say. "Clearly."

TO READ BRAD'S TEXTS, TURN TO PAGE 339.

⟵——⟶

TO READ BRAD'S EMAILS, TURN TO PAGE 237.

"HOW DO YOU feel about Layla's disappearance?"

"Terrible, of course." He sounds sincere, but a little flush creeps into his cheeks and he can't make eye contact with me.

"I don't think that's true," I say.

Now his face gets *really* red. He looks like a grape about to pop. "How dare you!" he says, banging his fist on his desk. "How dare you question my integrity?"

Do I press on—fully accuse him of being happy that Layla's gone because the TV ratings have spiked? Or do I back off, now that he's getting angry?

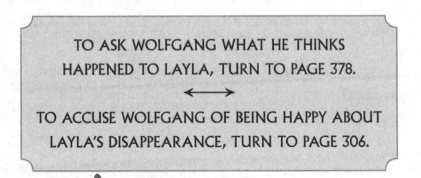

TO ASK WOLFGANG WHAT HE THINKS HAPPENED TO LAYLA, TURN TO PAGE 378.

←——→

TO ACCUSE WOLFGANG OF BEING HAPPY ABOUT LAYLA'S DISAPPEARANCE, TURN TO PAGE 306.

ELIZA'S RIGHT: THE best way to eavesdrop is to crawl in a vent. Luckily, the vent by Wolfgang's door is just big enough to fit us. We use the sandwich method, which means we put Frank in the middle of whatever we're doing. Mostly because we can't trust him to lead, and because we can't trust him to be the caboose either.

We stop when we're right above a ceiling grate. Not only are their voices coming through loud and clear, but I can see Mom and Wolfgang too.

"And how are Layla's relationships with the rest of the cast and crew?"

"Fine," Wolfgang says with a flick of his wrist. "She is respected and loved by most. But she doesn't exactly get along with the director or Brad Brad—"

Frank fidgets, and the grate buckles beneath him. It swings open, and his legs go falling straight through. He flails, his bottom half in Wolfgang's office, while Eliza and I desperately tug at his top half.

But we don't have a good grip—his shirt slips out of our hands, and he drops from the ceiling right onto Wolfgang's back. "PIGGYBACK!"

Wolfgang tries to shake Frank lose, but Frank holds on so tight that he constricts Wolfgang's airway. Wolfgang pulls at the arms around his throat. Frank shouts, "GIDDYUP, HORSEY!"

Mom starts yelling at Frank. "Let go, Frank! Stop

it!" She tries to pry Frank off, but it's making Wolfgang choke even more. Eliza and I watch in horror.

At last Wolfgang passes out, face-first, onto the floor of his own office.

"Dead horsey," Frank says.

Ten minutes later, when Wolfgang wakes up, he croaks, "You're fired!"

Straight from the horse's mouth.

CASE CLOSED.

I PULL WOLFGANG'S black coat over Frank and me. We huddle together in a tight hug as the door to the closet opens. I don't think Mom sees us, and suddenly I understand why Mom never lets me wear black clothes if I'm walking outside at night. Camouflage!

"Excuse me," says Wolfgang coldly. "But did I give you permission to search through my belongings?"

"I'm sorry," Mom says, the door still ajar. "I thought I heard . . ." But then she trails off and shuts the door again. I hold my breath until I hear Mom sink back into the chair. "I do apologize, Mr. Westover," she says. "You were saying . . . about Agatha Tuggle."

"Layla recently had a fight with her."

"Really," Mom says. "About what?"

"I don't know," Wolfgang says. "I just . . . I walked by Layla and Agatha shouting at each other. I was in a rush and on my way. It . . . it might have been about Miriam."

"Miriam Jay? Layla's mom? What about her?"

"She's a real piece of work. An overbearing stage mom gone horribly, horribly wrong. She used to sit behind Director Chen, shouting out acting suggestions and modifications. Filming took twice as long as it should have because Miriam would shout, 'Speak out, Layla!' during takes and ruin the whole shot. At some point during last season, Layla banned her mother from set."

"Because of that?"

"I don't know. Layla didn't say. But Miriam Jay is no longer allowed to come within the gates of the studio while Layla's working. It's kind of like an unofficial restraining order. The only reason Miriam is on set now is because we're exhausting every possible resource to find Layla. If Layla were here, Miriam Jay would not be."

"From what you're saying, it seems like Layla doesn't get along with anyone," Mom says.

"It's easy to be a good friend to someone who is down on their luck. It's much harder to stick around for someone's success," Wolfgang says wisely, sounding very much like he's quoting a movie. Quite possibly a movie he's worked on.

"So you think her professional success has created a lot of personal enemies?"

"I think this industry chews people up and spits them out. And when a sixteen-year-old hits it big like Layla, it can cause other people to resent her and blame her for their own shortcomings."

My head is spinning. Mostly because I don't really know what the heck that means. But luckily Mom translates it. "So . . . you're saying it isn't Layla's fault that she has a bad relationship with some of her coworkers and family members."

"Not in my opinion, no. She's pretty distraught about

it, too. Poor kid. Oh, I'm sorry!" Wolfgang says. "That fire alarm ate up our interview time—I have to get to a meeting with some of the other producers. I'll be back in an hour or so if you need me."

"I'll let you know."

There are footsteps, the sound of Mom and Wolfgang leaving. When I'm sure they're gone, Frank and I burst out of the closet. First thing I do is get Eliza out of that cupboard. She sighs in relief the second she rolls onto the floor.

"That was a tight squeeze," she says, stretching her neck. "But we learned some useful stuff. Like how Layla was fighting with her agent—"

"And her mom."

"Those are two really good leads," Eliza suggests. "Where do you think we should start?"

TO INTERVIEW LAYLA'S AGENT, AGATHA TUGGLE, TURN TO PAGE 125.

⟵——⟶

TO INTERVIEW LAYLA'S MOM, MIRIAM JAY, TURN TO PAGE 470.

NINE DOTS, FOUR lines, two possible paths, and I have no idea how we're supposed to figure out which path to take. "Eliza, what is this all about?"

She bites her lip, keeping her flashlight trained on the dots. "That's impossible," she whispers. "There's no possible way to connect all nine dots with only four lines, unless . . ."

She touches her finger to the carved wood. Then she whips around so fast that her hair smacks me in the face.

"We have to think outside the box!" Eliza says.

"Okay . . ."

"Our lines can stretch longer than the dots go . . . like this!" And with her finger, she draws a line from left to right across the top and then a diagonal line down that crosses two more dots.

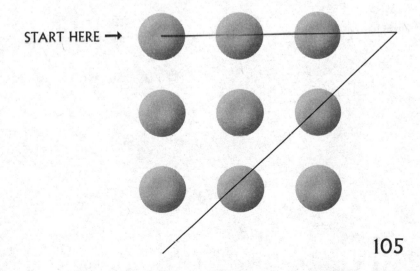

START HERE →

"Only two more lines are allowed," she says. "And we have four more dots to hit."

"And we can't pick up our pencil," I remind her. "It has to be continuous."

"But we can touch the dots twice!" Frank says. Then he pokes a dot with his finger, like it's a button. "Poke poke!"

"Exactly," she says. "If I'm right, the remaining two lines will be in the shape of an arrow, pointing to the correct path."

TO CHOOSE THE LEFT PATH, TURN TO PAGE 245.

←——→

TO CHOOSE THE RIGHT PATH, TURN TO PAGE 21.

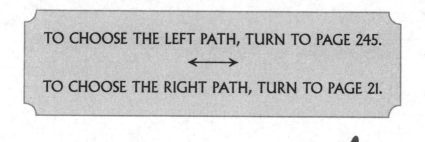

WOLFGANG'S BOX IS proving to be more challenging than I thought.

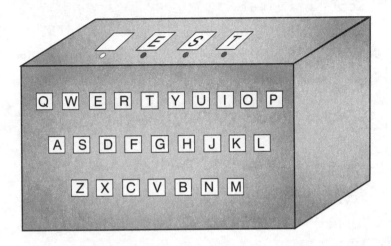

"Eliza, can you help me?"

"Sure," she says, and she digs into her backpack for a notepad. She scribbles words down, some of them I'm not sure I ever would have thought of:

> ZEST
>
> JEST
>
> LEST
>
> VEST
>
> FEST
>
> REST

"Is that all of them?" I ask.

"You're missing ME!" Frank says.

"Huh?"

"PEST!" Frank boasts, grinning wildly.

PEST, Eliza writes.

"And you're missing Carlos!" Frank says. *"BEST!"*

"Aww! Thanks, buddy!" That's the nicest thing I think he's *ever* said to me. Which he punctuates with one enormous fart. *That's* the Frank I know.

BEST

"We're missing a few. I'll leave you some clues. Want to fill in the blanks?"

"Sure," I say.

A BIRD'S _ _ _ _

NORTH, SOUTH, EAST, _ _ _ _.

A TIMED EXAM: NOT A QUIZ BUT A _ _ _ _.

"I think that's all of them," Eliza says. "Count 'em up!"

COUNT UP ALL POSSIBLE FOUR-LETTER E-S-T WORDS. ADD ONE HUNDRED, AND TURN TO THAT PAGE.

WE HAVE TO go in! Now that we know where Layla is—and that she's safe—we can't leave her.

Eliza, Frank, and I storm into the room, and I'm surprised at how small it is. Layla is tied to a wooden chair, and there are filing cabinets and a single desk. But otherwise, the room is plain and empty.

Layla looks at us with a mixture of surprise and relief—her eyes fill with tears. Just like when Brad's character, Sebastian, saves her from the Witch Queen's ice tower . . . it's so strange to see Layla in front of me. Almost like I stepped into *Teen Witch*.

"Oh, bless you!" Layla cries.

"But I didn't even sneeze!" Frank says, confused.

Tuggle is surprised to see us, but that surprise morphs into fear.

"What are you doing here?" she says.

"Saving Layla," I say, braver than I feel. I move toward Layla to untie her, but Tuggle steps between us.

"Here's the thing about sub-basements," Tuggle says. "They're so far below the ground that it's impossible to hear you scream. But . . ." She presses a button on the wall, and the floor rumbles. A square piece drops out. I can't tell what's below. From here it looks like a black hole.

"Wh-what's that?" I ask, trying to keep my voice from wobbling.

"Is it the sub-sub-basement?" Eliza whispers.

"Of course not. It's the sub-sub-sub-sub-sub-sub-sub-sub-sub-basement. Might as well be the earth's core. Goodbye, little detective."

And she pushes me in.

CASE CLOSED.

WITH OUR ELEVEN different four-letter E-S-T words, it's time to figure out which one is most likely to be Wolfgang's password: *zest, jest, lest, vest, fest, rest, pest, best, nest, west, test.*

"Stop!" I shout. "This is it."

I point to the spot in the notebook where Eliza wrote *west.*

"Why?" Frank says.

"Wolfgang *West*over. It's part of his name."

Eliza presses her finger on the W.

Click. The top of the box opens, and we're in!

I don't know what I'm expecting to find: photos, a secret letter, gems, something juicy maybe. Instead, there's only a scrolled-up blueprint of the studio.

"That's *it*?" Frank asks, voicing my thoughts. "How boring!"

Eliza lays the blueprint flat, and under her breath, she mutters, "Interesting."

"What?" I say, leaning over the document.

Eliza points to what looks like a different floor plan than the studio we're standing in. But at the top of the blueprint map, it still says Stage Eight.

"Here's where we are," Eliza says, pointing to an area that looks like everything we've already explored. "And this is an area of the building that we haven't seen yet. A basement, maybe."

"But we've explored this whole studio. There is no basement."

"Maybe not a basement, but there clearly is *something*," Eliza says. "It's in the blueprint of the building, and diagrams don't lie. According to this map, there's an entrance outside Brad's dressing room. Funny, we walked by there today and didn't see anyth—"

"Kids?" Maureen calls, her voice muffled. "Did you forget we're playing hide-and-seek?"

"Quick! Run!"

Eliza, Frank, and I dash toward Brad Bradley's dressing room, away from Maureen. Now that we know there's a secret underground basement around here, we *have* to find it. It might have important clues . . . or even Layla.

The dressing-room hallway has all the stars' dressing rooms on the right-hand side, while the left wall has pictures of the cast and crew at award shows, autographed headshots, and framed promotional posters.

I start taking the pictures off the wall, very carefully.

"What are you doing?" Eliza asks.

"Seeing if the secret entrance is behind any of these pictures. Come help."

Eliza goes to the opposite end of the hall and starts removing the pictures. Meanwhile, Frank waves us on like he's a conductor, probably because he's too short to reach the pictures.

"Strawberry shortcake, banana split! Carlos makes Eliza look like . . . shiiiiiiiift to the left, shiiiiiiiift to the right, stand up, sit down, FIGHT FIGHT FIGHT!"

"Can you stop that?" Eliza gripes. "This is extremely heavy, and your cheering is making it hard to concen—"

"GO, ELIZA! YOU CAN DO IT! PUT A LITTLE POWER TO IT!"

"Ughhhh," she groans. "Carlos, can you help with this one? It feels fused to the wall."

I ditch my promotional poster from season two and head to Eliza's photo, which—I've just noticed—is the only poster in the hallway that's *not* about *Teen Witch*.

"On the count of three, we pull," I say. "One, two . . ."

Frank knocks into me, and I trip forward. I pull down on the picture frame, the painting swivels, and the wall clicks open, revealing some rickety wooden steps that lead downward.

"COOL!" Frank says. It's kind of annoying how Frank has a talent for discovering all sorts of important clues when he's not even trying. Like the blueprint with the basement on it—and even this secret entrance. I'm glad he's on my team and all, but I feel like *I'm* the one with something to prove to Mom.

"Let's go," I say, hopping down the first three steps.

Eliza has concern written all over her face. She reaches into her backpack, pulls out a flashlight, and says, "I came prepared."

She goes in; Frank follows and closes the wall behind us.

This basement looks nothing like the set upstairs. The set is high tech, with that giant mechanical dragon and green screens and lights and cameras. Down here, it's dingy and old. We keep getting hit in the face with cobwebs.

"It seems like no one's been here for years," Eliza says.

I have the feeling she wants to turn back, but neither one of us suggests it. So we press on. But quickly we get to a fork in the basement, where our path divides. There's one road that leads to the left, and the other veers to the right.

"Now what?" Eliza says.

"We split up!" Frank says. "Banana splitsies!"

"Um, *no way*," I say. I know Frank is only six and way too young to have seen any horror movies, but the second people split up is the second everyone dies. So . . . we are sticking together, no matter what.

"We're not splitting up," Eliza says, shining her flashlight at the wall dividing the two hallways. There's something written on the wood, carved with a knife.

TO STAY IN STAGE EIGHT: WITHOUT PICKING UP YOUR PEN, CONNECT ALL NINE DOTS WITH ONLY FOUR STRAIGHT LINES. YOU CAN GO OVER THE SAME DOT TWICE. WHEN DONE CORRECTLY, THE ANSWER WILL POINT YOU TO THE ROAD YOU WANT TO BE ON.

START HERE →

"It looks like someone else started it for us," Eliza says, running her finger on the marks between the first three dots. "At least partially."

"We want to stay in Stage Eight, right?" I ask.

Eliza nods. "You know . . . I'm starting to think this is some sort of underground tunnel that connects all the different stages. So that people can walk across the studio lot in inclement weather."

"What inclement weather? It's Los Angeles."

"Come on," Eliza says. "Let's figure out which route to take."

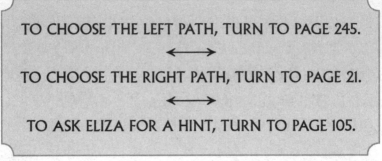

TO CHOOSE THE LEFT PATH, TURN TO PAGE 245.

TO CHOOSE THE RIGHT PATH, TURN TO PAGE 21.

TO ASK ELIZA FOR A HINT, TURN TO PAGE 105.

116

WE HAVE TO follow Guillotine. The only way he could look more suspicious is if he had a sign above him that read LOOK AT ME, I'M GUILTY!

We burst out of the prop room and run after him, just in time to see him turn another corner. It's a tricky balance: we have to hurry, so we don't lose him. But we also have to be quiet, so he doesn't detect us.

The quiet part is particularly hard for Frank, who stomps down each hallway like he's Godzilla.

"Frank! Shhhhh!" Eliza hisses.

"Shhhhhhhhh!" Frank repeats. He starts to tiptoe, but he's still as quiet as a lumbering hippo.

Luckily, Guillotine is too far ahead to hear. In the distance, I can see him fiddling with a lock. And as I get closer, I can see he's headed into his office, a door marked:

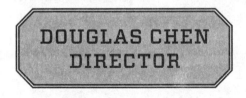

DOUGLAS CHEN
DIRECTOR

He opens the door, then pauses.

"Stop!" I whisper. I pull Frank and Eliza back by their shirts, and we crouch behind a potted plant in the hall.

Guillotine answers his phone. "What? Hello? I can't hear you!" he snaps. "Ugh, the service in this building stinks—hold on, I'm going outside!" He walks away, and the door is one of those heavy ones that starts to close on its own. I'm almost positive that once it closes, it will lock automatically too.

We could make a run for it, to try to catch the door before it closes and locks us out. But it's a risk: Guillotine could catch us. Or we could change course and do what Eliza originally wanted: snoop through Brad Bradley's dressing room before he's done with my mom.

TO CATCH THE DOOR TO GUILLOTINE'S OFFICE, TURN TO PAGE 31.

←→

TO GO INVESTIGATE BRAD BRADLEY'S ROOM, TURN TO PAGE 294.

I HAVE TO follow the shadow. I pull Eliza into the velvet red hall with all of the executive offices. "This way, quickly!"

I chase after the shadow. Every time I think I'm catching up, it whips around another corner.

"Tuggle?" I call. "Is that you?"

We weave through the potion table, the lockers, the classroom, the green screen area, the robot dragon. We pass the director's chair and the writer's room.

"Where do you think she went?" I whisper to Eliza.

We look around, but all is quiet.

Too quiet.

"THERE!" Frank shouts, pointing to the door of the sound booth, which slams shut. We run toward it, faster than I've ever run in my life.

I yank the door open, expecting to see Tuggle or Layla inside, but it's just a big padded room with sound-proof walls—empty except for a standing microphone and a door that leads to a tiny control room.

"Maybe they're in there," I say.

We go into the control room, but there's nothing.

SLAM.

We turn around, and through the glass we see Tuggle waving at us. I shove past Eliza to the door, but it's locked. Tuggle must have hidden behind the door and waited until we were inside to lock us in here. We've been tricked!

"Hey!" I bang on the door. "HEY!"

But Tuggle walks out of the sound booth.

"Don't ditch us!" I cry. "You can't just leave us in here!"

"She can, and she did," Frank says.

"Uh . . . Carlos?" Eliza says, her voice an octave higher than usual. "Not to make you panic, but . . ."

She gestures to something box-shaped underneath the sound table. Something connected to a timer, set to go off in three minutes.

"Is that what I think it is?" I gulp.

"I don't want to explode!" Frank says, tugging on my sleeve.

"So how do we disarm it?"

Eliza pops open a control panel to reveal a bunch of wires. They have color labels on them on the top, but all the wires are black.

Eliza and I gasp at the same time.

"Season three, episode seven!" we both shout.

"The one where Aurelia's brother dies!" Eliza says. She turns to Frank to quickly explain. "This character on *Teen Witch* was supposed to disarm the device, but he didn't do it in time."

"You think this is the same prop from the show?"

"It looks like it! I'm trying to remember how to disarm it. . . ."

"No pressure," I say, "but we have two minutes left on the clock. Actually, I take that back, *yes* pressure."

Frank moves his hands wildly around Eliza's head. "Okay, I just fastened your thinking cap!" he says very seriously.

"Thanks, Frank. From what I remember, I think we have to figure out which order they're plugged in at the bottom and cut the wires in that order. Am I missing anything, Carlos?"

"Sounds right to me! Now, Frank, find scissors!"

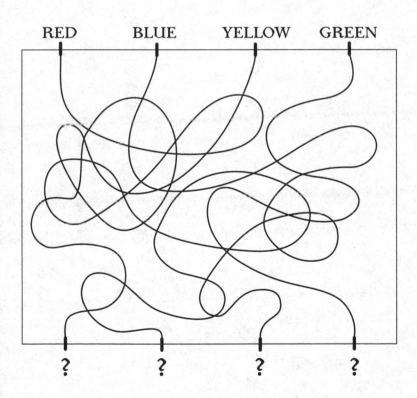

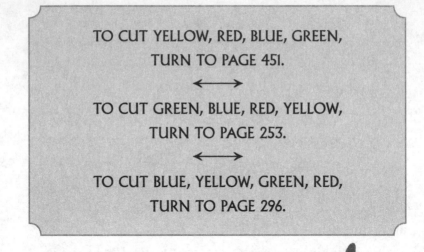

TO CUT YELLOW, RED, BLUE, GREEN,
TURN TO PAGE 451.

TO CUT GREEN, BLUE, RED, YELLOW,
TURN TO PAGE 253.

TO CUT BLUE, YELLOW, GREEN, RED,
TURN TO PAGE 296.

122

WE CAN'T GIVE up on Layla—we have to stay with her and search for a way in.

We ignore the fire alarm and continue knocking on the wall. But so far, nothing is working. I wish we had a sledgehammer to knock down the wall.

"NO!" we hear Layla suddenly scream. "GET AWAY FROM ME! NO—"

She cuts off suddenly, and we don't hear anything more from her.

"Layla?" I say. I pull my shirt above my mouth. The air is getting very thick and smoky. This is no false alarm! "Layla—answer us!"

Eliza has her hand over her mouth, and my eyes sting.

"Carlos, we have to get out of here!" Eliza coughs.

I grab Frank's hand and push forward—but the basement is filling up with dense black smoke, so heavy I can barely breathe. I taste it on my tongue. My eyes are streaming tears now. All three of us huddle together. And then we drop like flies: first Eliza falls to the floor. Then Frank passes out. Then my vision swims. Everything darkens. . . .

I wake up in the hospital with an oxygen mask over my face.

"Carlos!" Mom grabs my hand. "Eliza and Frank are okay. They're with their parents in the next room."

"Fire?" I manage.

Mom nods sadly. "Are you asking about the fire, or whether I was fired?"

I hold up two fingers.

"Yes to both. There was a fire, and I was fired. After the firefighters rescued you three, I went with you to the hospital and refused to leave your side . . . it's been three days. Wolfgang dismissed me in this very room, two days ago. I guess you can say my case went up in smoke."

CASE CLOSED.

I **HAVE TO** find out why Agatha Tuggle and Layla were fighting.

We corner Tuggle by the table of snacks for the crew. She is small, but she radiates confidence and power. It might be the pantsuit . . . or the tightly wrapped bun. But the effect is dulled by the way she has three pens sticking out of her bun, making her head look a bit like a pincushion.

"We're, er, detectives from Las Pistas Detective Agency, and we need to talk with you."

She blinks. Her owlish glasses make her eyes look twice their normal size. "What about?"

"Layla Jay," I say. "And why you've been fighting with her."

Instantly, Tuggle looks greenish. She glances nervously at a few of the crew members nearby. And I understand what she's saying: she doesn't want anyone to overhear. It could be dangerous to have rumors flying around.

"Let's go somewhere private," I suggest.

She nods and follows us as we take her somewhere away from the prying ears of the cast and crew. The writers' room is perfect for this. It gives us privacy and quiet, around an oval table.

"So . . . let's talk about you and Layla. What were you fighting about?"

"Who even told you we were fighting?" Tuggle replies.

"That's confidential," I say, right as Eliza says, "Wolfgang Westover."

"Oops," Eliza adds.

Tuggle snorts. "I would not trust any information that comes from Wolfgang Westover," she says, casually examining her nails. "He is positively giddy that Layla is missing. *Giddy*. His show has never been as popular as it has been in the past five days. Maybe he kidnapped her to boost the show's ratings."

"So you think Layla's been kidnapped?" I ask.

Tuggle chokes for a second, then quickly recovers. "Who said kidnap?"

"You just did," Eliza says.

"No, I didn't."

"Yes, you did!" Frank says, pointing at her.

"No, I didn't."

"YES, YOU DID!" Frank shouts.

"I think you misheard me," Tuggle says sweetly. "I was just piggybacking on what you were suggesting. I don't know what happened to my client. For all I know, she thought of this publicity stunt herself."

I frown. Tuggle is trying so hard to rewrite our conversation as we're having it. Is that suspicious behavior? Or is that just what agents are used to doing—spinning conversations to put themselves and their clients in the best light?

TO ASK TUGGLE WHY SHE WAS FIGHTING
WITH LAYLA, TURN TO PAGE 227.

←——→

TO ASK ABOUT LAYLA'S RELATIONSHIP
WITH THE CAST AND CREW, TURN TO PAGE 136.

"SO WE TALKED to Brad Bradley," I say. "And he seems really jealous of Layla."

Eliza's eyes widen, like she's surprised I'm being so blunt and forthcoming, but there's no time to tiptoe around. Not with a suspect like Guillotine, who's already eyeing the door, looking for an escape route.

"Is there a question here?" Guillotine asks.

"Yeah. *Why* is he jealous of Layla?"

"He's been insufferably jealous of her ever since she got promoted," Guillotine says. "But she's been insufferably domineering."

"What is *domino-ing*?"

"Not dominos, Frank," Eliza says. "*Domineering*. It means bossy."

"Bossy how?" I ask.

"Layla was—is . . . ," he says, quickly catching himself. Eliza and I gasp. Did he just use the *past tense* to talk about Layla? Like she is . . . dead?

Guillotine knows his little mistake hasn't gone unnoticed, and for a moment we are all paralyzed. Staring at each other. A standoff.

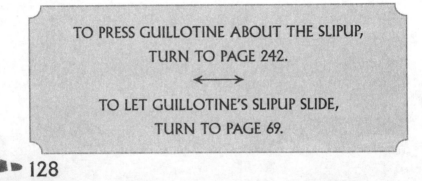

TO PRESS GUILLOTINE ABOUT THE SLIPUP,
TURN TO PAGE 242.

←——→

TO LET GUILLOTINE'S SLIPUP SLIDE,
TURN TO PAGE 69.

THE LOCK CLICKS open, and I loop it out of the locker. Eliza tumbles out.

"Hooray!" Frank cries.

Eliza is shaky. "I don't like small spaces," she admits.

"I thought you don't like bugs."

"And bats!" Frank says. "And booger flicking. And smelly farts."

"All of the above."

I look back over my shoulder, but Tuggle is long gone by now. We need a plan. "Any ideas?" I ask Eliza.

She snatches my phone out of my pocket. "First of all, I'm texting your mom."

I wince. "She's going to kill us."

"Well, I'd rather be killed by your mom than an agent kidnapper on the loose," Eliza says.

Louise volunteers. "I'll do it! I'll take your phone outside—the service is way better out there. That way we can be certain the text goes through."

I shove my phone into Louise's hands. "You go text my mom. You'll find her number in my contacts. Call the police too, while you're at it. We have work to do here."

"Are you going to be alri—"

"Go!" I say firmly, and Louise runs out with my phone.

I turn to Eliza and Frank. "We need to go after Tuggle," I say. "I thought I heard her footsteps headed to the right—in the direction of the writers' room and the broken freight elevator. If we hurry, we can catch up!"

Eliza frowns. "I don't know, Carlos. I think our best bet is to lay a trap for her here. We'll have more control over the situation."

"How do you even know she'll come back up here? What if she just takes Layla and escapes with her out another exit of the studio?"

Eliza smiles knowingly. "She has to come back here . . . we know all her secrets. She can't ditch us because we're too big a danger to her."

TO RUN AFTER TUGGLE, TURN TO PAGE 436.

←——→

TO LAY A TRAP, TURN TO PAGE 283.

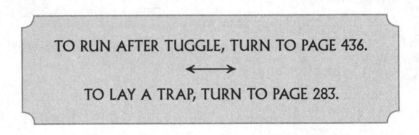

"WHAT'S GOING ON between Guillotine and Layla?"

"Lots."

"Well, *why* does Guillotine hate Layla?"

"How many hours you got?" Brad says.

"A hundred million zillion," Frank says.

Brad sighs and leans against the door. "Look, you know why everyone in the industry calls Douglas Chen 'Guillotine,' right?"

Eliza and I shake our heads no.

"Because of all the times he shouts 'CUT!' His clapper board slices right through our scenes, and heads go rolling."

At that, Frank starts to roll on the ground, clearly hungry for attention. I ignore him.

"So . . . he's a difficult person to work with?"

"Ha!" Brad Bradley snorts. "Difficult is an understatement. He's verbally abusive. Abrasive. Rude. Callous."

I don't know what some of those words mean, but I understand the gist: Guillotine is one nasty person.

"But what does this have to do with Layla Jay?" Eliza says, so quiet it's like she's mouthing the words. I nudge her, and she repeats herself louder, though she turns bright red in the process.

Brad sits down on Layla's makeup counter. And he leans forward like he's about to tell us a ghost story or something. "Guillotine and Layla are both really opinionated. They don't get along. And now that Layla's *star is rising* or whatever," he says with a scowl, "Layla's been extra bossy on set."

"Really?" Eliza whispers. "That's hard to imagine. She seems so sweet on TV."

"Yeah," I say. "She's always sticking up for her friends and helping the coven—she uses her magic to fight Evil Witch Wilhelmina!"

"That's just television, kid."

"But we've read all her interviews," Eliza says. "I mean, not *all*—I've only read a few. Well, not *so* few that I don't know what I'm talking about. Just the right amount."

"What she *means*," I say, glaring at Eliza, "is that even in her interviews, Layla doesn't seem like a diva or anything."

Brad scowls. "I know everyone thinks of her as Hollywood's *darling*, but she's *so* not."

ACCUSE BRAD OF HATING LAYLA ON PAGE 374.

WE HAVE TO scream for help. Or we'll all be stuck in this grave together . . . forever.

"Help! Help! Help! Help!" we call over and over again. "Help! Help!"

"HELLLLLLLLP!" Frank bellows.

"He—*ack!*" I bend over as I start to cough.

"I don't feel good!" Frank says, taking a few gulping, gasping breaths.

"The air feels thinner," Eliza says softly.

"We screamed too much," Mom chokes. "We've used up all our oxygen."

Dizzily, I lie on the floor. I know Mom is right. I can barely breathe. And even though we're in pitch darkness, a new kind of darkness is closing in. . . .

CASE CLOSED.

 **WE TELL FRANK** to turn box one.

Zzzzzzt!

I can almost *see* the current of electricity that jumps through him—and Mom, who is holding on to him. Next thing I know, they are both on the ground.

"Are you okay?"

"Great, Carlos, awesome, even! I think I have super lightning powers now, like Superman."

"Superman doesn't have lightning powers," Eliza whispers, examining her brother for cuts and scrapes.

But I'm too busy looking at Mom. She's breathing heavily like she just ran a marathon. Electrocution is very serious stuff, and I am relieved she's okay.

The circuit keeps sparking, and in the flickering light, Mom shakes her head. "We can't touch it again," she says. "It will electrocute you immediately."

We short-circuited, and it cut our mystery circuit short.

CASE CLOSED.

I PRESS THE buttons in the order yellow, black, blue, red, green.

"What's happening?" Eliza says. "Why isn't the gate closing?"

"I'll try it again!" I hit the buttons.

"Let me try!" Frank says. "I'll push them all! Just for funsies!"

"Frank, get off!"

"They're getting away, Carlos!" Eliza shrieks.

"Going, going, gone!" Frank says, like an auctioneer. "Can I push some buttons *now*?"

CASE CLOSED.

MAYBE TUGGLE WILL open up to us if we throw the spotlight off her. "Did Layla get along with everyone in the cast and crew?" I ask, even though we already know from eavesdropping on Wolfgang that she does *not*. "Does she have any enemies?"

Tuggle laughs. "I suppose it's no secret that Layla does not get along with her costar, Brad Bradley, and her director, Douglas Chen—though you might hear people call him Guillotine. Nasty name if you ask me, but an even nastier personality, so I suppose it fits."

"Nastier than this?" Frank says, and he spits out a loogie, dangles it a few inches below his chin, then sucks it back up again.

"No," Tuggle says, sounding disgusted. "*Nothing* is nastier than that."

"Ewwww, Frank!" Eliza yelps, and I kick him under the table. He loves being disgusting. I guess I should count myself lucky that he didn't fart. His farts *really* clear a room.

"Why doesn't Layla get along with Brad or Guillotine?" I ask.

Tuggle rubs her temple. "Where do I even begin?"

"At the beginning," Frank says. "Duh."

"Brad Bradley is a talentless hack who has always been jealous of my client's talent. And Douglas Chen is a power-hungry monster who doesn't want his actors or crew members to have any opinions. It's always his way or the highway. You take a smart, savvy, incredibly mature sixteen-year-old like Layla, and pair her with someone petty and vindictive like Chen? It's just a bad match."

"If it's a bad match," Eliza says, "then why did you get Layla an audition for this show?"

"Are you kidding? *Teen Witch* has *made* Layla's career. She's a household name—you couldn't pay for that kind of fame and exposure. A few years of terrible coworkers is well worth the trouble, if you ask me."

A few years seems like a long time to be miserable, but I don't fight Tuggle on this one. "Does Layla get along with Wolfgang Westover?"

"Famously. But she shouldn't. The man is all about the bottom line, and I don't trust him one bit."

"Bottom line?" I ask.

"Money," Eliza explains. "You're saying he only cares about money, right?"

"Indeed."

"And does Layla get along with her mom?"

Tuggle makes a zipped-lips motion and smirks. I'll take that as a "No, they don't get along," but Tuggle doesn't elaborate.

TO ASK WHERE LAYLA MIGHT BE,
TURN TO PAGE 148.

←——→

TO ASK ABOUT LAYLA'S RELATIONSHIP
WITH HER MOTHER, TURN TO PAGE 297.

138

I KNOW I shouldn't look in Miriam's car, but I'm getting desperate to find Layla. I take a deep breath, try the driver door, and . . . it opens.

I search the passenger seat, Eliza takes the driver's side, and Eliza pops the trunk open for Frank to explore. For a second, I don't think he'll go in there, since it's filled to the brim with caviar cans and furs. But I forgot how much Frank likes gross things, even fish eggs and dead animal skins.

I look inside the glove box: car manual, registration, and first-aid kit. Boring, boring, and more boring. Then I switch to the armrest in between the seats and pop it open to find a GPS. Now *this* is more like it.

It's one of those old ones that runs on batteries, that you put on your car dashboard. I press the power button on the side of it. And it lights up.

"Hit previous destinations," Eliza says, over my shoulder.

I'd call Eliza a backseat driver, but she *is* sitting in the driver's seat.

I obey, and Eliza starts writing down the last five addresses into her notebook. "We can look these up online later. And then we'll get a sense of what Miriam's been up to the week before Layla went missing—and where she's been since."

She continues to scribble.

And then she stops.

"Eliza?"

Eliza's voice is hoarse. "Look where she went the day before Layla vanished."

The GPS reads: LOS ANGELES COUNTY SUPERIOR COURT.

I look up at Eliza, and her gray eyes are wide.

"She went to court, Eliza!" My mind drifts to a few trial shows I know Eliza's mom likes to watch. The ones with dramatic lawyers and super-hokey twists. "So . . . does that mean Miriam is a criminal?"

"Maybe," Eliza says. "Or maybe not. It could be anything: a speeding ticket, small claims court. She could be getting sued. Or maybe she's suing someone else. But the timing really *does* seem too convenient." She pauses. "I wonder if it has something to do with whatever Miriam was looking for in Layla's dressi—"

Screech!

Vroom!

BOOM!

We both look up. There is a giant hole in the wall of the studio building—like it's just been blown up or crashed into. Smoke is billowing from the building, and suddenly the whole parking lot reeks of burning rubber.

"What just happened?" Frank calls from the trunk.

"Mom!" I whisper. I can barely feel my hands as I

fumble with the car handle—can barely feel my feet as I run to the studio door. Blood pumps in my ears. Please be all right, I plead. Please, Mom!

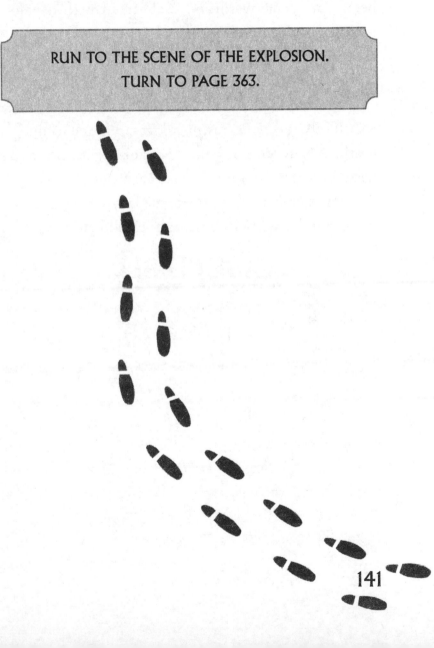

RUN TO THE SCENE OF THE EXPLOSION.
TURN TO PAGE 363.

I'M CERTAIN LAYLA'S message to Wolfgang wants us to go to the prop room closet. We slip inside the prop room, and we study the closet. There's a ton of stuff in here. The whole wardrobe is cluttered with needless junk. I wonder what, specifically, Layla wanted us to look at.

Thunk!

A footstep behind us. I whip around in time to see a shelf of wigs come crashing down, pinning us underneath. A gray Washington wig lands right on Frank's head, and then more pile on. The wigs are all over, pressed against my face, my hands, my whole body.

I guess this is the definition of a bad hair day.

CASE CLOSED.

FRANK'S SAFETY COMES first.

"Help!" he says, his gray eyes wide.

"Let him go, please!" I say.

Eliza whimpers beside me.

Miriam's eyes narrow on the stack of documents on the floor. "Give them here. No harm will come to him—just slide me the papers."

"Which ones?" Eliza says.

Miriam snorts, and her grip around Frank's neck gets a little tighter. Her acrylic nails dig into his skin, and he is stiller than I've ever seen him. "Which ones? *Which ones?* All of them. I'll take every paper you have, so I can destroy it."

"Destroy it? Why?"

"Why do you think? It looks positively terrible for me. Don't want people to get the wrong idea . . . very incriminating. All the evidence stacked against me. Give me those papers, and all that evidence goes away."

"So you admit that you took Layla?" I say.

"What?" Miriam says, her nostrils flaring danger-ously. "Maybe you're not listening. I said this looks terrible for me, and I don't want people to get the wrong idea. I have no idea where my daughter is—but if I don't destroy those papers, I'll be suspect number one."

"I'm sure there are digital copies, though," Eliza says logically. "I mean . . . Layla filed this with a lawyer and

143

the county court. Even if you destroy this, you can't destroy them all."

"Watch me!" Miriam says, and she shoves Frank at us. We topple over like bowling pins as Miriam yanks the papers out of Eliza's hands and runs. I scramble after her—Miriam took a left, toward the set. We could chase her. Or, if we took a right, we would reach the parking lot before her. We could cut her off.

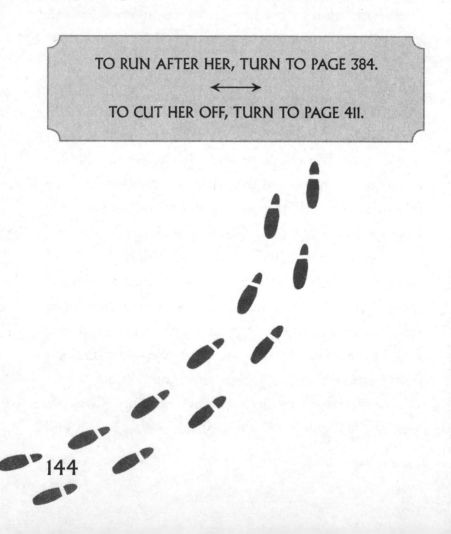

TO RUN AFTER HER, TURN TO PAGE 384.

⟵——⟶

TO CUT HER OFF, TURN TO PAGE 411.

WE HAVE TO disarm the robot, and I think I have an idea how.

"Remember when we were hiding under the robot yesterday, and there were those gears Frank wanted to touch? I bet if we could break the gears somehow, we'd stop this robot."

Eliza touches my arm. "We'll follow you," she whispers. "But be careful."

The papers Tuggle wants are all over the floor after Miriam got tossed. So I pick them up. Then I walk forward slowly, carefully, and calmly, with the agent-termination papers in hand. I know Eliza and Frank are behind me. I can hear Eliza's sharp, nervous breaths, and I can see Frank's bouncy steps out of the corner of my eye.

Closer . . . closer . . . "NOW!" I cry, and the three of us drop to the floor and start crawling toward the underbelly of the robot beast.

Tuggle tries to swipe at us with the dragon tail and snap at us with the mouth, but we're too low to the ground to reach. I feel like a worm, but it works: I roll right under.

Eliza follows. Then Frank, holding something in his hands.

"What's that?"

"A pen!" Frank says. "I found it on the floor."

145

It says TUGGLE AND TICKLER ASSOCIATES. One of Tuggle's bun pens must have fallen out of her hair as she was shoving Layla into the belly of the dragon.

"Let me have that," I say. Frank pouts, but he hands it over.

We stare straight up into the gears. Yesterday they were still, but now they are spinning dangerously fast. I know I have to stop them, and—as a special kind of poetic justice—I'm going to use Tuggle's own pen to do it. If I can stick this pen in between the final two gears, in just the right spot, I think I can manage to jam them.

The problem is, the end gears are spinning so fast that they're like blurs. I know the first gear is spinning to the right, clockwise—that's the only thing I can tell.

Eliza points up. "If we know the way the first gear turns, we can figure out the rest, since their teeth are intertwined," she says. "Just think about which way each gear would push the one after it. The one all the way on the left is clockwise, so the last one—all the way on the right—has to be . . ."

IF THE LAST GEAR TURNS CLOCKWISE,
TURN TO PAGE 301.

←——→

IF THE LAST GEAR TURNS COUNTERCLOCKWISE,
TURN TO PAGE 391.

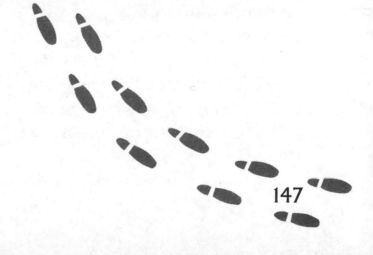

147

"WHERE DO YOU think Layla is?"

"I haven't the foggiest," Tuggle says, with a shrug that makes her shoulder pads bounce.

"Okay, but if you had to guess," I insist.

Tuggle sighs, her face sinking into her hands. And for a second, she looks tired and annoyed. But then she perks up again and says, "Look. I understand why everyone is making a big hullabaloo about this. Layla is a very special, very important young talent. Her star shines bright. But take it from someone who has known Layla for years: everything is fine."

"But how do you know that?" Eliza says. "Where is the proof?"

"I just know. Layla is flighty and unpredictable, and—hold on. *Brrrrrng brrrrrrng!* Do you hear that? *Brrrrrrrng brrrrrrrng!* I think that's my phone."

"You're making those noises," Frank says. "I can see you saying *brrrrrrng.*"

"Oh, I'm sorry, kids. A very important client is calling, and I have to take this." She holds the phone to her ear. "Agatha Tuggle speaking! Oh, yes, *hello!* So good to hear from you." She gathers her things and quickly scurries from the room.

Eliza, Frank, and I stare after her, dumbfounded.

"Did she just *fake a call* to get out of talking to us?" Eliza says.

"There's not even cell service in the building!" I say.

148

Frank whistles.

"So what next?" Eliza asks.

"Fart in her briefcase! Or sneeze in her tea! Put her hand in warm water while she sleeps, so she pees the bed!"

"Frank, I was talking about who we investigate next." She blanches. "You wouldn't really do the hand-in-warm-water thing, would you?"

Frank grins wickedly.

Okay, time to break up this exchange before it turns into a full-on sibling fight. "Frank, you're currently sharing a hotel bed with Eliza. If you make her wet the bed, you'll be sleeping in it too."

Frank considers this for a moment. "Worth it."

"*Frank!*" Eliza yells.

"As for who we investigate next," I say, still trying to keep them from fighting, "Miriam Jay is a good possibility. Or maybe we could find Wolfgang Westover . . . to question him ourselves. Especially since Tuggle said we shouldn't trust him."

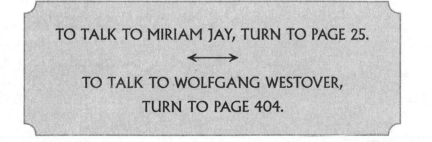

TO TALK TO MIRIAM JAY, TURN TO PAGE 25.

←——→

TO TALK TO WOLFGANG WESTOVER,
TURN TO PAGE 404.

I'M FINALLY STARTING to understand how creepy Louise really is. And how terrifying. If she's *this* obsessed with Layla, maybe she wanted to "keep" Layla for herself, kidnap her and lock her away somewhere.

I shudder at the thought.

"This is the scariest thing I've ever seen," Eliza says, as if reading my thoughts.

"Nuh-unh!" Frank says. "Not the *scariest*. What about the time we saw the spider as big as my face? What about the ghost that lives in the backyard? What about the time we were stuck in the car for four hours and Dad kept farting?"

"Oh, yes, that was definitely the scariest!" Eliza says, and Frank giggles.

"So," I say, getting back to the mystery at hand, "is this enough evidence to show that Louise is—"

"What are you doing?" asks a sharp voice. Guillotine.

Eliza, Frank, and I stiffen. Being around him is like hanging out with an actual guillotine. The man seems dangerously moody, and I never know when he's going to slice right through us.

"I said," he snarls, "what are you doing?"

"Looking for Lola," Frank says.

"Layla," I correct.

"Potato, tomato," Frank says, yawning.

Only Frank could yawn at a serious kidnapping case.

Guillotine's lips are in a thin, tight line. Like pressing his lips together will keep him from exploding at us. "I was directing my star, Brad Bradley, and I come into the prop room to get *one* thing and find that it's been turned into a kiddie day care."

"Hey!" I say, pointing at Guillotine. Grown-ups are always underestimating kids, but this seems especially rude.

"How are you proceeding without Layla?" Eliza asks. "Don't you need Layla for, like, every scene? And besides, I thought *she* was your star!"

Guillotine's mouth drops open in surprise that someone would talk to him like that, but we're not actors, so we don't have to suck up to him.

Watching Guillotine, my gut tells me we won't have long to interrogate him before he closes like an oyster guarding a pearl. But maybe we can get in a question or two before that point.

I have two ideas: I could follow the clues Layla Jay left for us, which means I should ask Guillotine about Layla's secret chest. Or I can follow my suspicions about shady possible suspects. And so far, Louise seems shady. And so does Brad Bradley. Maybe Guillotine could tell us why Brad is so jealous of Layla.

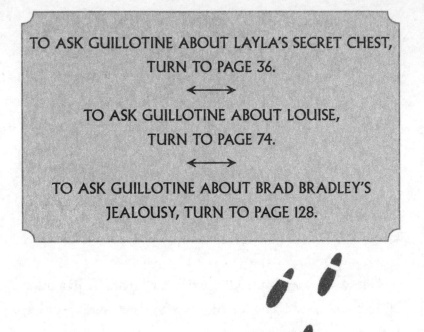

TO ASK GUILLOTINE ABOUT LAYLA'S SECRET CHEST,
TURN TO PAGE 36.

TO ASK GUILLOTINE ABOUT LOUISE,
TURN TO PAGE 74.

TO ASK GUILLOTINE ABOUT BRAD BRADLEY'S
JEALOUSY, TURN TO PAGE 128.

I OPEN THE door and have to blink five times before I register what I'm seeing.

Wolfgang Westover is standing there, looking absolutely furious. He's so tall—and the ceiling is so short—that he has to hunch to fit in.

"*You?*" I say.

"I could ask you the same question," Wolfgang growls. "What are you doing down here?"

"Looking for Layla."

"That's what I'm doing."

I protectively step in front of Layla, and so do Eliza and Frank. With my hand pressing the walkie-talkie button, for Mom to hear, I say, "You have to answer our questions first, Mr. Westover."

"This is *not a game*," he bellows. "And I am no longer entertained! Now let me at my star!"

"Not until we understand why," Eliza says firmly.

"Why what?"

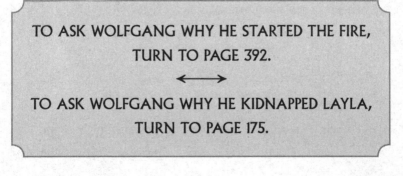

TO ASK WOLFGANG WHY HE STARTED THE FIRE, TURN TO PAGE 392.

←→

TO ASK WOLFGANG WHY HE KIDNAPPED LAYLA, TURN TO PAGE 175.

IF LOUISE IS stalking Layla, then we have to go question her.

Eliza, Frank, and I wander through the set until we reach the side door. We burst through, out into the studio parking lot. The Los Angeles sun is blindingly bright, which makes me wish I had a pair of cool shades so I didn't have to squint to see the girl holding the sign:

> # LAYLA'S NUMBER ONE FAN!
> # XOXO, LOUISE

Louise seems to be about sixteen or seventeen. Just about the same age as Brad Bradley and Layla Jay. She has brown eyes, freckly skin, and messy light brown hair—or maybe it's a dark blond. She smiles, revealing a mouth full of braces.

But she's not smiling at us. In fact, she barely seems to notice us. She's watching the door eagerly, like Layla Jay could walk out at any moment.

"You think that's Louise?" I ask.

"It has to be," Eliza says.

We walk over, and Louise starts pacing.

"We want Layla! We want Layla!" she chants in our

faces. "We demand to know where she is!"

Who is this "we" Louise is talking about? She's the only one out here.

"Uh . . . hi," I say. "Are you Louise?"

Her eyes narrow. "Who wants to know?"

I have to get her to warm up to us. "We are detectives, looking for Layla Jay. We were told you're the Layla expert."

She *loves* that. Her eyes light up, and she claps her hands together. "Yes, of course. I am the utmost authority on Layla. As the official president of her unofficial fan club, and as her soul twin, I can tell you anything you need to know that will help you find her."

"What's a soul twin?" Eliza says.

"A soul twin!" Louise says. "You know, we're like practically the same person. There are just too many coincidences for it to be anything but *fate*. Like . . . we have the same initials: L.J. Layla Jay and Louise Jenkins. Isn't that something?"

"What else?" Frank says.

"We're both only children. Well, if you don't count my stepsister."

"What else?" Frank says.

"We were both born in Portland. Well, she was born in Portland, Maine, and I was born in Portland, Oregon . . . but it's close enough."

Close enough? Maine and Oregon are on opposite sides of the country.

"What else?" Frank says.

"Her birthday is August fifth, and mine is May eighth."

"Uh-huh . . . ," I say, scratching my head.

She sighs. "Get it? August fifth is 8/5. May eighth is 5/8. It's reverse! And we both like to dip French fries in ice cream; I love photography, and she loves to model; and she was in a dinosaur movie, and I love dinosaurs. See? Uncanny, right?"

I don't see how *any* of this makes them soul twins or whatever.

"Have you ever told Layla about the whole soul-twin thing?"

"Of course!"

"And how did she react?"

"She . . . she was excited about it. Obviously," Louise says defensively. "You'd be excited too, if you met your soul twin!"

Uhhhh. Right.

"Layla and I are BFFs," Louise continues, "and I even have an autographed picture to prove it!"

My eyes dart to the camera around Louise's neck. Does she possibly have pictures of Layla? Anything that might help us figure out what Layla was doing right before her disappearance? Maybe she caught a clue on camera.

156

Or maybe I should just confront her about her creepy stalking habit.

TO CONFRONT LOUISE ABOUT STALKING LAYLA, TURN TO PAGE 368.

←——→

TO ASK LOUISE IF SHE HAS ANY PICTURES OF LAYLA, TURN TO PAGE 75.

WE HAVE TO go investigate the woods. It's the only part of the set we haven't seen yet, and maybe there's a clue there.

We wander the path Louise told us to follow, which leads up a hill. The farther we go, the more trees there seem to be. And eventually we reach a point where there are so many trees that we can't see the studio buildings. I guess they need the woods to be super dense, so that when they film, it seems like a real forest.

Up at the crest of the hill, there is a small clearing with camera equipment and a graveyard with fake gravestones that I've seen on the show.

"Where do we start?" I ask Eliza.

"Let's just comb the area for clues."

I wander around, and Eliza takes the other end of the clearing. Frank goes off on his own too. It takes about two minutes before Frank starts shouting.

"Hey, look! I found something!" Frank says. "In this tree!" He sticks his head inside a tree hollow. "Oh, wait, nope. That was just tree sap."

I roll my eyes.

"Uh-oh," Frank says. "I think my head is stuck."

Eliza and I run over to him, and he is face-first inside the tree hollow. This reminds me of when Frank gets his head stuck in the banister at his house. Which has happened on multiple occasions.

158

"Carlos, help me pull him out!"

Eliza and I heave and ho and pull and tug, but Frank is stuck in there good. Now we have to wait for a lumberjack to come (which is going to take hours). And we have to wait for Frank to be carefully cut out (which is going to take even longer).

I guess we barked up the wrong tree.

CASE CLOSED.

"**I THINK WE** have everything we need," I say. "Thank you."

I look to Mom to make sure it's okay I ended the conversation without her permission, and she follows my lead. Standing up and shaking both of their hands, Mom wears a cheerful grin. It's totally fake and forced. But to anyone who doesn't know her very well, Mom comes off charming.

"Thank you both very much. Some interesting information here. We appreciate your time, and we will keep in touch."

Miriam seems satisfied with herself as she marches out of the office. Tuggle is a bit more guarded. She inspects us as she leaves. I swear she's looking at me like I'm a math equation. At last she walks out, her high heels clicking.

"It's getting late," Mom says.

"Did I do okay? With my questions?"

Mom presses her lips together. "Yes," she finally answers. "You did well, Carlos."

"Is the trial over, then? Am I part of the Las Pistas team?"

"We'll see," she says. Which we *all* know is Mom code for *no*.

DAY TWO

IN THE MORNING, I lie in bed for ages, just looking at the ceiling. I don't understand. What more can I do to prove myself? I've got passion and talent and experience. What more does Mom want?

It's hard to stop thinking about me—but I have to remind myself that this is about *Layla*. The more time that passes, the more I'm convinced she's in serious trouble.

Sure, we made progress on the case yesterday, but it's not enough.

As I listen to Mom's light snores and Frank's occasional sleep muttering, I run through everything we found out.

First, we know that Louise has been stalking Layla . . . or, at the very least, has been a super-creepy fan.

Brad Bradley is jealous of his costar.

Guillotine hates Layla, for some unknown reason. He also seems to hate *everyone*.

Tuggle seems to be way too casual about Layla's disappearance.

Miriam seems to be way too fake with her sobbing.

Wolfgang Westover is acting like Layla's disappearance is a good publicity opportunity.

Tuggle, Miriam, Guillotine, and Brad have all been fighting with Layla.

With all those potential leads and suspects juggling in my head, I can't possibly lie here one second more when there's a case at hand.

I roll out of the bed I'm sharing with Mom and jump on Eliza and Frank's hotel bed. Eliza groans and tries to put the pillow over her eyes. She's never been a morning person. But Frank pops up like a pogo stick, and he and I jump on the bed together before lying in a dog pile on Eliza.

Frank licks her ear, which I think is going a little too far, and she growls, "Get off me, you monsters!"

"Rawr!" Frank replies.

All the noise wakes Mom up. "Cool it, kids," Mom says, rolling out of bed with a yawn. "Save the energy for your detective work."

While Mom changes in the bathroom, Eliza, Frank, and I discuss the case again. Well, Eliza and I discuss the case, while Frank crawls under the bed to look for dust bunnies.

"We talked to so many people yesterday," Eliza says. "And each one seems guiltier than the next."

"We almost have too many leads," I say. "Where

should we start today?"

"You start where I start," says Mom, the bossy over-lord micromanaging my life. But the universe has other plans in store. When we arrive on set, we know some-thing is wrong right away.

"Thank goodness you're here!" Wolfgang Westover booms. "Follow me!"

"What's wrong?" Mom asks.

"It's ruined! All ruined! I'm going to kill whoever did this!"

Eliza, Frank, and I have to run to keep up with his long legs. He walks through the set with the lockers and classrooms, past the green screen area, all the way to the back of the studio. There's a huge crowd of cast members and crew alike. They part for us, right down the middle, and I feel their stares as we pass. All our major suspects are here: Miriam Jay, Agatha Tuggle, Guillotine, Brad Bradley—even Louise is inside the studio today. My guess is that she was hanging with her uncle Wolfgang this morning.

At last we're standing in front of a door I recognize: the prop room. And when we go inside, I gasp.

The whole place is a disaster. It's not just messy: it's completely broken. Wands are snapped. Wizard cos-tumes are shredded to ribbons. Furniture is hacked into pieces, like someone went at it with an ax. The crystal ball that gives witches their prophecies is in ten thousand shards on the floor, and all the hair has been pulled out of the wigs. Not a single prop has been untouched, not a corner of the room undamaged.

I turn around to look at the cast and crew.

"WHO DID THIS?" Wolfgang bellows. "Thousands of dollars in damage! How dare you!"

"Is this the only room that's been destroyed?" Mom asks.

"Layla's dressing room," Wolfgang says. "It's the same way. Ripped-up clothes and makeup all over."

"I wonder," Eliza whispers in my ear, "if the culprit was also looking for Layla's chest."

My stomach plunges. If that's true—if someone was *so* desperate to find the chest that they'd destroy everything in two rooms—then I bet they found it.

"Nobody move," Mom says. "I will be questioning everyone one-on-one, one by one."

One-on-one? Hey, wait a minute! What about *us*?

I turn to Mom, and she must see the hurt on my face because she says softly, so only I can hear, "I have a very important job for you, Eliza, and Frank. I'm trusting you to be my eyes and ears."

Eyes and ears? Does she think I'm stupid? That doesn't mean *anything*. All I'm going to do is stand around and wait . . . when I could be investigating and participating! I feel like I just got demoted.

"Carlos? I'm trusting you." Mom kisses my cheek. "Stay here, guard this room, and keep your eye out for any suspicious behavior." She quickly dials the police, and when she's done, she stands up and announces to the crowd of onlookers, "You are all to stay put in this hallway. The prop room is now a crime scene. Do not go in there. Do not leave the hallway. If you do either of these things, you will jump right to the top of my suspect list."

"Come on," Brad Bradley says, flipping his hair. "I left my phone in my dressing room. Can't I run back to get it? I'm going to be bored here—"

"No," Mom says. "No one leaves. As long as this takes, I need your cooperation."

Everyone groans, Guillotine loudest of all. He slumps against a support beam and rolls his eyes.

"I'll go alphabetically. Mr. Bradley, you first."

Brad runs a hand through his floppy hair again. "If I must."

He and Mom disappear around the corner, and I'm stuck here guarding the prop room. I look around. I wonder if we can find any clues in here. Maybe the culprit left something behind accidentally.

I nudge Eliza. "We should shut the door and investigate the prop room."

"Really? Because I was thinking we should investigate Brad Bradley's dressing room, now that he's tied up with your mom."

"But shouldn't we sift through the clues at the crime scene?"

"This may be our only chance to get into Brad's dressing room."

"Uh . . . Eliza? Carlos?"

"But maybe we could—"

"HEY!" Frank says, so loudly that the whole hall goes silent for a moment. Thankfully, Frank waits until people start muttering among themselves again before saying, "Guillotine just sneaked away! Snuck away! Snuckered away! Anyway, he's gone!"

I peek out the door, and sure enough, I just catch sight of Guillotine turning the corner of the hall before he disappears from sight. He is clearly disobeying my mom . . . in a highly suspicious way. We could follow him.

Or we could snoop through Brad's room.

Or we could investigate the prop room, comb for clues at the scene of the crime.

I have to act fast!

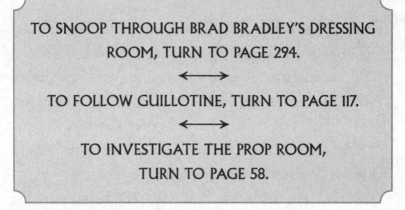

TO SNOOP THROUGH BRAD BRADLEY'S DRESSING ROOM, TURN TO PAGE 294.

←——→

TO FOLLOW GUILLOTINE, TURN TO PAGE 117.

←——→

TO INVESTIGATE THE PROP ROOM, TURN TO PAGE 58.

"FRANK!" I SAY. "Rotate box two . . . but be careful!"

Frank reaches his tiny fingers in, and *click*.

He moves the pipe clockwise, and all the lights switch off. Then with a hiss, the door above us releases.

"GET ME OUT OF HERE!" Frank shouts.

"Shhhhhh, Frank," I say. "We don't know where Tuggle is. We have to be quiet."

"QUIET AS A MOUSE! SQUEAK!" he says loudly.

Still on Mom's shoulders, Frank pulls down the door, and this time it pops right open. Frank scrambles up. Then Mom and I lift Eliza. Then Mom lifts me, while Eliza and Frank tug from above.

But then . . . there's no one to lift Mom, and she's too deep in the hole for us to pull. I look around the set, but there's nothing here to help us.

"Go!" Mom says, throwing her phone at me. "You have to get back to where there's service and call the police. If you see Tuggle, run and hide! Do *not* confront her! Be careful, hijo!"

"But Mom!" I say. "I can't just leave you here—"

"I'll be fine. Tuggle's not coming back here, and I can wait. Layla's in trouble . . . saving her is our top objective."

I nod, and Eliza grabs my hand and squeezes tight.

"We won't let you down, Mom."

We run down the hill toward Stage Eight, but a flash

168

of car lights catches my eye and the trunk of a green car pops open. In the distance, someone is carrying a bundle across the parking lot . . . a *person-sized* bundle.

"Eliza!" I gasp, pointing that way.

"We told your mom we'd call the police."

"And we will! But if Layla is wrapped in those blankets, then we *have* to get her out or stop that car. If we don't, they'll be miles away before the police can arrive!"

"Well?" Frank says impatiently. "Any ideas, Mr. Idea Man?"

Two are running through my head, actually. The car is going to have to drive out of the lot . . . and the only thing standing between the car and the open road is the security gate . . . which is unlocked for people leaving the studio. If we went to the guard's booth, there might be some way to lock the gate.

Or we could go right to the source and break Layla out of the trunk of that car. As Mom said, saving Layla is our top objective.

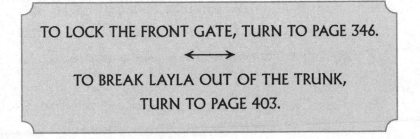

TO LOCK THE FRONT GATE, TURN TO PAGE 346.

←——→

TO BREAK LAYLA OUT OF THE TRUNK,
TURN TO PAGE 403.

IT MIGHT SOUND crazy, but I'm going to follow Frank's lead . . . and pull the fire alarm. Yep, it *definitely* sounds crazy.

I nod at him, and he yanks on the lever.

BRRNNGG!!! BRRNNGG!!! BRRNNGG!!!

The sound of the alarm is deafening. We all hold our ears, scurry down the hall, and duck into the adjacent hallway just in time—because Wolfgang Westover storms out of his office.

"WHAT IS GOING ON?" he bellows in his deep voice. "Where's the fire?" I peek around the corner. He stomps in the other direction, toward the set—with Mom on his tail.

"Let's go!" I say, pulling Eliza and Frank. "We have to follow Wolfgang."

"No, Carlos," Eliza says firmly. "When they figure out there's no fire, they're going to come back here and continue the conversation in his office."

"So we did all that for nothing!"

Eliza walks over to Wolfgang's door and opens it, a sly grin on her face. "We can hide inside his office and wait for them to come back. You know, this wasn't the plan I would have gone with, but it did the trick. Good job, Frank."

"Frank is the bestest smarterest person in the world!" Frank says. "And don't you forget it!"

Inside, Wolfgang's office is just what I would expect of a TV executive producer. A deep red carpet, velvet curtains, and promotional Hollywood posters everywhere—probably some of the projects he's worked on.

His office isn't big, but there are places to hide. I usher Eliza into a cabinet. Frank and I hide in a coat closet. We spread out, just in case we still can't hear through the closet door. I don't want this all to be a waste. Eliza gets the cramped spot in the cabinet because she's a bit smaller than me . . . and I definitely don't trust Frank on his own. Knowing him, he'd burst out randomly into song the second he got bored. At least if I'm with him, I can put a hand over his mouth when he starts to get too fidgety.

We wait for what seems like *forever* before the alarm finally shuts off. And then another forever before Wolfgang and Mom come back into the room. I can't see anything in the darkness of this closet, but I can definitely hear them clearly. Mission accomplished.

"What a waste of my time," Wolfgang grumbles as he finds his way back to his squeaky chair. "As soon as I figure out who pulled that alarm, I'll fire them."

There's a silence from Mom, and I can only imagine she's giving him a sympathetic look.

"What was I saying before this whole fiasco?"

"Layla," Mom gently reminds Wolfgang. "You were

telling me about some of the troubles she faces on set."

"Right," Wolfgang says. "For one, she and Brad Bradley do *not* get along. I think there's a bit of competitiveness. Maybe some professional jealousy from Brad. It gets in the way of their work. And to be honest, our director, Guillotine—I mean . . . Douglas Chen . . . only makes matters worse."

"How so?" Mom asks.

"He's an instigator. He wants Layla and Brad to fight. He . . . he has no interest in creating a harmonious working experience."

Mom is silent, and Wolfgang fills the pause with more words. I need to take notes on Mom's interrogation habits, because this is amazing. Who knew that sometimes not asking any questions could get the suspect to blab all their secrets?

"To be honest," Wolfgang continues, "Douglas Chen and Layla don't get along either. Guillotine has a problem with me giving Layla a producer's credit in the show, but what else could I do? That girl is a star in the making. I have to satisfy her agent's demands."

"Demands?" Mom says, jumping on that. Just like I would have done. "What demands?"

"Producer's credit, salary increase, more creative control over her character . . . annoying, but all pretty standard. But then there were the weird ones. Like a basket of vegan cookies are to be delivered to Layla on the first day of every month. She is to be served sparkling water chilled to exactly forty-two degrees. No hotter, no colder. And Agatha Tuggle . . . she just keeps complicating everything."

"Complicating," Mom repeats.

"I'm here every day. Tuggle is not. And let me tell you: Layla *seems* happy most of the time. But every time Tuggle drops by during filming, somehow I end up in an office with Tuggle talking about how dissatisfied and unhappy Layla is. And I'm not sure how true it is. I mean, Layla's never said anything to me!"

"Isn't that what an agent is for, though?" Mom says gently. "To have those hard conversations that would be uncomfortable for her? To make necessary but reasonable demands on behalf of their client?"

Wolfgang bristles. "No, you don't understand. Tuggle creates unnecessary drama. It's like she isn't satisfied unless everyone's upset, angry, or both. I like to leave the drama on the set, but Tuggle takes it with her. Look, Detective Serrano, we love Layla here at Burbank Productions, but working with her agent"—he drops his voice to a whisper—"is a nightmare."

"*Achoo!*" Frank sneezes.

Oh, no! Frank!

"What was that?" Mom snaps. I can *tell* she's looking

173

our way. I could stay really silent and hope she just ignores the noise and moves on. Or I could hide us beneath Wolfgang Westover's black coat. We definitely wouldn't be seen under the coat in the back of this dark closet. Only . . . it might make noise to rustle it over ourselves.

Neither option is great, but I have to choose fast.

> TO HIDE UNDER WOLFGANG'S COAT,
> TURN TO PAGE 102.
>
> ← →
>
> TO STAY VERY STILL, TURN TO PAGE 348.

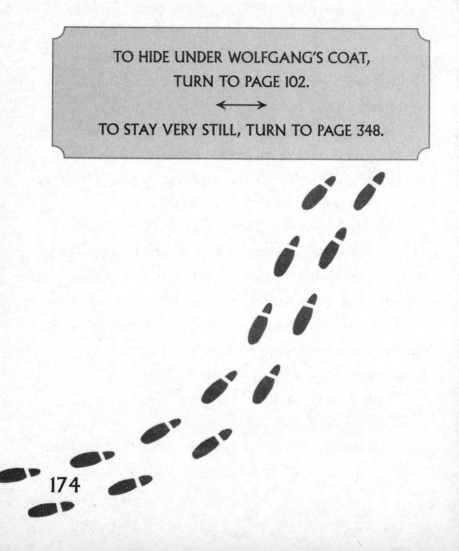

"WHY DID YOU kidnap Layla?" I ask, my fingers still gripping the walkie-talkie, so Mom can hear it all. Next to me, Eliza folds her arms, and Frank menacingly puts up his fists.

"What?" Wolfgang says. He dabs his clammy forehead with a handkerchief from his suit pocket. "I did no such thing!"

I nod at Eliza, and she consults her notebook of clues. "First," she starts, "you were very happy that Layla was missing—you saw this as a publicity opportunity."

"Tuggle told us you were untrustworthy," I add.

"And yesterday, we heard Layla screaming in this secret part of the studio that isn't even on the official map. And today here *you* are in this secret part of the studio, not even on the map," Eliza says. "That's awfully convenient."

"And you won't tell us where you were during the fire," I say. "We know that the kidnapper started the fire as a diversion to get us away from here. Then the kidnapper— you—used the smokescreen to move Layla to a different location. I have to believe that since you knew about this secret basement and you have a clear motive, you're the kidnapper."

"BOOM, WE GOT YOU!" Frank shouts.

Wolfgang looks blank for a second . . . and then he chuckles. He actually *chuckles*. Which is not the reaction I was expecting. "Wow, when you spin it like that, I look guilty. There's only one problem."

"What's that?"

"I'm not guilty."

Eliza and I exchange a confused glance.

"There are holes in your account," Wolfgang says. "For one, I actually *didn't* know about this secret basement, as you call it, until about ten minutes ago. When I received an anonymous note with directions into this disgusting cellar."

"Tell us where you were when the fire started."

Wolfgang's expression darkens. "I can't."

"You have to," Eliza says. "Or we're going to assume you're lying to us."

Wolfgang gulps. "It's so shameful. I . . . I . . ." He dabs his forehead again. "Please don't think badly of me when I tell you."

I raise my eyebrows. What could have he been doing that was so bad?

"I was on the phone with the press," he says hoarsely. "I was drumming up interviews and articles and publicity for the show."

"Layla was in serious trouble," I say, pointing to where she is lying, unconscious. "You could have been looking for her or making posters or placing ads or spreading the word about her disappearance on the internet, but all you can think about is your show's performance and how to make an extra buck off her pain?"

"I know," Wolfgang says, burying his face in his hands. "But you have no idea what pressure I'm under, as a producer, to get the ratings up. And with the delayed shooting schedule, it's even *more* important to drum up buzz."

I take the walkie-talkie out of my pocket. "What do you think about this, Mom?" I let go of the button for the first time since Wolfgang came in.

"—not Wolfgang! I repeat, NOT WOLFGANG. Take your hand off the button, so you can hear me! Stop interviewing Wolfgang!" Mom curses a string of words so foul that Frank perks up. "Carlos, can you hear me? Code red, CODE RED."

I fumble the walkie-talkie. Code red! But code red is our emergency term! How long has Mom been trying to get through to me? I've had my hand on the button the whole time. As long as I'm transmitting to her, she can't transmit to me. I'm so stupid!

"Carlos, COME IN!"

"Mom, I'm here. You said code red?"

"You're in danger! I'm trapped, and she's coming for you! It's—"

The line cuts off.

"Mom?" I shout into the walkie-talkie. "MOM!"

Eliza takes the walkie-talkie out of my hands and puts it down. "Carlos, we have to leave . . . now."

"Mr. Westover, please carry Layla and follow us down—"

"Not. So. Fast."

I whip around, and I'm face-to-face with a woman in a dark pantsuit with intense shoulder pads. Her hair is smoothed into a perfect bun, pens sticking out the top. With one hand, she adjusts her round glasses. The other is holding some sort of remote.

"Agatha Tuggle!" I say.

"You're behind this?" Wolfgang bellows, and he stands up so fast he clunks his head on the low ceiling. "Ow!"

"Spare me the reaction reel, and hand me my client."

"NO WAY, JOSE!" Frank says.

Tuggle smiles. "I don't think you understand. I pulled an all-nighter last night. And during that all-nighter, I rigged the basement with about twenty different movie-grade explosives."

Wolfgang cries out, and Eliza gasps.

"Do not test my patience. Now hand me my client, and I promise I'll let you go. No harm, no foul."

We can't trust her. If we give her Layla, then she's just going to blow up the basement anyway. We mean nothing to her. In fact . . . we're four people who know her dark secret. She'd probably *want* to blow up the basement.

I have to keep her talking while I think up a plan.

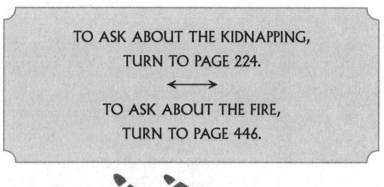

TO ASK ABOUT THE KIDNAPPING,
TURN TO PAGE 224.

$\longleftrightarrow$

TO ASK ABOUT THE FIRE,
TURN TO PAGE 446.

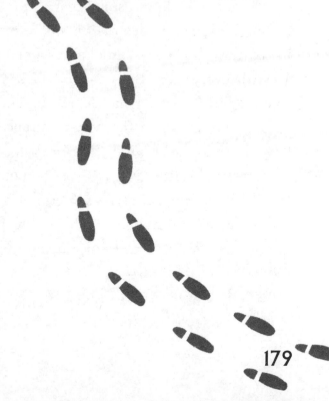

WE CAN'T IGNORE the fire alarm. We have to get out of here.

"We'll be back!" I shout through the wall.

"Don't leave me, please don't leave me!" Layla sobs through the wall. And it breaks my heart. But we have to run. We're no help to Layla if we've been barbequed.

Besides, Layla is on the other side of the wall, and we have no idea how to reach her. Maybe we should get help. Maybe we do need Mom after all.

We run back the way we came. As we get closer to the exit, my nose twitches—not with a sneeze, though. With something that makes my stomach drop.

"Eliza, Frank, do you smell that?"

"He who smelt it, dealt it!" Frank retorts.

"No, not *that*," I say. "Smoke! It's a real fire!"

With every step, the air gets thicker and denser, smoke pouring into the small basement hallway through the cracks in the secret entrance. "Everyone, drop down to the ground!" Eliza instructs.

"STOP, DROP, AND ROLL!" Frank says. And instead of crawling, he starts somersaulting and rolling.

"Frank, no!" Eliza shouts. "That's only if your clothes are on fire! We have to keep moving . . . we have to escape!"

"STOP, DROP, AND ROLL! STOP, DROP, AND ROLL!" he keeps screaming.

Eliza reaches the secret door and puts her hand on it gently. If it's hot, there might be fire on the other side of the wall.

"It's cool to the touch," she confirms, and she pulls the exit open. Smoke billows in much more thickly now. I'm walking through a wall of heavy black smog to get out. Back in the nonsecret hallway again, we crawl on our hands and knees through the smoky studio.

Outside, the fire trucks are already here, but I ignore them as I scan the crowd for Mom. She's way in the back. The moment she spots us, she screams our names, and she elbows her way through the crowd to get to us.

"Thank goodness!" she whispers as she pulls us all into a hug. Then her relief turns to anger, quicker than I've ever seen. "Where were you three? I was worried sick! I tried to go in after you, but the firefighters won't let—"

"Mom," I interrupt. "I know you're going to be mad at me, and you can ground me later, but right now, there's no time."

"What's wrong, Carlos?"

I take a deep breath. "We ditched Maureen and went investigating . . . we actually *found* Layla, but she was on the other side of the wall. She's still trapped in there."

Mom nods. She doesn't even look angry. I guess

emergency mode trumps disobedience. "Follow me."

We run to the fire chief, who's directing a team of firefighters into the building. Mom is *amazing*—it's incredible to watch her in action. Right away, she commands the chief's attention, and tells him exactly what we told her.

"We can take you to her!" I say. "It's hard to describe, but very easy to show."

The fire chief considers for a moment. Then he says, "By George, what are you waiting for? Get suited up!" He has four officers help us into flameproof suits and oxygen masks. In no time, the four of us are ready to go in.

With the firefighters beside us, we head to the picture frame outside Brad's dressing room, where the smoke is so thick it clouds my mask. Then we lead the firefighters through the secret entrance behind the picture, through the tiny rickety hall, to the wall of bricks.

"Here!" I say. She was right here . . . but on the other side of the wall. "LAYLA!"

"Layla!" Eliza shouts.

"LAYLA, IF YOU DON'T ANSWER ME, YOU'RE IN BIG TROUBLE, MISSY!" Frank shrieks.

Silence.

"Please!" I say. "Break down the wall, and you'll see! She's there! Maybe she passed out from the smoke."

182

The firefighters move forward with a sledgehammer and a pickax, and they start chipping away at the wall. They destroy the brick wall in no time, and we step through a misshapen hole into a hidden room—it has a chair, a filing cabinet, and a tiny desk. All covered in dust and cobwebs. Whatever this place is, it looks like no one's been there in years.

And there's certainly no Layla Jay.

"She was here!" I say. "I swear she was!"

"We're so sorry for wasting your time," Mom apologizes to the firefighters. "We'll be on our way now."

The firefighters grumble as we file out of the secret passageway.

On the walk to the parking lot, Mom is quiet, and I can't tell if she's mad or disappointed. Honestly, I'm not sure which one's worse. We file into the car, and it isn't until we roll off the lot that I say anything. "She really *was* there, Mom!"

"I believe you," she says.

"You do? But . . . but I've been lying to you about investigating. I ran away from Maureen!"

Mom flicks on her turn signal. "True, but you aren't a boy who cries wolf."

"WOLF!" Frank cries. "WOLF!"

"Clearly that's Frank's job," Eliza says, leaning against her little brother.

We pull into the parking lot of the hotel, and Mom puts the car into park. She purses her lips together. "I'm very upset with you. I can't pretend I'm not very angry that you've lied to me multiple times and sneaked around behind my back. But . . . I believe you found Layla Jay, and if that's the case, the culprit started the fire because of how close you were getting. I can't deny your talent."

I feel like I could cry, but in a good way. I grab Mom's hand. "It's in my blood."

"I'm not happy about letting you back inside Stage Eight with a kidnapping arsonist on the loose. But . . ." Mom takes a deep breath. "In this line of business, a detective is foolish if she refuses help. And I could use your help."

"Whatever you need, Ms. S," Eliza says. "We're all yours."

DAY THREE

SINCE THE FIRE only ruined the prop room, Wolfgang Westover insisted that everyone continue filming to stay on schedule. "The show must go on!" were his exact words on the phone to Mom. And the investigation must go on too. Our plan is set. Since cell phones get poor reception inside the building, Mom and I have our walkie-talkies ready. And when we arrive back at Stage Eight, we split up right away. Mom gives me a tiny nod of acknowledgment, and my heart swells.

No having to avoid her. No lies between us. No babysitter.

Just two Serranos and two Thompsons working together. This is the way detective work *should* be.

While Mom goes to check alibis for the fire yesterday, we head to the secret passageway. She's the bait . . . we're leading the hunt for clues in the room where I *know* Layla was. Our only rule is to page Mom when we find something important.

The rubble in the secret passageway is even worse than I remember. Broken chunks of brick lie all over the hall, and the chalky dust is everywhere. We step

185

carefully through the hole into the empty room, the size of a closet.

Is this the room Layla was kept in—before the fire gave the kidnapper a chance to move her? There's a wooden armchair and an old desk with a computer monitor on it. And the computer looks *ancient*. A radiator that keeps spitting out steam. A bunch of filing cabinets. A locked door, with a number pad next to the handle. Dust and cobwebs everywhere. Whatever this room is, it doesn't look like it's used much anymore . . . except possibly as a hideaway for kidnapped film stars.

As Eliza and I look around, Frank lies down on the floor, kicking up at the desk.

"Why don't you help us search?" I snap at him.

"This is *boring*. I miss the fire."

"Seriously, Frank?" Eliza says. "Fire isn't fun—it's dangerous!"

"At least it was much more exciting than this empty room. And this boring paper."

"Paper?" I ask.

"Yeah. It's stuck to the underside of this desk with chewed-up bubblegum." He pauses. "Can I eat the bubblegum?"

"Ew, Frank, *no*!" Eliza says.

"Too late!" Frank says, his mouth full of ABC gum.

Eliza gags, and I pull the paper out of Frank's hands. "It's a letter!"

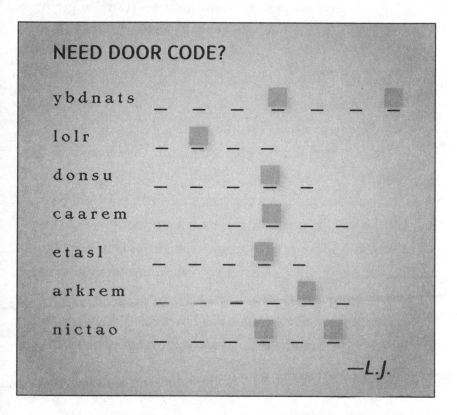

"L.J.," I say. "This note is from Layla Jay! She must have written it in code, then stuck it under the desk with some gum, so that whoever kidnapped her wouldn't see. Then anyone looking for her would be able—"

"This doesn't feel right," Eliza interrupts.

I sigh. Sometimes Eliza wants to make everything

so complicated, when it seems straightforward to me. "What is it now?"

"Layla just *happens* to write us a secret note giving us the *exact* thing we need to explore the basement further, and the kidnapper just *conveniently* overlooked it?"

"Accidents happen."

"No way, Carlos. Not like this."

"It's a trap!" Frank yells. "A TRAP! A VENUS FLYTRAP!"

Eliza nods and gives the tiniest of shrugs. "Well, yeah. While we were making a plan last night with your mom, the kidnapper was making plans of their own. They were on the defensive yesterday, and the fire was a stupid, desperate move. They don't want that to happen again. So they're playing offense today."

"Can I be goalie?" Frank says. "Or orange eater? That's my favorite soccer position."

My head is spinning with everything Eliza's said. "Say you're right—"

"I am."

"Okay . . . but even if it *is* a trap, we still have to follow the bait. It's the only way we'll find out who is behind this. And it's our only chance of getting Layla back. Don't you think?"

"I guess you're right," Eliza says with a gulp.

188

"So what do we do with this code?" I ask.

Eliza takes the paper from me and holds it very close to her nose. "Unscramble," she says confidently. "First we unscramble each of these words. Then we take the highlighted letters and unscramble *those*, and we will have our passcode."

"Let's do it," I say.

THE SOLUTION TO THE PUZZLE WILL TAKE
YOU TO YOUR NEXT PAGE.

←——→

TO ASK ELIZA FOR A HINT,
TURN TO PAGE 272.

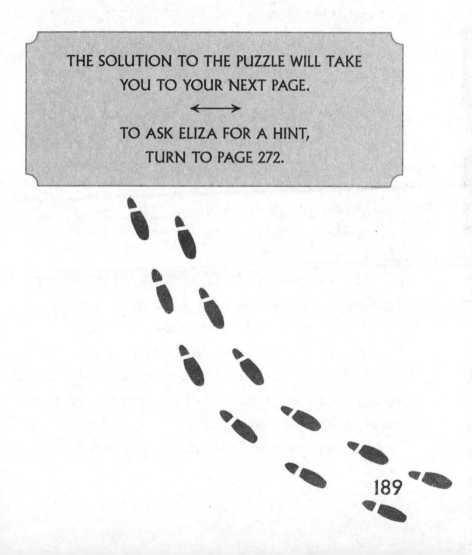

I **BANG ON** the pipes. I have to make as much noise as possible to draw Tuggle out of the room. It reminds me of an episode in *Teen Witch* where Layla's character Aurelia distracts the headmistress to keep her best friend out of detention. Obviously the stakes are *way* higher here.

Instantly, Tuggle rips open the door and sticks her head into the hallway. "You!" she gasps. Then she charges at us.

Uh-oh. I did not think this through.

"RUN!" I shout.

Frank and I are in the lead; Eliza lags behind. But we all hop back over the rope and dive into the open elevator. I press the button to go up repeatedly.

Come on, doors . . . close!

They start to shut, but then Tuggle lunges forward and sticks her arm out. She gets inside the elevator, and the doors shut behind her.

Three's a company, four's a crowd. Especially when the fourth is an evil, maniacal kidnapper.

"I was wrong to take my eyes off you," she says. "I won't make the same mistake again."

The elevator starts to go up again. We stand around, each in our own corner. I can almost see Tuggle calculating her odds of winning a barehanded elevator brawl. But I know: her odds aren't good. If she tried to attack one of us, the other two would jump her.

But I'm more concerned about what happens when we get back to the set. Who knows what sorts of weapons she'll have stashed nearby?

We can't let this elevator get to its destination. We have to jam it. I could jump up and down to put stress on the cables. The elevator is so rickety—it might work. But just as I'm bending my knees to jump, I see Eliza, and she's staring right back at me.

"Man," Eliza says, "I really hope you don't have a hatchet upstairs, Tuggle. That would be really unfortunate for us."

"Really?" Frank says. "Because I think death by a million needles is worse. Death by poisonous slugs. Death by killer farts!"

"Oh, no," Eliza says slowly, still staring lasers at me, "a *hatch*et is way, way worse."

Tuggle is barely registering Eliza, but suddenly my heart beats fast. I can read my best friend like a book. The elevator wall panel is right next to me. I'm the only one who can do what I think she's telling me to do. But should I go with her idea, or my original one?

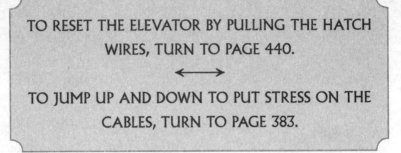

TO RESET THE ELEVATOR BY PULLING THE HATCH WIRES, TURN TO PAGE 440.

←——→

TO JUMP UP AND DOWN TO PUT STRESS ON THE CABLES, TURN TO PAGE 383.

I HAVE TO tackle her to the ground. It's the only way to stop her.

I run after her, and when I'm close enough, I dive. We go soaring into Guillotine's director's chair, which collapses under us. Maybe I should consider football, in the baseball off-season.

"Go get help!" I shout at Eliza and Frank, and they disappear.

I've got Tuggle around the legs, but she squirms with more ferocity than I imagined. She reaches out, stretching toward Guillotine's chair.

Then she turns around and smiles wickedly, the TV clapper board in her hands.

"Cut!" she cries, and chops the clapper board on my arm.

Ouch!

In that split instant, I let go, and she scrambles to her feet. She throws the clapper board at my head, and I duck instinctively. A split second later, she is gone. I let her slip through my fingers.

CASE CLOSED.

"WE'VE BEEN INVESTIGATING," I admit, and I stare deep into Mom's eyes. She doesn't look angry or confused or hurt or betrayed. She doesn't wear any expression at all.

"I know," she says. "I'm a detective, remember?"

"Right," I say, feeling stupid.

She sighs. "So . . . you want to tell me what you found?"

"Really?"

"If we combine your clues and my clues, maybe we can piece together this puzzle."

So I tell her all about our discovery with Miriam: how we found her snooping in Layla's room for something. How she left a coded note for a mystery person, asking for money from Layla's paycheck. And how we found, in her car, that she was at the courthouse the day before Layla went missing.

Mom's eyes grow wide. "I—I think our clues *do* fit well together," she says. "Because I found Layla's written calendar. And you'll never guess when *she* had a court date."

"The day before she went missing!" Eliza and I say together.

While Frank shouts, "November thirty-third!"

"So did Layla take Miriam to court, or the other way around?" Eliza asks.

194

"I'm not sure," Mom admits. "In any case, I had a thorough look around Layla's dressing room, and I can't imagine what Miriam was looking for. Unless she was looking for this . . . I found it in a pocket of Layla's coat."

Mom pulls out a scrap of paper. It's folded into fourths vertically . . . not a single horizontal fold. I start reading.

DEAR WOLFGANG,

PLEASE, HELP ME, AS YOU ARE MY ONLY FRIEND IN THIS PLACE. I AM AT MY WITS' END AND DO NOT KNOW WHAT TO DO. SOME PEOPLE THINK "WHAT A DIVA," BUT YOU KNOW I'M NOT LIKE THAT. I DON'T REALLY ENJOY THIS DRAMA. I'M SO SICK AND TIRED OF THIS TERRIBLE TREATMENT. BELIEVE ME WHEN I SAY: I VERY MUCH WANT TO GET ALONG WITH GUILLOTINE AND BRAD, BUT HOW DO I MAKE THEM STOP SABOTAGING ME? I CAN'T *DEMAND* RESPECT. TUGGLE IS NO HELP, AND MIRIAM . . . WELL SHE IS OUT OF MY LIFE NOW . . . I DON'T KNOW WHAT TO DO.

-L.J.

I've barely finished reading the note when Wolfgang hollers to Mom from the wreckage of the set. "Detective Serrano!" he yells. "A word?"

"Flubbernoodle!" Frank replies. "There's your word."

Eliza and I shake our heads.

"That's not a word, Frank," Eliza says.

"Yuh-huh, it is!"

"Then use it in a sentence," I challenge.

"A really cool word that I know is *flubbernoodle*." Frank sticks his tongue out at me.

"Yes, of course, Mr. Westover," Mom says loudly. Then she drops her voice so only we can hear. "Take it," Mom insists, thrusting the note at us. "You know what to do. Be careful."

"But, Mom, what about y—"

"Go!"

We run away from the set and tuck ourselves near Brad Bradley's dressing room. That's when I unfold the note, and all three of us stare at it again.

"I hope she's a better actress than writer," I say. "Her sentences are kinda awkward."

"I agree!" Frank says.

"Uh . . . Frank? You can't read yet."

"Anything you can do, I can do BETTER!"

"Except read."

"Hmmm," Eliza hums, wearing a thoughtful expression. Her eyes are distant . . . like she's a million miles away. "I wonder whether there might be a secret message hidden *within* the letter."

IF THE SECRET MESSAGE SAYS TO EXPLORE UNDER THE FLOORBOARD, TURN TO PAGE 81.

←——→

IF THE SECRET MESSAGE SAYS TO LOOK IN THE PROP ROOM CLOSET, TURN TO PAGE 142.

←——→

TO ASK ELIZA FOR A HINT, TURN TO PAGE 299.

WE CAN'T WAIT for the person in the rafters to come down. Who knows how long that will be? We have to follow them!

The ladder into the rafters is on the side wall of the studio, and I grab on, climbing rung after rung. Frank follows me, and Eliza goes last.

When I get up to the catwalk, everything is shaky. And I have some major vertigo when I look down. It's a really long way to fall. At least fifty feet.

As Frank hoists himself onto the bridge, I turn to find the mystery person. And they are right in front of us. Dressed in all black, with a blank white mask. The person is not tall, and not broad, but I still can't tell if it's a man or woman.

"Hey! Who are you?" I ask.

But instead of answering, they charge right at me. The lighting bridge shakes with each thundering footstep, and I trip over the edge.

"AHHHHHHHHHHHH!"

Plop.

I land directly in a giant human-sized cauldron, in a vat of sticky potion pudding. I try to wiggle my arms or legs, but I'm practically glued. "HELP! Eliza! Frank!"

"We're coming, Carlos!" Eliza shouts, climbing down the ladder, while Frank catapults himself over the edge, landing in another cauldron next to me.

"Weeeeee! That was fun!"

In all the commotion, the person in black slips out the Stage Eight door.

"Get them!" I yell to Eliza, but it's too late. They're gone.

CASE CLOSED.

WE'RE RUNNING THROUGH the hall, past the green screen room, toward the lockers. But I stop short and put my arms out to protect Eliza and Frank.

There are six fancy TV cameras, shattered to smithereens. The glass is all over the floor, and the different pieces of plastic or aluminum—or whatever cameras are made of—are in a thousand shards, too.

Everyone in the cast and crew is deathly silent, and Mom is across the room, holding her hand to her mouth in surprise.

"WHO DID THIS?" Wolfgang Westover bellows, pointing around the crowd. "How dare you! This is thousands of dollars of damages!"

There are a lot of confused faces. And then there are all our suspects.

Wolfgang Westover, who is obviously livid.

Guillotine, who is shrinking away.

Brad Bradley, who looks mildly relieved.

Agatha Tuggle, who looks afraid.

Miriam Jay, who looks triumphant.

Louise, who is excitedly snapping pictures.

"Move over, Uncle Wolfie," she says. "You're creating a shadow on my perfect shot."

"Not now, Louise!" he says, brushing her off. "I demand to know who damaged these cameras, and *why*."

Why? That is the question I have. This is obviously a distraction . . . but from what?

"You will pay," Wolfgang Westover says, shaking, spittle flying from his mouth. He looks almost like a wild boar. "When I find you, and I *will* find you, you will pay for this."

"Calm down, Westover," Tuggle says. "You don't want to give off a threatening air, do you? Not while Layla's still missing—"

"Who gives a hoot about Layla? This is costing me money!"

The whole studio is hushed. On a knife's edge.

"Heh heh." Wolfgang chuckles. "I'm just kiddi—"

"See?" Miriam Jay shrieks. "See! I told you he's not doing anything to find my baby girl! I told you he doesn't care!"

"Take a joke, lady," Brad says.

"I will wash your sass mouth out with soap, boy! Then we'll see how fresh you are!"

The whole room erupts into a fight. Miriam Jay is poking a long, bony finger at Wolfgang, who is shouting back at her. Brad and Louise are raging at each other. Cast members and crew members alike are yelling about stupid stuff that doesn't relate to Layla at all:

"You always steal my morning bagel off the food tray!"

"Last time you did my makeup, you made me look like a raccoon!"

"You call *that* music, Bob? Your new score sounds like a dying cat."

Tuggle is trying to soothe the room, but no one is listening. And Guillotine is still pretending he's part of the wallpaper.

"We need to calm them down," Eliza says in my ear.

"How?" I say sarcastically. "With some jazz hands and a musical number?"

"YES!" Frank says. "THAT."

Eliza frowns. "I was thinking more like creating a common enemy. . . ."

"Like who?"

"Maybe we can pretend we saw a rat or something. Everyone hates rats."

"I don't!" Frank says.

We have to act fast: Miriam seems ready to strangle Wolfgang with her necklace.

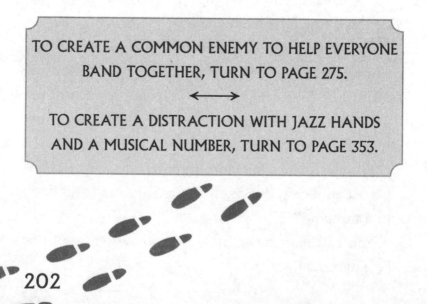

TO CREATE A COMMON ENEMY TO HELP EVERYONE BAND TOGETHER, TURN TO PAGE 275.

←——→

TO CREATE A DISTRACTION WITH JAZZ HANDS AND A MUSICAL NUMBER, TURN TO PAGE 353.

WE HAVE TO see who it is. Finding out who is under the mask is our only priority.

I reach forward, toward her mask, arms out-stretched . . . almost there . . . my fingers curl around her mask, and I yank.

Whump!

The mystery person knocks straight into me, and I fall onto my butt. But she doesn't stop—before we even know what's happening, she is out the studio door. I look down at my hands. I'm holding the mask . . . but fat lot of good that does me when I didn't see her face. Whoever it was—whether it was Miriam Jay, Louise Jenkins, or Agatha Tuggle—saw that my guard was down and took advantage of the moment.

I never thought I'd say this . . . but maybe I should have tickled her first.

CASE CLOSED.

ONCE I'VE DECODED Miriam's secret letter, I step back and admire my handiwork.

LAYLA CHANGED HER BANK ACCOUNT NUMBER. IT IS NO LONGER OH TWO OH FOUR. STUCK FOR CASH. I NEED YOUR HELP. PLEASE WIRE ME TWO THOUSAND DOLLARS FROM LAYLA'S INCOMING PAYCHECK.

—YOU KNOW WHO

"Two thousand dollars!" I choke. "But—that's not even her money! That's Layla's money!"

"When you're a minor," Eliza explains, "your parent has to cosign all legal contracts with you. And I'm sure Miriam set up Layla's bank account. Sometimes the parents of child actors dip their hands into that money . . . they feel entitled to it."

"So it *is* stealing!" I say.

"Unfortunately, it's not technically seen as stealing. It's not illegal. Just immoral."

A flash of anger runs through me, and for a moment,

I really feel for Layla. Imagine working eight hours a day, only to have your hard-earned money taken by your parents without permission.

"Do you think Layla knows that Miriam has her hands in her bank account?"

Eliza rolls her pigtail braid between her fingers. "Well, that would certainly explain why Miriam is banned from set. But there's something even more concerning."

"More concerning than theft?" I say, surprised.

She nods. "Clearly, Miriam is plotting with somebody. We don't know who this letter is for. Why would Miriam leave it in the cauldron? Who would have access to Layla's money?"

"Well . . . who?" I ask her.

"Yeah, who?" Frank demands, rolling onto his back and kicking his feet up into the hollow body of the dragon.

"Agatha Tuggle. Or Wolfgang Westover. Possibly Guillotine."

"So one of them is working with Miriam to steal money from Layla," I say. "But . . . that doesn't explain why Layla's disappeared or where she's gone."

"Or what Miriam was looking for in Layla's dressing room," Eliza says. "Don't forget—we caught her snooping, red-handed."

I admit, we still have lots of investigating to do.

"Let's go," I say, crawling out from underneath the metal dragon. The first thing I see when I inch out are an old pair of blue Chucks. I recognize those shoes. Those shoes are attached to some legs that I recognize, which are attached to a torso I know, which is attached to a head wearing a disappointed expression that I am all too familiar with.

Uh-oh.

"Hi, Mom," I say.

"Hi?" she says. "*Hi?* I've been looking everywhere for you, Carlos." She bends down and pulls Eliza out from under the dragon. Then she yanks Frank up.

"What are you three doing under here?"

"Er . . . ," I say.

"Um . . . ," Eliza hesitates.

"Saltines in a can!" Frank says confidently.

"He means sardines in a can," Eliza translates.

I try to hide my surprise at how quickly Frank came up with that lie *and* at how credible it sounds. "Right," Frank says. "We hide and we mush together and just stay put for hours. Like sardines do." He pauses. "By the way, what's a sardine?"

"It's a fish," Mom says, squinting at me. She's using her human lie-detector face on me. Usually when she looks at me like that, I crumble and tell her everything.

But I have to stay strong. For Layla's sake. For my own too.

"We got bored, Mom," I finally say. Because that *is* a truth: it's the most boring thing in the world, waiting around for someone else to solve a juicy mystery.

"Okay," Mom finally says, but I can tell she doesn't fully believe us. "It's time to go home for the day."

"You're done detecting?"

"For now," Mom says.

"Did you figure it out yet?" I ask, following her as we weave through the lockers and toward the door.

"Not quite, but I have some good leads."

Us too, I want to say. We had a really productive day, I want to say. Let's compare notes, I want to say. But I don't say anything.

I'm terrified of disobeying my mom. But hey, at least I know she doesn't steal my money.

AS WE HEAD back to the studio in the morning, I know Mom's suspicious of us. For one, she is *very* quiet. And two, she keeps trying to separate Frank from Eliza and me. Which is a good strategy. Of all the secret-keepers in our trio, Frank is the weak link. He always blurts out things he's not supposed to.

But so far so good. We walk through the studio door, and head inside—

"Detective Serrano!" says a young woman we've never met before. She's round, with a purple streak in her reddish hair. "And *you* must be wittle bittle Car-wos," she says to me, reaching forward to pinch my cheek. "Coochie coochie coo!"

I side-eye Mom, who is looking triumphant.

"Meet Maureen." Mom pauses, like an executioner before delivering the final blow. "Your babysitter."

"Babysitter!" I splutter. "This is so unfair!"

"We don't need a babysitter, Ms. Serrano," Eliza says.

Maureen smiles. "You two look like siblings, so you must be Eliza and Frank—what cutie patooties!"

"I'm not cute," Frank says. "I'm a ferocious monster!"

And he bites Maureen's arm.

"Owwww!"

"FRANK!" Eliza cries. As she goes to pry her brother off Maureen, I turn to my mom.

"A babysitter, Mom? Seriously?" I try to keep the betrayal out of my voice, but I can't help it. Stab me in the back, Mom, why don't you?

"Maureen is an intern at the studio. I hired her to watch you three. I know you've been investigating behind my back—don't deny it!" she says, when I open my mouth to argue. "And you lied to me about it. That's the thing that breaks my heart, Carlos. You lied last summer, and now you're lying again. It's a pattern now."

I feel lower than dirt. "I'm sorry. I just thought if I showed you how good I was at detective work, you'd see that I'm *meant* to be doing this. And maybe you'd let me help—instead of always blocking me."

Mom frowns. "Carlos, I don't ask you to stay away from investigating because I'm mean, or because I want to kill your passion. I do it to protect you. My job can get very dangerous. I don't want you in harm's way." She hugs me tight.

"Still, Mom, a babysitter? How can I prove that you can trust me?"

"Trust doesn't work like that, hijo," she says, ruffling

my hair. "Trust takes time and repeated honesty. It takes two seconds to break down the wall of trust you've built with someone—and years to repair it again."

I stare down at my feet. I think the worst thing about this lecture is that she's right: I haven't kept her trust, and I have been lying to her, and I want to do better. But at the same time, the need to investigate is a wild hunger inside me.

"I still love you to pieces, Carlos," she says. "Be good."

Then she slips across the desks, where they're setting up to film a classroom scene, and disappears behind a crowd of costumed wizards.

I scowl after her.

"Don't worry, kiddos," Maureen says, crouching down to our height. "We're going to have so much *fun!*"

"I like fun!" Frank says. "What kind of fun?"

"I have toys for you!" She digs into her bag and pulls out teething rings, rattles, and toy trucks. Eliza and I exchange a glance, and we both fold our arms. Frank grabs a rattle and starts making music with it.

"What are we supposed to do with this?" I ask, glaring at Frank. But he's too busy rocking out to notice.

"This stuff is for babies," Eliza adds.

Maureen digs deeper into her bag. "I have coloring books. How about we color together?"

"How about not?" I say. I don't mean to be nasty to

Maureen . . . it's not *her* fault she's babysitting us. But I'm having a hard time hiding my anger and frustration. I feel like we're on to something, now that we know Miriam Jay is taking Layla's money. Layla's depending on us to see that lead through.

"How about hide-and-seek?"

How about leave me alone?

TO PLAY HIDE-AND-SEEK WITH MAUREEN,
TURN TO PAGE 23.

←——→

TO TELL MAUREEN TO BUZZ OFF,
TURN TO PAGE 319.

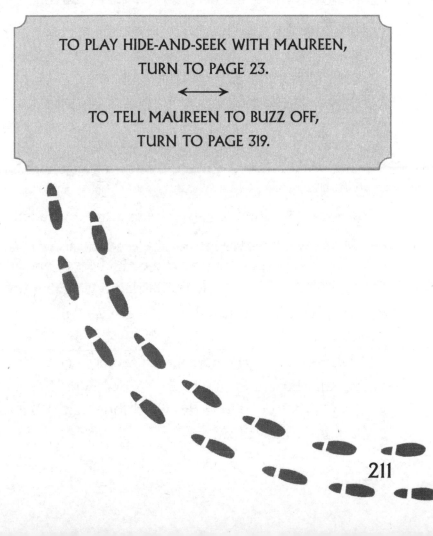

211

IT CAN'T BE a coincidence that Layla Jay used the word *grave*, and there's a spot in the on-set graveyard with fresh dirt. We have to dig it up.

Since we don't have a shovel, we dig with our hands. I feel like a gopher, and dirt is getting all over my clothes. I hope Mom doesn't kill me for this. I hope we find something important.

The hole is three feet deep now, and I'm starting to give up hope.

Tap.

Eliza's hand hits a hard piece of wood. We both peer over the hole, and then look at each other in excitement.

"X marks the spot," I say, and Eliza laughs.

Frank whines from the tree. "When are you going to come up *here*?"

But we ignore him as we excavate a small wooden trunk from the hole we've dug. It's pretty plain. It has a lock on the front that requires three numbers to open.

"It's locked!" I cry. "How the heck are we going to get in? Where in the world are we going to find the combination?"

"We already have the numbers to get into her chest, remember?" Eliza says. "From Layla's first note."

"Oh yeah!" I say. Honestly, I had forgotten. What would I do without Eliza?

212

I turn the lock to two five six, and it clicks open.

Inside, there are a few pieces of paper with some random dots and dashes.

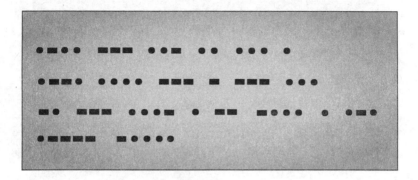

"Well, this is hopeless!" I say, looking at the scrap paper. "What a waste of time!"

"What do you mean?" Eliza asks, genuinely confused as she looks at me. "This is in Morse code."

"More code?" Frank groans as he dangles upside down from a tree. "Not more code!"

"No, *Morse* code. It's a series of dots and dashes that spell out the alphabet. Here, let me borrow your phone, Carlos." I hand it to her, and she searches the internet. When she's done, she hands me what I'm guessing is the key to Morse code.

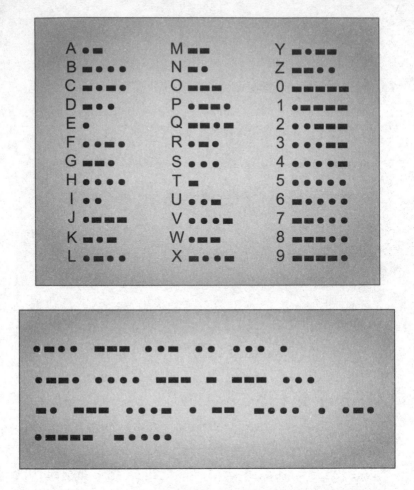

"Oh!" I say, after I take a good look. I've never actually seen Morse code before, but it doesn't look any harder than any of the other ciphers and codes we've cracked. "We can do this, no problem!"

ADD TWO HUNDRED TO THE NUMBER IN
THIS MESSAGE, AND TURN TO THAT PAGE.

BRAD'S PHONE UNLOCKS. We're in!

His home screen is pretty ordinary, and out of instinct, my finger moves toward Brad Bradley's texts. But then I notice that his recorder app has a new notification. Which is weird to me, since I never record anything on my phone. But I'm definitely curious. . . .

Should I start with my first instinct? Or go with what piqued my curiosity?

TO LISTEN TO BRAD'S RECORDER,
TURN TO PAGE 96.

←——→

TO READ BRAD'S TEXTS, TURN TO PAGE 339.

ONCE WE'VE DECODED the message from Layla's chest, I just stare at it:

> *LOUISE*
> *PHOTOS*
> *NOVEMBER*
> *16*

Even though it's warm outside, I can't help but shiver. Partially because this is super creepy. And also because I have this uncanny feeling that someone is watching us. Only when I turn around, no one is there.

"Does this note mean," I say quietly, "that Louise is the kidnapper?"

Eliza hums thoughtfully. "I don't know. It's possible."

"What do you think November sixteen means?"

Suddenly, there's a screech and the sound of creepy music playing. I look around for the source of the sound and notice a few speakers built into the trees. The hair on my neck stands on edge as the music—if I could even call it music—echoes around the woods. It's like a dying-cat string quartet, full of minor chords. Something about it is just *off*.

I pull Eliza and Frank close to me, wrapping them in a protective hug. It feels like Halloween, and I've just stepped into a haunted house where something is going to pop out at me.

The music cuts off, and then there is ringing silence. None of us says anything—not even Frank. After a few minutes, Eliza breathes, "Do you think we should go back now? Find your mom?"

"Mom, schmom," Frank says. "I want the music back!"

He weaves through the trees, and we follow him, because if there's one thing I know about Frank, it's that we *always* have to keep an eye on him. Tree after tree, we run through the woods until Frank stops abruptly, which makes Eliza smack into him, and me smack into Eliza.

"What's the big idea—" I start to complain. But then I see it: a note tacked to a tree, addressed to "Dear Detectives." I pluck the note off its nail, fold it open, and read the contents.

STOP INVESTIGATING, OR YOU'LL BE NEXT.

That's it.

"Next!" Frank says. "Next for what? A prize?"

"No, Frank, not a prize. Or at least not a good one. The culprit is threatening to . . ." I look to Eliza.

"Kidnap us," she offers weakly. "Or . . ."

"Or?"

She doesn't answer. But I can fill in the blank with my worst nightmares.

As we walk back to the studio, I think I hear the crunch of footsteps behind us. Could it be the person who gave us that threat? Or is my imagination running wild, now that I know the culprit is tracking our movements? It seems obvious that we're in danger now.

Footsteps crunch in front of us, in addition to behind us. I seize up, frozen on the spot.

"Carlos? Eliza? Frank?" Mom says, bounding up the hill. I let out a sigh of relief and run to her. "What are you three doing out here? I thought I told you to stay inside!"

"We found a secret passageway in the prop room," I explain. "We thought we might be able to find her."

"Any luck?"

I shake my head.

"Just as well. Luck is pretty temperamental when it comes to detective work. Better to rely on instincts and deduction."

"What are you doing out here, Mom?"

"Looking for you three, of course. Time to go back to the hotel."

DAY THREE

BRRRRRRNG! BRRRRRRRNG! BRRRRRRRNG!

I groan and look over at the clock: 5:30 a.m.

Mom rolls over and gets the hotel phone. "Yes, this is she . . . yes . . . mmm. *What?* We'll be right there." She flicks on the light.

"NO MORE SUN!" Frank says, slipping his head inside the pillowcase.

"I'm sorry—I could let you three sleep if you want. I thought for sure my junior detectives wouldn't be able to resist . . . but if you want to stay here all day instead . . ."

"Resist what?" Eliza says with a yawn.

"We have a ransom note for Layla."

"What?" Eliza and I shriek, and Mom shushes us.

"And," Mom says, "it's a video ransom note, left on the green screen on set. Mr. Westover just told me the video was made with the show's equipment too. Which means we may be able to discern more clues."

Eliza puts on her shoes and is at the door in record time.

"Hurry up, hijo! Get dressed. Put your shoes on," Mom says.

I throw off the covers to reveal my feet—with my shoes tied up and ready to go. "I never took mine off in the first place."

At the studio, Wolfgang Westover is waiting for us outside, along with his niece Louise. At once, I remember the clue from Layla's lockbox: Louise. Photos. November 16. We have to know what Layla's note meant. She wouldn't have left us this clue if it weren't important. But before I can ask Louise about it, Wolfgang Westover runs to Mom and clasps her hands.

"Come quick!" he says. "The police are here dusting for fingerprints on our video editing equipment, but I think that will be useless. Lots of people handle our equipment. Not just one. I'm hoping *you'll* find something, Detective. Since you're quite familiar with the case by now."

"Of course. Take me to the screen, Mr. Westover."

He holds the studio door open for Mom, and she ducks under his arm.

"Wait just one second," I say. "We have to talk to Louise—"

"No time!" Wolfgang cries. "Layla's in danger!"

Mom quirks an eyebrow at us. "Are you kids coming, or did you want to stay out here and talk to Louise?"

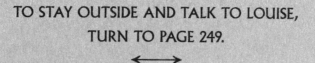

TO STAY OUTSIDE AND TALK TO LOUISE,
TURN TO PAGE 249.

←——→

TO FOLLOW MOM INSIDE AND LISTEN TO
THE RANSOM NOTE, TURN TO PAGE 413.

I ENTER THE code 4395. The lock clicks, and the door pushes open.

"Go! Go! Go!" I whisper, as Frank and Eliza scurry in. The footsteps behind us get heavier and louder, but I get on my hands and knees to crawl.

Something grabs my shoe—and is pulling my leg like an octopus dragging me down into a dark sea.

"Help!" I cry. "Eliza! Frank! They've got me!"

They each grab one of my arms and pull.

"HEAVE HO!" Frank shouts, and they yank me so hard that I slip out of my shoe. I scamper inside and shut the door before the culprit has a chance to grab me again.

"Are you okay?" Eliza asks, panting.

"They got my shoe," I say, wiggling my sock at her.

We are inside some sort of broom closet. There's nothing here but cleaning supplies and an old tarp scrunched in the corner. There's only one way in, which means there's only one way out. Uh-oh.

"Do I get candy if I find Layla?" Frank says.

"Sure," I say. "Hey, Eliza, how do we—"

"GIVE ME CANDY," Frank shouts, pulling up the tarp in the corner. Underneath is Layla, unconscious but breathing.

Eliza and I lean over her.

"Hey! Where's my candy?"

"Not now, Frank—it's an emergency!" I look at Eliza. Even in the dark of the cupboard, I can see the concern in Eliza's eyes.

KNOCK KNOCK KNOCK.

The sound comes from the door behind us.

And now Eliza's concern is full-on panic. She grips my arm, while I grip the walkie-talkie in my pocket.

"Who iiiiiis iiiit?" Frank sings.

There is *no* way I'm answering that door.

KNOCK KNOCK KNOCK.

"Not by the hair on my chinny-chin-chin!" Frank replies.

I feel sick. A million different thoughts are running through my head, and a couple of our suspects jump to the top of my head. But—as the knocking gets more violent, rattling the door on its hinges—my loudest thought of all is a nagging worry:

Are we in more trouble if we answer the door? Or if we don't?

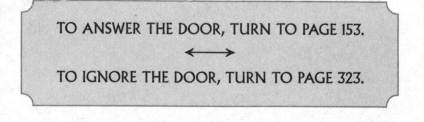

TO ANSWER THE DOOR, TURN TO PAGE 153.

←——→

TO IGNORE THE DOOR, TURN TO PAGE 323.

"OKAY," I SAY very soothingly. "We'll give you Layla. But first we need to know why you kidnapped her. It doesn't make any sense."

"Doesn't it?" Eliza says grimly. "Carlos, it actually makes *perfect* sense. Remember how Mr. Westover told us that Tuggle was causing all sorts of trouble on the set—instigating fights between Brad and Layla?"

This is all flooding back to me. "She always described Layla in the total opposite way than Mr. Westover and Miriam Jay."

"And speaking of Miriam—the note in the cauldron she left? Who else would have access to Layla's bank account but her agent?"

"You were working with Miriam Jay to steal money from Layla?" I say.

"No," Tuggle says, "I was transferring money from a minor to her legal guardian."

"Without Layla's permission, though. You were doing it behind her back!" I say. "No wonder Layla was upset with Miriam—and had that fight with you."

"A fight big enough to fire you as her agent?" Eliza says, looking at Tuggle, who nods once. Eliza groans. "We should have known. All the signs were there! I mean, she faked a phone call to get out of talking to us."

"She was a liar liar pants on fire," Frank says.

"You might want to hang up your detective hat, kid,"

Tuggle says. "Your mom got there first. She was trying to radio. If *only* you had listened."

"Where. Is. She?"

"None of your concern," Tuggle says, and I slump down to my knees. Eliza bends down and whispers in my ear, "I'm sure she's okay, Carlos. I'm sure of it. Come on. The only way we help her is to get out of this." I wipe my watery eyes on my sleeve and stand up again, still sick and shaky.

"Why lure *me* down here?" Wolfgang asks.

"Because you had all the puzzle pieces. I couldn't tell if you suspected me or not."

"I can confirm: I did not."

"Well now, I guess that's just rotten luck for you, then. Because *now* you know too much . . . and I can't have that. I just need a clean start with my client."

"So you're going to murder five people?" Eliza scoffs. "That's your clean start?"

Her nostrils flare. "If this gets out, I'm ruined."

"I think that ship has sailed," I mutter.

"And sunk!" Frank adds.

"Enough," Tuggle says. "You hand me my client. Now."

Obviously, that's the one thing we can't do. There's nothing in the room we can use . . . there's just the tarp, Layla, and all of us. And none of us are carrying weapons . . . unless you count the gaseous stench Frank

225

sometimes uses to assault my nose.

I perk up. Could a fart really save us? Or should I go with something more reliable—like tackling Tuggle and wrestling the remote out of her hands?

"Well?" she says sharply. "I'm waiting!"

TO USE FRANK AS A STINK BOMB,
TURN TO PAGE 51.

←——→

TO TACKLE AND WRESTLE AWAY THE REMOTE,
TURN TO PAGE 90.

226

TUGGLE IS PROVING to be a bit trickier than I thought, considering we already asked her why she and Layla were fighting, and she didn't answer! Time to try again.

"Why were you fighting with Layla?"

Tuggle coughs. "Excuse me?"

"We need you to answer the question," I say. "We have a witness that claims you and Layla were having some pretty loud, pretty public arguments."

Tuggle shifts uncomfortably. "That, well . . . really, it's nothing. You don't understand what it's like to work with actors. You give and you give and you give, and sometimes they just take and take—"

"Excuse me," Eliza interrupts. Polite but firm. "But it's not like you're working for Layla out of the goodness of your heart. As a talent agent, you have a commission—a ten percent cut from everything Layla makes, right?"

Tuggle smiles tightly. "Someone's done her research."

"Don't change the subject," I say, tapping my pointer on the table, like I've seen interrogators do in movies. "What were you and Layla fighting about?"

"Nothing," Tuggle says, her glasses flashing. "Absolutely nothing at all." She's closing up on us. But I haven't gotten enough out of her. I have to keep the conversation going.

TO ASK ABOUT LAYLA'S RELATIONSHIP WITH THE CAST AND CREW, TURN TO PAGE 136.

←—→

TO ASK WHERE LAYLA MIGHT BE, TURN TO PAGE 148.

228

"WHAT'S YOUR PROBLEM with Layla?"

"Me?" Guillotine says. "I have no problem!"

"You just said—"

"I said we were peachy."

"Sarcastically!" Eliza says.

"That's a matter of opinion!" Guillotine says, scowling.

"We know what we heard," I say. "We heard it with our own ears."

Frank perks up. "I heard it with my own ears! I saw it with my own eyes! I smelled it with my own nose! I touched it with my own hands! I tasted it with my own tongue!"

Guillotine's lips curl into a mean-looking smirk. His eyes dart to his right. "You know, it seems like you three hear what you want to hear. So hear this!" And he cranks up the speaker in the prop room.

The theme song to *Teen Witch* plays so loudly that I cover my ears. I even close my eyes, just to escape the piercing sound.

Suddenly something cold wraps around my ankle. . . . I look down, and they're the golden handcuffs used on the Witch Queen in season one—the ones that are supposed to be unbreakable with magic. Guillotine has buckled me to the leg of a prop shelf so heavy it'd probably take an elephant to move it.

229

He's gotten Eliza and Frank too, with two spare pairs of the same prop. We're stuck! Even though my ears are bleeding from the *Teen Witch* theme song, I hear Guillotine loud and clear now: "Don't push too far, or this case will end on a bad note!"

CASE CLOSED.

WE DECIDE TO snoop through Layla's dressing room. If we want to know what happened to Layla, then we have to get inside her head.

Only . . . when I open the door to her dressing room, I realize it's going to be much harder than I thought. Because it's an absolute mess. A complete and total pigsty. Mom would *kill* me if I ever let my room get this messy.

"Yay, dirt!" Frank says, diving headfirst into a pile of discarded costumes.

Eliza—who likes everything clean and organized— is twitching.

"This is hurting you, isn't it?" I say.

"It's really not that hard to keep things sanitary," she says, throwing a blackened banana peel into Layla's trash can.

Layla's dressing counter has two drawers: one has nothing but a book inside, and the other is locked. On top of the counter, there are open tubes of lipstick, eye shadows with powder everywhere, and fake eyelashes just lying on the table like caterpillars. Her closet is open, with no clothes on the hangers. I guess they're all on the floor. And there's a purse hanging off the back of Layla's makeup chair.

I unzip the purse and reach my hand in.

"You thief!" Frank shouts at me. "You burglar! You

robber! You . . . if you find a quarter in there, I CALL DIBS!"

But her purse is empty. No wallet. No phone. No scrap of paper with an address. Nothing. I'm about to throw the purse aside when I notice a little rip in the lining at the bottom of it.

I reach my fingers down into the hole in the lining and feel something cold, hard, and metal against my fingertips. I coax it out of the rip in the purse, and into my palm.

It's a key.

My hands are practically shaking as I take the key and put it in the keyhole of the locked dressing-room drawer. The lock clicks—we're in.

"What are you doing?" Eliza asks.

"I found a key," I say. I pull the drawer open and find . . . a single sheet of paper. I try not to be too disappointed. But then my heart beats fast when I see it's a hand-lettered note.

"Eliza!" I say. "Come look!"

Frank sings from his costume pile on the floor, "I see London, I see France! I see Eliza's underpants!"

Eliza and I glare at him, then turn to the note. It's in secret code—and we have to decipher it. There's no reason Layla would go through the trouble of coding a message and hiding the key unless this was super important.

ABCDEFGHIJKLMNOPQRSTUVWXYZ
||||||||||||||||||||||||||
ZYXWVUTSRQPONMLKJIHGFEDCBA

Ru blf ziv ivzwrmt gsrh, gsvm R nfhg szev yvvm prwmzkkvw. Blf droo mvvw gsv kzhhxlwv gl nb xsvhg: gdl urev hrc. R'n rm tizev wzmtvi.
KOVZHV SVOK.

TURN TO THE PAGE NUMBER IN THE SOLUTION.

←——→

OR TO ASK ELIZA FOR A HINT,
TURN TO PAGE 312.

"SO HOW EXACTLY do we tackle this?" I ask Eliza. "It looks like gibberish."

Eliza hums. "I think I remember something about Layla—I mean, Aurelia—using the chart to decode the message." She walks up to the wall and traces her fingers along the chart as she thinks out loud. "We can use the rows and columns to make all the letters of the alphabet. So if we look at the first part of the message, it says B1. If we go to the B row and the one column, we see the first letter is F."

"Oh!" I say. "So the second part of the message is C4. So we look where C and four meet, we get the letter O, right?"

"And the next one is purple!" Frank shouts.

"What? No, Frank," Eliza says. "There are no colors in this passcode!"

"Well, there should be," Frank pouts.

Eliza turns back to me. "The third letter is D2, which is R. The first three letters of the first word of this puzzle are F-O-R."

"I think we're getting the hang of this decoding thing!" I say.

	1	2	3	4	5
A	A	B	C	D	E
B	F	G	H	I or J	K
C	L	M	N	O	P
D	Q	R	S	T	U
E	V	W	X	Y	Z

B1-C4-D2-A5-E1-A5-D2 E2-B4-C1-C1 E4-C4-D5
D3-D4-A1-E4 B3-A5-D2-A5,
    E2-B4-D4-A3-B3,

B4-C3 A4-A1-D2-B5-C3-A5-D3-D3 C5-C1-A5-
C3-D4-E4, B4-C3
    D3-B4-C1-A5-C3-D4 C5-B4-D4-A3-B3

D5-C3-C1-A5-D3-D3 E4-C4-D5 B3-A1-E1-A5
D4-B3-A5 D3-A5-A3-D2-A5-D4
    B5-A5-E4,
D4-B3-A5 C4-C3-C1-E4 E2-A1-E4 D4-B3-A1-D4
E4-C4-D5 A3-A1-C3 B1-C1-A5-A5:

A1 C2-A1-B2-B4-A3-A1-C1 C3-D5-C2-A2-
A5-D2, D4-B3-A5
    D3-D4-D2-C4-C3-B2-A5-D3-D4 C4-D5-D4
    D4-B3-A5-D2-A5

	1	2	3	4	5
A	A	B	C	D	E
B	F	G	H	I or J	K
C	L	M	N	O	P
D	Q	R	S	T	U
E	V	W	X	Y	Z

D4–E2–B4–A3–A5 C2–C4–D2–A5 D4–B3–A1–C3
A1–C1–C4–C3–A5;
   C4–C3–A3–A5 C2–C4–D2–A5 D4–B3–A1–C3 A1
   C5–A1–B4–D2.

D1–D5–A1–D2–D4–A5–D2 A1 A4–C4–E5–A5–C3,
D4–D2–B4–C5–C1–A5 A1 C4–C3–A5,

D3–B3–C4–D5–D4 B4–D4 C4–D5–D4, A1–C3–A4
E4–C4–D5 A1–D2–A5 A4–C4–C3–A5.

ADD THREE HUNDRED TO THE SOLUTION OF THIS
PUZZLE, AND TURN TO THAT PAGE.

←→

OR TO ASK ELIZA FOR ANOTHER HINT,
TURN TO PAGE 468.

LOOKING AT BRAD'S emails, the first thing I see is one from Layla, dated just a few days before she went missing.

> Brad,
> Stop emailing, stop texting, stop calling, stop show-ing up at my house with a string quartet. I do NOT want to date you. I'd rather date a slug. I'm sick to death of telling you I'm not interested. For the millionth—and last—time, leave me alone!
> L. Jay

"Maybe he's holding a grudge about being rejected," I say. "Maybe he kidnapped Layla for revenge."

"Could be," Eliza says, leaning in to look at the next email. This one was from Wolfgang Westover:

> B.B.—
> If you can't get along with your costar, then maybe we should rethink your position on this show. I expect you to come back with an attitude adjust-ment. Remember that Layla is the star, and you have to make her happy.
> W.W.

"Wow," I say. "Do you think Brad was close to being fired? Wolfgang Westover seems pretty upset."

"Mr. Westover definitely made it clear which of his lead actors is more important to him. . . ."

"Who? Who? Is it the robot dragon?" Frank asks.

"Uh . . . Frank," I say gently, "you know the robot dragon isn't real, right?"

"YOU AREN'T REAL."

READ BRAD'S TEXTS. TURN TO PAGE 339.

I BET THE key to Guillotine's filing cabinet is in his desk drawer. That's where *I'd* put a key, anyway. I open the drawer and dig around.

Frank does too, idly chattering as he rifles. "Junk, junk, junk, secret box, gum, paper clip, junk."

"Wait!" I say. "Go back!"

"Paper clip?"

"No, back again," Eliza says.

"Gum!" Frank says. "You're right, I'm keeping that!" He shoves four strips in his mouth.

"No, Frank—the secret box! What do you mean?"

"Oh, yeah," Frank says, blowing a bubble. "Secret because it's locked."

"Again?" I groan. "So now we have *two* things to unlock!"

Eliza eases the lockbox out of the drawer. She tries to pry it open, but it won't budge. It's wood around the sides, but the top is smooth and glassy. "Interesting," Eliza says. "It's a touch screen on top. Let's hope it doesn't operate on fingerprints. . . ." She wakes up the touch screen and a single word stares us in the face:

STARTLING

"What's that mean?" I say.

"No idea."

Eliza touches the screen again, and a box pops up with two words now:

*PASSWORD HINT

"Click that!" I say. "Let's see what the password hint is."

DELETE ONE LETTER AT A TIME, WHILE STILL ALWAYS CREATING A NEW WORD.

"Oh!" Eliza says. "I've done this before with the word *snowing*. First, I deleted the N to create *sowing*. Then I erased the O to create *swing*. Then got rid of W to make *sing*. Deleted G to make *sin*. Then *in*. Then *I*. You get the picture."

"Each time we delete a letter, what remains still has to be a word?"

Eliza nods.

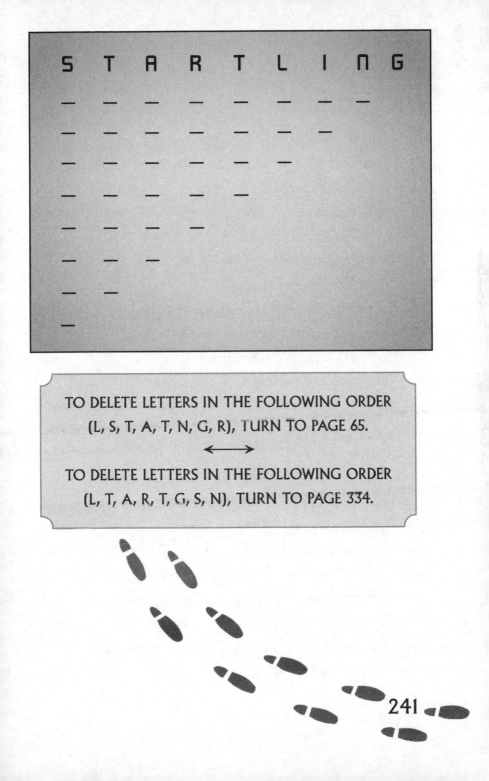

S T A R T L I N G

— — — — — — — —

— — — — — — —

— — — — — — —

— — — — —

— — — —

— — —

— —

—

TO DELETE LETTERS IN THE FOLLOWING ORDER
(L, S, T, A, T, N, G, R), TURN TO PAGE 65.

←——→

TO DELETE LETTERS IN THE FOLLOWING ORDER
(L, T, A, R, T, G, S, N), TURN TO PAGE 334.

241

I CAN'T LET Guillotine get away with that major slipup.

"Was?" I say.

"Was what?" he snaps.

"You said, 'Layla *was*.' Do you know something about Layla that we don't?"

He bares his teeth. "What exactly are you implying? That I *killed* Layla? That I'm a murderer?"

The silence between us is electric.

"Well, are you?" Eliza asks.

"I can't believe you're asking me that. I can't believe you're accusing me of that. How *dare* you!"

I say, "It's a simple question—"

"That you're avoiding," Eliza points out.

Guillotine's mouth twitches. "Follow me," he says. "I need to show you something . . . you may be right, actually."

I follow him through the hall, so excited I can barely breathe. What does he need to show us? What are we right about? I look to Eliza for a clue, but she gives me a thumbs-up as we walk. At last we stop at the part of the set where there are bubbling potions. "Step right here . . . that's it. Perfect. Now, you said you were fans of this show, yes? Well, I want to show you one of the special effects. It may be relevant to your case. And as a bonus, you may remember this

242

magic effect from season two, episode four. . . ."

He reaches onto the shelf in the potions room, retrieves a small ball, and throws it on the ground. It erupts into bright neon smoke, so thick I can't even see my own hands. I cough as the smoke fills my lungs.

"I don't like this magic trick!" Frank whines. "Where's the rabbit in the hat?"

When the smoke clears, I blink a few times, because I have no idea how I got here—I'm in a small room I've never seen before, dark and tiny and cramped.

I gasp—partly from surprise and partly for air. "Where are we? How did he do that?"

"With a very high-tech lift," calls a voice above us. When I look up, Guillotine is leaning over a big square-shaped hole in our ceiling, his floor.

"Hey!" I scream. "Let us up!"

"YEAH, YOU POOP FACE!"

"Not just yet. I think I'll give you a little time-out . . . until you can learn not to falsely accuse people of crimes they didn't commit."

"But . . . *this* is a crime! What you're doing right now!" Eliza argues. "Imprisonment and reckless endangerment!"

Guillotine doesn't make any indication that he heard Eliza. "And now, for my final act, I shall make you disappear . . . now I see you, now I don't!"

And with a *thump*, he closes the hatch on us, and everything goes dark.

CASE CLOSED.

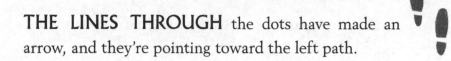

THE LINES THROUGH the dots have made an arrow, and they're pointing toward the left path.

START HERE →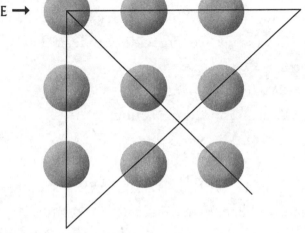

Without even waiting to see if Eliza and Frank are in agreement, I veer off to the left.

In the flashlight beam, I can barely see, but the wood floor looks rotting and old; it groans beneath our feet. The peeling walls are tight around us—there's barely enough room to walk without having to turn slightly sideways. And worst of all, there are no doors or windows or any sort of ventilation. I never thought I'd miss the tunnels in Guinevere LeCavalier's mansion so much. At least *those* tunnels were wide and breezy, and I wasn't in constant danger of eating a spider—

"AHHHHHHHHHHHHHHHHHHHHHHHHHHHH!"

The bloodcurdling scream makes my hair stand on end.

"HELP! HELP! SOMEONE HELP ME!"

My stomach swoops. It's *her*! Layla Jay. I recognize her voice from TV. Only . . . right now, she isn't acting.

Eliza's gray eyes are wide with fear. "Layla," she whispers.

"We have to help!"

We run toward the sound.

"LAYLA!" we shout. "LAYLA, WHERE ARE YOU? CAN YOU HEAR US? LAYLA!"

"HELP! HELP ME, PLEASE!" she shrieks again, and I realize something that makes my stomach drop like a stone—her voice is coming from the other side of the wall. Only there are no doors. No windows. No way to get to her. I start knocking all over the wall—maybe there's a trick wall or some sort of secret passageway that will open up.

"Hold on, Layla!" Eliza cries.

"PLEASE! SAVE ME! WHOEVER YOU ARE, PLEASE—I'M TRAPPED!"

And just when I think I can't get any more panicked, a deafening alarm starts ringing through the hall. *Brrr-rrrrrrng! Brrrrrrrrng! Brrrrrrrrrrrng!*

"The fire alarm!" Eliza says in panic.

"Ashes, ashes, we all fall down!" Frank sings.

246

"Carlos, do you think it's real? Or did someone just pull the alarm again, like Frank did yesterday?"

My instinct says it's dangerous to ignore a fire alarm . . . but it is *also* dangerous to ditch a clearly kidnapped person in a dingy basement just to save our own skins.

"What do we do?" Eliza says, grabbing on to my arm too tight.

"Don't leave me, please!" Layla cries.

"But it's a *fire*," Frank reminds me.

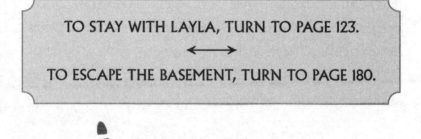

TO STAY WITH LAYLA, TURN TO PAGE 123.

⟵⟶

TO ESCAPE THE BASEMENT, TURN TO PAGE 180.

"SO WHERE IS Layla?" I ask. "What did you do with her?"

"I didn't—"

"LIAR LIAR PANTS ON FIRE!" Frank shouts into the mic.

"You already gave us motive!" Eliza says.

"M-motive!" Like a rubber band, Tuggle snaps back to herself. "I didn't do anything!" she says. "How dare you accuse me? I've done nothing wrong!"

Then she runs.

Locked in this booth, we scream and shout and yell and shriek until we lose our voices. And *still* no one comes for us. It's hours before someone finds us, and by that time, Tuggle is long gone.

Though the soundproof booth mutes all noise, I can still hear failure ringing in my ears.

CASE CLOSED.

WE HAVE TO find out what Louise knows about Layla's mysterious note.

We wait until the door closes behind Mom before we turn to Louise. She gets so nervous she takes a step backward.

"Wh-what can I help you with?" she says.

I reach into my pocket and pull out our translated version of Layla's Morse code note: Louise. Photos. November 16. "Does this mean anything to you?"

Louise's eyes grow wide. "That day . . . it was five days before Layla went missing. There was a special screening of the season three finale, which Uncle Wolfie snagged me a ticket to, and omigosh, it was *so awesome*!" She pauses. "You know . . . I have pictures from that day!"

"Pictures of what?" Eliza asks.

"Mostly just pictures of Layla." She blushes furiously. "I know I'm not supposed to go near her after that incident at the Kids' Choice Awards last year . . . you know, when I accidentally cut off a lock of her hair . . . but I couldn't help taking pictures of her last week. She looked so graceful. So poised." She self-consciously twists her hair. "She's everything I'm not."

"What do you mean?" I say.

Louise looks down at her shoes. "She's so perfect. I'm so . . . unperfect."

"Imperfect," Eliza corrects automatically.

"You see!" Louise cries. "I'm even imperfect at being imperfect!"

"Celebrities aren't perfect," Eliza says. "I can forget that too, sometimes. But actors are just . . . people. People with very visible jobs."

"Nobody's perfect," I add. "We're right there with you, Louise," I say. "I can get moody sometimes."

"I always put my foot in my mouth," Eliza offers.

"I pick my nose," Frank adds.

Louise smiles. A big mouthful of braces shines at us. "Thanks," she says. "Here, let me get the photos for you." Louise digs into her bag and pulls out a bunch of pictures. "Some of the photos are a little underdeveloped, though. My dad accidentally let light into my darkroom, which, like, completely kills your photos."

She hands us her stack, and I flip through the pictures: Layla posing on the red carpet, Layla signing autographs for fans, Layla glancing nervously behind her on an empty sidewalk, Layla waving at the paparazzi.

"Wait!" Eliza says. "Go back to that other photo!"

I turn back to the picture of Layla glancing behind her. The image of Layla is clear, but the background of the picture is shadowy.

"Yeah," Louise says. "I took it right before she ran

smack into me—I nearly dropped my camera!"

"What?"

"Yeah. Layla bumped into me." Louise grins. "I'm never going to wash that outfit again!"

"Half of the picture isn't clear."

"Like I said," Louise says with a shrug, "my dad ruined this batch."

"We can see enough," Eliza says. "You know, if we took a pen and outlined the shadowy areas, I wonder if we might be able to detect what Layla was looking at—what she was so scared of!"

"Time to connect the dots in this mystery," I say.

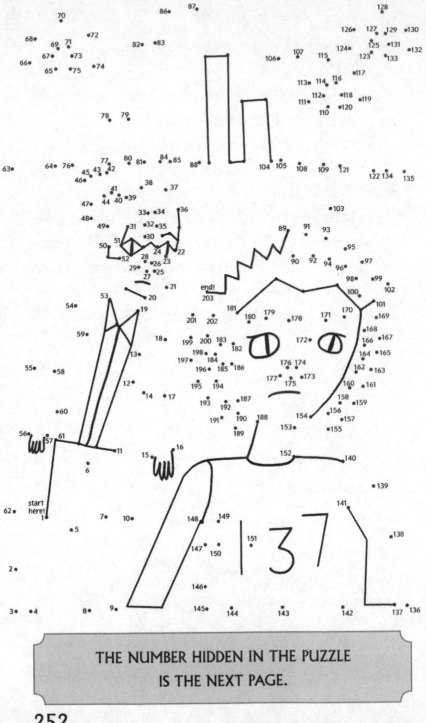

THE NUMBER HIDDEN IN THE PUZZLE
IS THE NEXT PAGE.

I CUT GREEN, blue, red, yellow. I expect something to happen, but the timer just keeps counting down. One minute left before this thing goes off.

"Uh-oh!" I yell. "Everyone hide!"

In this room the size of a closet, though, there really aren't any hiding spaces. The only thing I see is a small cabinet. Inside, there are reels of footage. I throw them all on the floor.

"Thirty seconds left!" Eliza squeaks.

Eliza, Frank, and I squeeze inside, crouching in the dark. My pulse pounds in my ears.

BOOM!

The sound of an explosion is unmistakable. Instinctively, I grab Eliza and Frank to protect them, and they both huddle closer. Something thumps against the cabinet door. And then . . . I think the worst is over.

"Are we safe?" Eliza whispers.

"I think so. Let's check it out."

I push on the cabinet door, but it is stuck. Uh-oh. I bang, thud, kick—I'm like a tornado against the doors. Frank and Eliza too. But it's no use. The door is sealed shut.

"I think there's a chair or something in our way," Eliza says between gritted teeth as she shoves the door again. "Something heavy got knocked into place, and it's keeping us trapped."

We keep pushing, but it's a useless effort. I'm certain

by the time we get out, Layla will be gone for good. If only the cast and crew were still on set! I just hope they can find us . . . before they have three skeletons in the closet.

CASE CLOSED.

I GRAB MOM's hand and Eliza's hand and run in the opposite direction. Frank follows, leaping from rock to rock like a ballerina.

"If you run, you'll never see Layla again!"

That stops Mom in her tracks, but I pull her along. We have to get help!

When we reach the studio, we call the police right away, who say they'll be back after the ransom exchange. They don't believe us when we say the ransom exchange is just a decoy!

But a few hours later, they do believe. And by the time they get back to the set and into the woods, it's empty. Even the tombstones with our names on them have disappeared.

A whole lot of good it does, knowing who kidnapped Layla if we don't have the kidnapper *or* the kidnappee in our custody. And the worst part of all? Tuggle was right: no one ever saw Layla again.

CASE CLOSED.

WE FINALLY HAVE Layla's message deciphered.

> If you are reading this, then I must have been kidnapped. You will need the passcode to my chest: two five six. I'm in grave danger.
> PLEASE HELP.

We have a creepier mystery on our hands than I thought.

"Passcode to her chest?" I say. "What chest?"

"This is a chest," Frank says, pointing to his front.

I shake my head. "No, Frank, I think Layla means a *chest*. Like a treasure chest. It's a, uh, synonym."

"Cinnamon?" Frank says.

"You mean homonym," Eliza corrects.

And . . . this just goes to prove that Eliza *is* the smartest person I know. In every subject, not just math. I pass the letter to her.

She points to the first line of the letter. "Look at this, Carlos. Layla knew she was going to disappear before it happened. This letter is proof—"

"What are you doing in here?" says a voice from the doorway. I turn, and Brad Bradley, teenage superstar, is standing there with his arms folded. "Who are you? Who told you you're allowed to be in here? Are you . . ." He trails off, looking like he swallowed a bug. He gulps before continuing. "Are you friends with Louise?"

"Who is Louise?" I ask.

"Layla's psycho stalker."

Layla has a *stalker*?

"What do you mean, stalker?" I ask.

"No, wait," Brad says. "If you're not with Louise, then who are you?"

"We're defectives!" Frank says proudly.

Brad Bradley's eyebrows shoot up.

"He means detectives," I correct. "We're here to figure out what happened to Layla. Right, Eliza?"

I elbow Eliza, and she lets out a tiny squeak. I look at her, and she's about ready to faint as Brad Bradley runs a hand through his floppy mop-top hair.

"Erd, skigget, woggum, quark," she whispers.

Yikes. She's more starstruck than a solar system.

"Guillotine hired *you*?" Brad says. "You're a bunch of babies!"

"Humph!" Frank pouts. "I am rubber, you are glue. Whatever you say bounces off me and sticks to you!"

"Guillotine didn't hire us," I say.

Brad frowns. "Yeah, that didn't seem like him. I doubt he'd want to find her anyway. He's probably happy she's gone. He *hates* her."

Why would Guillotine hate his lead actress? Could he have a motive to make her disappear? Then again, maybe I should ask Brad about Louise, the stalker. That also seems like a promising lead.

TO ASK FOR MORE INFORMATION ABOUT GUILLOTINE, TURN TO PAGE 131.

←——→

TO ASK FOR MORE INFORMATION ABOUT LOUISE, TURN TO PAGE 76.

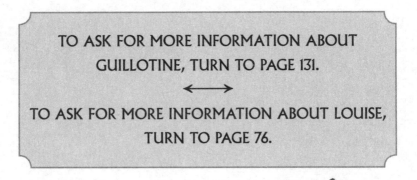

I **ENTER THE** code 8567, and a giant net drops from the ceiling.

"Weeeeee! Look at me! I'm a tuna!" cries Frank.

My first thought is Mom. She can get us out of this mess! I need my walkie-talkie. But the net is pulling my arms in tight—I'm too caught up in this web to reach my pant pocket. I have to get out of the net first. Eliza and I try to disentangle ourselves from the net, but the more we try to get out of it, the more we get stuck. Not only are we twisted up in the net, but the three of us are tangled together too.

"That was too easy." The masked kidnapper shoves us off to the side and enters the small door. Moments later, the kidnapper is dragging an unconscious Layla out of the basement and away for good, while we're still trying to undo fifty million stupid knots. And let me tell you: I am *knot* amused.

CASE CLOSED.

IF OUR BUTTS aren't in those chairs when Mom gets there, Eliza, Frank, and I will be toast. We don't have time to poke through Wolfgang's office—not if we want *any* shot of investigating in the future.

I pull Eliza and Frank through the long hall and across the set, where Guillotine glares at us as he's working with Brad Bradley. We go to sit on the chairs, behind the cameras.

"You've returned," Mom says. I didn't even see her, standing behind the robot dragon. But now Mom steps toward us slowly, like she's the evil witch that Layla's character, Aurelia, keeps trying to defeat. "Where were you?"

"I had to go to the potty," Frank says.

"Right," I say. "He was doing a bathroom dance, and so I took him to the bathroom, so he wouldn't get into any trouble. And Eliza . . ."

"Used the girls' potty!" Frank says. "Because she's a girl."

"Carlos, what you did back there—you disobeyed me, you embarrassed me, you embarrassed Las Pistas Detective Agency. I don't even know what to say."

"I'm sorry," I mutter, but she steamrolls over my apology.

"If you step out of line one more time, I'll make sure you're as far away from any investigation as you can get! You know, hijo, after that stunt you pulled in the summer—stealing and solving my case while I was sick—I thought we were working back to a place where we could trust each other. I want to trust you, Carlos."

"You can trust me, Mom," I say softly.

"I wish that were true," she replies, and my eyes sting. Mom has the world's best "I'm disappointed in you" shame speeches. "I'm giving you one last chance to earn my trust. Do not make me regret it. I expect you three to stay *right here* while I keep doing my job." Frank poses in a very awkward position, freezing into place. "Just like that," Mom says with a satisfied nod. And then she's off.

"I'm sorry," Eliza says, gently putting a hand on my back. "Are you okay?"

"Fine," I say, more aggressively than I'd intended. I don't *want* to disobey Mom. And I do want her to trust me. But I also wish she'd let me help find Layla. Doesn't Mom realize that she's keeping me away from the thing I enjoy—and the thing I'm good at? This is who I am.

"I know what will make you feel better," Eliza says.

"Ice cream?" Frank shouts.

"Even better than ice cream." And she points across the room to Agatha Tuggle.

"*How* is that better?" Frank gripes. "Tuggle doesn't

taste like chocolate-chip cookie dough!"

"I think she'd be a good person to interview. After you two got caught," Eliza says, "I heard a lot more about Tuggle and Miriam Jay, Layla's mom."

"Okay, spill!" I say.

"Yeah, spill!" Frank says.

"You know you can stop copying me now, right, Frank?" I say, trying to hide the annoyance in my voice.

"Right, Frank?" he repeats, a grin spreading across his face.

Eliza hushes him and pulls us all into a tight huddle. "Layla has been getting into fights with her agent. From what I understood, Tuggle is angry that Layla is so ungrateful, when Tuggle puts in a hundred and ten percent effort into getting her auditions."

"But it's Agatha's job to do that! That's what she gets paid for, right?"

Eliza nods. "But that's not even the biggest thing." Her eyes light up like she has a big, juicy secret. "I found out that Layla banned Miriam Jay from set."

"Banned?"

"Banished. Expelled. Took away her access badge. Her mom isn't allowed to cross the front gate of the studio lot, or Layla has a major fit."

"But we saw her mom earlier!" I say. "Why is she here today?"

"Probably because Layla is missing. All bets are off when Layla isn't here."

"So . . . is Layla in a fight with her mom?"

"I guess that's what we have to find out," Eliza says. "Anyway, I thought that those were two good places to start. Tuggle's right there—we could talk to her and come back to these chairs before your mom even knows we were gone."

"And what if I want to talk to Layla's mom instead?"

"Then we'll just have to be sneaky!" Eliza says. "Find her without getting caught."

TO INTERVIEW AGATHA TUGGLE,
TURN TO PAGE 125.

← →

TO INTERVIEW MIRIAM JAY,
TURN TO PAGE 470.

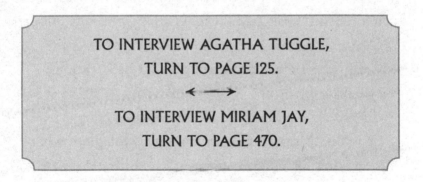

SORRY, ELIZA, BUT I am all over Frank's sledge-hammer idea. I have to admit . . . it sounds *way* more fun to sledgehammer a math puzzle than to solve it.

We carry the box into the prop room, and I make sure to close the door behind us. We move through the shelves. Luckily, it's well organized. We move past the fake weapons to where there are a few *real* weapons. I drag the sledgehammer off the shelf, but it's so heavy, I can barely lift it.

"For the record," Eliza says, "I think this is a terrible idea."

"Noted," I say. But then Frank and I turn to each other. "SLEDGEHAMMER TIME!" we both shout, then we high-five.

I pull the sledgehammer up as far as it can go . . . then I drop it.

BINK.

It makes a small dent in the safe. Not *quite* what I was looking for when I suggested smashing the safe to smithereens. But it's a start.

CLUNK. TING.

I smash it over and over again until finally there's a misshapen hole where I can reach in.

"Let me! Let me!" Frank says, and since I was the sledger, I let him do the honors. He reaches inside and pulls out—

264

"A stack of papers?" he groans, passing them off to me. "How boring!"

"Give me those," Eliza says. When I look up to hand them to her, I see that the door is open just a crack . . . when I am a thousand percent *sure* I shut it.

I hand the papers to Eliza like I'm passing off a football—I keep running toward the door, our end zone. I hear someone back away and run. Someone was watching us. And the footsteps were heavy . . . which leads me to our biggest suspect. The one who hired Mom.

"Eliza—"

"I'll read as we run!" she says. "Hurry!"

In the distance, someone dives into the freight elevator . . . the one with the big sign on it that says OUT OF ORDER. The elevator doors are closing, so I guess that sign is a hoax, and it is in perfectly good order.

We wait until the elevator comes back again, and hop in.

"Wait!" Frank cries. "I lost my shoe!"

"No time!" I say as the elevator doors close. "We'll get it later!"

"But it was *right* outside the elevator," Frank pouts.

"We'll be back soon," I say, looking at the buttons. There are only two: one for the floor we're on. And one to go down.

I gulp and press the other button. The elevator starts

descending. The lift is so rickety that we're swaying all over the place. Eliza grabs on to Frank, who squirms away from her with a "Get off me!"

It'll be a miracle if the elevator cables don't snap.

The elevator stops with a jerky motion. "Let's get out of here!" Eliza whimpers.

I press the button to open the elevator doors, only they won't open. Well . . . they open, but only about two inches. Enough for us to see into a dark and creepy hallway. But not enough for us to get out of this stinking elevator.

"We're gonna die in here!" Frank says cheerfully.

"No, we're not. A cool, logical head will help us out of this," Eliza says with a deep breath. "We just have to . . . get the doors open somehow."

"Cool, let me just pull my handy-dandy pliers out of my pocket," I say sarcastically.

"Really?"

"No!"

"Right, of course, you were kidding," Eliza says with a nervous chuckle. "Well, I think we should look at the instruction manual for the emergency brake."

"Found it!" Frank says, opening a panel on the sidewall of the elevator. "Well, I *maybe* found it. I can't read."

Eliza leans in closer to the panel and squints at some

tiny printed instructions. "To reset elevator settings," she reads out loud, "pull lever."

I look around for a lever, but there is none.

"Great, no lever!"

Eliza keeps reading.

"In the event that the lever is jammed, you can unplug and then reattach wires along the H-A-T-C-H buttons inside this panel. Make sure all wires are attached."

She stops reading.

"That's it?"

"That's all we need, I think," she says, gesturing toward a bunch of mismatched, tangled buttons and wires in the open panel box.

"So . . . we have to make the word *hatch* in one continuous line? A straight line?"

"No, I don't think it has to be straight. Just continuous. It can zigzag." Eliza hums. "It seems like there are a bunch of different ways we can connect those wires. Just make sure you don't repeat the H when you connect the last button; I have a feeling you'll need five separate knobs for this thing to work."

"Okay. I think that makes sense."

"You work on that, Carlos, while I try to read through the documents we got out of Layla's safe."

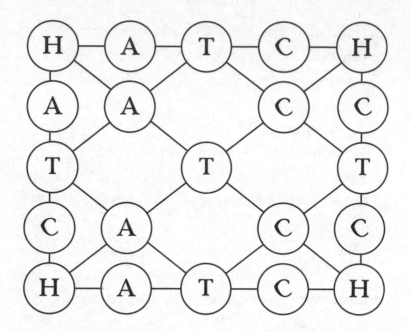

ADD THREE HUNDRED TO THE NUMBER
OF TIMES THE WORD *HATCH* CAN BE MADE IN A
CONTINUOUS LINE, AND TURN TO THAT PAGE.

←→

TO ASK ELIZA FOR A HINT, TURN TO PAGE 87.

I PRESS THE big red *record* button.

"We know you kidnapped Layla. We know you were stalking her for at least a few days before you snatched her. But why?"

Tuggle hesitates. "Where's your proof?"

"What?"

"Where's your proof?" she repeats.

Alarm bells go off in my head. That's not what an innocent person says. An innocent person would deny, deny, deny! She's not denying. She's just . . . calculating. Seeing how much we know will help her figure out what to do next. The problem is, the photo of Layla running from Tuggle isn't exactly hard evidence. It doesn't *prove* that Tuggle is the kidnapper. What we need . . . is for Tuggle to admit it. Out loud.

"We have proof," I lie. "In my pocket."

"I—what is it?" she says, looking greenish.

"So why did you kidnap her?" I say, leaning into the microphone. "Were you jealous of her? Did you want to strike her down?"

Tuggle glares at us. I bet she's wondering whether she would win a physical fight, three children against one adult. But finally she answers. "You have it all wrong. I love my client! I always want to build her up—do whatever is best for her career!"

"So then why did you kidnap her?"

"I didn't."

"You did."

"I . . . did you know she was threatening my livelihood?" Tuggle whispers. Her usually tight bun has come loose, and she tucks a coil of hair behind her ear. "She told me she'd drive my agency into the ground."

Good. If we can't get an outright confession, we can at least start with motive. "Why would Layla say that?" I ask, trying to make my voice as sympathetic as possible. Eliza flashes me a thumbs-up from an angle Tuggle can't see.

"I don't know. But I don't . . . I can't be threatened like that. My business is everything to me. I spent fifteen years cultivating my reputation . . . and it could all come crumbling down with one famous little girl."

We're getting really close to a confession . . . but we don't have it in the bag yet. I have to be careful with my next move. If my question is too blunt, I could put Tuggle on the defensive. And if she's defensive, she'll close up like a clam. But if my response is too roundabout, I might never get a confession out of her. She could walk away, and we'd be left with no proof at all.

TO DEMAND TO KNOW WHERE LAYLA IS,
TURN TO PAGE 248.

←——→

TO SYMPATHIZE WITH TUGGLE'S SITUATION,
TURN TO PAGE 395.

"THIS DOUBLE-SCRAMBLED passcode problem is harder than it seems," I say. "Give me a hand?"

Eliza leans in.

y b d n a t s	_	_	_	_	_	_	_
l o l r	_	_	_	_			
d o n s u	_	_	_	_	_		
c a a r e m	_	_	_	_	_	_	
e t a s l	_	_	_	_	_		
a r k r e m	_	_	_	_	_		
n i c t a o	_	_	_	_	_		

"Standby," she says.

"Standby for what?" I look around, but the secret basement is dead silent.

Eliza chuckles. "No, *standby* is the solution to the first unscramble. Which means that N and Y are the letters we're going to have to come back to in the final scramble."

"The second one," I say. "Two Ls, an R, and an O. *Roll*?"

Eliza nods.

"I can roll!" Frank says, and he starts to roll and writhe and wriggle on the ground.

"Skipping ahead," Eliza says, ignoring her brother, "the fifth one down is *slate*. That's what they call the clapper board that the director holds." She gasps suddenly. "Standby, roll, slate! These are all things that have to do with TV. All things the director calls out before they start taping."

"So these words have a television theme," I say, rubbing my chin. "That might help me figure out the rest of them."

"True," Eliza says. "But in the end, when we unscramble the highlighted letters, it might be something different. We'll keep an open mind for the last scramble."

y b d n a t s	S	T	A	N	D	B	Y
l o l r	R	O	L	L			
d o n s u	_	_	_	_	_		
c a a r e m	_	_	_	_	_	_	
e t a s l	S	L	A	T	E		
a r k r e m	_	_	_	_	_	_	
n i c t a o	_	_	_	_	_	_	

THE SOLUTION TO THE PUZZLE
WILL TAKE YOU TO YOUR NEXT PAGE.
←→
TO ASK ELIZA FOR ANOTHER HINT,
TURN TO PAGE 27.

WE HAVE TO create a common enemy. It's the only way everyone's going to stop fighting and come together.

"RAT!" I shout. "RAAAAAAAAAT!" I point to the floor wildly.

A few people let out very high-pitched screeches. "Rat? Rat!" everyone's shouting. People start dancing on their tiptoes. A few people grab the witches' brooms and start swatting around.

"WHERE DID IT GO!"

"UNDER THE TABLE!"

"LET'S GET IT!"

"TEAR THIS PLACE APART!"

"BURN IT DOWN!"

"Wait, no!" I shout. "Stop! There isn't really a—"

But it's too late. Everyone starts tearing apart the studio, brick by brick, limb by limb. Cushions are ripped, walls are toppled, machinery disassembled, props crushed—until there's nothing left but debris. And if there's no more set, then there are no more clues to find.

CASE CLOSED.

AS MUCH AS I hate to admit it, Frank's wild methods sometimes produce results. So . . . I grab a feather from him and prepare to tickle monster this masked woman.

"Attack!" I shout, and all three of us dive toward the mystery figure, wiggling our feathers.

"Hahahahahahahahahha!" she cries, doubling over. "Ohmygod stop it! I can't breathe! Hahahahahahahahaha!"

I know that voice. I know that laugh.

"Stop . . . it . . . or I'll tell—Uncle Wolfie!"

I reach forward and rip the mask off our mystery person, and there she is: Louise Jenkins. Wiping the tears off her face and standing upright again. Something falls out of her jacket pocket: camera film.

She gathers it up frantically and looks at us with an expression that's half defiant . . .

And half terrified.

"GOTCHA!" Frank yells.

My stomach drops as I look from Louise's mask to the camera film to her guilty face. "You!" I say. "What . . . how . . . you . . ."

"I know what happened," Eliza says. "You started selling photos of Layla Jay to tabloid magazines. Then that incident happened on the red carpet, when you tried to snip off a lock of Layla's curls. And that was a step too far. Suddenly, you weren't allowed to get anywhere near Layla, and you had no photos. So you kidnapped Layla. Not only can you have an unlimited number of photos to sell now, but you finally get your wish: to spend time with your celebrity idol, Layla."

"You don't know what you're talking about!" Louise spits. Her whole face is puckered and flushed red. "You . . . you have no idea . . . Brad Bradley asked me to take those photos—I was doing it for Layla."

"Yeah, right!" Frank shouts.

I snort. "Like Brad Bradley would ever do anything that didn't help himself!"

"What I don't understand," Eliza says, "is what you're doing here in the dead of night, Louise, dressed in all black and a faceless mask."

"I'm getting my pictures back!" Louise says. "And I'm here at night wearing this outfit because I wasn't supposed to set up pictures in the first place. I don't want to get in trouble with Uncle Wolfie."

"So," I say, standing over her, "now that you have Layla all to yourself, you don't want to share your pictures with Brad anymore? You want all the fame and glory for yourself?"

Louise looks wounded. "No, you have it all wrong! I want the pictures back because Brad Bradley was using Layla—and me—for some good publicity. Look, a few

277

months ago, Brad Bradley told me that I'd be helping him and Layla if I just got photos of the two of them together to go viral online. So I hid cameras around the studio and put them on automatic timers to capture behind-the-scenes photos of *Teen Witch*, but I *just* found out what Brad Bradley was doing to Layla, so I am collecting my cameras and my footage before he has a chance to hurt her even more."

"Hurt her!" Eliza says. "How? What are you talking about?"

"He's going to stab her in the back!" Louise shouts. "Uncle Wolfie just told me that he's trying to sell Layla down the river. He is demanding his own *Teen Witch* spin-off . . . and that Layla be fired!"

"He can't do that," I say. "And Tuggle would never allow that."

"That's the thing!" Louise says. "Tuggle is begging Uncle Wolfie to do it! I'm the *only one* who has Layla's back right now! She needs me!" Louise has a maniacal look in her eye.

But something she just said is bouncing around my head on repeat: "Tuggle is begging Wolfgang to do it."

"I . . . that doesn't make any sense! Why would Tuggle want her biggest client to be fired?"

"Yeah," Eliza says, her eyebrows scrunching together. "How does that benefit her?"

"Yeah," Frank says. "Wait . . . what am I yeahing?"

Louise puts her hands on her hips. "I'm telling the truth, I swear. And I'll prove it!" She pulls out her phone and dials a number.

At first I think she's calling her uncle, but then she puts the phone on speaker, and I can see plain and clear who she is calling: Agatha Tuggle.

Brrrrring brrrrrring!

A cell phone goes off from across the set.

Brrrrring brrrrrrring!

I hear a curse word and someone fumbling, and then the phone goes silent.

"Was that a coincidence?" Eliza says quietly. "Or is Tuggle in the studio with us?"

Chills prickle up my spine, and I turn around to look for her, and—

Boom. The lights go out.

Eliza and Louise shriek, and I wave my hands around and smack something fleshy. "OUCH!" Frank says. "You stepped on my face!"

"Where are you?"

"Carlos, I can't see!"

"Be brave," Louise whispers to her herself. "Like Layla Jay."

"What's going on? Carlos, is that you?"

"No—Eliza, where's your flashlight?"

"Eeeeek! Something touched my foot!"

"Three blind mice," Frank sings. "Three blind mice . . ."

Suddenly, I'm shoved backward. I try to scramble to my feet, but I'm grabbed under the armpits and pulled back.

I struggle, but the person who has my life in their hands is strong and fast. There's a clanging noise . . . and then I'm pushed again. A slamming noise.

I feel metal all around me—above and below too. I'm in a small box. A coffin? No . . . not a coffin. A *locker*. One of the school lockers they have on set . . . maybe even the one Layla's character uses.

Look, I love *Teen Witch*, but I do *not* want to become a prop skeleton for their set. I bang the sides and stomp the floor and jiggle the handle, but I'm locked in.

TO ASK THE MYSTERY PERSON WHERE LAYLA IS,
TURN TO PAGE 423.

←——→

TO TRY TO CALL MOM FROM INSIDE THE LOCKER,
TURN TO PAGE 430.

I'M GETTING MY best friend out of this stupid locker. "Don't be silly, Eliza. I would never ditch you."

Eliza sighs in relief. "You're the best, Carlos."

"Less talky, more savey my sistery!" Frank shouts, tapping his foot.

"Eliza, you said you know how to get out?"

"Yes," Eliza says. "I think the key to the code is actually in here with me." She slips a piece of paper through the vent, and I stare at it.

Code to lock: XXX

3 5 9 One of these numbers is correct and in the correct spot.

3 0 2 One of these numbers is correct but in the wrong spot.

2 9 7 Two of these numbers are correct but in the wrong spot.

8 5 4 All of these numbers are incorrect.

4 1 8 One of these numbers is correct but in the wrong spot.

"Oh, Eliza!" I groan. "It's a logic puzzle."

"Don't look at me," Louise says. "I'm terrible at these."

"NOT IT!" Frank cries.

"You can do it!" Eliza says. "Get me out of here, you three! And quickly!"

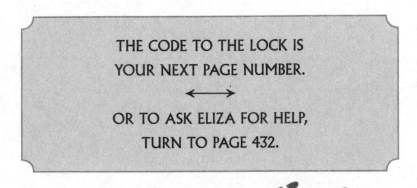

THE CODE TO THE LOCK IS
YOUR NEXT PAGE NUMBER.

←——→

OR TO ASK ELIZA FOR HELP,
TURN TO PAGE 432.

ELIZA'S RIGHT: WE'LL have more control over the situation if we lay a trap.

And I have an idea. . . .

"Frank, go to the room where they have the set storage pieces. Bring back as many paint cans as you can possibly find."

"Empty or full?" Frank says.

"Full, of course!"

He nods once and scampers across the open atrium, toward the prop room.

"Eliza, help me figure out how to get the cans up to the catwalk."

She smiles and looks up. Directly up, like she's praying to the heavens. "You know how Layla flies around, pretty much every episode."

"Yeah?"

"People can't fly."

I'm totally confused—but she scurries to the vertical ladder that leads up into the rafters, where all the lights are. Where we'd found Louise earlier. I go to follow her, but she says, "No! Stay there."

I look around anxiously for Tuggle . . . but she's nowhere to be seen. How much time do we have to save Layla? And what about Louise? And what about us?

Something taps me on the head, and I swat it away.

"Carlos!"

I look up. The thing tapping me is a carabiner—one of those metal loops, attached to a thin rope. Of course—Layla uses this device to fly! And that's exactly how we're going to get those paint cans to fly too.

Frank turns the corner, wheeling a whole cart of paint cans. He speeds up the closer he gets to me, and nearly bowls me over. I hook the harness to the handle of a paint can, and Eliza pulls it up. Rinse and repeat. We work silently and quickly, because we don't know how much time we have.

After our sixth paint can, I shout. "That's enough! Let's go!"

I help Frank onto the ladder, then follow him up. And I can breathe easier now that we're all suspended on the bridge.

I gesture for Eliza and Frank to follow me, and we weave through the lighting bridges until we find a spot just above the lockers. Yes, this spot will do perfectly.

"What are we doing here?" Eliza whispers.

"Tuggle thinks we're still trapped in the lockers, right? So we know for a fact that she'll come back here to get us . . . and that she will have her guard down until she opens them. So . . . that's when we pour the paint."

"Carlos, that's brilliant!"

"We just have to be quiet."

We both look at Frank.

"Hey! I can be quiet!" he says loudly.

Suddenly, the doors to the freight elevator open. I guess it isn't broken after all. Inside is Tuggle, holding a bundle of clothes . . . no, wait . . . it's Layla. Unconscious. Tuggle sinks her into Guillotine's director's chair and comes for us.

I hold my breath. . . . I can see her bun right below me, and she whispers something I can't hear into the locker where I was trapped. Here we go! I tip my paint can over, and Eliza and Frank follow.

For a moment, Tuggle is stunned. She blinks. She takes off her round glasses and looks up at us, an expression of shock and fear on her multicolored, painted face. Then she starts to run.

"NO!" I shout. I didn't count on her running. We don't have anything up here that could stop her . . . except maybe unscrewing some of the fancy Hollywood lights. They look like they would drop like rocks.

"Carlos, strap me in!" Frank says, grabbing hold of a harness in the rafters. But I've never harnessed anyone before—what if it's too dangerous for Frank?

I have to make a choice, and *fast*—Tuggle is already halfway across the set!

285

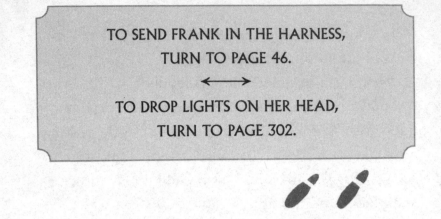

TO SEND FRANK IN THE HARNESS,
TURN TO PAGE 46.

←——→

TO DROP LIGHTS ON HER HEAD,
TURN TO PAGE 302.

286

I HAVE TO tackle her. I charge straight toward her. She presses the button in her hand.

Suddenly, the floor opens up—like a sideways door—and we fall straight into a hole, six feet deep.

"Dumb move," Tuggle says.

"You brought back the steel tomb?" Eliza says, her voice full of fear and anger.

"What's the steel tomb?" Mom asks.

"In season three, Aurelia and Sebastian build this . . . this steel tomb. They try to trap the Witch Queen in here. It's said to be inescapable."

"I spent all night reinstalling it," Tuggle gloats. "Works marvelously, doesn't it?"

Mom, Frank, Eliza, and I claw at the dirt walls, trying to scramble up.

"Stop that, or I will be forced to seal you in."

I stop clawing. That does *not* sound good.

"Where is Layla?" Mom asks, her voice surprisingly calm.

"Safe," Tuggle says. "I'd never hurt my star client."

"Then why are you doing this?" Eliza asks.

"I'll do anything to keep her," Tuggle says. I can hear her walking forward, and the shadow of her pencil-stuck bun is in the hole with us. "She was going to leave me, you know. For a different agency with more oompf and power. She was going to leave me destitute, and sully my good name with all her celebrity friends. I'm in danger of losing everything. I *made* her out of nothing. She owes me."

"What!" I choke. "That's ridiculous! It is your job to help her career."

"And she paid you," Eliza says. "You get a commission. It's her right to change agents if she wants to. And she *should* change agents—"

"Because you're a poopybutt!" Frank finishes.

There's a silence that rings through the woods. Then, Mom asks, "Where is Layla?"

"That's none of your concern."

"I think I understand," Eliza says. "You threw her to the wolves with Brad Bradley and Guillotine and even Louise. You put her in a terrible working environment, and she was unhappy, and you didn't do anything to help her. Louise said she overheard you two arguing about her contract."

"Layla found out I was taking a little extra side money from the production company. My agency was in jeopardy. I needed some more money to stay afloat. Layla called it a breach of contract. Layla was not happy about that, to put it lightly. She was going to besmirch my reputation. And in this business, that's all you have."

"So, when Layla left your agency, you planned to

kidnap her. That's logical!" I say sarcastically.

"You think I *planned* this? It happened in the moment, out of sheer panic. But now that I've come this far, I have to keep going."

"Where is Layla?" Mom repeats.

"That pesky question again?" Tuggle says. "I think you'll find you have bigger things to worry about than the location of my client. Like, maybe, running out of oxygen." Tuggle presses the button in her palm, and the doors above us snap closed, trapping us inside our own graves.

TO SCREAM FOR HELP, TURN TO PAGE 133.

←——→

TO LOOK AROUND THE HOLE,
TURN TO PAGE 359.

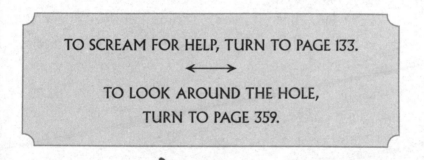

"ALL RIGHT, LAYLA Expert, what's the gossip on set?"

Louise grins ear to ear. "You wouldn't believe me if I told you! First, Brad. He's been really moody lately because he and Layla both had their contracts open for renegotiation this past summer. And now Layla is making a couple hundred thousand dollars more than him per episode. They used to get paid the same, but now she's worth a lot more than he is. And rightly so! The show is called *Teen Witch*, not *Teen Witch and Friend*. But Brad can't handle being second fiddle. His ego is the size of Jupiter."

Frank launches into song. "Frank goes to college to get more knowledge! Brad goes to Jupiter to get more stupider!"

"Frank," Eliza says. "Be respectful! That's *Brad Bradley* you're talking about."

"Poop Poopley, you mean!"

I groan. "Sorry, Louise. You were saying?"

"And that's why Douglas Chen has soured on Layla too. Because Layla was also awarded an executive producer credit, and she has been exercising her creative control more and more."

"What does that mean?" Eliza asks.

"It means that Layla has opinions, and she's making those opinions heard! She's an inspiration to us all,"

290

Louise says with an awed sigh. "Mr. Chen told Uncle Wolfgang that Layla's getting too big for her britches and someone ought to knock her down a peg. But if you ask me, I think Mr. Chen and Brad are both threatened by a smart, savvy, business-minded young woman like Layla. And I think he's mad that she gets to be a producer before she's eighteen. Mr. Chen didn't get to produce anything until he was, like, thirty-five."

For a second, I'm wondering whether I'm getting an accurate picture of what's going on. Louise is *full* of information. But it seems a little . . . biased. Is it possible that Louise's admiration of Layla skews her perspective?

"There's more," Louise says proudly. "The tabloids caught Layla and her mother shouting at each other in a restaurant before Layla stormed out. And *I* caught Layla having an argument with her agent, Agatha Tuggle, in the woods."

"The woods?" Eliza asks just as I say, "What was the fight about?" Just as Frank says, "What's a blabloid?"

Louise points at Frank. "It's a magazine or website that just focuses on gossip." Then Louise turns to Eliza. "Part of the show is filmed outside, in the woods. The set inside is just for the school scenes, the inside-the-home scenes, and the green screen. If you want to investigate the woods, it's back along this side road. It's still in the studio lot, just not *in* the building. And . . ." She points to me now. "Which fight are you curious about?"

"Both," I say.

"Well, I can't tell you what Layla's fight with her mom was about. The tabloid never said. But the one with her agent—the one *I* overheard—was about Layla's contract."

"Her contract!" I say. "What about it?"

"I don't know. I think Layla wanted more money from Uncle Wolfgang or something. Maybe her last promotion isn't cutting it anymore. I know I'd want more money if I was as big a star as Layla. And *that*," she says, with a note of finality, "is everything I know."

I lean against the concrete wall of the studio. I'm not ruling Louise out as a suspect, because she's creepier than a spider in wait, but we have so many other leads we need to explore. If Louise is telling the truth—that Agatha Tuggle and Miriam Jay both got into fights with Layla recently, and that Brad Bradley and Guillotine are angry about Layla's pay raise and executive producer credit—then we have to follow up on that.

"Thank you so much for your time," I say to Louise.

"No problem," she says. "I'll be here if you need to ask me anything else. And if you *do* find Layla, please tell her how much her fans love her. But especially *me.*

And maybe get her autograph for me. And a picture. And a lock of her hair—kidding!" she says quickly, at the stricken look on Eliza's face. But Louise definitely isn't kidding.

I pull Eliza and Frank to the middle of the parking lot, out of Louise's earshot.

"This is making my head spin," Eliza says. "There are so many promising suspects, it's hard to know who to go after first. What do you think?"

"We could see who we run into first. Inside the studio."

"Or," Eliza says, looking out into the distance, "we could go explore the woods, where Louise said Layla Jay had that fight with her agent, Tuggle. We haven't seen that part of the set yet, and maybe there's a clue there."

"YES!" Frank says. "That one! I want to be outside!"

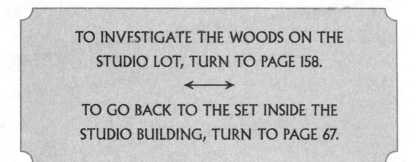

TO INVESTIGATE THE WOODS ON THE
STUDIO LOT, TURN TO PAGE 158.

←——→

TO GO BACK TO THE SET INSIDE THE
STUDIO BUILDING, TURN TO PAGE 67.

WE HAVE TO investigate Brad Bradley's dressing room. This could be our only chance.

We leave the prop room and mosey down the hall. When we're sure no one's paying attention to us, Eliza quietly turns the doorknob to Brad's room, and we slip in. Brad's dressing room is filled, floor to ceiling, with posters of himself. Brad smiling, Brad on the cover of magazines, Brad making duck lips at the camera, Brad smoldering, Brad, Brad, Brad, Brad, Brad.

"Barf," Frank says.

"I'm sure he's just proud of his achievements," Eliza says softly. "It must be exciting to get so many inter-view requests. I bet he's just trying to keep a record of all the magazines he's talked to."

"On his wall?" I snort. "Admit it, Eliza. This guy would marry a mirror."

We get to work, poking around. Brad has three dressers devoted to fan mail. Most of them are sealed with a lipstick kiss. I roll my eyes.

At last, in the top drawer, I find Brad's phone. I wake up the screen—only Brad's numbers are in the wrong order . . . and a few of the numbers are missing.

8	3	?
1	?	?
?	?	2

I tap the spot in the middle, where the five usually is, but instead, it's asking me to pick a number one through nine.

"I think it's encrypted with extra steps," I say. "It's not a four-digit passcode . . . it's something else."

Eliza takes the phone from me and squints at the screen. "I think I know what this is. It's a magic square! You have to use the numbers one through nine only once. And each row, column, and diagonal all add up to the same number!"

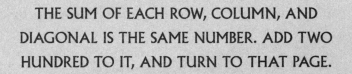

THE SUM OF EACH ROW, COLUMN, AND DIAGONAL IS THE SAME NUMBER. ADD TWO HUNDRED TO IT, AND TURN TO THAT PAGE.

←——→

TO ASK ELIZA FOR A HINT, TURN TO PAGE 407.

BLUE, YELLOW, GREEN, red. That's the order I cut.

Instantly, the device explodes.

BOOM!

We're blown back off our feet from the force, and there's something stinging my eyes. Really painfully. I can't even see—my vision is blurry. And I can't stop blinking. I touch my face, and my cheeks are all wet, and my nose is running. I wipe my face on my sleeve and clear my throat to relieve the tickle. "What was that? Poison?"

"No . . . I think that was pepper spray," Eliza coughs. "I can't see a thing."

"I can't stop crying," Frank says. "Tastes salty. And peppery."

"Well, how long does it last, Eliza?"

"I don't know. I've never been pepper sprayed before."

We can't do anything with irritated lungs and painful, stinging eyes. There's nothing left but to sit here and cry until the pepper spray wears off.

I hate to say it . . . but this really blew up in our faces.

CASE CLOSED.

"SO WHY DON'T Layla and her mom get along?"

"Look, you've met Miriam Jay, right?"

Briefly. Barely. But I nod anyway.

"Right. So you know she's not exactly the maternal type. She doesn't really care about her daughter as a person. She cares about her as a product."

"What does that mean?" I say, looking to Eliza to translate for me.

Eliza opens her mouth, but it's Tuggle who answers. "Momager," she mutters.

"What's that?" Frank asks.

"It's a word for a mom who's also a manager," Tuggle says. "And Miriam is one of the worst ones too."

"Why?"

"I've never met anyone more controlling or less caring. About two years ago, Layla got a hairline fracture in her wrist during a stunt, and you know what her mom said to her as she was writhing on the ground? Not 'Are you okay?' Not 'Do you need to see a doctor?' Not 'Let me dry your tears.' Miriam Jay said, 'How much is this going to cost you, Layla? Time is money, money is time, and a broken actor can't work.'"

"What!" I say, and Eliza looks concerned.

"Tip of the iceberg," Tuggle says, her eyes wide behind her round glasses. "I don't know what's going on between them, but I'm telling you, it's not healthy."

ASK WHERE LAYLA MIGHT BE.
TURN TO PAGE 148.

298

"HUH? WHAT DO you mean, message within a message?"

"Within a message within a message within a message within a message!" Frank says.

Eliza lets out a deep breath and begins to think out loud. "At first I thought there might be a hidden message because of the weird spacing and indentations. But . . . I don't see anything there."

"Right," I say. "And there aren't any particular words or letters that stick out." I look to her for confirmation, and she nods. "I mean, this letter is pretty ordinary. Other than the way it's folded."

"What?" Eliza says.

"Look," I say. "Folded three times vertically. No horizontal folds. It . . . I don't know . . . it stuck out to me because that's a weird way to fold up a letter. You can't carry it in your pocket like that. It's still too long."

Eliza looks up suddenly, grinning ear to ear. "Maybe you can't put it in your pocket, but you *can* include a secret message with folds like that!"

"What do you mean?"

"Let's read *only* the letters on the folds. Straight down the line!"

DEAR WOLFGANG,

PLEASE, HELP ME, AS YOU ARE MY ONLY FRIEND IN THIS

PLACE. I AM AT MY WITS' END AND DO NOT KNOW WHAT TO DO.

SOME PEOPLE THINK "WHAT A DIVA," BUT YOU KNOW I'M NOT

LIKE THAT. I DON'T REALLY ENJOY THIS DRAMA. I'M SO SICK AND

TIRED OF THIS TERRIBLE TREATMENT. BELIEVE ME WHEN I

SAY: I VERY MUCH WANT TO GET ALONG WITH GUILLOTINE AND

BRAD, BUT HOW DO I MAKE THEM STOP SABOTAGING ME? I CAN'T *DEMAND*

RESPECT. TUGGLE IS NO HELP, AND MIRIAM . . .

WELL SHE IS OUT OF MY LIFE NOW . . . I DON'T KNOW WHAT TO DO.

-L.J.

IF THE SECRET MESSAGE SAYS TO EXPLORE
UNDER THE FLOORBOARD, TURN TO PAGE 81.

←→

IF THE SECRET MESSAGE SAYS TO LOOK
IN THE PROP ROOM CLOSET, TURN TO PAGE 142.

I'M CERTAIN THAT the last gear turns clockwise. Which means I have to put the pen underneath the last two gears. I stick it in, but it doesn't stay. It flies out from under the machine, halfway across the set.

"Now what?" I ask Eliza.

Suddenly, the metal dragon sinks lower, smooshing on top of us, trapping our legs. We try to twist out, but I might as well be trapped in between two sheets of concrete. Even Frank, a wiggle master, can't get free.

I hear footsteps by my head, and I crane my neck to see. Please let it be Mom's blue sneakers . . . please let her be coming to save us. . . .

But it's not: my heart sinks when it's shiny black heels. "Never thought you'd lay your own trap!" Tuggle says gleefully. "Thanks for assisting me in your capture."

CASE CLOSED.

I THINK DROPPING lights on her head would be the best option.

I run across the catwalk, to the very edge of the set, and start unscrewing a light. Only . . . it's much harder than it looks. The lights seem to be fastened pretty tight. After much wrenching and wiggling, I finally pry one loose. And perfect timing, too . . . because here comes Tuggle.

I let the light fall. It smashes next to her, missing her by inches. Tuggle jumps—and when she realizes that the light drop was no accident, she leaps off the set. She's too far away from the lights and the lighting bridge. There's no way I can get her from here.

"Missed me, missed me!" she taunts.

"Now you gotta kiss me!" Frank sings in reply.

Tuggle sweeps up poor unconscious Layla like a baby in her arms, runs out the door, and disappears for good.

CASE CLOSED.

I'M CERTAIN THE deciphered riddle on the cave wall is telling us that three is the magic number. I have to agree: three is pretty magical. After all, me, Eliza, and Frank are a three, and we're the best team out there.

"Three!" I shout.

Immediately, the wall opens up right in the middle, like elevator doors.

"Wow!" Eliza marvels. "Talk about Hollywood production values!"

We walk forward, and to my surprise, we're outside in a wooded area with tall, skeletal trees and patchy grass and mossy rocks. I turn back to look at the tunnel that we just walked out of, but the doors have already closed behind us, and there doesn't seem to be a way back in. I don't even see the studio building. I guess there's no choice but to go forward.

"Is this . . . part of the studio?" I ask. "Where are we?"

"Up your butt and around the corner!" Frank replies, giggling.

Eliza steps forward, peering out into the distance. "I think this is the woods, where they film the outdoor scenes. Remember?"

"There's *no way* the cast and crew crawl through a tiny hole behind a mirror in the prop room to get here."

"There must be a different way," Eliza says. "But this looks so familiar, from the show, right? Come on!"

She runs forward, and we follow. I keep tripping

over rocks, wishing that I had joined the track-and-field team instead of baseball.

At last we reach what must be the main area of the set. The land is more level, and in one spot, mushy, like it had just been filled in with fresh dirt. There are some camera stands set up, a few chairs for the crew, and some wires connected between trees, which were either for levitating the cameras or levitating the actors.

There are still plenty of trees—but there's also a mini graveyard, which I've seen in the show. Can't have a show about teenage wizards without some moody cemetery scenes.

"I can't believe I'm seeing this *in person*!" Eliza marvels, running her hands over the gravestones. "When the Witch Queen rises from the dead and puts a curse on Sebastian's father so fast that Aurelia can't even stop it?" She squeals. "I even see the feathers from when he was turned into that owl! Aurelia—I mean, Layla—was standing *right here*."

"Hey, Eliza. Doesn't this dirt look fresh to you?"

She comes over to examine the spot on the ground. We both poke it with our shoes. Definitely soft to the touch.

I feel sick. "Do you think," I whisper, "that it's Layla's body?"

Eliza is silent for a moment, and she paces. Suddenly she stops dead. "Carlos." Her eyes get really wide—bugging out and everything. "Carlos. *Carlos.*" She grabs my arm.

"Carlos!" Frank echoes, as he starts to climb a tree.

"What?"

"'I'm in grave danger,'" Eliza says. "*Grave* danger."

Suddenly, I understand what Eliza's trying to tell me. I reach into my pocket and pull out our first clue from Layla. My hands are shaking, and my fingers fumble to open the folded paper.

If you are reading this, then I must have been kidnapped. You will need the passcode to my chest: two five six. I'm in grave danger.
PLEASE HELP.

Grave danger. Graveyard. Is the word *grave* a clue? Or just a coincidence?

"Holy macaroni!" Frank shouts from the top of a tree. "Eliza, Carlos! Come here! I found a clue, and it's a *big* one! Bigger than big . . . the biggerest!"

TO DIG UP THE DIRT, TURN TO PAGE 212.

$\longleftrightarrow$

TO CLIMB THE TREE, TURN TO PAGE 44.

I'VE COME THIS far . . . I might as well keep going down this path with Wolfgang. "You're happy Layla's gone, aren't you?"

"What?" he says. "That's preposterous!"

"Is it?" Eliza says coolly. "Suddenly, the buzz around this show is immense. Your ratings are through the roof—people are watching episodes on every conceivable platform and device. This show has never been more popular. Layla's disappearance is great for publicity, isn't it?"

"I'm paying for the investigation!" Wolfgang bellows. "Why would I do that if I didn't want Layla found?"

It's a good point. "To throw us off the scent?"

"Want a scent?" Wolfgang says through gritted teeth. "I'll give you a scent."

"That'd be great, yeah!" I say.

He leads us through the studio—to the makeup room. "Stay there," he says as he pores over bottles in a cabinet.

"What are you looking for?" I ask.

"The perfect scent," Wolfgang says, quickly turning around and dousing us with a whole bottle of perfume. Only . . . it's not perfume. It's the foulest, nastiest, most nose-splitting, brain-withering odor.

I can't breathe. I immediately start coughing—and can't stop.

"I'm going to faint!" Eliza chokes. "I'm going to die."

"Ahhhhh," Frank says, as if he smells a flower. "What is it?"

"Skunk funk," Wolfgang says. "Extracted, of course, from the glands of a skunk. Let's see you stick your noses in other people's business smelling like *this*."

He runs out of the room, covering his nose with his sleeve.

Wolfgang is right: we smell so horrible that none of the suspects want to talk to us. *We* don't even want to talk to us. All I want to do is crawl out of my own skin. When Mom finds us, she takes us to the hotel right away, and we bathe in tomato juice. It's supposed to stop the aroma of skunk, but it makes it worse. We have to stay in the tomato bath for a whole week, with Mom delivering our food and water. Mom even spoon-feeds us because our hands are too prune-y to hold utensils.

This stinks.

CASE CLOSED.

I DECIDE ELIZA'S right: we have to talk with Wolfgang Westover. Especially after Agatha Tuggle called him shady. But this time, we question him ourselves—instead of listening to him and Mom talk through a closet.

When we knock on the blurry glass door to his office, he answers right away. "Come in."

But when we open the door, he's shocked to see us.

"What are you doing here?" he asks, mouth hanging open.

"We'd like to question you about Layla's disappearance."

"Huh? But your mom . . ." Comprehension dawns on his face, and he chuckles. "Oh, right! I think it's adorable that you kids want to play detective, just like your mommy." His tone is so sickly sweet that I want to shrivel up and die.

"Not *my* mommy!" Frank says.

"Sorry, kids. I don't have time to play pretend; I've got so much to do. Even if Layla wasn't missing in action, being a producer is hectic. But now that she *is* missing, it's twice as frenzied. Hold on a second." He pulls out his cell phone from a drawer and speaks into it. "New show idea: *Frenzied Frenemies*. Copyright Wolfgang Westover, Burbank Productions, LLC." He puts the phone away. "That idea is top secret, kids. If you tell anyone, I'll have to kill ya."

His tone is jokey, but he clearly didn't think about how bad that would sound. Eliza and I stare at him with our jaws open, while Frank shouts, "I'm TELLING!"

"That might not be an appropriate joke for the occasion," Eliza says.

Wolfgang frowns. "Oh. Right. Of course not. My apologies."

I steal our detective casebook from Eliza. "Like I said, just a few questions, and we'll be on our way."

"You kids are so cute," Wolfgang says. "Wittle bittle investigators."

Somehow I manage not to cringe, and I can tell Eliza is trying not to roll her eyes. Adults talking down to kids might be the number-one most annoying thing in the universe.

Wolfgang returns to his work, and I look helplessly at Eliza. She gives me an encouraging nod and a nudge. "Mr. Westover, we really think we can help with the Layla case."

"And we're not taking no for an answer," Eliza adds.

Mr. Wolfgang looks up at us, sighs. "Then you'll leave me in peace?"

"Promise," I say.

"Cross my heart, hope to die, stick a needle in his eye!" Frank says, looking all too eager to poke a needle into an eyeball.

Wolfgang smiles at Frank. "You know, you have a lot

of energy. You should be a stuntman."

"You're not the boss of me!" Frank yells.

Wolfgang chuckles and turns to me, his brown eyes twinkling over the frames of his reading glasses. "I can give you five minutes."

All the things we know flash through my mind like fireworks:

1. Wolfgang and Tuggle hate working with each other.

2. Tuggle and Layla were fighting about something.

3. Tuggle faked a phone call to get out of talking to us.

4. Layla banned her mother from the set and is fighting with her too.

5. Miriam has been stealing money from Layla's bank account.

6. Miriam was clearly looking for something in Layla's dressing room.

7. Guillotine and Layla don't work well together.

8. Brad Bradley is jealous of Layla.

9. Wolfgang is delighted about Layla's disappearance because the show's ratings got a huge boost.

My instinct is to ask about that last one. If we don't have much time with him, I don't want to get bogged down in individual suspects . . . what if we ask about the wrong person? Or we could ask him what he thinks happened to Layla. I'd be interested to hear what theories he's come up with.

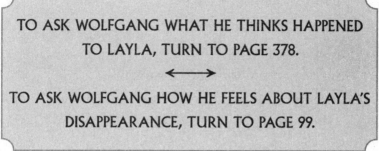

TO ASK WOLFGANG WHAT HE THINKS HAPPENED TO LAYLA, TURN TO PAGE 378.

←——→

TO ASK WOLFGANG HOW HE FEELS ABOUT LAYLA'S DISAPPEARANCE, TURN TO PAGE 99.

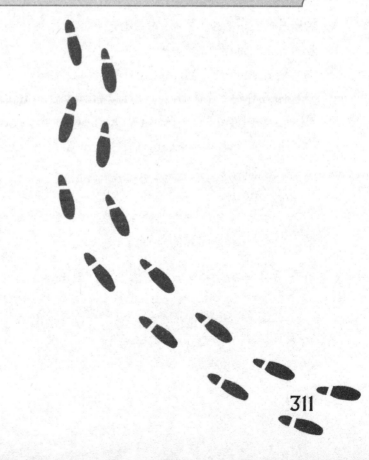

"**WHAT *IS* THIS** gibberish?" I ask Eliza. "I don't understand this at all."

Frank squeezes between Eliza and the piece of paper. "Carlos, it's the alphabet. Duhhhhhh."

I roll my eyes. "I can see *that*."

"L-M-N-O-P!" he sings. "X-Y-Z!"

"Uh . . . you missed a few in there."

"I'm saving them for later," Frank says.

"Hmmm," Eliza says. I know she's two seconds away from talking through her thought process . . . like she always does. She even does it during tests in class, which *would* get her into trouble if she wasn't every teacher's favorite student.

"You see how the alphabet is written normally on the first line," she says, "and then written backward on the second line? I think it's the key to the code."

"So . . . you're saying . . . that when we see an A written down, it's actually a Z? And a B is really a Y?"

Eliza nods.

A B C D E F G H I J K L M N O P Q R S T U V W X Y Z
| | | | | | | | | | | | | | | | | | | | | | | | | |
Z Y X W V U T S R Q P O N M L K J I H G F E D C B A

Ru blf ziv ivzwrmt gsrh, gsvm R nfhg szev yvvm
prwmzkkvw. Blf droo mvvw gsv kzhhxlwv gl nb
xsvhg: gdl urev hrc. R'n rm tizev wzmtvi.
KOVZHV SVOK.

"Look at the first word," Eliza says. "*Ru*. The key
tells us the letter R is really an I, and the letter U is
really—"

"F," I interrupt.

"F for Frank!" Frank cries.

"That's right, Frankie," Eliza says. "Which makes the
first word *If*."

I steal a pen off Layla's messy countertop and write
down the first word. "We can do this."

TURN TO THE PAGE NUMBER IN THE SOLUTION.

ONCE I ATTACH the wires in all fourteen combinations of *hatch*, the elevator blinks back to life. The doors burst open, and we climb out of there as fast as we can. But the only thing worse than being stuck in a creepy elevator is being in this hallway.

"Where are we?" Eliza whispers.

"Sub-basement," I say, pointing to a sign that reads SUB-BASEMENT NO LONGER IN USE.

The whole sub-basement is roped off, but I step over the rope and keep going. There's one flickering light bulb in the whole dungeon-y basement. It's so dark I can barely see, and the walls aren't walls at all, just pipes. The floor is dirty and creaky. And the ceiling is so low that I'm tall enough to touch it without standing on my tiptoes.

"I can't read in this flickering light," Eliza huffs. She gets a flashlight from her bag. "Much better."

"Anything good yet?"

"All legalese," she says. To be honest . . . I have no idea what that means.

We inch forward. Halfway down the hall, I hear a girl's voice shouting, "LET ME OUT OF HERE!"

My heart stops. It's Layla Jay. I run forward, but Eliza pulls me back.

"Carlos."

"Eliza—what are you doing? Layla is screaming. Layla needs us."

314

She taps her flashlight on the page she's reading, and I grab it from her impatiently. The top reads NOTICE OF TERMINATION OF REPRESENTATION.

"What does that—termination? So Wolfgang fired Layla? So it is him after all?"

"More like *Layla* fired *Tuggle*."

My head is spinning. "But how—why?"

Frank groans. "Even *I* know why. Money, money, money."

Of course! The cauldron with the money Miriam was taking out of Layla's account. Tuggle, as her agent, would have access to Layla's money. She'd be able to wire some to Miriam Jay. So it was *Tuggle* that Miriam was trying to contact.

"Very clever, Frank!" Eliza whispers. "And remember how she told us and Wolfgang and everyone on set about what an irresponsible diva Layla was? But it was all lies. But why would she kidnap—"

"YOU! LET ME GO!" Layla shrieks.

"Shhhh!" I say to Eliza and Frank, and we peer around the pipes to listen.

"Calm down, Layla," Tuggle says. They both sound like their voices are muffled, like they're in a room somewhere, not in this hall. "Please. Let's talk about this rationally—"

"Rational?" Layla shrieks. "You lost all chance of *rational* when you knocked me out and kept me hostage!"

I only know Layla from her character on TV: Aurelia, the dragon-taming, earth-saving, evil-queen-fighting, troublemaking teen witch. But it seems like the actress has just as much guts as her character.

"I need you to stay with me," Tuggle says. "I know you haven't been happy lately, but I swear, I'll do whatever you want to change that. I'll cut off ties with your mom and stop sending her money. I'll intervene in your argument with Guillotine. I'll stop trying to get Brad Bradley a spin-off show without you. I'll even get Wolfgang to give you a raise."

"It's too little, too late," Layla says. "You should have been doing this all along!"

"Layla, I need you. Financially, my agency won't survive."

"You should have thought about that before you conspired to steal my money and tried to tank my career behind my back with Brad! You know how much I despise him! How could you? And we aren't even discussing any of this, because you *kidnapped* me."

"Layla, please. You know it was an accident—I didn't mean to. Heat of the moment. I was only trying—"

"I know what you're trying to do!" Layla snarls. "You sweet-talk your way out of everything, don't you? Not this time. HELP! HEEEEEELP!"

Tuggle waits until Layla has screamed herself out

before saying, "No one is around to hear you. No one will ever find you. I can make this all go away, if you just say yes to being my client and letting this little incident slide. I'll release you and spin a great story about your spontaneous vacation. All you have to do is remain my client."

"You can't blackmail me into being your client, Agatha. It doesn't work like that. Not only am I leaving Tuggle and Tickler Associates, but after this kidnapping, I'll make sure you go to prison. And you'll never work in this industry again!"

"Is that a threat?" Tuggle says, her voice shaky.

"It's a promise," Layla retorts.

There's a pause that's so long and so intense that I can only hear the pulse pounding in my ears.

And even though I'm only listening from in the hall, I can feel the mood change. The silence is sinister.

"Please," Layla whispers. "Don't."

We have to do something. I look around, and all I see are exposed metal pipes. I could bang on them to make a racket. That would lure Tuggle out of the room, away from Layla. Or we could storm into the room and try to intervene.

Is it better to separate the culprit from the victim? Or is it better to make sure I don't leave the victim all alone?

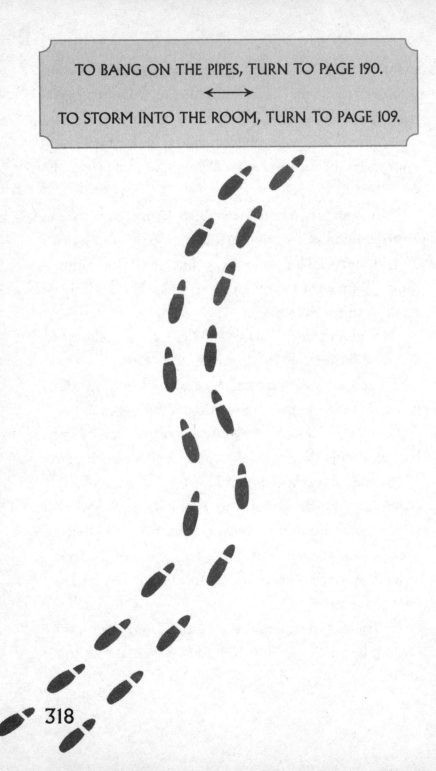

TO BANG ON THE PIPES, TURN TO PAGE 190.

←→

TO STORM INTO THE ROOM, TURN TO PAGE 109.

318

"WE DON'T WANT to play hide-and-seek," I say to Maureen. "We don't want to play any kiddie games with you. Buzz off!"

Maureen looks wounded, her eyes pooling with tears like I just slapped her in the face. But then she blinks them back. "It's okay. I know you're probably just cranky because you're sleepy."

She ushers us into the writers' room and lays down three yoga mats.

"Shhhhhhh," Maureen says. "It's naptime. Rock-a-bye babies in the treetops, when the wind blows—"

"We're not babies!" I say.

"Somebody's fussy!" Maureen says, shoving a bottle into my mouth.

"Can I have one?" Frank says. And at my outraged glare, he adds, "I'm not a baby—I just like milk."

Maureen gives him a bottle, and then she plops herself right in front of the only exit, and every time I peek an eye open, she starts singing lullabies.

Rock-a-bye baby? More like say goodbye case-y!

CASE CLOSED.

WE DECIDE TO search for Layla's secret chest. Layla obviously wanted someone to find it, and she might have hidden something important in there. Something that will let us know who might have taken her . . . and why.

The only problem? We have absolutely no idea where it is.

The set is almost too big—Layla could have hidden it anywhere. We wander around, first looking through Layla's dressing room, but I don't find anything. Then we move to the carefully organized prop room, but there is no chest of any kind there.

But there is a drawer in some sort of cabinet that's labeled LAYLA PROPS.

"I don't think this is what she meant by *chest*," Eliza says.

"I know," I say. "But we might as well look, right?"

I dig through the drawer, which has items I've seen on the show before: identical versions of the wand Layla's character, Aurelia, carries. A few witch hats. A patch that is part of Aurelia's school uniform. A locket that she always wears.

"I can't believe I'm touching the Locket of Doom!" I say to Eliza.

"I can't believe *I'm* holding Brad Bradley's cape! *Eeeeeeeeeeee!*" She squeals at a pitch not yet known to human ears.

"I can't believe I'm wrestling a snake!" Frank says,

rolling around on the floor, choking a rubber snake.

I open the locket—I've *always* been curious about what's inside, and *Teen Witch* never shows the audience what's in there. I've been thinking there must be a picture of the Witch Queen or some other show spoiler . . . but inside, there's a tiny wad of paper.

I unroll it, and my eyes grow wide. "Look at this!" I shove the paper at Eliza while Frank jumps between us for a better view:

Dear Layla, I am your number one fan!!! I know you probably hear that a lot, but I am really your greatest fan. I've watched everything you've ever been in 150 times each, no exaggeration. I know everything about you, from your strawberry allergy to your favorite brand of face cream. I know where you were born, where you live, what your daily routine is like, your library card number. Not saying you owe me anything, but maybe a little bit. Without your fans, you'd be nothing. We make you who you are. We make you famous. You should be grateful. You don't want fans like me to think you're snooty, do you? I know you gave me an autograph before, but I want some of your time. If only we could meet, I know we would be best friends forever. I'll be watching you . . . on TV and in real life. Love love love, Louise Jenkins

HOW MANY TIMES DID LOUISE WATCH LAYLA'S SHOWS? TURN TO THAT PAGE.

WE CAN'T ANSWER the door! There's no way the person on the other side of that door is friendly, and I'd bet anything it's the kidnapper.

No, we have to figure out how to get out of this without letting them in. I need a way out. I need Eliza.

I turn to her. "How can we get out of the room?"

"I—I don't know, Carlos. There doesn't seem to be another exit."

"But maybe there's a shovel or someth—"

KABOOM!

The explosion comes from outside the room, but the force of it is still so strong. I'm blown off my feet, and Eliza and Frank crash into me. The ground feels like it's shaking.

"Everyone okay?" I ask.

Frank brushes himself off. "Thumbs-up!"

"Why would they explode *outside* the room, instead of inside?" Eliza asks.

The question is answered when we open the door. The basement has caved in completely. The explosion caused the whole place to collapse; boulders and stones of all sizes block any way out.

"I told you this was a setup!" Eliza cries. "We walked right into a trap! And now we're stuck!"

This is what rock bottom feels like.

CASE CLOSED.

I CAN'T FIND any pattern in this math problem. I groan.

"Everything okay, Carlos?" Eliza says, eying me with an X-ray kind of glance.

"Not really," I say. "I can't figure this out."

"Let's do it together," Eliza says, tracing her finger over the numbers.

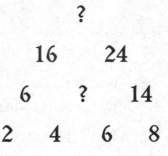

"Let's see," she says, twisting her braid between her fingers. "Let's look for a pattern."

"Well," I say. "I saw two, four, six, eight at the bottom . . . which is just counting by twos. I thought it was something, but the second row goes back down to six. So I don't think it's anything anymore."

"It's a good start, though!" Eliza says. "That six is interesting to me. Because it's the top of a mini pyramid between two and four. See that?"

"Two plus four is six," I say.

"Exactly!" Eliza says excitedly. I can tell the math nerd in her is getting revved up. "So if we move to the other side of the pyramid, we have six and eight at the bottom . . . and fourteen between them."

"Six plus eight is fourteen!" I say, and I feel like I'm catching Eliza's excitement in a baseball mitt. "So if this pattern is true, then four plus six would make the middle number ten."

?

16   24

6   10   14

2   4   6   8

"It's simple addition, when you get down to it," Eliza says. "Little addition triangles within the big triangle. The sum of the two numbers next to each other makes the number above and between them."

"Six plus ten is sixteen," I say, testing it out on the middle rows. "And ten plus fourteen is twenty-four. It seems to work, Eliza!"

"Which of course, would make the top number . . . sixteen plus twenty-four. In other words . . ."

"TEN THOUSAND!" Frank cries.

THE NUMBER THAT BELONGS AT THE TOP OF
THE PYRAMID IS YOUR NEXT PAGE.

MOM CAN SMELL a lie from across state lines. She *is* a professional detective, after all. There's just no way I'd be able to fool her, so I might as well be truthful. Even if it means admitting that I've betrayed her trust.

"Yes . . . we've been investigating behind your back," I say. For a moment, it feels good to get it off my chest, but then I wince, close my eyes, and wait for the lecture of the century.

Only it doesn't come. I peek one eye open.

Mom is wearing a frown, but her one eyebrow is cocked real high, and she says, "Well? What have you found?"

"What?" Eliza and I say together.

"I'm not in trouble?" I say.

"Oh, *of course* you're in trouble, hijo. But you were, at least, eventually honest. And I'm glad for that." She sighs. "It's clear to me that none of you are particularly obedient kids. You three have strong wills and curious minds." She pauses. "Those are the qualities of a good detective."

My grin grows and grows—is this really happening?

"This is important to you, isn't it, Carlos?"

I nod. "The most important thing in the world. If only you could see how good we are, Mom. If only you gave us a chance. I think you'll agree . . . we're naturals."

Am I imagining it, or is that a smile at the corner of Mom's lips? My heart beats fast.

326

"Perhaps trying to ban you from investigating was a mistake. Maybe I should be helping you and supervising you. That way, I can make sure you are safe. So what have you found?"

"A chest!" Frank says. "Except not a chest. A non-chest chest, and a secret number note."

Mom winks at Eliza. "Translation?"

"He means this," Eliza says, handing her the cypher we found in Layla's dressing-room drawer. "She mentions a chest, only we haven't found it yet."

We tell her what we've discovered: about Brad, Guillotine, and Louise. And when we're done catching her up, I'm *shocked* to see my mom beaming.

"If we put our findings together, I think we've covered a lot of ground." She pulls out her detective notebook, which she always pores over whenever she's on a job. "Let's see." She hums. "Wolfgang Westover has told me that none of the crew members harbor any resentment toward Layla. And Layla gets along with the crew famously. Which does help us narrow it down, since there are so many people who work on a set."

"Did he have any idea who might have kidnapped Layla?" Eliza asks.

"He's not convinced she was kidnapped. Remember," Mom says, "he hasn't seen this note."

"So he thinks Layla is, what, hiding?" I say. That seems far-fetched.

"Mr. Westover wonders if Layla and her agent, Agatha Tuggle, are working together in this stunt to try to get Layla another salary increase. Maybe if Layla disappears for a few days, the production company will realize how valuable she is . . . and offer her more money. I'm not saying he's correct—it's just a theory," she adds, at the sight of my scrunched-up face.

"One that doesn't fit with our big clue."

"True," Mom says. "But Mr. Westover's next theory might: he says that Layla's mother has been acting odd."

"Odd?"

"Even," Frank says.

"Apparently Layla has asked the security guards to escort her mother off the premises during filming on multiple occasions. Ms. Jay has left kicking and screaming."

Eliza frowns. "She kicked her own mother out? Why?"

Mom shrugs. "That's what we're about to find out in this next interview, with both Agatha Tuggle and Miriam Jay."

"Both?" Eliza says.

"Wait, *we*?" I say.

"Wee wee!" Frank giggles.

Mom squints at me. "We're trying this out . . . on a *trial* basis only."

"What . . . what does that mean?" I whisper. Do I even dare hope?

"You told me you wanted a chance to prove yourself," Mom says. "So here's your shot."

Suddenly the knot in my stomach tightens. If I only have one shot, then the pressure is *on*.

"I'm taking the lead on this," Mom says.

Disappointment settles. How do I prove myself if I'm following Mom's lead? I guess I'm closer to the action, but I still feel like I have a babysitter . . . when I want free rein and trust. I've never felt so close to—and so far from—my goal, at the same time.

Mom leads us to the writers' room. It's really exciting to be here. I mean, this room is where the magic happens. I read this interview that said at the end of season two, the writers realized the finale was all wrong, and they had to rewrite it so that Layla's character had a bigger cliff-hanger ending after her first duel with the Witch Queen. The writers spent six days in this very room, not even leaving to sleep or eat. Talk about dedication!

Whatever sleeping bags used to be in the writers' room, they're all gone now. The room is empty except for our two suspects. Layla's agent, Agatha Tuggle, and the mother of the starlet, Miriam Jay, are waiting for us, sitting on opposite ends of the long table. The mood is strained and awkward, even before we take our seats: Mom and Frank on one side of the table, Eliza and me on the other.

Agatha Tuggle is smiling widely. She's got this casual expression, like nothing is wrong. Miriam Jay is the opposite. She's got a whole wad of tissues in her hands, and she looks very much like she's been snotting all morning into them.

"We've been waiting here forever!" Miriam cries. "What have you been doing? Where have you been? Are you going to find my baby girl or not?"

"Not," Frank says, and I kick him under the table.

"Miriam, you have to calm down," Agatha says, smoothing her pantsuit. "I work with so many actors, and they are all flighty and impetuous. This is part of the artistic process. You'll see—Layla will turn up again in a day or two, rejuvenated from her creative adventure—"

"Not my Layla." Miriam sniffles. "She's always responsible! She never misses a rehearsal. She's always on time. My baby girl is like a little adult."

"True as that may be," Agatha says, "I think we all need to calm down. There's no evidence that anything's wrong."

"Actually," Mom says, "we found a letter from Layla."

We lay the decoded letter on the table, and Miriam and Agatha both scramble to read it. When they're done, they both step back, wearing different expressions on their faces.

Agatha Tuggle is surprised, her mouth in a perfect O shape. But then her expression morphs: her forehead scrunches and her lips pinch together, and she looks worried, anxious. Is this the worried face of someone guilty? Or just the crumbling face of an agent who just realized her attitude toward her client's disappearance has been way too casual?

I can't get a good read on Miriam Jay . . . she has no expression at all. She looks like she could be playing poker with a hard face like that. For someone who was just crying and whining and carrying on about Layla when we walked in the room, her stillness now is jarring. But is it suspicious?

Mom opens her mouth to ask a question, but I have to throw my hat in the ring first. How will Mom see me as a detective if she doesn't see me detect?

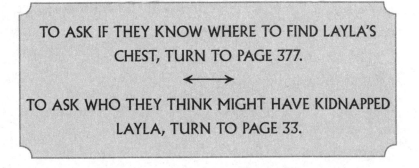

TO ASK IF THEY KNOW WHERE TO FIND LAYLA'S CHEST, TURN TO PAGE 377.

←——→

TO ASK WHO THEY THINK MIGHT HAVE KIDNAPPED LAYLA, TURN TO PAGE 33.

I DECIDE TO search inside the TV cabinet for the key to the filing drawer. When I open the cabinet drawer, there's a whole bunch of junk inside. Guillotine definitely doesn't have organizational skills.

"What's this?" Frank says, leaping forward, grabbing a small, circular shiny disc and holding it in the air. "An alien ship? TAKE ME TO YOUR LEADER."

"It has Layla's name on it," I say.

"It's a CD or DVD," Eliza says. "It's like . . . an old-fashioned way to play music or a video. Haven't you ever seen Mom's collection, Frank?"

He shakes his head no.

"Should we watch it?" I ask.

"PLAY!" Frank agrees.

We pop the disc into the player beneath the TV.

"MY MAGIC IS GONE! WHAT HAPP—"

The TV's volume is so loud that the room shudders. Maybe even the whole building. I think my eardrums have burst!

I lunge at the remote, and I lower the volume as fast as I can.

"Do you think anyone heard?" I ask, my ears still ringing.

Eliza walks over to the door, peeks it open a crack, and squeaks. "Oh, they heard."

She opens the door. Outside Guillotine's office is

the entire cast and crew—at least sixty people. And they look angry.

"Er . . . hi," I say.

"What did I tell you?" Guillotine cries. "While the detective lady distracts us, she's unleashed these three on our stuff without a warrant! They'll be going through all your private, personal things!"

There's a rumbling through the crowd. Then someone from the back shouts, "GET THEM!"

The mob grabs me, Frank, and Eliza, and lifts us over their heads. I try to wiggle away, but I'm floating in a sea of hands. They carry us to the door, angrily yelling and being generally moblike the whole time. They march us out of the studio lot, down the street, across town, to the beach. They throw us in the Pacific Ocean to cleanse themselves of us, where we drift out to sea, later to be rescued by pirates.

But that's another story.

CASE CLOSED.

I'VE CRUSHED THIS letter deletion puzzle! *Startling* to *starting* to *staring* to *string* to *sting* to *sing* to *sin* to *in* to *I*. With the right combo, Guillotine's box clicks open, and inside is a single key.

"I think I know what this goes to!" Eliza says with a grin. She puts the key into the lock on the filing cabinet, and turns.

The drawer slides out, and inside are a bunch of files, each with the name of an actor or crew member working on the show.

"Who do we read about first?" I ask Eliza.

"Me!" Frank says. I wonder if he'll throw a temper tantrum when he realizes there's no Frank Thompson file.

Eliza's gray eyes twinkle. "We have to start with the source herself: Layla Jay."

Layla Jay's file is thick and heavy. I set it down on the table and open it.

The first page is a printed email from Miriam Jay to Guillotine, from a few months ago.

I know Mr. Westover has refused this request a hundred times before, but you've got to do something about his niece, Louise. That photo of Layla storming off set—how did that end up in *Celebrity Watcherz* magazine? I even caught Louise outside the windows of my house, wearing camouflage and hiding in a bush.

You do something about it . . . or I will.

"Wow," Eliza says.

"Um . . . Eliza, we already knew Louise was a creepy stalker."

"Yes, but, Carlos, she's profiting off Layla's success. Louise takes these sneaky photos without Layla's permission, and then she is selling the photos to magazines and online gossip sites. Who pay her for these photos. It's really unethical!"

"Shady stuff," I agree. "Do you think this email was before or after Louise tried to snip a piece of Layla's hair at the red carpet event?"

"I don't know," Eliza says. "But I think it's clear that when it comes to Louise, we're dealing with a real fanatic. She clearly doesn't know right from wrong."

"Or up from down," Frank adds. "Or left from right. Or backward from forward. What are we talking about again?"

I sigh and flip through the folder again. There seem to be lots of negotiation-type emails from Tuggle—and a few contracts from the first four seasons of the show. A few memos from the producers, a script change or two.

"What's this?" Eliza asks, plucking a paper out of the pile. It's all crumpled, like someone went to toss it in a trash can but then thought better of it. Frank and I lean closer, as we all look down on the note. It's hand-written, on Wolfgang Westover's stationery.

D.C.,
Is this a joke? You and Tuggle are really pitching me a spin-off show starring Brad Bradley? You do know Layla Jay is our moneymaker, right? You can't pitch a spin-off that cuts Layla out of the show!

You need to have a talk with Bradley, by the way. His unrequited romantic advances are making Layla Jay very uncomfortable and creating a hostile work environment. This needs to stop. And you need to stop resenting her for becoming famous. It's not her fault she's young and successful.

Remember, SHE is your star. Without her, the show is nothing. I need you to put aside your anger toward Layla. Because if you can't fix this, I'll find a director who can.

W.W.

336

"Wolfgang threatened to fire Guillotine!" I say. "And Tuggle and Guillotine pitched a spin-off idea starring Brad Bradley? Isn't Tuggle Layla's agent, not Brad's? And Brad is asking Layla out, but she doesn't want him back? There's so much to think about—I am so confused."

Eliza puts her hand over the letter, and there's a look on her face I can't quite read. It's like she's part upset, part horrified, and part shocked. She shakes her head no.

"It can't be," she whispers.

"What?" Frank asks.

"Brad Bradley."

I roll my eyes. "He's a pig, Eliza."

"But . . . he's so lovely on TV!"

"Yeah, but that's TV. It's not real. Someone tells him what to say and how to act."

"But his interviews—"

"Eliza, *this* is what Brad Bradley is really like."

She puts the letter from Wolfgang back into Layla's file and closes the folder gently. "I . . . I just thought I knew him."

"Well, you DON'T!" Frank says. "You don't know ANYBODY. You don't even know ME."

Eliza stares at her brother. "You have a point, Frank."

Huh? He does? "What are you talking about—you know Frank!"

"No, I mean . . . if we don't know Brad, then we don't know Layla either. We don't know anything about any celebrity. And I was still obsessed with him. When it comes down to it, am I any different from Louise?"

I snort. "Of course you are! You don't stalk—"

CRASH!

Eliza grabs my arm in panic. "Was that on accident . . . or on purpose?"

"Only one way to find out," I reply, pulling Eliza and Frank out of the room . . . and toward the sound.

RUN TO THE CRASH! TURN TO PAGE 200.

338

I OPEN BRAD'S texts, and before I can even read anything, I get an incoming text message from Guillotine.

> Wolfgang said no.

Then three dots appear, and I hold my breath while I wait for Guillotine's next text.

> I'll work on him. Just stick to the plan.

My heart is thudding. Wolfgang said no to what? And what is this plan they're talking about? Does it have anything to do with Layla?

I swipe out of the texts from Guillotine.

Next, I see texts from a number that Brad hasn't saved . . . but the texts are signed with the initials A.T.

"A.T.," I say. "Is this from Agatha Tuggle?"

Eliza hums. "It seems likely. What other A.T. would there be?"

> Get ready to see your name in lights, you STAR! Can you stop by later to sign the contracts? —A.T.

> Sure. But when am I going to see results?

Soon.

Vague. And unhelpful.

Well, Brad, you know we have to take care of the Layla issue first. Can't have a spin-off while the original's still running.

Is there anything I can do to help . . . speed up the process?

Don't you worry about that.
Very soon, the *Teen Witch* franchise will be all about you.

It better be. BTW, that *Teen Witch* title has got to go. I'm thinking something more manly. How about *Most Powerful Warlock in the Whole Wide World and Pretty Handsome to Boot*?

"What's this about?" I say, staring at the conversation. "The *Teen Witch* franchise will be all about Brad? But . . . Layla is the star of the show."

"Brad has his eye on a spin-off," Eliza says. "And apparently they can't move forward with this new show until Layla is out of the picture. This could be a solid motive for kidnapping . . . or worse."

I gulp.

"The other thing that strikes me as odd," Eliza says, "is that Brad is talking to Agatha Tuggle. She's *Layla's* agent, not Brad's. They shouldn't be communicating at all, let alone conspiring."

"And *that*," Frank says, ripping the phone out of Eliza's hands, "is a stinky name for a show. I like the name *Warlock Octopus* better."

"But . . . the show isn't about octopuses, Frankie," Eliza says.

"It should be." Frank folds his arms. "Everyone likes a good octopus."

"Should we look at more texts?" I say, steering us back. Eliza nods.

I scroll down, and my finger stops dead on texts from Miriam Jay. But what would Layla's mom be doing texting Brad?

> Stay away from my girl. I know what you're trying to do. And if you don't back off, I will make it my life's mission to ruin you.

"Wow," I say. "That's pretty threatening."

"Mmmm," Eliza agrees.

"MORE!" Frank cries.

Up next, we have a text from Brad Bradley to Louise. Which is *unbelievable*. Didn't Brad call Louise a stalker?

Hey, Louise. You know that pic you took of me kissing Layla on the cheek? Can you sell that to *Celebrity Watcherz* magazine?

The gossip tabloid? I don't know, Brad. Did Layla say it was okay?

Oh, yeah. She wants the publicity. All publicity is good publicity, right? Don't you want to help her career? This will be good for her, promise.

I'm not sure. . . .

You can keep the money, Louise.

What's in it for you?

Nothing. Just publicity for me too. It's a win-win. We're friends, right? Right. So help me out. Hey, I'll get you another used tissue for your Layla shrine. . . .

Okay. I guess.

"Stop reading," Eliza says. "I feel sick."

Frank perks up. "Are you going to throw up?" he says excitedly.

"I just . . . I can't believe how different Brad is when the cameras are on him. But that's not who he is, not on the inside." She looks like her head is spinning. "It's all just an act."

"Well . . . he *is* an actor."

"How much do we know about any celebrity, Carlos? How much do we really know about Layla?"

"What are you saying?"

"We've been hearing so many things about her—she's a diva, she's easy to work with, she's opinionated, she takes direction well, she's responsible, she's impulsive, she's smart, she's a headache. Everyone has something different to say about her. How do we even know what's tru—"

CRASH!

"What was that?" I say.

"Sounds like shattering glass. Let's go!"

RUN TO THE CRASH! TURN TO PAGE 200.

"WHERE DO YOU think Layla could be?"

"At first I thought she ran away, but the way you're talking, it seems like there might be foul play. Was she kidnapped?"

"We can neither confirm nor deny," I say, which is something my mom says to avoid answering a question. And *if* Louise is the kidnapper, I don't want to give away our leads.

Louise's bottom lip quivers. "Oh, Layla! Hear my prayers and come back to me safely!"

Eliza clears her throat. "So, do you have ideas on who might've taken her . . . if she was taken?"

"If I had to guess, I'd stick close to Douglas Chen if I were you."

"Who's that?" Frank asks, tugging on my shirt.

"That's Guillotine's real name," Eliza says. "Remember?"

"No. Why does he get fifteen names? I want more names! Frank . . . Frankie. Frank the Hot Dog! Frankenator Three Thousand!"

"Frankenstein's monster," I mumble, turning back to Louise, who looks pointedly down at my shoes. She has a look about her . . . the "I'm keeping a secret that's going to burst out of me at any moment" look. Mom calls it the Confession Face. There are big confessions and small confessions, and I don't know which is about to come pouring out of Louise. But I have to help it along.

"You have something else to tell us, don't you, Louise?"

She runs her tongue over her braces and says, "Also, look, not to give you too many leads and derail your case, but Layla has been going through a tough time lately, and nobody seems to have her back. There's stuff brewing with her director, her costar, her agent, even her mom. I could tell you the secret behind-the-scenes gossip . . . if you want." She looks eager. Like she's been waiting her whole life for someone to ask her about Layla Jay.

ASK LOUISE ABOUT THE ON-SET GOSSIP
ON PAGE 290.

345

WE HAVE TO lock the gate. It's the only way to keep the car on the premises until the police arrive.

We run to the front booth, where a guard usually sits. But there is no guard. Did *everyone* go with the police to watch the fake ransom exchange?

Vrroooom! The engine is purring.

Lights turn our way.

The car is coming fast.

"Carlos! Close the gate! Hit the button!" Eliza shouts.

"Which one?" There's a whole row of buttons.

GREEN   BLUE   YELLOW   RED   BLACK

"I can hit them for you!" Frank says gleefully.

"NO!" Eliza and I both shout.

"Carlos! There's a note on the switchboard!"

To Security Guard Kippler:

If you need to close or open the gate, here's the order you've got to press these buttons:

Red must be pushed sometime after blue and

immediately after black.

Yellow and green cannot be pushed one right after the other.

Christmas colors should be pushed one right after the other.

Bumblebee colors should be pushed one right after the other.

Green is pushed last.

Come on—you knew you'd be getting hazed, new guy. Good luck and welcome to Burbank.

Irv

"Seriously?" I shout. "That's all we get? This is an emergency—no time for coworker jokes!"

"Keep cool, Carlos. We can figure out the order."

TO PUSH THE BUTTONS IN THE ORDER YELLOW, BLACK, BLUE, RED, GREEN, TURN TO PAGE 135.

←——→

TO PUSH THE BUTTONS IN THE ORDER BLUE, YELLOW, BLACK, RED, GREEN, TURN TO PAGE 456.

I FREEZE, AND Frank copies me.

Two seconds later, the door to the closet opens, and I'm face-to-face with Mom. And it is *not* pretty. Her mouth quivers angrily, and her nostrils flare. "Carlos! Frank!" She yanks us out by the arm. "And where's Eliza?"

"Where you told her to be. We ditched her."

"We ditched her," Frank repeats.

"She didn't want to break the rules," I say.

"She didn't want to break the rules," Frank copies.

"Why is he doing that?" Mom asks.

"I don't know," I say.

"I don't know."

Mom turns around to Wolfgang. "I am so sorry about this," she says. "My son and his friend like to play detective."

"Play? I'm not playing!" I say. I can feel my anger rising, but I wither under Mom's intense glare.

"Play?" Frank echoes. "I'm not playing! Also! Either! Too!"

"It's okay," Wolfgang says kindly. "I have three kids of my own. Not to mention all the child actors I've worked with. I know how it goes."

Mom walks Frank and me to the door. "Go wait for me by the chairs behind the director—where I *told* you to wait in the first place. When I'm done here . . . ,"

348

she says, and she doesn't finish the threat. That's how I know I'm in *big* trouble.

Then Mom closes the door in our faces.

"We did good!" Frank says.

"We did *not* do good, Frank. We got thrown out!"

Frank shrugs. I pull him down the hall, so we can watch for when Mom leaves. Our only hope for finding out more is Eliza. I really hope she can contain her sneezes.

A little later, Mom and Wolfgang walk out of the office. They both head down the hall, talking together, and they walk right past Frank and me, hiding behind a pretty thick potted plant. I hesitate. Mom is headed for those chairs, and if Frank and I aren't with Eliza, she'll know something's up. I have to get her out of Wolfgang's office—and fast!

I run to Wolfgang's door, and the knob turns. Eliza emerges, looking breathless and disheveled. "I have so much to tell you," she says, keeping the door propped open with her foot. "But first . . . do you want to take a look around Wolfgang's office?"

"What about Mom?" I ask. "She's on her way to find us! If we're not where she told us to be, we're so dead. Worse than dead."

"I hear you," Eliza says, "but this might be our only chance to search Wolfgang's office."

349

TO SEARCH WOLFGANG'S OFFICE,
TURN TO PAGE 55.

←—→

TO GO BACK TO THE CHAIRS LIKE MOM SAID,
TURN TO PAGE 260.

"SO," I SAY, asking Miriam a question we already know the answer to, "does Layla get along with her cast and crew?"

"Of course she does!"

"Really?"

"Really really!"

"Really really really really really really really," Frank says. "Do you ever notice how words sound weird the more you say them? Really really really really really—"

I elbow him.

"What about Layla's relationship with Guillotine?"

"Oh, they love each other. They get along swimmingly."

I look at Eliza with confusion. Eliza raises her eyebrows at me.

"Okay," I say. "Does she get along with Tuggle?"

"What kind of question is that? Of course she does!"

"What about with Brad Bradley?"

"*I* don't like that Brad Bradley. I think he's a social climber, and he's willing to walk all over Layla to get to A-list celebrity status . . . but she has no issues with him."

Wrong, wrong, and wrong. Miriam keeps getting every question about her daughter incorrect!

"Do you even know your daughter at all?" Eliza says.

"Excuse me?"

"You are not excused!" Frank says. "Now, eat your peas."

Miriam scowls. "Well, I *never*—"

But whatever she nevers, we don't get to hear . . . because Miriam hoists up her heavy skirt and marches out of the room.

"Oh, I'm sorry!" Eliza says, covering her mouth with her hands.

TURN TO PAGE 453.

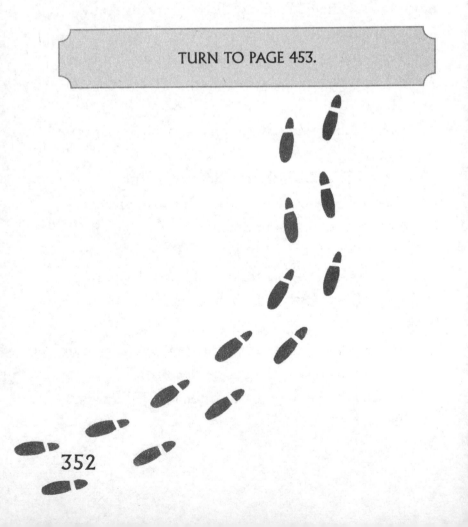

I DECIDE THERE'S nothing like a showstopper to catch everyone's attention. Here goes nothing!

I shimmy my arms, and Eliza—catching on fast—does a pirouette. And Frank, our lead vocalist, bursts into rousing song: "Old MacDonald had a farm! Eeeeeee-I eeeeee-I oh!"

Not quite the song I had in mind. Not quite a *song*. But it does the trick. Everyone turns toward Frank to watch his shrill rendition of the most annoying jingle on the planet.

"Here a QUACK! There a QUACK! Everywhere a quack quack—" He cuts off suddenly. "I can't hear you! I *said:* everywhere a—"

"Quack quack," everyone in the studio parrots back to him.

"Very good, maestro!" Frank says. Then he bows, and everyone offers him weak applause.

But it works. Frank has become the new gossip of the cast and crew, and every fight seems to have fizzled. As everyone exits the studio for the day, I can't help but give Frank a hug, which he squirms right out of.

We leave the broken cameras just the way they landed as we head back to the hotel for the night. We eat room service, and I'm waiting for Mom to tell us about her interviews, so I can tell her what we found out while we were snooping around.

353

But then she says, "Maybe it was a mistake to let you three run around unsupervised."

"What?" I say. "But I thought you were going to trust me! I thought we were a team!"

"We are . . . I want to be. But those crashing cameras shocked me back to reality. This case is dangerous. Even more dangerous than I thought. We have a missing person—and possibly a murder."

"Murder!" Eliza gasps. "What makes you say that?"

"Statistically," Mom mumbles, "after seventy-two hours of being missing . . . statistically . . . all I'm saying is, I would never forgive myself if something happened to you kids. If you could pause all your detective work—just for now."

"Sure," I mutter. "And cut out my heart while you're at it."

Mom flushes. "You *will* stay at the hotel tomorrow, and don't you dare take that tone with me, alborotoso! Respétame, hijo!"

Sometimes she starts speaking Spanish when she's mad.

I mumble an apology, even if I don't mean it. Because I *don't* mean it. Eliza, Frank, and I did amazing detective work today, but Mom doesn't know. She keeps treating me like a little kid. What's it going to take for her to really see me? And most of all—when is she going to start trusting that I can do this?

Our hotel room is cramped, and there's nowhere for me to go, so I sulk in the chair in the corner.

Hours later, after Mom and Frank have both fallen asleep, Eliza puts her hand on my arm. "Want to talk about it?" she whispers.

But I shake my head no. "I want to talk about the case," I say, soft as a hush.

Eliza raises her eyebrows, but she says nothing. So I continue.

"The crashing cameras have to be important somehow. We're so close to figuring it out. I can feel it."

"I know, Carlos, but what can we do? You heard your mom. Tomorrow we have to stay in the hotel. There's no way she'll let us come to the studio lot."

"If only we could investigate a little more." If only we had more time. If only we could poke around without anyone interrupting us—without the culprit getting scared and smashing cameras. . . .

I grab Eliza's hand. "Put your shoes on!" I hiss.

She squints at me, and I can see the question on her face. I answer before she even has to ask. "We're going back to the studio right now, to poke around while everyone's sleeping."

"What about Frank?" Eliza mouths.

"We can't wake him," I whisper. "Too loud, too risky."

"Too risky not to," Eliza says. "If he wakes up from a nightmare and sees us gone, he'll make a big stink about it—and ruin our cover. Besides," she adds, "he always finds good clues, even if accidentally."

"Okay, fine," I grumble.

Eliza puts the blanket over her brother's mouth to muffle the sound, then lightly shakes him. His eyes pop open in a very abrupt, creepy way. But for once, he doesn't shout.

Mom lets out a snore, and my stomach twists. I'm not betraying her; I'm *helping* her. Maybe if I can crack the case, she'll see that I'm as capable as she is. Maybe she'll see I don't need to be protected—I need to be involved.

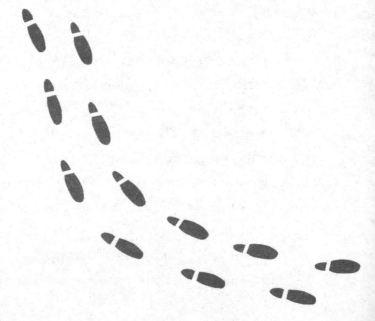

WE ARRIVE AT the studio just after midnight. Our Uber drops us off at the gate, and we walk the rest of the way. We pick a spot away from the security guard and start shimmying up the fence. It's hard because it's made of vertical poles—nowhere to stick our feet. But I take a cue from *Teen Witch*, actually . . . an episode where Layla and Brad were climbing a smooth wall after their wands had both snapped. Layla climbed on Bradley's back and then pulled him up.

Except, when Frank gets to the top, he doesn't pull us up. He just unlocks the side gate. We're in without detection!

Inside, Stage Eight is empty.

"It's a ghost town!" Eliza says.

"Knock knock!" Frank says.

"Who's there?" I reply.

"Boo."

"Boo who?"

"I'M A GHOST!" Frank shouts.

"Frank, that's not how the joke ends," Eliza corrects. "It's supposed to be 'Don't cry, it's just a joke.'"

"Don't cry, I'm a GHOST! Boo!"

"Shhhhh!" I snap. I hear a creaking noise coming from above. I look up into the rafters, and there's a figure in shadow. "Look!" But the second I point, the figure is running across the catwalk. "Quick! We need to get up there!"

"No we don't, actually," Eliza says, bending over to pick up a piece of rope. "I think we should ambush them at the bottom of the ladder, once they come down."

TO FOLLOW THE FIGURE UP INTO THE RAFTERS, TURN TO PAGE 198.

←→

TO TRY TO STOP THE FIGURE AT THE BOTTOM OF THE LADDER, TURN TO PAGE 29.

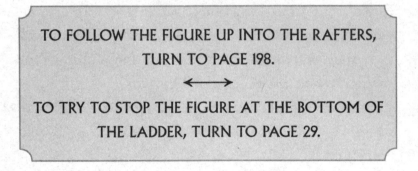

"DON'T PANIC," ELIZA says, breathing heavily. She is clearly panicking. "I hate small spaces . . . and the dark . . . and running out of oxygen."

"Well, let's solve one of these problems!" I say. "Mom, we need your phone flashlight."

"But, Carlos, that drains the battery. What if I need to call the police?"

"You said yourself you don't have service out here. Please, Mom, we don't have much time."

Mom flashes the light up at the ceiling. Whatever kind of doors are above us, they have, in fact, sealed shut. "Okay, Frank," I say. "You're up!"

Frank climbs up onto my shoulders and Eliza holds him by the ankles to keep him steady. He pulls on the door above, but it won't budge.

"Wait a second," Eliza says. "Ms. S, shine your light over at that corner."

Mom obeys, and we find a weird box in the upper corner.

"I bet it's a hydraulic door!" Eliza says.

"If that's true," Mom says, "then we're stuck in here. The pressure in hydraulic equipment can build up to create an incredible amount of force. We can never pull it open manually."

I have no idea what they're talking about. "Uh . . . English please!" I say.

"A hydraulic machine," Eliza says, "uses liquid that becomes pressurized through a series of motors and cylinders and circuits. Construction cranes that lift an insane amount of weight? They use hydraulics to do it. I won't go into the physics of it—"

"Yeah, hard pass," I say.

"But a door like this should have a control panel. And if we disable it, we should be able to pull open the doors above us, like they are normal doors."

"And that's the control panel?" I say, grabbing Frank by the hand. I drag him to the corner and hoist him up again.

He grunts as he stretches. "Can't . . . reach . . ."

"Stop! Put him down!" Mom says. "Carlos, take the flashlight. Frank, get on my shoulders." Mom crouches down, so Frank can climb on. While Mom isn't exactly tall, she's got height on Eliza and me. Now Frank can just barely reach the metal box, which pops open when he flips the switch on the side.

Inside is a circuit board with a bunch of tubes and shining buttons.

"Now what?"

"I . . ." Eliza breathes deeply. "When a circuit is lit up, it means it's connected. We have to disconnect them in order to turn the power off on the hydraulic door."

"Great, so disconnect them all!"

"Well, we have a bit of a problem," Eliza says. "Circuits have lots of electricity running through them. That's why they're all lit. So the more we play around with the circuits, the greater our chance of getting electrocuted."

"So, smashing them is off the table?"

"I'm afraid so," Eliza says. "We need to find one channel to turn . . . one spot to rotate that would disconnect the whole grid all at once. But we have to hurry—I already feel lightheaded from lack of air!"

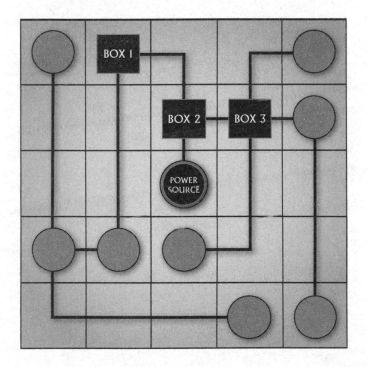

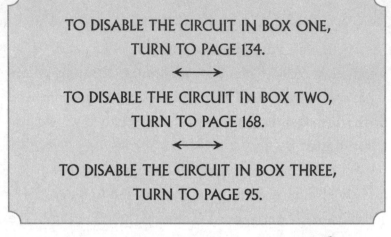

TO DISABLE THE CIRCUIT IN BOX ONE,
TURN TO PAGE 134.

⟵⟶

TO DISABLE THE CIRCUIT IN BOX TWO,
TURN TO PAGE 168.

⟵⟶

TO DISABLE THE CIRCUIT IN BOX THREE,
TURN TO PAGE 95.

362

INSIDE, THE STUDIO is frantic. Cast and crew members are running around like chickens with their heads cut off. Which sounds a bit gruesome, but thankfully everyone's head is firmly attached so far.

Eliza grabs my hand as I scan the crowd for Mom. Nothing . . . nothing . . . nothing. My palms are getting sweaty.

Something pushes me forward.

"Carlos!" Mom says from behind me, giving me a big squeeze around my chest.

"Mom!" I wrap my arms around her . . . tight. And she kisses my face a million times. I can't even be embarrassed about it—I am *that* relieved.

"Are you kids okay? Were you in the room? Did you get hurt?"

As if on cue, we can hear Brad Bradley loudly complaining. "A piece of rubble hit me in the face. I could have a *scar*. They don't pay me for my brains, you know! They pay me for my looks!"

He's not the only one grumbling. Crew members and cast members alike are sharing battle scars and exaggerated stories already. And all our major suspects are scattered throughout the crowd: Miriam Jay is clutching her necklace, looking like she might faint. Wolfgang Westover looks livid, his nostrils flaring. Agatha Tuggle keeps edging through the crowd to get a closer look. Guillotine seems almost bored. I swear, more than once, I catch him looking for the exit. Even Wolfgang's niece, Louise, is here—her mouth so wide a whole person could probably crawl in.

As the dust clears, I gasp: someone drove a car through the studio wall. The smashed-up car is damaged beyond repair, and that's what's causing all the smoke.

"Back up!" Mom says. As usual, she is good at commanding a room when she needs to. "The car might still explode!"

"Who was driving this thing?" Wolfgang demands.

"No one," Tuggle says, standing on her tiptoes to get a better look. She's so short that she probably can't see through the crowd.

"What do you mean, no one?" Wolfgang says.

"It was a ghost!" Brad cries. "The ghost of Layla is out to get me! To get all of us!"

"What?"

"Ghost!"

"A ghost! Cool!" Frank says.

"Is she dead? Do we know that for sure?" someone shouts.

"Is there a body?"

"My baby!" Miriam wails.

"STOP IT!" Mom bellows, getting control of the room again. "We have *no* evidence that Layla is dead. This has a logical explanation, not a paranormal one: someone put a brick on the gas pedal, which made the car drive straight into the wall. So who was in the parking lot in the past ten minutes?"

I look to Louise in panic, and she looks back at me with suspicion in her eyes. Don't tell, Louise! I am desperately sending her panic brain waves. Please don't tell, please don't tell!

Louise opens her mouth. "I was in the parking lot ten minutes ago!" she says with a sideways glance at us. There's a pause. I'm holding my breath and wishing, hoping, praying. Maybe she won't tell after all. Maybe we're safe!

"And so were they," Louise tattles, pointing directly at us.

Uh-oh.

"What does she mean? What were you doing outside?" Mom snaps. "Wait a second—where's Maureen?"

I shrug.

"Maureen?" Eliza calls.

"OLLY OLLY OXEN FREE!" Frank shouts.

From the part of the set that's a fake kitchen, the door to the lazy Susan cabinet pops open, and there's Maureen, folded up like a pretzel, contorted in ways I didn't think humans could bend.

"You three are very stubborn seekers!" she says. "I'm glad you finally gave up, though; my leg was falling asleep." She climbs out of the lazy Susan like nothing's wrong. Like a car didn't just crash through the wall of the studio, like it isn't still smoking and in danger of exploding at any moment.

While everyone's focused on Maureen and Mom, though, Guillotine starts to sneak out the exit.

"HOLD IT!" I shout, pointing at him. "Nobody move!"

"Carlos!" Mom says.

"We'll discuss it later, Mom. First let's call the police."

Mom looks at me in surprise . . . but then walks over to the landline on the wall and dials the police.

"They're on their way," she says a minute later, hanging the phone back on the wall.

"My set is ruined!" Wolfgang cries. "RUINED! Look at this rubble! We weren't supposed to have rubble on set until three episodes from now, when Aurelia's rival coven—"

"La la la la la," Eliza whispers.

I shake her. "What?"

"I don't want any spoilers!" she says. "I still want to be surprised by all the twists and turns when I watch it on TV. La la la la!"

Frank, who thinks Eliza's just singing for the fun of it, chimes in. "LAAAA LA LA LA LAAAA LA!" Only he's so loud, he draws the stares of everyone on set.

Mom pulls us aside as Wolfgang starts directing the writers on how to change the script. She brings us into a corner that's supposed to be the couches in the *Teen*

Witch school common room.

She gives us her mommiest Mom glare. It's so severe that even Frank curls himself up into a tiny ball. "Even after I told you no, even after I caught you in a lie, even after I hired a babysitter to supervise . . . you kids have been investigating, haven't you?"

She looks at me, waiting for an answer. I can't help it—I begin to sweat. I've never felt more like my life was hanging in the balance. I've been so afraid that she would take this away from me . . . that I would never have the chance to show her what I could do.

If I tell her the truth, I could be risking *everything*. It feels like too much to risk. I have to lie to her.

Suddenly, Eliza links her arm in my elbow, and I remember what she said earlier this morning: "You're not alone. You have a team. You have us."

That's right. If Eliza, Frank, and I do better together, then maybe the same is true with Mom.

Maybe Mom has a place on my team too. But only if I open up.

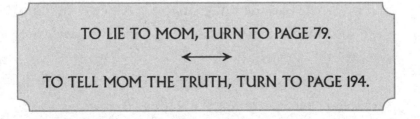

TO LIE TO MOM, TURN TO PAGE 79.

←——→

TO TELL MOM THE TRUTH, TURN TO PAGE 194.

"YOU SEEM TO be obsessed with Layla . . . a little *too* obsessed."

Louise's smile melts into a frown. "Are you accusing me of something?" she says, suddenly aggressive.

"YES," Frank replies, and I elbow him.

She glowers. A memory pops into my head. Last year, Eliza and I found a cute stray cat at recess, but when it knew it was surrounded, it arched its back and hissed until we ran away. Louise looks just like that: a cornered cat about to attack.

"I—I'm just passionate!" Louise says. "There's nothing wrong with that! I mean, it's not a *crime* to be a fan of someone's work."

"We know," I say soothingly.

"It's just," Eliza cuts in, "we heard from Brad Bradley—"

"You're going to listen to that two-faced, backstabbing wannabe? Jeez, did he tell you about that Kids' Choice Awards incident? Because I can explain that! I didn't mean to cut a lock of Layla's hair off—I just had scissors in my hand, and I slipped onto the red carpet, and in panic, I accidentally snipped. A perfectly innocent mistake that could have happened to *anybody*!" she says.

Okay, but it's not an accident if Louise *brought* scissors to a red-carpet event. Who does that?

368

Eliza steps protectively in front of her little brother. I can tell she's nervous.

"No, wait," Louise continues. "Did he tell you I have a shrine to Layla, made from her dirty old tissues? Because that's a lie!"

What a relief!

"It's not a *shrine*—it's just a collection!" she explains.

I'm not sure that's any better. Frank makes a gagging noise.

Louise is at fever pitch now. "You can't believe anything Brad says! He's an absolute phony. I know things about him that would make your hair curl, and I can tell you all about it. I know *everything* about what happens backstage! Between Uncle Wolfgang, all the exclusive interviews I read, and my own, er, detective skills," she says, patting her camera, "I've got the 411 on all the drama."

TO ASK LOUISE ABOUT THE ON-SET GOSSIP,
TURN TO PAGE 290.

←——→

TO ASK LOUISE ABOUT PICTURES OF LAYLA,
TURN TO PAGE 75.

369

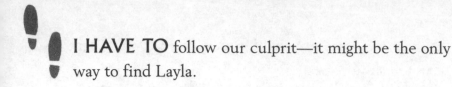

I HAVE TO follow our culprit—it might be the only way to find Layla.

"I'm so sorry, Eliza," I say into the locker slit. "I'll be back for you!"

I sprint after Tuggle. She dashes through the set and—to my surprise—exits Stage Eight through the side door. We run into the studio lot. She's weaving between concrete stages, and I'm very careful to stay out of sight.

Eventually Tuggle stops at Stage Twenty-Four, which is a museum full of old props from movies that came out before Abuela was even born. Is this where Layla is hidden?

Tuggle looks around nervously before ducking inside, and I follow her. She climbs up some stairs, stands on an overhang, and seems to be looking into some sort of deep-water tank. But the tank is metal, not glass, so I can't see in. I climb after Tuggle.

"Freeze!" I say from behind her. "Step away. Is Layla in the tank?"

"Oh, no! You found me!"

"I followed you," I say, edging closer to the edge of the overhang. Tuggle steps back to let me pass through. At last I can see inside the tank, and it's filled completely with *goop*, a gooey green gunk that one TV channel likes to pour on people. Frank always laughs hysterically when they do.

But I don't see any ripples . . . or bubbles. Is Layla even in there? Tuggle is grinning at me—in a way that makes me feel like I'm an antelope at the watering hole.

"Kid, it'd be foolish to take you on when it was four on one. But one on one? Those are odds I can handle."

She runs forward and gives me the biggest shove. I fall forward into the goop tank; it sludges *everywhere*, sticky and slimy and gross. I wriggle in the tank, trying to get to the edge but the wall is too tall for me to climb. All I can do is float in the green glop.

I shouldn't have run ahead without my friends. What a mess!

CASE CLOSED.

I HIT AS many buttons as possible, and the noise is a loud disharmony of gibberish. There are bells and sirens and horns and laughter and train whistles and elevator music. All played at the same time. Frank is enjoying being the maestro of sound. He plays the buttons like a piano.

Tuggle bends over, holding her hands over her ears. Yes! All we have to do is keep playing this nonsense.

But then Tuggle stands up, holding her stomach and cackling with laughter. "What do you think you're doing? You honestly think some annoying noises are going to stop me? I've kidnapped Layla Jay, the biggest starlet in Hollywood, and you think some sound effects—*ha!*" She wheezes.

"So you admit it!" I say. "You took Layla Jay?"

"Yes. I think we both know that by now."

"Excellent!" Eliza says. "When the authorities come back—"

"I'll deny everything," Tuggle says. "*If* they ever find me. It's your word against mine."

Some sort of noise between a snort and a gasp escapes me. "But . . . you've already confessed! We heard it with our own ears!"

"Sure," Tuggle says, striding toward the side door. She slips halfway out before popping her head back in, one last time. "You know I confessed, and I know

I confessed. But without any concrete proof, who will believe you?"

CASE CLOSED.

"YOU HATE LAYLA, don't you?"

Brad's eyes flash dangerously. "I don't."

"Sure you do."

"No, I *don't*."

"Well, maybe not *hate*, but you strongly dislike her."

Brad says nothing. Just folds his arms and glares. "What, am I on trial now or something?"

"GUILTY GUILTY GUILTY!" Frank cries.

Brad blows his bangs out of his face. "All I'm saying is: everyone thinks she's sooooooo talented. She's not so great. I can perform circles around her."

Suddenly, a voice echoes across a loudspeaker system. "Brad Bradley! Report to the fitting room immediately!"

"Wonderful," Brad says sarcastically. "Guillotine is calling me. Try not to disturb too much of Layla's stuff, okay? Don't want you to get sued by the Ice Queen." And he walks out.

The second he's gone, Eliza groans. "He probably thinks I'm such an idiot." She slinks down into Layla's chair. "I don't know what's wrong with me. It was like the second I saw Brad, I just froze. But I can't help it . . . it's Brad Bradley! I can't believe I met *Brad Bradley*!"

"Yeah, and Brad Bradley could very well be guilty."

"GUILTY GUILTY GUILTY!" Frank cries again.

374

"Not Brad," Eliza says. "No way."

"You never know," I say. "We can't rule out any suspects. So where do we go from here?"

Frank raises his hand. "Crawling! Sneaking!" But I look to Eliza.

"Well, here's what we know. Layla Jay seemed to know she was about to be kidnapped. She's hidden something important in a treasure chest or lockbox, with the code two five six. We know Layla has a creepy stalker, Louise. We know Guillotine and Layla don't get along. And we know Brad . . ." She takes a deep breath like she's readying herself for the end of the sentence. "Is jealous of Layla."

That's a lot of things we found all at once. My head is spinning. For a split second, I wonder if Mom has made as much progress as we have, but then I feel guilty.

Lately Mom's been going on and on about trust and honesty. And honestly? I'm not so trustworthy right now.

"What next?" Eliza says to me, and I snap to attention. I'll worry about Mom later.

"We could question Louise or Guillotine. Or," I say, waving Layla's cryptic note in the air, "we can follow this clue."

"But, Carlos, we have no idea where Layla's chest is."

"We could start looking. We have to try."

TO QUESTION LOUISE,
TURN TO PAGE 154.

←→

TO QUESTION GUILLOTINE,
TURN TO PAGE 37.

←→

TO SEARCH FOR LAYLA'S CHEST,
TURN TO PAGE 320.

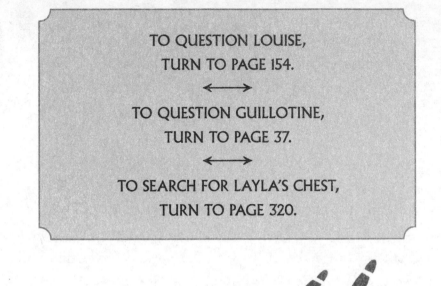

"SO, IN HER letter, Layla mentions a chest. Where do you think it is?"

"I haven't the foggiest!" Miriam says. "A chest! What . . . what do you think she's keeping in that chest?" Beads of sweat cling to her forehead and slowly drip down. "Could it help us find her? Oh, I would give *anything* to find my sweet, darling daughter!"

Tuggle's eyebrows pinch together. "How do we know this letter is verifiably from Layla? Is this her handwriting?"

"Well?" I say to Layla's mom. "Is it?"

Miriam shrugs. "How am I supposed to know?"

"For that matter," Tuggle continues, "even if it *is* Layla's handwriting, how do we know this isn't just some silly prank or practical joke?"

I just blink at her. Really? Layla writes that she's afraid she's about to be kidnapped, then she disappears, and her agent thinks it's a *prank*?

"You didn't answer their question," Mom says, tapping her fingernail on the table. "Do you, or do you not, know where Layla's chest is?"

"Not," Miriam says miserably.

"Not," Tuggle says, sitting up stiffly in her seat.

TO ASK WHO THEY THINK MIGHT HAVE KIDNAPPED LAYLA, TURN TO PAGE 33.

"WE ARE WONDERING if you have any hunches or instincts about where Layla went."

"Wish I could help," Wolfgang says. "But that's why we called in Las Pistas. There are no clues, no notes, not a single indication of where Layla has gone. If I had any idea at all, I'd be exploring it right now. Detective Serrano is our only hope."

"What about the police?" Eliza asks. "Why aren't they involved?"

"They too have nothing to go on," Wolfgang says. "The more time that passes, the more interested the police are in this case. But when we first called them, they were convinced that she just ran away from the pressures of famous life."

Suddenly, Frank slips out of his chair, plops down on the floor, and begins to rummage through drawers in Wolfgang's cabinet.

"Frank," I say warningly. But Wolfgang waves his hand. "He's fine. Don't worry. I don't keep anything valuable in there." For someone who is so condescending to kids . . . he's also kind of a warm and patient guy. Is it just an act?

"Do *you* think she ran away from the pressures of famous life?" Eliza asks, getting our questioning back on track.

"No. That girl has never missed a day of filming in

her life. Not even when she's sick. She always knows all her lines. Last week, during filming, she was even helping Brad Bradley memorize *his* lines. She shows up on set early every day and leaves late. I've never seen anyone more responsible—sometimes I think she's an adult in a kid's body." He pauses, pulls out his phone again and says, "New show idea: *Body Swappers*. Copyright Wolfgang Westover, Burbank Productions, LLC." He looks back at us. "What was I saying? Oh, right! Layla! She's completely well adjusted—she's even a straight-A student with her private tutor too."

Huh? That is the *exact opposite* of what Tuggle told us about Layla.

"Both of you look very confused," Wolfgang says. "What's going on?"

"It's just . . . Agatha Tuggle told us the opposite. She said Layla was—"

"Unreliable," Eliza jumps in. "An impulsive airhead."

Wolfgang's brow scrunches. "Tuggle said that? Why, that's off the mark! A complete mischaracterization of her client! Let me tell you something about Agatha Tuggle—she is causing so much trouble on set, pitting Layla and Brad against each other."

"Tuggle also said not to trust you," Eliza says.

Wolfgang's eyes narrow. "I think we're done here,"

he says, suddenly colder than he's ever been. "I have a lot of work to do."

Then he holds the door open for us. Eliza, Frank, and I have no choice but to leave.

In the hallway, Eliza, Frank, and I walk a loop around—through the hallway full of offices and then passing the dressing rooms, the prop room, the makeup room, the costume room, the green screen area, the robot dragon, the set built like a high-school hallway. And back around again.

The place seems empty—not a single cast or crew-member in sight. Mom too is nowhere to be seen. Which makes me nervous . . . because she could pop up at any moment. I keep looking over my shoulder. I know I'm probably paranoid, but Mom can't know we ditched our babysitter.

"I thought we could question Guillotine next—hey, what's that you're looking at, Frank?"

"A lockbox."

Eliza frowns. "Where'd you get a lockbox?"

"I stole it."

"Where'd you steal it, Frank?" I ask, even though I know exactly what he's going to say.

"From Wolfgang Mozart," he replies.

"Wolfgang Westover," Eliza corrects, while I groan. "What's inside?" she adds.

"I dunno. Haven't opened it yet."

"Then why'd you steal it?" I say.

Frank shrugs.

I sigh and take the box from him. It's smooth and wooden. On the side of the box, there seems to be a keyboard. And on the top, there are four slots with a tiny light underneath each one. The first slot is blank, and the light isn't on. The second, third, and fourth ones have the letters E, S, and T with a glowing green light underneath.

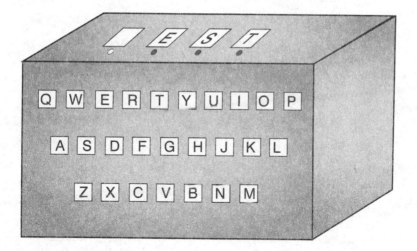

"Green for go," I whisper. So it seems like we only need to figure out the first letter of the password. The problem is, there are a lot of four-letter words I can think of that end in E-S-T.

Eliza hums thoughtfully. "We should make a list of

all the blank-E-S-T words we can think of."

"Like *BEST*!" Frank says.

"Yes, that's one!" Eliza says proudly.

"And *CHEST*!" Frank says.

"No, Frankie. That's not right. Four-letter words only."

"*SHEST!*" Frank cries.

"That one isn't even a word," I say. I turn to Eliza. "Should we start plugging in random letters? Trial and error?"

"I wouldn't do that," Eliza says. "We don't know if this box has a fail-safe device. If we plug in the wrong answer, maybe it would self-destruct or release some sort of alarm. We better play it safe."

"How?"

"If we can list all the possible solutions, we can make a more educated guess to determine which word would most likely be Wolfgang's password."

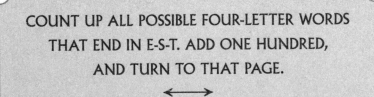

COUNT UP ALL POSSIBLE FOUR-LETTER WORDS
THAT END IN E-S-T. ADD ONE HUNDRED,
AND TURN TO THAT PAGE.

⟵⟶

OR TO ASK ELIZA FOR HELP, TURN TO PAGE 107.

IF WE JUMP up and down on the elevator, maybe we can get it to jam. I start hopping up and down, and the elevator jiggles. Frank joins in, while Eliza grips the side, and the elevator wobbles wildly.

"What are you doing?" Tuggle says sharply.

I don't answer—I just keep jumping.

"Stop that!"

Tuggle lunges at me to make it stop. Got to keep jumping—

Snap!

The sound of elevator cables breaking—we go plunging straight down the shaft.

CASE CLOSED.

WE HAVE TO run after her. We can't let her out of our sight.

Miriam runs as fast as she can in her high-heeled shoes, but she's no match for Frank's boundless energy. He catches up to her quick, with Eliza and me trailing right behind.

She heads toward the set, but it's empty. Everyone must have evacuated from the car wreckage. Miriam races toward the door. But suddenly, she flies to the side—the papers in her hands flutter in the air and scatter everywhere. Miriam soars across the set—and crashes against the wall. She does not move.

"What was *that*?" I shout, while Eliza grabs Frank by the shirt and yanks him back.

With Miriam out of our line of sight, I can see the giant robot dragon powered up, flashing different lights, red eyes glowing, its tail whipping around. But we are just out of range.

"But . . . who's controlling the dragon?" Eliza asks.

"COME OUT, COME OUT, WHOEVER YOU ARE!" Frank yells.

The chest of the dragon opens, and the person at the controls is a tiny woman, with big round glasses, a tight bun, and three pens sticking out of her hair.

"You?"

"Me," Tuggle says, taking a smack at us with the

384

dragon. She just narrowly misses crushing Eliza to a pulp.

"Where is Layla?"

Tuggle opens the other side of the dragon's chest, and *there*, next to her, is a too-still Layla. "If you care what happens to Layla, don't run."

"What are you doing?"

"I need those papers," she says. "And I need *you*."

"Us?" Eliza says, surprised. "Why us?"

"Because you know too much. Because you put the puzzle pieces together faster than I ever could have imagined."

Did we? Because I have no idea what she's talking about. "I don't understand . . . you crashed the car into the studio?"

"I had to get this place to clear out somehow."

"*You* kidnapped Layla?"

"I thought we'd been over this already," she says impatiently.

"But why?"

"I think I know," Eliza says, and she grabs my arm. "Carlos, she's right—we *do* have the puzzle pieces. The note we found in the cauldron—from Miriam to a mystery person? Meet our mystery person."

"You took money out of Layla's bank account and gave it to Miriam?"

"Miriam is her legal guardian. She has a right. Besides, she said she was going to use it on lessons and outfits to make Layla Jay the biggest kid star since Natalie Wood."

"Who's that?" Frank asks.

"I don't care if Miriam took that money to buy Layla a pony—it's still Layla's money!" I say.

"Everything suddenly makes sense," Eliza says grimly, "about how *nothing* made sense."

"You're not even making sense now!" Frank cries.

"I mean . . ." Eliza looks up at Tuggle. "Wolfgang Westover told Carlos's mom that you were causing all sorts of unnecessary drama on set, on behalf of your client. And then you told us that Layla was irresponsible and flighty, when Wolfgang said exactly the opposite. So . . . it's more than just money. You're purposely doing a bad job for your client."

Tuggle frowns. "I've known that Layla's been unhappy with my representation for a few months now . . . ever since she found out that I was feeding her mother money and didn't intervene when she was having issues with her director and her costar. I found out Layla was shopping around for another agent. She is my agency's main source of income. I need her to stay afloat. I . . . I tried to delay her from switching by tanking her reputation. So other agents

386

wouldn't want to work with her."

"That's terrible—*you're* terrible."

"I thought I could convince her to stay." Her expression darkens. "I thought wrong." The dragon's tail swipes toward us again. And I can feel Tuggle itching to be done with us. Any moment now, that dragon is going to attack. And from what I can remember about when Layla's character, Aurelia, battles it on the show . . . it breathes fire.

"When Layla came to me a few days ago wanting to terminate her agent agreement, she told me she was planning to besmirch my business and my reputation. . . . She was going to drag my name through the mud! And I couldn't have that. I needed to convince her to stay with me or keep her mouth closed . . . or both. This little . . . *action* was born out of necessity. You don't understand. My reputation is everything to me. If that's gone, I won't make a dime in this industry."

"Good," I say. "You don't deserve it."

Tuggle scowls. "Enough talk! Bring me the papers. I have to get rid of any kind of evidence that Layla and I weren't on the best terms."

Eliza grabs my arm and whispers. "We're evidence now. She's going to want to get rid of *us*."

I have to stop Tuggle—and fast!

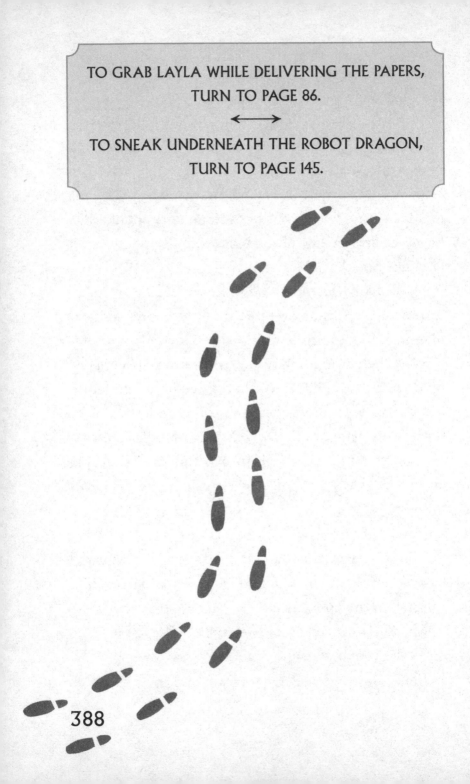

TO GRAB LAYLA WHILE DELIVERING THE PAPERS,
TURN TO PAGE 86.

⟵——⟶

TO SNEAK UNDERNEATH THE ROBOT DRAGON,
TURN TO PAGE 145.

388

ELIZA'S RIGHT; IF Miriam is here, we should talk to her directly. We slip back inside Stage Eight and walk around the classroom scene they're currently trying to film—with Brad Bradley and a bunch of the *Teen Witch* side characters.

It's actually easy to find Miriam, because she's right behind the camera people and Guillotine and the throng of crew members crowded around the area. Miriam is in the back, where the cauldrons are. She's peering—headfirst—into the large cauldron.

I wonder if she's looking for a reply to the letter she left yesterday. Or maybe she already has her reply.

"Looking for this?" I say softly.

She yanks her head up fast, like she's been caught doing something naughty. I wave the secret code in her face, and she pretends to be confused. Miriam Jay is a pretty good actress—I guess Layla had to get it from somewhere.

"And what is that you have?" She goes to snatch it, but I pull my hand back.

"Snooze you lose!" Frank gloats.

"We saw you leave it there yesterday," Eliza says. "And we've decoded it. We know that you're stealing money out of Layla's bank account. And this is proof."

Miriam scowls. "Proof? You've got *nothing*." She tosses an open bottle of potion at us, and the liquid starts smoking the second it makes contact with our clothes and skin.

It sizzles on my hand. "OUCH!"

"YOW!" Eliza howls.

"IT BUUUUUURNS!" Frank yells, so loudly that Guillotine has to yell "Cut!"

But that's the least of my worries. "The paper!" I cry. The potion is reacting with it, and it's shriveling up into nothing. By the time Guillotine comes over, it's gone.

"You!" Guillotine snaps. Miriam is grinning behind the director. "That was a *perfect* take. Perfect! A one-in-a-million kind of take! And now it's ruined! I—I'll ruin you!" Guillotine chases us out of Stage Eight with the rest of the burning potion—he's right on our tails, sloshing the bubbling, burning liquid all over—and we can't stop until we're safely beyond the studio gates, out of his reach.

CASE CLOSED.

THE LAST GEAR has to turn counterclockwise. I stick the pen in *right* where it will do maximum damage. The gears stop turning.

There's a splutter that is unmistakably the sign of a robot powering down. We've done it!

I crawl out from under the robot as fast as I can. Tuggle has climbed down from the control pit, leaving Layla behind. For a moment, Tuggle just stares at me through her round glasses, looking more frightened than evil.

Then she runs.

TO CHASE HER OUTSIDE, TURN TO PAGE 464.

←——→

TO TACKLE HER TO THE GROUND,
TURN TO PAGE 193.

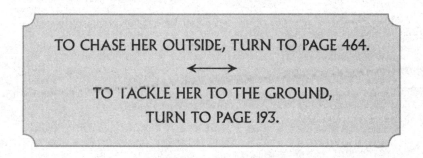

391

"WHY DID YOU start the fire?"

"Are you insane?" Wolfgang says. "This set cost a few hundred thousand dollars and took months of work! I would never torch my own production!"

"Then you got someone to set the fire for you," I accuse.

Wolfgang scrunches his eyebrows in a very confused-looking expression. "Now I *know* you're playing make-believe. The studio would murder me—I'd be blacklisted from Hollywood. I don't understand what you're getting at."

Now *I'm* confused. "You had to have started the fire!" I shout. "We were getting too close to Layla, and you needed to get us to evacuate!"

"There's an easy way to settle this," Eliza says. "We need your alibi, Mr. Westover. Where were you when the fire started?"

Wolfgang's eyes dart between Eliza, Frank, and me. "That's none of your business," he whispers.

Very suspicious.

ASK WOLFGANG WHY HE KIDNAPPED LAYLA.
TURN TO PAGE 175.

I CAN'T TELL Mom the truth. She'd be angry at me for investigating, and she'd take me off the case for sure. The problem is, she has proof: Eliza's notebook. I have to explain it somehow. . . .

"No, Mom, of course we haven't been investigating," I say. "This is just stuff we made up. We're writing a fake story using real people."

Mom squints at me far too long. Her face is blank, and I can't tell whether she believes me. "Follow me," she says at last, ushering us into the parking lot. And in two minutes, Mom has hooked me up to a bunch of wires and some weird machine.

"What is this?" I ask.

"A polygraph."

Eliza gasps. "Carlos . . . it's a lie-detector test."

Uh-oh. I'm a sitting duck.

"Can I go next?" Frank says. "This looks FUN!"

Mom smiles. "I always keep one with me, just in case. I never dreamed I'd be using it on my own son, though."

The machine starts beeping.

"Now, Carlos," Mom says calmly. "Tell me. Were you investigating Layla's disappearance today?"

"No," I say quickly, but the needles of the machine move up and down, betraying my verbal answer.

Mom smiles grimly. "We're off to the hotel to pack

your bags. I'm sending you three to Abuela's house while I solve this one on my own."

This is so unfair. I want to argue, but I know—from Mom's expression and her firm tone of voice—that she has her mind made up. "Will you at least tell us what you find?"

"No," Mom says. "I don't associate with liars. And that's the truth."

CASE CLOSED.

"I CAN'T BELIEVE Layla would say that to you," I say soothingly. "After everything you've done for her!"

"Right?" Tuggle says. "*I'm* the victim here!"

I resist the urge to roll my eyes.

"She was going to fire me," Tuggle says. "My little boutique agency would have a hard time without her. She's our major source of income. Maybe I could survive if Layla left . . . but she was going to give me bad press. She was going to collapse my world."

"Why?" I say, trying to hide the eagerness in my voice.

"She found out I was taking a little side cash from the production company."

"Money that should have been Layla's?"

"It's not like Layla isn't filthy rich!" Tuggle says. "I *needed* the money. She didn't. My company needed a bailout, while her star was soaring! I mean, if you think about it, Layla owes me. It's because of me that she even has a name in Hollywood. *I* made her famous." She scowls, and the bitterness radiates off her. She is unraveling. "I did everything for her. I worked my hindquarters off! Ungrateful little brat!" she says. "The least she could do is keep her mouth shut. The least she could do is not tank my company."

One thing from the joint interview we did with Tuggle and Miriam comes floating back to me: Miriam had said Tuggle was getting awfully chummy with Brad Bradley. And Tuggle had said she was trying to solve the fights between Layla and Brad on set. But now that I know she's a liar. . . .

"You weren't smoothing over fights between Layla and Brad, were you?"

Tuggle tilts her head, like she can't believe I'm asking the question. "Like I said, Layla was going to leave me. I needed another star."

"Who is Brad's agent?" It's a question Mom asked her, which she lied about. I know the answer now.

"As of last month? Me."

"Does Layla know?" Eliza asks.

Tuggle nods, which the microphone can't pick up. "Layla called it a betrayal, that I courted one of her rivals. But what else was I supposed to do? She already knew about the extra money and was upset . . . I could tell I was losing her. My greatest project—my top earner—was slipping through my fingers. I needed someone else."

"But Brad?" I ask.

"Brad makes a good sum, but he's not the *Teen Witch*, you know? But he could be. It was up to me to make him the star."

"But you had Layla."

"Not for long. Layla was not thrilled with my representation, but Brad was. So I had to position Brad for a lead role . . . and ruin Layla's reputation before she ruined mine. It was just a little rumor here and there. I poisoned Guillotine against her, and I was on my way to getting Wolfgang Westover to turn sour too. But then Layla found out what I was doing and confronted me."

This is sick. This is twisted. This is . . . all making sense. Tuggle's been going around saying things like Layla's flighty and irresponsible . . . and then Tuggle needed her to *be* flighty and irresponsible. It's like Tuggle created problems between Layla and her coworkers, then pretended to solve these problems in a way that painted Layla in a terrible light.

Eliza moves to the microphone to say something, but I hold my hand out. A *stop* gesture. Tuggle is on the edge. She's close . . . and we have to let her lay her own trap.

"It's not like I *hurt* her," Tuggle says. "Okay? It's not like I've done anything really wrong! I mean, I just needed a little time . . . to get Layla to agree to stay with me . . . and not to trash-talk my company publicly. Let's not blow this out of proportion. I mean, *kidnapped* is such a drastic, dramatic term."

"What would you call it?" I ask.

Tuggle throws her hands in the air. "An accident!" she cries. Eliza snorts, but luckily I've taken my hand off the mic button. "It wasn't premeditated—I didn't *mean* to do it. It happened so fast. A spur-of-the-moment mistake! A momentary lapse of judgment!"

It's not a *moment* if Layla's been missing for six days. Even if Tuggle didn't mean to do it at first, she's been keeping her hostage for almost a week now. "So you admit it?" I say. "You have Layla?"

"What are you talking about? I just told you I do!"

BINGO! We have our evidence. Eliza transfers the audio file onto my phone, and I lean forward into the mic. "That's a wrap," I say with a laugh.

"What?" Tuggle says.

"That's a wrap," I repeat. "We got everything we need. You were great, by the way. I wonder if they'll deliver your Academy Award to your prison cell." I gesture to my phone and then the microphone, and Tuggle looks whiter than a snowstorm when she realizes we've been recording this whole conversation.

She lunges for the door. "GIVE ME THAT PHONE!" she snarls as she grabs my arm and wrenches it.

"GET OFF ME!" I try to wriggle out of her grip, but she's got me tight. Her nails dig into my arm, and she's squeezing me like I'm made of Play-Doh.

The door is open, but she's blocking the exit. I can't get around her. Especially not while she's turning my arm into mince meat.

"Go, Frank, go!" Eliza says, and he's so small that he slides under Tuggle's arm without even having to duck. Eliza tries to follow her brother, but Tuggle flings out her other arm to stop her.

"NO!" Tuggle says, slamming the door on my arm. I hear a sickening crack—and feel a sharp pain. But the door pops back open, thanks to my bone.

Tuggle doesn't notice. Her eyes are on the prize: my phone in Eliza's hands. We have to get rid of it.

"Frank! Go long!" I cry, and Eliza throws the phone.

For a second that feels like forever, the phone arches in the air, and Frank runs toward it, arms outstretched. . . .

Please don't drop it! *Please don't drop it!*

He catches it, and he runs out of the sound booth. I don't know where the cast and crew are, or where Mom is, or where Frank's headed—but he can run faster than any of us. And by the time Tuggle even turns around, he's out of sight.

Defeated, she lets go of my throbbing arm. It's over.

One hour later . . .

"Your radius saved the day," Eliza says, as a paramedic is wrapping up my arm. They're treating me on set.

"My . . . what?"

"Your radius! It's the forearm bone that runs from your elbow to your thumb."

I grin, even though my arm is throbbing. "That should be our new slogan: 'I'll give an arm and a leg for your case!'"

"Speak for yourself," Eliza says with a playful nudge.

"Plus you still have a leg!" Frank says, his mouth full of chocolate. He reaches into his giant stash and rips another bar open with his teeth. "Anyone want my reward candy?"

"It's all yours," I say. "You deserve it."

"That's true, I'm amazing!"

After Frank ran out of the sound booth with my phone, the set was still empty. And Frank did the absolute best thing he could have done: he used the phone to call my mom.

Where were Mom, the cast, and the crew? While we were talking to Louise, Wolfgang Westover had shown everyone the ransom note that had been left this morning. Everyone then left the studio to drop off the ransom and pick up the hostage. But this "exchange" was all a hoax. Tuggle had left a message to lure everyone away from the set, so she could get Layla away without anyone interfering. If we hadn't stayed behind, I don't know *what* would have happened.

When Mom got the call from Frank, she came right away, with the police and the paramedics. And she bought Frank fifteen candy bars from the vending machine and called them his reward for doing the right thing.

Positive reinforcement makes Frank even more unbearable.

"Nothing beats my sweet treats, how I love to EAT!" he sings.

"You should get him to a hospital," the paramedic tells Mom, as she examines me. "That arm is broken. He needs a real cast, not a splint."

Mom is beside herself. "Are you okay, does it hurt, are you all right, I'm so sorry."

"I'm fine."

"I'm so sorry," Mom says for the millionth time. "I really tried to find you three before I left the studio, but we were all in such a rush to get to Beverly Hills for the ransom drop-off. I shouldn't have left you alone. I thought you'd be safe here."

"Don't worry, Ms. S," Eliza says. "Broken bones actually grow back stronger."

"See that?" I manage to smile without wincing, which is a big feat, considering. "I want you to know we have your back."

"Really? Because I thought you lent me a hand," Mom says, and Eliza, Frank, and I all groan. "How would you three like to lend me a hand again on my next case?"

"Detectives don't usually ask questions they already know the answer to!" I tease, and Mom kisses the top of my head.

There's no sign of Layla yet, but it should be any minute now. . . .

See, with her confession taped, Tuggle had no choice

but to lead us to Layla, who was hidden in the studio—underground, in a place that no one, not even Wolfgang Westover, knew about.

At last, the police come swarming onto set with Layla in their arms. She blinks slowly, like she's unused to being under all the lights. I'm sure it will come back to her, though; it's like finding her sea legs.

"And these," says Wolfgang grandly, pulling Layla in our direction, "are the detectives that saved your life."

Layla grabs Mom's hand. "Thank you," she says.

"I know you want to rest, but we need you to hang tight for just a little longer," Mom says to Layla. "We'll be back soon for a debrief with you. But my son broke his arm catching your captor, and we need to get his arm in a cast right away."

I shuffle closer to Layla. "Can . . . can I ask you a favor?"

"Anything!"

"Can I have your autograph . . . for my cast?"

My cheeks get flush, but Layla simply beams. "I'll sign it ten times for you, Detective!"

CASE CLOSED.

WE HAVE TO break Layla out of the trunk!

I run toward the parking lot, just as the engine starts to rumble. The car moves into reverse—headed straight for us.

"DIVE!" I shout.

Eliza, Frank, and I all lunge out of the way, so the car doesn't run us over. I skid across the parking lot and skin my knee. But then, as we're lying on the pavement, the car rolls right through the open gate, out of the studio lot. It speeds down the street. And there's no way we'll ever catch up.

CASE CLOSED.

I WANT TO find Wolfgang Westover. Sure, we eavesdropped on his conversation with Mom, but I think we should question him ourselves.

Only . . . when we get to his office, we find a sign on his door.

> WENT TO A PRODUCERS' MEETING.
> WILL BE BACK IN THIRTY MINUTES.

I stare at the note. "So . . . thirty minutes from now? Or thirty minutes from thirty minutes ago?"

Eliza shrugs.

"Where are producers' meetings anyway?"

Eliza pulls up her map of the studio lot. "I'm guessing the building labeled 'executive offices'?"

I snatch the map from her, cross the set, and walk outside. We have to go all the way to the other end of the studio lot to get to the executive offices, a building slightly smaller than the big set stages that surround it. We walk coolly into the lobby.

"We have to see Mr. Westover," I say to the receptionist. "It's urgent."

He stares at us. "Are . . . you actors? Or his kids?"

"Yes," Frank says.

404

"Okay, follow me."

He leads us to a conference room where twelve producers are sitting around a long table. They look like they're yelling at each other. The receptionist opens the door, and we walk in awkwardly.

"What are you doing here?" Wolfgang Westover says. "I'm in the middle of an important meeting."

Suddenly, a murmur rolls through the office. "Why—look at him!"

"The perfect size."

"What a perfectly shaped head!"

"He's just what we've been looking for—for Gubernick's new show."

"Little one," a woman says to Frank, "how would *you* like to be a *star*?"

"Oh, boy, would I!" Frank says. "No, wait. Would I?"

"Of course you would," a different woman says. "We'll put your face up everywhere—you'll see your name in lights!"

"I do like lights," Frank says. He holds hands with two of the producers, and he's whisked away in a crowd of suits.

"Frank! Wait!"

Eliza and I chase after him, but one of the twelve producers steps in our way. This guy is even bigger than Wolfgang Westover, and that's saying something.

"Excuse me," he says coldly, "but this exit is for the talent only. You can't follow this way."

We're forced to go back the way we came. On the streets of the studio lot, Frank is nowhere to be found, and I have no idea which stage they've taken him into.

Frank's been discovered, and now we're stuck recovering him.

CASE CLOSED.

MY EYES GLAZE over, looking at Brad Bradley's phone password. This looks way too much like a math problem, and I'm not a math kid. I turn to Eliza, who is more excited than when the *Teen Witch* season three finale aired . . . and that's saying something.

"Isn't it exhilarating? No matter which way you add—vertically, horizontally, or diagonally—it will always add up to the same number!"

"Yes, but what number is that?"

"I can't remember," Eliza says. "But we'll figure it out together!" She bites her lip and starts filling in some more numbers.

8	3	?
1	?	9
?	7	2

"Three spots remaining, and the numbers we have left are four, five, and six."

"Why was six afraid of seven? Because SEVEN ATE NINE!" Frank shouts.

"Yes," Eliza says, "but *why* did seven eat nine?" She pauses. "Because you're supposed to have three squared meals a day."

Frank doesn't get it, but I groan.

"Here," Eliza says, passing the phone back to me. "Place four, five, and six so that each row, column, and diagonal all add up to the same number."

"But," I say, "still I don't know what that number is!"

"A little trial and error won't hurt. Sometimes that's all problem-solving is."

I take a deep breath. All I have to do is figure out where four, five, and six go. I can do this!

THE SUM OF EACH ROW, COLUMN,
AND DIAGONAL IS THE SAME NUMBER. ADD TWO
HUNDRED TO IT, AND TURN TO THAT PAGE.

←→

TO ASK ELIZA FOR ANOTHER HINT,
TURN TO PAGE 19.

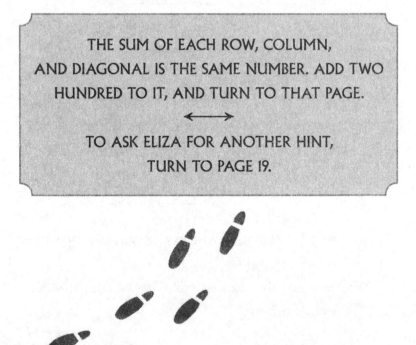

WE HAVE TO eavesdrop on Wolfgang and Mom's conversation. It's important that we know what Mom knows. Especially if we're going to investigate alongside her.

"Come on!" I whisper, putting my ear to the door. I listen closely, but Mom and Wolfgang sound muffled.

"Do you hear anything?" Eliza whispers.

"Yeah," Frank says. "Womp womp wump wump womp womp."

I groan. "We heard Miriam and Wolfgang because they were shouting. But the door's too thick to hear a conversation at normal volume. We have to get inside, or we're never going to hear anything!"

Eliza points upward. "We can climb through a vent to eavesdrop. I'm sure we'll be able to hear better with the grates instead of this pesky door."

"That could work. What do you think about crawling, Frank?" I look to my left, and he is gone. "Frank? Frank, *no*!" He is standing right by the fire alarm, his fingers curled over the lever.

Eliza's eyes bulge. "Frankie. Don't. You. Dare."

"But it's a distraction!" he says.

A distraction! That's not such a terrible idea. We could use the distraction to force Wolfgang and my mom out of this office, so they have this conversation somewhere else. Somewhere where it's easier to eavesdrop.

"Come on," Eliza says, tugging on my arm. "Let's get Frank into the vent before he does something bad."

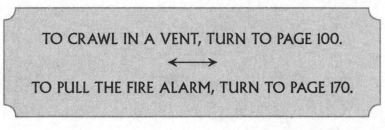

TO CRAWL IN A VENT, TURN TO PAGE 100.

←——→

TO PULL THE FIRE ALARM, TURN TO PAGE 170.

WE HAVE TO cut Miriam off. We run to the right, go out an emergency door, and—

"Where have you been?" says a stern-looking woman, walking over to us from a different soundstage: Stage Nine. "All child actors are supposed to be in lessons right now! Your tutor is waiting! You're not trying to cut school, are you?"

"We're not child actors," I say. "We're detectives—and we need to go!"

"I don't care *what* you play on TV," she says, grabbing our arms, dragging us toward Stage Nine. "You can't skimp on your education."

CASE CLOSED.

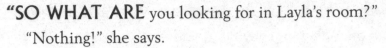

"SO WHAT ARE you looking for in Layla's room?"

"Nothing!" she says.

I squint at her. I'm attempting the tactic my mom used with Wolfgang: just let your suspect fill the uncomfortable silence with words and truth. But before Miriam says anything, Eliza pipes up. "I don't believe you. You're clearly rummaging around in here, and we need to know why."

"If you *must* know," Miriam says with a sniff, "I-I was looking for one of her scarves . . . something that smells like her. So that I could have her n-n-nearby!" She bursts into sobs.

Yeesh, Layla isn't the only one in the family who is trying for an Oscar. Miriam's performance is *so* over the top that it's hard to swallow.

TO ASK MIRIAM WHERE SHE THINKS LAYLA IS, TURN TO PAGE 78.

←——→

TO ASK MIRIAM WHY LAYLA BANNED HER FROM THE SET, TURN TO PAGE 43.

LAYLA'S FACE IS everywhere, on all sides of the green screen—the floor and the three walls. Four different Laylas, all facing each other.

She is blindfolded, and her black hair has tons of flyaways. Even though it's nighttime in the video, everything is clearly visible. Layla is sitting on a stool, with trees behind her. She is trembling and her voice is shaking, and for an actress, she sounds very monotone. Almost as if she's being forced to say these words.

"My name is Layla Jay. I'm being held captive against my will. In return for my safe release, two conditions must be met:

"One, after today, no attempt will be made to contact my captor.

"Two, a suitcase filled with one million dollars cash should be left at the corner of North Larchmont Boulevard and Melrose Avenue at ten o'clock this morning.

"I will be returned safely two hours after the ransom is collected. If you try to trace or follow or arrest my abductor, if you fail to show up with the money, if anything goes wrong with the drop-off, then . . ." Layla sobs and doesn't finish the sentence. Instead of shutting off, the video loops over again.

"Get all teams in Beverly Hills at North Larchmont Boulevard and Melrose Ave. FBI too," says a policeman into his walkie-talkie. "We have to figure out the ransom—"

He walks away.

"So, what do you think?" Wolfgang Westover asks Mom.

"It seems like the police have this under control," Mom replies.

Wolfgang looks almost disappointed. He pauses to watch all the chaos before he says, "Well, if you think of anything." And then he strolls off.

"That's it, Mom?" I say. "After all that, we just step back and let the police take care of it?"

Mom pats my head. "Carlos, the police are far better equipped to handle a ransom and hostage situation than we are. Our job is to figure out who took Layla and where she is. Not to be action heroes."

"But who took Layla? And where is she?"

"I know," Eliza says quietly.

I turn to look at her so fast that my neck cracks. "What?"

"I know where she is, and she's not in Beverly Hills. That's a decoy." Eliza points at one of the multiple videos of Layla that keeps playing on a loop. "I thought it was weird, how this was filmed. With fantastic production-quality lighting. And look at the background—"

"Trees!" Frank says.

"The woods," I realize. "This was filmed in the woods? Right here on set?"

"It's really hard to transport a hostage. There is no

way the kidnapper would be able to get Layla through the front gate without anyone noticing, especially since we're on high alert. And why would the kidnapper come here to film this ransom note unless Layla already *was* here?"

Eliza's right: if Layla really was kidnapped in the greater Los Angeles area, it wouldn't make any sense for the kidnapper to bring Layla back to the set where everyone is looking for her, it's really crowded and busy, and Layla knows her way around.

"So," Eliza continues, "if it follows that Layla is actually here on set, the only thing this ransom note accomplishes is to get everyone away from the studio. At ten o'clock—the time of the ransom drop-off—the kidnapper will be free to flee. This is all just a distraction, a decoy. Which means we have to stop these officers from going to Beverly Hills."

Mom stares at Eliza with her jaw ajar. "That's really clever, Eliza," Mom says, a note of awe in her voice. "I—I think you're right!"

"Unless," I say, and all three of them turn to stare at me. "Well . . . I was just thinking . . . the culprit might back down from their plan if everyone stays on set. They probably won't make a move unless the set clears out. And then we might *never* catch them. If the police officers go, and we stay, we might be able to discover who's behind Layla's kidnapping and stop them once and for all."

Mom hums. "An astute observation, Carlos."

I don't know what *astute* means, but it sounds good.

Mom smiles at all three of us in turn. "Okay, let's try it your way."

After all the police officers are gone, when the set is completely empty, we head to the woods to search for clues.

Leaves crunch under my feet as I bound up the hill to the spot where I know Layla was filmed—where we uncovered the chest yesterday that had the clue about Louise. As the trees thicken, Mom holds her phone up in the air and waves it around. "I don't like this at all. I don't have any cell service. Look, no bars."

At last we round the hill and arrive at the graveyard set. But my heart drops to my stomach when I see four tombstones that weren't there yesterday.

"What is this?" Mom asks, and Eliza lets loose a shaky laugh.

"Hey! That's ME!" Frank says.

There's a big rug in front of our tombstones, and we walk across it. I can't help but notice that the ground beneath the rug doesn't feel like earth at all—it feels an awful lot more solid.

I put my hand on my own tombstone and trace my name. The hair sticks up on the back of my neck. I can't think of any reason why *our* names would be on the tombstones. And these gravestones weren't here yesterday, and *are* today. Who would spend time, effort, and energy, with Layla missing, to set up these totally unnecessary tombstones? The answer comes to me instantly.

"It's a trap!" I shout, grabbing my mom's arm. "Mom! IT'S A TRAP!"

"Of course it's a trap," says a cool female voice. From behind a tree, out steps Agatha Tuggle. She's holding something in her hand—a button maybe? A remote?

My heart is thrumming, and all I can think is I have to run and get help. Or I have to tackle her to the ground—wrestle that remote thing out of her hands.

TO RUN AWAY, TURN TO PAGE 255.

←——→

TO TACKLE HER, TURN TO PAGE 287.

 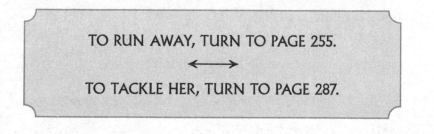

I DECIDE TO follow my gut: we have to investigate Miriam. And that means checking with the front gate to see if Miriam has arrived yet.

But first we have to ditch the babysitter.

"Do *you* see Maureen?" I say loudly.

"No!" Eliza feigns. "She's a really good hider."

"Let's search over here!"

We slip outside. Hopefully by the time Maureen realizes we're not coming to find her, she won't be able to find us. Hide and *don't* seek.

Outside, there's a teenage girl sitting on the blacktop in front of the door. The same teenage girl we saw yesterday, on our way into the studio—the one who had the sign claiming she was Layla Jay's number-one fan.

Only today she's bent over a poster board, making a sign that reads WHAT'S THE WORD ON LAYLA?

When we pass by, she stares at us. "Who are you?" she asks. Her mouth is full of braces.

"We could ask you the same question," I say.

"Louise Jenkins," she says. "My uncle is Wolfgang Westover, one of the producers, so I'm allowed to be here!" she adds defensively.

"Okay? Cool?" I say.

"We're detectives," Eliza explains. "Trying to find Layla Jay."

Her eyes bulge. "OhmygoodnessIloveLaylaJayso-much!" Louise says, like it's all one word.

"A LIKELY STORY!" Frank says, pointing his finger in her stomach.

"Sorry about him," Eliza says, pulling him away from Louise. We continue to walk toward the front gate.

"Wait!" Louise calls out after us. "Is there anything I can help with? Any way that I can help you find Layla Jay?"

I turn around. "We just need to know if Miriam Jay is on the studio lot. We . . . er . . . have some business with her."

"Oh!" Louise says, clapping her hands together. "Yeah, she arrived this morning. That's her car over there." She points to a row of cars parked along the side of the Stage Eight building. "The red one!"

Of course Miriam Jay would drive a flashy red convertible. It's like adding insult to thievery.

I walk to the car and stare into the windows. Frank follows me, only he puts his nose right up against the window. "It's full of DIRT!" Frank says gleefully, and he begins to draw smiley faces in the grime with his finger.

"Frank, no!" Eliza says. "And, Carlos, what do you think you're doing?" It's almost like she can read my mind—that's how close we are.

"I want to peek inside," I admit, cringing as I say it. I know it's breaking and entering to investigate inside her car without a search warrant or permission. But on the other hand, Layla's been missing for five days now. And if we want any shot at saving her, we may just have to bend the rules a bit.

"Come on," Eliza says. "It makes no sense to snoop through her car when we could talk to Miriam herself."

TO BREAK INTO MIRIAM'S CAR,
TURN TO PAGE 139.

←→

TO CONFRONT MIRIAM ABOUT THE NOTE IN
THE CAULDRON, TURN TO PAGE 389.

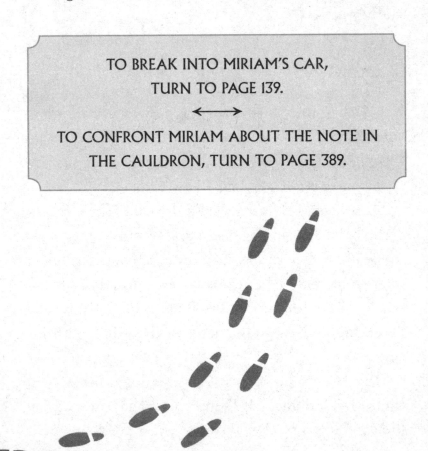

I ENTER THE code 5934. Nothing happens. Then I enter it again. And again.

"Something's wrong," I say to Eliza.

We crowd closer to the code, and Eliza shines her flashlight onto the door. I think I hear a footstep behind us. But when I turn around, I don't see anything. A shiver goes up my spine. But I have to focus on this puzzle.

"Carlos?" Eliza whispers.

"Maybe we need to press enter or something," I say.

"Carlos?"

"Or maybe we're doing it wrong."

"Carlos?"

"What?"

"Where's Frank?"

My stomach drops, and I look around, but she's right. He is gone.

Eliza moves the flashlight all around—*THWACK*. Without noise or warning, something knocks me smack in the face. My vision swims, and then goes dark. . . .

I wake up sitting on a branch. Eliza is on my right, and Frank is on my left. Eliza whimpers beside me, and Frank swings his legs casually.

"Where are we?" I whisper.

"I don't know, Carlos. It looks like some sort of jungle.

421

But it's too well lit, don't you think?"

I squint. Through the thick trees I can just make out a camera.

"Stop looking at the camera!" a voice says through a megaphone. "It ruins the effect."

"Effect of what? Please—you have to help us. We were kidnapped and need to be returned to my mom."

"That's some good fake backstory. Love it! But save it for when we're rolling film."

"No!" I shout. "You don't understand! We don't belong here."

"Of course you don't belong here!" the voice in the megaphone says. "That's the whole point of the show *Endurance*. We throw you in the jungle for a week and film it. Can you survive?"

"But—"

"Enough talk! Release the tiger! And . . . lights, camera, action!"

CASE CLOSED.

"WHERE'S LAYLA?" I shout through the locker vents.

But I don't hear a response—only some grunting and Eliza's scream, and then a locker right next to mine slamming shut.

"Eliza?"

"Carlos!" she cries. "I'm locked in!"

"You guys?" Louise says, her voice quivering. "Witch-craft, magic, hear us plead; help us in our time of need."

It's something Layla and the witch gang say on the show right before they battle the baddies . . . but I don't think it's going to help here.

"GET OFF ME, YOU VILLAIN!" Frank shouts. "I'M GOING TO BITE YOU!"

For a second, I have a glimmer of hope that Frank actually *will* bite Tuggle, but a moment later, I hear a fourth locker slam shut.

"Night-vision goggles from the prop room," Tuggle explains. "I knew they'd come in handy one day."

There's a pause, and then the lights in the studio go back on. I can see it—just barely—through the slits in my locker.

"What are you kids doing here?" Tuggle asks.

"We could ask you the same question!" I reply. "Where is Layla?"

"Safe," she says curtly.

423

"And us?" Eliza asks. "Are we safe from you?"

There's a silence, which I take to mean no.

"You ruined everything," Tuggle says at last. "Why couldn't you just leave it alone? Now you know too much. What do I do? *What do I do?*"

I have to soothe her—get her to see reason. I talk to her like she's a spooked deer. "Let us out," I say quietly. "Don't make this situation any worse. One kidnapping charge isn't as serious as five kidnapping charges. You have to fess up."

She laughs gruffly. It's more like a short bark. "My life is over," she says. "After this, there's no coming back. There's only one way out. And that's to make sure Layla obeys me, and you four disappear."

"What do you mean by *disappear?*" I ask with a gulp.

"I think you know exactly what it means," Tuggle says. "You're smart kids, so don't play dumb."

Is it just me, or is the air a little thinner in here? I can barely breathe.

"We have a right to know why," Eliza says. "Why did you do this?"

"I—I didn't mean to!" Tuggle whispers. "It all happened so fast! Layla . . . she said she wanted to leave me. The agency—we'd crumble without her. She's our star client! I didn't want to lose my business."

"Oh!" Louise gasps. "I overheard you and Layla fighting about her contract. Is this why?"

"Yes, Layla wanted to cancel it."

"Why?" Eliza asks.

"She . . . she found out about the kickbacks I was taking from the studio."

"Kickbacks?" I ask.

Tuggle clears her throat. I can tell she's uncomfortable, but she plows on like she needs to get this off her chest. Guilty conscience syndrome. "It costs a lot of money to run a business. I just needed extra cash flow . . . a little money, off the record, that wouldn't get accounted as Layla's income."

"Why would Wolfgang agree to that?" Eliza asks.

"I told him that's what Layla demanded, but on the condition that it was secret. That way I could get extra help, and Layla wouldn't need to know about it. It wasn't supposed to be forever . . . it was just for a little bit. But Guillotine blabbed to Layla about the arrangement, and next thing I know, Layla is firing me." Tuggle lets out a strangled cry, and suddenly her voice sounds nasty and twisted. "But I *made* her. She was nothing before me. *I* got her commercials, *I* got her auditions, that ungrateful little brat." There's a pause, and then Tuggle says, sweetly, "Is it so wrong that I needed a little extra time to convince her to stay with me? Is it a crime to want to keep my star client?"

"It is when you kidnap her!" Eliza says, aghast.

"You tore the prop room apart," I say.

"I had to. I can't find Layla's copy of the termination papers—the document she used to dismiss me. It's the only evidence that could possibly incriminate me."

"And you destroyed all the cameras? Why?"

"I couldn't keep my eye on you three and Detective Serrano at the same time. I needed to keep this confined, under control. I couldn't have you running all over the place snooping through whatever, and her finding out anything she could from people who know Layla well. Or finding that termination notice before I did. Smashing those cameras was the only way to stop everyone in their tracks and buy me more time. That's all I ever wanted—more time." She bangs her fist on my locker, and the clang echoes loudly in my ears. Ouch.

"If I don't have Layla," Tuggle cries, "my whole career is destroyed. I tried to see if I could get Brad instead. I thought maybe—just maybe—if I could replace Layla with another star, I could keep my agency and reputation afloat. But he only seemed interested in dating my client. Wanted me to put pressure on her. I realized he lacks star power. He is no Layla Jay."

"Where. Is. Layla?" It feels like the millionth time I've asked.

"Here," Tuggle admits. "On the studio lot. I hid her here, so I could have plausible deniability if she was found."

"So," I say, jiggling the locker door to no avail. "What now?"

"I can't allow you to go," Tuggle says. "For me, the only way out is to cover up this whole inconvenient ordeal. If I can convince Layla to stay with me . . . one last shot with her . . . but if she still refuses . . . and well, you four, obviously I have to . . ."

I don't like the way she trails off. Not one bit.

"I'm very sorry. I have to go. I'll be back. Look, kids, if I can think of a way out, I will take it. I don't *want* to go through with it. But if I have to, I promise, it'll be painless."

"What will be painless?" I ask, my stomach twisting as her footsteps get farther away. "*What* will be painless? WHAT WILL BE PAINLESS?"

But I'm met with silence.

"Eliza," I say, when I'm sure Tuggle is gone. "We have to escape these lockers . . . quickly!"

"I don't know how," she replies. "I'm locked in!"

"Me too."

"Me three," says Louise.

"I'm not!" Frank says. Suddenly, his voice is right outside my locker, and when I look through the vent, there are his shoes.

"Wait, what? Frank, you could have escaped this whole time?"

"Yup!" he said. "The back of my locker was loose. I pushed it out."

"Why haven't you escaped already?"

"I was playing dead. Like a possum. Or was it opossum? Opossum blossom! I play dead, and whatshername doesn't pay attention to me. She pays attention to you."

"Wow, Frank," Eliza marvels. "That's actually pretty smart."

"Of course it is," he boasts. "I'm the SMART Thompson, and don't you forget it!"

I push on the back of my locker, and Frank's right—it's a little wobbly. So I push it harder, and with a loud clang it smashes open. "It's a prop. It's fake! Come on out, Eliza! Louise!"

Louise pushes the back of her locker out too, and crawls out. But Eliza doesn't move.

"I think mine's stuck!" she says. Frank, Louise, and I go to the back of Eliza's locker and start to pull.

"Push!" I cry to Eliza.

"I'm trying!"

But it just won't budge. Just our luck that Eliza is the only one sealed in tight. Without the combination to the lock or some kind of metal-melting power tool, there's no way to get her out.

I look over my shoulder, down the hall. I know I should probably bust Eliza out, but Tuggle ran to deal with Layla. If I follow her quickly, I might get to Layla in time.

"If you have to go, then go," Eliza says, reading my mind. "But if you're going to stay and help me out, I think I know how you can break me free."

TO BREAK ELIZA OUT OF THE LOCKER,
TURN TO PAGE 281.

←——→

TO FOLLOW TUGGLE ALONE, TURN TO PAGE 370.

429

I HAVE TO call Mom. She's our only hope right now.

I dial her number as I hear Eliza get pushed into a locker. Come on, phone—work with me here! But the cell reception is truly awful. It's not even ringing.

Frank yells as he's put in his locker. I wave my phone frantically around my locker. I *have* to get cell service . . .

Finally, in the top left corner of the locker, I've hit the spot! The phone rings and rings. Pick up, Mom! But she doesn't pick up. It's her voice mail. "This is Cat Serrano. Please leave a message after the beep." *BEEP.*

"Mom, please pick up the phone!"

Tuggle curses and fumbles with my locker door. I have seconds left. "We're at the studio! The kidnapper is—"

The locker opens, and Tuggle snatches the phone out of my hands, smashes it on the ground so hard it shatters, and drags me out of the locker.

"You sneaky little brat," she says to me. The lights are back on, and I am face-to-face with Tuggle. And I expect her to look evil and snarling . . . but she just seems nervous. Her hands are shaking. "I was going to leave you kids in here while I figured out what to do with you and Layla. But now I see you are way too resourceful to be left alone."

She drags me to the prop room, pulls my hands

behind my back, and throws some prop handcuffs on my wrists. Then she tapes my mouth closed. She does the same to Eliza, Frank, and Louise—one by one—and when we're all cuffed and muffled, she shuffles us into a van. She leaves for a few minutes and comes back with Layla, whose eyes are wide in panic. We're all in the van together now, but we all are in need of rescuing.

The car starts, and Tuggle drives the five of us for hours. I can't move, can't escape. When the van finally stops, she opens the back doors. I gasp. We're in some sort of snowy tundra. Alaska, maybe? Or Canada? But it seems even colder than that. Is it possible to drive to the North Pole?

"Wh-where are we?" I shiver.

"Somewhere no one will ever find us," she says, shoving us all into an igloo. "We'll stay cool while the investigation is hot. You'll all learn to enjoy the simple life of ice fishing, polar-bear dodging, and ice-floe surfing. It's like a vacation . . . only forever."

CASE CLOSED.

"ELIZA, THIS LOCK is too hard! I need your help!"

"Well, I'm a little preoccupied, being stuck inside a locker," Eliza says, "but I'll try to help." I slide the paper back through the vent. "It's so hard to see in here. But . . . hmm . . . ," she says, and I know the gears of her super-smart brain are turning. "I think we should start with what we definitely know. Look at the fourth clue: All of these numbers are incorrect."

She slips the paper back to me, and I see what she's talking about. "So if eight, five, and four aren't in the combination at *all* . . . then you can cross them out wherever you see them."

Code to lock: XXX

3 5̸ 9 One of these numbers is correct and in the correct spot.

3 0 2 One of these numbers is correct but in the wrong spot.

2 9 7 Two of these numbers are correct but in the wrong spot.

8̸ 5̸ 4̸ All of these numbers are incorrect.

4̸ 1 8̸ One of these numbers is correct but in the wrong spot.

432

"Great," Eliza says. "Now you know, if you look at the last clue, the number one is definitely part of the code. But not in the middle spot. So it's either the first or last number in the code."

"Cool!" I say.

"Wow!" Louise says.

"Yawn!" Frank says.

"Next . . . I think we should look at the first two clues. Because the first two are a paradox."

"Pair of rocks?" Frank says.

"No, paradox. It means inconsistent, contradictory. So, in the first clue, it says one of the numbers is correct and in the right spot. And in the second clue, it says one of the numbers is correct but in the wrong spot. So . . . since the three is in the first spot in both of those, we know that the number three isn't a number in the code."

"Why not?"

"Because," she explains, "the number three can't be in the right spot and the wrong spot at the same time. That's a—"

"Bear of socks!"

Louise snorts with laughter, and Eliza mumbles, "Close enough."

We're getting close to cracking the code—I can feel it. "If the number three is out, and we've already crossed out five because of the fourth clue, then the first clue tells us that the number nine is correct and in the correct spot. And!" I say excitedly, before Eliza can jump in. "Since we knew that the number one was either in the first spot or last spot, we can definitely confirm that the number one is first."

"One blank nine," she confirms. "We're just missing that middle number."

Code to lock: 1X9

~~3~~ ~~5~~ 9   One of these numbers is correct and in the correct spot.

~~3~~ 0 2   One of these numbers is correct but in the wrong spot.

2 ~~9~~ 7   Two of these numbers are correct but in the wrong spot.

8 5 4   All of these numbers are incorrect.

~~4~~ 1 ~~8~~   One of these numbers is correct but in the wrong spot.

"Last piece of the puzzle," Eliza says thoughtfully, mulling over the last steps. She sends the paper my way again through the locker vent—we're playing an endless game of pass the puzzle. "The key to figuring out that last number is the third line down. It's most illuminating. Two of the numbers in the third clue are correct. We already know nine is correct. So the other correct number is either two or seven."

"Right," I say. "But either two or seven could be the middle number. Unless . . ." My eyes drift up to the second clue. There is only one number that would make clue two and clue three true. Only one number they have in common. . . . Eliza! I think I've cracked it!"

THE CODE TO THE LOCKER IS YOUR
NEXT PAGE NUMBER.

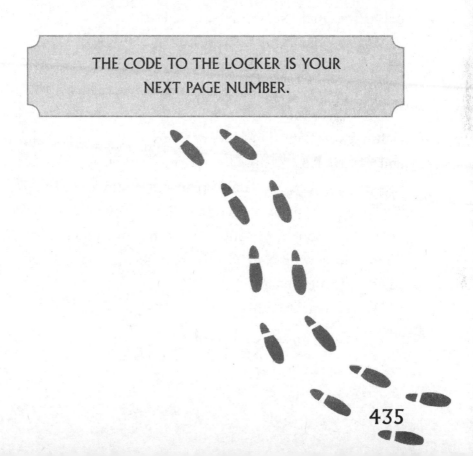

I DON'T CARE what Eliza thinks—we have to go after her.

I'm almost certain Tuggle ran in the direction of the writers' room and the broken freight elevator, so I drag Eliza and Frank to that corner of the studio.

Suddenly, the freight elevator doors open. So much for it being out of order! Staring us in the face is a loader—one of those construction trucks that scoops things up.

Tuggle is in the driver's seat, and the person in the passenger seat is bundled up tight and wearing a ski mask. Ten bucks says I know who it is.

Tuggle looks at us disbelievingly. She blinks slowly twice, with a nervous expression on her face, but then it changes to steely resolve. She drives toward us.

"RUN!" I shout.

But it's too late. The loader scoops us off the ground, and the truck backs up. Down the freight elevator, onto the ground floor . . . Tuggle picks up steam and drives like a maniac out of the studio. There's nowhere for us to run—it's too dangerous to move out of the scooper. She could run us over. So we huddle together, doing the only thing we can . . .

We keep on trucking.

CASE CLOSED.

WHEN WE'RE DONE outlining the underdeveloped parts of Louise's photograph, my mouth drops. The shadowy silhouette behind Layla is clearly a woman—and there's the outline of a bun, with pens or pencils sticking out of it.

"Tuggle," I say. "Agatha Tuggle."

"What?" Eliza says.

"He said, 'Tuggle! Agatha Tuggle!'" Frank shouts.

"I heard him the first time!"

"Then why'd you say, 'What?'" Frank complains.

"Layla was running when you took this?"

Louise nods. "But I didn't realize she was running away from something, or I would have handed in the picture earlier, I promise!"

Things are starting to click. In the coded note we found in Layla's desk, she knew she was going to be kidnapped. Layla knew it couldn't be Louise, because she was running from someone (behind her) and bumped into Louise (in front of her). Which means that Layla must have led us to Louise, hoping that Louise would have caught her *other* stalker on camera.

And Tuggle—she had been up and down the studio, telling everyone that actors were flighty and fickle. She had been saying that Layla's disappearance was no big deal—that it was nothing. Well, of course she would say that. She was trying to stop people from looking for Layla!

My head is spinning, and when I look at Eliza, I can see the wheels turning in her head too. Her gray eyes flash.

I hold the photos out to Louise. "Thanks for your help. Please keep that photo safe for now. And don't tell anyone about it."

She silently takes the photos back.

"We should go tell your mom," Eliza says.

"Absolutely."

We head into the studio, but I gasp when I walk inside. The place is empty. Not even a ghost would set up town in here.

"Hello?" I call.

"HELLO HELLO HELLO!" Frank calls. "ECHO ECHO ECHO!"

"Where is everyone?" Eliza whispers, huddling closer to me.

I know we have our group of prime suspects, but the set has always been crowded with, like, a hundred other people. Without them here, everything is creepy. The lights above us seem creaky, and the lockers give me the shivers. Out of the corner of my eye, I spot something moving in the hall, but by the time I whip my head, it's a shadow. A person-shaped shadow.

"H-hello?" I say.

438

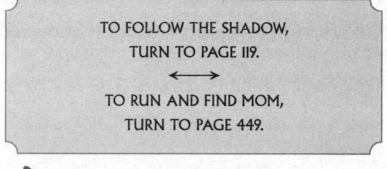

TO FOLLOW THE SHADOW,
TURN TO PAGE 119.

←→

TO RUN AND FIND MOM,
TURN TO PAGE 449.

I OPEN THE side panel in the elevator and start pulling the wires out between the letters H, A, T, C, and H. Pretty much undoing all our hard work from before. But it's necessary.

As soon as I disconnect the wires, the elevator jolts. It stops dead.

"What did you do?" Tuggle says, panicked.

"I stopped the elevator."

"Start it up again," she demands.

"No."

Tuggle screams in frustration. She paces the elevator so fast that it shakes on its cables. Then she grabs Eliza and turns to me with an angry snarl on her face. "I'm going to kill her!"

Eliza whimpers, but somehow she remains very, very still.

"Go ahead," I bluff, and I manage to keep my voice from wobbling. "But you'll be stuck in here with her body—and then my body, and Frank's body, assuming you want to get all three of us. And when the police rescue you from this elevator, you can add three murders to your kidnapping charge. I'm sure a jury would love that."

Tuggle throws Eliza at me, and I catch her. Eliza wraps her arms around me.

"Hey! She's *my* sister!" Frank says, wiggling his way into our hug.

Tuggle runs a hand through her hair, trying to smooth her bun. Then she slips around me and plays with the emergency box, trying to get the elevator started again. She has no idea where the wires need to go, and I'm not telling.

I don't know how long we sit in a corner together, watching her. But suddenly I hear a *thump* on top of the elevator. Tuggle and I both freeze and watch the ceiling . . . a square becomes dislodged, and someone is reaching their hands in.

The fire department!

"Stay calm," a man says. "We're here to rescue you. Come on, kid, you first."

"No," I say. "Take her first. She's Layla Jay's kidnapper. I don't trust her on her own."

"I . . . I don't . . . these wild accusations . . . I need an attorney," Tuggle mumbles.

The firefighters reach in to grab her. At first she struggles and wiggles and thrashes, but when it's clear the firefighters have a firm grip on her, she goes boneless and limp. And then she's gone.

After Tuggle is out, the firefighter reaches for Frank, then Eliza, then me.

When he brings me back to the studio floor, I'm surprised by the crowd of people. But before I can take stock of who's there, Mom rushes at me, red as a beet.

"I knew something was wrong when I couldn't find

you on set!" she says. "Thank goodness Frank left his shoe. It was the perfect bread crumb."

"We found Layla, Mom."

Mom calls Wolfgang and the fire chief over. "Where is she?"

"She's in the sub-basement."

"The *what*?" Wolfgang says.

"Haven't you ever wondered where the elevator goes?" Eliza asks.

"That old thing has been broken since I started working here—since before you kids were even born. I've never even touched it."

"Well, it works. And it goes to a basement," I explain. "And that's where you'll find Layla. Alone now. She's okay, I think."

"GO GO GO!" the fire chief says, and they all start rappelling down the elevator cables.

Meanwhile, a police officer clicks handcuffs on Tuggle and recites her Miranda rights. "You have the right to remain silent, anything you say can and will be used against you in a court of law. . . ."

Mom grips my shoulder. "I don't know how to feel about this, Carlos."

I look down at my shoes. "Are you going to take me off future cases?"

"I was serious when I let you help me investigate.

But, hijo, it's always more important to me that you are safe. You were lucky—something really bad could have happened to you. Next time, we'll have to have an emergency plan in place. And we'll have better communication, right from the start. I'll share everything—but that means you have to share everything with me. This is a two-way street."

I can hardly breathe. I look at her, and I'm sure the eagerness is written all over my face. "Next time?"

"You heard me."

I wrap my arms around her and bury my face in her neck.

An hour later, Stage Eight is hopping. Wolfgang Westover has brought in a bunch of reporters, and he's setting up a press conference.

Layla doesn't look too happy about it. "It's not like I have a choice," she whispers as she powders her face. "Wolfgang Westover pays my bills."

She turns to me, Eliza, and Frank—her temporary bodyguards. We were assigned by Mom, who thought it'd be important for Layla to be around nonthreatening people, who are younger and smaller than her.

That's what she *said*, anyway. The real reason, I think, is that Mom knew how excited Eliza and I were to meet our favorite actress. And even more exciting?

She's talking to us like we're friends!

"You're right," I say, trying so hard not to get tongue-tied while I talk to *Layla Jay*. "I mean, Wolfgang could give you a day to recover. Kidnapping is no joke."

"How do you make a tissue dance? Put a little boogie in it!" Frank says. "Now *that's* a joke."

Layla actually laughs. "Good one!"

I can't believe she laughed at a Frank joke . . . and a gross one at that. It's crazy how she's so much like her character Aurelia in some ways: she's brave and strong. And yet . . . the more I talk with her, the more I realize how different Layla is from her character. Aurelia never would have laughed at a booger joke. I guess that's why they call it acting.

"Are you going to be okay, Layla?" I ask.

She nods as she leans close to the mirror to attach fake eyelashes. "I just have to get through this press conference, and then filming the rest of season four and then a court date, and then maybe I can sneak in another movie before a press tour for the premiere of season four, and then season five will start filming. . . ."

"That sounds nice," Eliza mumbles, still too star-struck to even look at Layla.

"Yeah," I say. "Just . . . be careful who you hire as your agent next time."

Layla stops applying her makeup and glances at all

444

of us in turn. "I hear you three were responsible for catching her. I just want to say . . . thanks."

"No problem," I say, surprised. I guess I didn't expect such sincere gratitude.

"Um . . . welcome. You're welcome. I mean, of course you're welcome, I mean, we're welcoming you, omigod, stop talking, Eliza," Eliza says, a flush rising in her cheeks.

"I'll see you guys later, okay?" Layla says, and she walks out onto the stage, greeting the press with an easy wave. She's a natural in front of a camera. Just like we're naturals behind a mystery.

This one's wrapped up nicely, and I can only hope that—as they say in Hollywood—there will be another act.

CASE CLOSED.

"SO YOU SET off that fire to stop us?" I ask.

"Well, I definitely needed a fast way to get you away from Layla . . . before you figured out where the lever was that would flip that wall around. I never imagined you'd have the firefighters knock down the wall entirely. It made me glad I spent my time in the chaos moving Layla to this room."

"And you left that door combo for us," Eliza says. "You wanted to lure us here purposely?"

"I wanted to lure all *four* Las Pistas detectives here. You see, you had information about my behavior on set—information that Mr. Westover here provided you. You told me when you were interviewing me exactly what he'd said about me."

"Right," I say. "You were causing fights between Layla and Brad. You were creating all sorts of unnecessary drama and blaming it on Layla."

"But why would you do that?" Eliza asks. "If Layla's your top client?"

"Layla was going to leave me. For a while she's been threatening—"

"Because you were the one wiring money to Miriam from Layla's bank account," Eliza says. The look on her face is the same one she gets when she cracks a puzzle. "That note we intercepted from Miriam—that was for you, wasn't it?"

"I didn't do anything illegal," Tuggle snaps. "Her

mother and I were in the right."

"Layla clearly didn't think so," I say. "Not if she wanted to leave you."

"She can't leave me . . . I would never let her. I fought back. Ruined her reputation, so that other agents wouldn't want to work with her. But that was only part of it. Your mother had the other piece of the puzzle."

"Which is?"

"Detective Serrano found out that I was working with Guillotine to get Brad Bradley his own show—a show that didn't star Layla. With Layla's show gone and her reputation ruined, only *then* would she be allowed to leave me. Because I *made* her. I *own* her."

"That's sick," Eliza says.

"I was worried what would happen when you talked—once you put all that information together. So I wanted to get you all at once. But your mother had to make it difficult."

I step closer to Tuggle. "Where is my mom? What did you do with her?"

The right corner of Tuggle's mouth lifts. She's smirking at me! "I took care of her first. And now I'm moving on to you."

I'm so afraid I can't even move. What does "took care of her" mean? I look to the walkie-talkie—I have to reach her. I have to do something. I have to get out and find Mom!

"And, um, why am I here?" Wolfgang Westover says.

"Who did I pitch the Brad Bradley spin-off show to? Who did I lodge Layla's complaints and demands with? You are the only other one who had all the pieces together—it's not my fault you were too stupid to put them together."

"Oh," Wolfgang says. "Yeah, you probably didn't need to lure me down here. I wouldn't have pieced that together."

"It's too late," Tuggle says. "You know too much." Tuggle rubs the remote in her hand menacingly, like she's going to press it. I don't know how explosives work. The only bomb I know is a stink bomb, courtesy of Frank's butt. But that's crazy—and who knows if that would even work? Maybe I should tackle Tuggle and try to wrestle the remote out of her hands. With Eliza and Frank and Wolfgang behind me, we could overtake her!

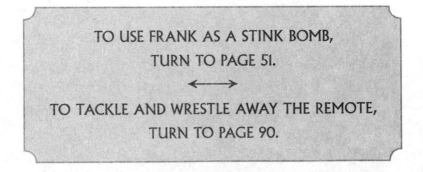

TO USE FRANK AS A STINK BOMB,
TURN TO PAGE 51.

←——→

TO TACKLE AND WRESTLE AWAY THE REMOTE,
TURN TO PAGE 90.

WE CAN'T FOLLOW some mysterious shadow! Between the scary note we got yesterday and now the disappearance of everyone in the studio, I know it's too dangerous for us to keep going without backup.

I walk out of the studio to find Louise leaving. "Where are you going?" I ask, chasing after her.

"While we were talking, Uncle Wolfie showed everyone the ransom note we got last night. Everyone's gone downtown for the ransom drop-off. Uncle Wolfie texted me the address. I can give you a ride if you want! I just got my license last month."

We hop in. Her driving isn't great . . . but she does get us downtown safely. Everyone from *Teen Witch* is waiting crowded in a hotel lobby, across the street from the drop-off. I find Mom almost immediately.

"Mom!" I say. "We have something crazy to tell you! We know who—"

"Look across the street! It's our kidnapper!" the police chief cries, waving his binoculars in the air. I squint out the window. It seems like there's someone in a trench coat, but it's hard to tell. "What are you waiting for, everyone? ATTACK!"

We all dash out of the hotel lobby toward the figure in a trench coat, picking up the suitcase. In the heat of the moment, I'm elbowing people out of my way. But Frank is the fastest.

He zips between people's legs until he's at the front of the charge.

"NEVER FEAR, FRANK IS HERE!" he shouts as he leaps forward and tackles the mystery trench-coat person to the ground.

Only . . . they both bounce.

The trench coat slips off, and it's not a person under there at all! Beneath the trench coat was a blow-up shark toy. It was taped to a remote-control car, so it looked like it was walking from far away.

"A decoy!" cries the police chief.

My stomach sinks. Eliza, Frank, and I know the truth: we were all lured away from Stage Eight on purpose. The ransom note was the lure, and the shark toy was the bait.

We fell for it hook, line, and sinker.

CASE CLOSED.

WE CUT YELLOW, red, blue, green.

The countdown timer stops, and I exhale a huge sigh of relief. I literally wipe the sweat off my brow. Nothing like disarming a dangerous device to get my heart rate going!

I get to my feet to assess the situation. The control room is closet sized, with lots of controls and switches on a panel. There is one door that leads to the sound-proof, wall-padded room with the one microphone.

Shouting won't work. Not only is the studio deserted, but the soundproofing will also block our screams. I pull out my cell phone. No service. I guess this room blocks out a signal. I grab the landline, but when I pick it up, the line is dead. The vents are too small in this room, even for Frank. I wonder if we could break the glass—

"THERE SHE IS!" Frank cries as the door to the sound booth opens.

Tuggle looks almost disappointed to see us alive. I flick the microphone on, so she can hear us from the control room.

"You locked us in here with a bomb!" I growl. "We could have died!"

Her face hardens. "Don't be so dramatic," she says. "You're reminding me of Layla."

"Where is she?" I demand.

KABOOM!

An enormous thunderstormy noise echoes through

the sound booth, and I jump back from the mic in surprise. Frank has his little fingers on a sound-effect button. *"Frank!"*

"Sorry," he says, but then he presses another button anyway. This new sound effect is a laugh track, and Tuggle looks befuddled.

"Look, it's working!" Eliza says. "She's getting confused!"

"Then . . . should I keep doing it?"

"Carlos," Eliza says. She points to a big red button on the soundboard. It's labeled RECORD.

"But where—"

Eliza nods at my microphone and widens her eyes—and without having to say a word, I think I know what Eliza is telling me. There is a standing microphone in front of Tuggle. In a sound booth. And we're in the control room.

"Ohhhhh," I say in realization. "Oh!"

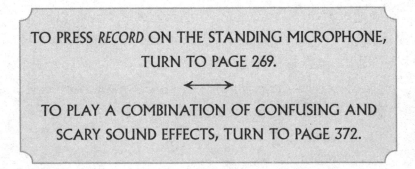

TO PRESS *RECORD* ON THE STANDING MICROPHONE, TURN TO PAGE 269.

←——→

TO PLAY A COMBINATION OF CONFUSING AND SCARY SOUND EFFECTS, TURN TO PAGE 372.

"SORRY, CARLOS," ELIZA says. "That was my fault. I startled her."

"It's not your fault," I assure her. "Miriam is just a jumpy witness."

"I didn't see any jumping," Frank says.

"Come on," I say. "We have to go after her! We're not done with her yet!"

Miriam Jay rounds the corner just as we leave Layla's dressing room. We follow her toward the set. We're pretty far behind her, but we're keeping an eye on her.

There's an area of the *Teen Witch* set with three different cauldrons, where Layla often cooks up potions. And that's where Miriam Jay is headed. We're still a good distance away, and Miriam doesn't realize we're on her tail.

Layla's mom stops, opens her purse, and looks around to make sure no one's watching.

"Wait!" I say, holding Eliza and Frank back.

No one looks around to make sure no one's watching unless they're about to do something suspicious.

Sure enough, Miriam pulls out a piece of paper and leaves it in the largest cauldron. Then she looks around again—and heads toward the side door of Stage Eight.

When we're certain she's gone, we run to the cauldron and peer in.

"Who do you think she's leaving a note for?" I ask.

"Let's find out," Eliza says, digging her arm in and pulling out the paper.

"Quick! Hide it!"

Frank snatches the note out of Eliza's hands and stuffs the paper down his pants (ew). And the three of us run to find a safe place to look at the note. We actually hide on set—beneath the giant robot dragon. We are all small enough to wiggle under the body of the beast for a private space.

"What's that?" Frank asks, pointing up at some cogs under the robot dragon.

"Don't touch those gears," Eliza says sharply. "It's probably something that controls the machine."

"I wish you hadn't said, 'Don't touch,'" Frank whispers. "Because now I wanna touch it."

Once we're sure that no one else is around, we lay the paper flat.

"What's this?" I say, looking at a note typed out from a computer. But the message is just a random collection of letters that don't make any sense.

"A secret code?" Eliza says excitedly. "Obviously Miriam doesn't want anyone to know the contents of this message—but who is she trying to communicate with?"

I cozy up to the letter. "I guess it's up to us to decode this!"

LZAYLZA CZHZANGZEZDZ ZHERZ BZAZNZKZ ZACCOZUZNT NZUZMBZZZER. ZIT ZIS NOZ ZLONZGZEZR ZOZHZ ZTWZO ZOHZ FZOZZURZ. STZUZCK FOZRZ ZCAZSHZ. IZ ZNZEEZD ZYOZURZ HZELZP. PZLEAZSE WZIREZ MEZ TZWZO THZOUZSZANZDZ DZOZLLZAZRZS FZRZOZZMZ ZZLZAZYZZLZA'SZ ZINZCOMZINGZ PZAYZCHZEZCK.

—YOU KNOW WHO

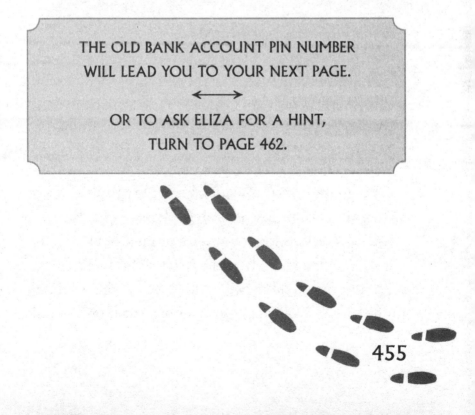

THE OLD BANK ACCOUNT PIN NUMBER
WILL LEAD YOU TO YOUR NEXT PAGE.

⟵⟶

OR TO ASK ELIZA FOR A HINT,
TURN TO PAGE 462.

I PRESS THE buttons in the order blue, yellow, black, red, green to close the gate, and it swings shut just in time—for the car to run straight into it!

The front of the car crunches, the airbags deploy, and Tuggle lurches forward. But I'm more concerned about the trunk, and the person inside it.

"Let's go!" I say. "We have to help Layla!"

When we reach the car, Tuggle hasn't moved. For now, we ignore her—and pop the trunk. Layla is in there, thrashing wildly, her wrists and ankles tied together with duct tape.

When she sees us, her brown eyes get really wide and watery.

"Who are you?" she whispers, her voice trembling.

"Detectives," I say. "Don't worry, you're safe now. We're here to help."

Ten minutes later, the studio is chaos. The police and EMTs are taking care of Tuggle. There are a few paramedics tending to Layla, but she's mostly just shaken. There are also a *ton* of paparazzi and reporters at the gate of the studio, trying to snap photos of Layla Jay.

I should have known the buzz around her would be big—she *is* famous, after all. But I didn't realize that we'd all be national news. Until Layla is done talking to the police, Wolfgang Westover has taken on the task of talking to the reporters. I just hope he mentions Las Pistas Detective Agency.

Eliza, Frank, and I sit on the steps of the door to the set, watching everything.

"We did it again," Eliza says. "Maybe we should start a competing business with Las Pistas."

"Very funny," I say. "Thanks for your help, both of you."

"Thank you for thanking me!" Frank says.

"You're welcome?"

"Thank you for thanking me for thanking you for thanking me," Frank says.

Eliza rolls her eyes.

"It wasn't what you think!" Tuggle shouts as the paramedics help her into a police car. "She is my client!"

"*Was* her client," Layla says from behind us. We whip around. "She is fired, obviously. Hey, thank you for everything. I hear you three were the reason why our car crashed. I . . . I don't know what I would have done if . . ." She trails off and shudders. "If you ever need anything from me, please don't hesitate to get in touch with my agent."

We raise our eyebrows, and Layla smiles. "My *new* agent, of course. Just as soon as I land one. I'll have to do a better job vetting this time, though."

"Good luck," I say, making eye contact with my shoes.

"Eeeeep," Eliza says, turning red.

"Hey! Wait a minute! I see you on TV every week!" Frank says, like he's just now recognizing Layla for the first time.

We all shake hands with her, and from a few yards away, Louise is staring at us with envy. Then Layla disappears into the studio. We survey the lot outside. The sound crew, camera crew, video editors, and the cast seem relieved—crowds of people chattering excitedly together. Wolfgang is especially boisterous with the journalists. I'm guessing he's happy that no one *he* hired was responsible for the kidnapping. Still, even though they weren't responsible, Guillotine and Brad look annoyed that Layla's back, and Layla's mom has been escorted from set. It seems like things at Burbank Studios will go back to normal soon.

"Carlos, come with me," Mom says, escorting me away from Eliza and Frank. Eliza raises her eyebrows, and my stomach drops. Am I in trouble?

But instead of lecturing me, Mom kisses my head. "Proud of you, hijo," she says. "You were honest with me, you investigated wisely, and we combined our strengths to work together. You took on a lot of responsibility, and you stepped up to the plate when I needed you."

"Does this mean you trust me again?" I ask.

"It just might."

"Does this mean you'll let me work as a junior detective on another case with you?"

"I just might." She smiles, and gives my shoulder another squeeze. And even though I'm not a movie star, I still feel like a million bucks.

CASE CLOSED.

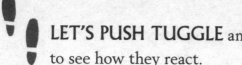

LET'S PUSH TUGGLE and Miriam a bit further, just to see how they react.

"You two are working together, aren't you?" I say. "You both kidnapped Layla."

"How dare you!" Tuggle splutters, while Miriam Jay bursts into big, blubbering sobs.

"I don't like where this investigation is going," she says tearfully.

"Why? Because you're guilty?"

"How dare you!" Tuggle says again, her chair scraping against the floor as she gets to her feet. "Come along, Miriam. We're going to have a chat with Wolfgang Westover about this . . . *highly* unprofessional accusation."

"Mr. Westover hired us," Mom says. "He won't fire us."

"Oh, yes, he will!" Miriam says through her sniffles. "When we're done with him. I am Layla's legal guardian! I can make her do whatever I want, including quit the show if Westover doesn't fire *you*."

They storm out of the room and slam the door behind them.

"You went too far," Mom says, pinching the bridge of her nose. She can't seem to meet my eyes. "It's my fault, really. I shouldn't have let you take the lead so soon."

460

"Wolfgang won't really listen to them, will he?"

We get our answer twenty minutes later, when Wolfgang comes to find us.

"I'm sorry, Detective Serrano," Wolfgang says as he takes our badges. "I know they're bullies, but they have leverage. My hands are tied."

Mom's failure with such a high-profile case is the gossip of the detective world. Her business collapses almost instantly. Mom gets a job as a cat walker, pulling reluctant cats down the street on leashes. Mom pulls, even though I was the one who pushed one question too far.

CASE CLOSED.

"I DON'T UNDERSTAND," I say to Eliza. "What are all these random letters? Why are there so many Zs?"

Eliza is staring so intently at the paper that I swear she's about to burn a hole through it with her eyes. At last her head pops up, so fast that she hits it on the base of the robot dragon we're hiding beneath. "Owww!" she howls.

"Do you have it?"

"Have what," Eliza groans, "the answer or a headache?"

"You don't need Eliza, because *Frank* figured it out!" Frank says, shocking me and Eliza both. Is it possible he's finally growing up to be a brainiac like Eliza? "It's bee language! Buzzzzzz zzzzzzz zzzzzzz!"

Okay, maybe not so much. I roll my eyes.

"You're definitely on to something with the Zs," Eliza says. "But the opposite—we need to get rid of the Zs."

I grab a pencil out of Eliza's backpack. "Let's go!"

LZAYLZA CZHZANGZEZDZ ZHERZ BZAZNZKZ
ZACCOZUZNT NZUZMBZZZER. ZIT ZIS
NOZ ZLONZGZEZR ZOZHZ ZTWZO ZOHZ
FZOZZURZ. STZUZCK FOZRZ ZCAZSHZ.
IZ ZNZEEZD ZYOZURZ HZELZP. PZLEAZSE
WZIREZ MEZ TZWZO THZOUZSZANZDZ
DZOZLLZAZRZS FZRZOZZMZ ZZLZAZYZZLZA'SZ
ZINZCOMZINGZ PZAYZCHZEZCK.

                              —YOU KNOW WHO

THE OLD BANK ACCOUNT PIN NUMBER
WILL LEAD YOU TO YOUR NEXT PAGE.

I **HAVE TO** chase her toward the door. Every time she tries to run in a different direction, Frank, Eliza, and I corral her back toward the side door. I feel like we're cattle dogs, herding a single sheep. We flank her from both sides.

Tuggle knows she's surrounded. She opens the side door and runs out.

"She's getting away!" Frank cries.

We follow her outside, and . . .

There are a hundred people standing in the parking lot. Mom, the cast, the crew, *everyone* who had evacuated the building after the car crash. Tuggle is trying to elbow her way through the crowd.

"STOP HER!" I shout. "SHE KIDNAPPED LAYLA!"

Everyone surrounds her, linking arms Red Rover–style, creating a fence. Tuggle turns around frantically, but she's enclosed. Caught in a circle—a human jail cell.

Mom runs over to us. "She's the kidnapper? Where is Layla?"

"Layla's inside. So is her mom. I think they both need a doctor."

"I'll call right away," Mom says, rushing away with her phone.

We watch as Tuggle thrashes about, throwing a temper tantrum in the middle of the human shield. But none of the cast or crew lets her off the hook. Even Brad Bradley shouts, "I can't believe what you did to my costar! She is *famous*!"

"And you threw off my filming schedule," Guillotine complains. "That's a lot of extra work you caused me."

"How dare you hurt Layla!" Louise shouts. "The official president of the unofficial Layla Jay fan club will not stand for this!"

People start shouting at Tuggle, and the inner circle around her gets tighter. Meanwhile, the crew members in the outer circle start lobbing their shoes at her.

Wolfgang Westover comes over to us. "I don't understand," he says, rubbing his strong chin. "I thought your mom was the detective."

"She is," I say. "And so are we."

"It runs in the family," Mom says, rejoining us and putting a hand on my shoulder. And I know, in that moment, that the mistrust and lies are behind us. We're a united team again. Stronger than ever.

"That's right," I say, beaming up at her. "It's in the genes."

Two weeks later . . .

It's a lazy Saturday morning at my house with Eliza and Frank. Winter break is coming, and it's shaping up to be a relaxing two weeks. But man, I wish it weren't. I'm already itching for another mystery.

I know the Thompsons don't feel the same: Eliza

465

is too preoccupied with homework and last-minute-before-break tests to even think about another mystery, and Frank has continued his upbeat no-matter-what attitude.

"Carlos!" Mom says, coming in from outside. "You have a letter."

A letter? But nobody has my address. . . . Nobody has ever written me before. "Who is it from?"

Mom simply smiles at me and waves the envelope.

I grab it from her hands and look at the return address. Layla Jay.

"Layla . . . is writing *me?*"

I rip the letter open.

"She's writing *us!*" Eliza squeals. "She wrote my name! She *knows* my name! I'm going to die!"

Dear Carlos, Eliza, and Frank,

"Hey! That's me!" Frank says, finally catching on.

Thank you so much for saving me. When Tuggle and I argued on November twentieth in the studio, I had no idea that she could ever be capable of kidnapping me and holding me hostage. I had no idea that I needed to watch my back in my own place of work.

Because this case is so high profile, the court

466

is moving the proceedings up to January tenth. Which means I'll be spending the month of January in court: first, getting my freedom from my mom, and second, making sure Tuggle gets locked away for a long time.

Filming has resumed, of course. Director Chen and Brad are so glad I've returned to the set safe and sound. (Not.) But Mr. Westover has my back more than ever, now that I've unintentionally brought his show lots of publicity. In three weeks, when we're done filming *Teen Witch* season four—and after the court cases, of course—I'm going on a vacation. I surely need it.

Thanks again for all your help. You three are great friends!

"Friends!" Eliza cries. "She called us *friends*!"
"I am framing this letter!" I shout.
Frank yawns. "Can I have some spaghetti?"
Typical Frank. Spaghetti! At a time like this!

If you ever need anything, just give me a call.
Your pal,
Layla Jay

CASE CLOSED.

THIS CHART IS *super* hard. Eliza's busy writing the translated code down in her notebook. I lean closer. If I can just peek over her shoulder, I can see what she's writing—

"CHEATER CHEATER PUMPKIN EATER!" Frank bellows.

Eliza looks up and laughs. "It's not cheating if we're on the same team, Frank!"

"So, did you decode it?" I ask her.

"I think so? I'm on the last sentence. . . ."

I wait for her to finish the last little bit, and then she hands me her notebook. The message on the cave wall reads:

FOREVER WILL YOU STAY HERE, WITCH
IN DARKNESS PLENTY, IN SILENT PITCH
UNLESS YOU HAVE THE SECRET KEY,
THE ONLY WAY THAT YOU CAN FLEE:
A MAGICAL NUMBER, THE STRONGEST OUT THERE
TWICE MORE THAN ALONE; ONCE MORE THAN A PAIR
QUARTER A DOZEN, TRIPLE A ONE,
SHOUT IT OUT, AND YOU ARE DONE.

"IT!" Frank cries.

Eliza and I both turn to stare at him.

468

"What?" Frank says, grinning in the flashlight beam. "You said shout it, so I shouted IT!"

"That's not what the riddle meant, and you know it! I . . . Eliza?"

She's staring up at the cave wall, thoughtfully twirling her braid. "This is starting to come back to me," she says. "I think I know the number we're looking for . . . and it's something we can count on one hand."

ADD THREE HUNDRED TO THE SOLUTION TO THIS PUZZLE, AND TURN TO THAT PAGE.

WE HAVE TO find Miriam Jay. It takes us a few loops around the set to find her—but we finally see her outside Wolfgang Westover's office. She's probably waiting to give him another piece of her mind.

"Who are you?" she says as we approach her.

"Nice to meet you," I say, holding out my hand to shake. "We're detectives from Las Pistas Detective Agency, charged with finding your daughter."

"You've *got* to be kidding me," Miriam says. "I tell Wolfgang to hire the best of the best—that money is no object—and he gives me . . ." She looks us up and down and doesn't finish the sentence.

"We are the best of the best," Eliza says coldly. "And we have questions for you."

"Then shoot," Miriam says.

Right here in the hallway? Okay, she asked for it. "We need to know what your fight with Layla was about."

Miriam tenses. Her mouth, especially, gets very tight. "I haven't the foggiest what you're talking about."

"That's not what we heard."

"Then you heard wrong. Goodbye," she says, stomping off down the hall.

We follow.

"If you don't stop following me, you'll be sorry."

"If you tell us what happened between you and Layla, we'll stop following."

470

Miriam heads out the door of Stage Eight, and we follow her next door into Stage Seven, which is bright and warm. There doesn't seem to be anyone filming, but there are a bunch of hairy, bird-eating, puppy-sized spiders in terrariums on the soundstage.

Face Your Fears! reads the show's banner.

Miriam puts her hand on top of a terrarium, tilting it threateningly.

"Stop," I say. "Just talk to us."

"Be reasonable," Eliza says.

"You poop face," Frank adds.

Miriam pauses for a moment. Then out of the blue, she cries, "GET THEM!" and topples the terrarium over. There must be at least five hundred spiders that all swarm toward us. Within seconds, they're crawling all over us, tickling us to death, while we try to be perfectly still to keep from being spider lunch.

CASE CLOSED.

Mysteries by
LAUREN MAGAZINER

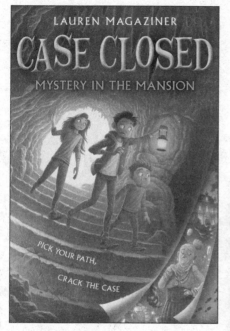

Pick your path,

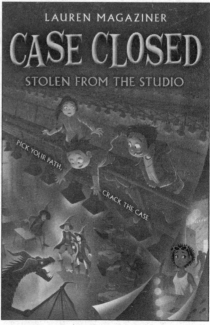

Crack the case!